Evermeet:
Island of Elves

Elaine
Cunningham

EVERMEET: Island of Elves

Distributed to the toy and hobby trade by regional distributors.

Distributed worldwide by Wizards of the Coast, Inc. and regional distributors.

Cover art by Ciruelo Cabral

FORGOTTEN REALMS and the TSR logo are registered trademarks owned by TSR, Inc.

All TSR characters, character names, and the distinctive likenesses thereof are trademarks owned by TSR, Inc.

TSR, Inc. is a subsidiary of Wizards of the Coast, Inc.

First Printing: April 1998
First Paperback Edition: March 1999
Printed in the United States of America.
Library of Congress Catalog Card Number: 96-60812

9 8 7 6 5 4 3 2 1

ISBN: 0-7869-1354-1
21354XXX1501

U.S., CANADA, ASIA,	EUROPEAN HEADQUARTERS
PACIFIC, & LATIN AMERICA	Wizards of the Coast, Belgium
Wizards of the Coast, Inc.	European Headquarters
P.O. Box 707	P.B. 2031
Renton, WA 98057-0707	2600 Berchem
U.S.A.	Belgium
+1-800-324-6496	+32-70-233277

Visit our website at **www.tsr.com**

Dedication

The Realms has a thousand historians, and this book owes an enormous debt to three of the finest. Much that is good in this story grew from their suggestions and research; any flaws that remain are entirely my own. In gratitude for their expertise and their enthusiasm, I'd like to dedicate this book to Steven Schend, herald and historian; to Eric Boyd, the Realms's answer to Thomas Aquinas; and to Moonsong, Sage of Arabel, wherever he may be.

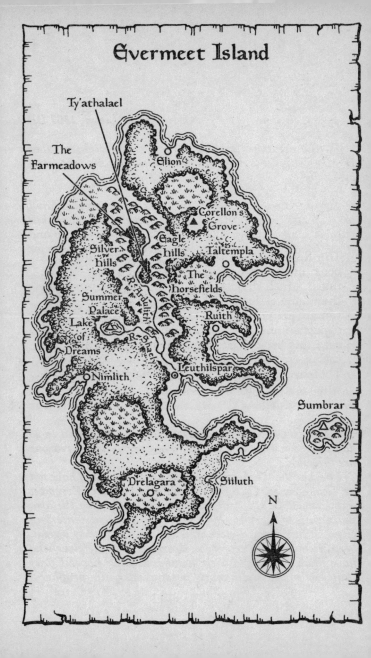

To the esteemed scholar, Athol of Candlekeep, does Danilo Thann, his erstwhile and unworthy student, send greetings.

My old friend, it is with enormous satisfaction that I take up quill and parchment to begin an endeavor that may, in some small measure, begin to justify the care and effort you once lavished upon my education. I thank you for that, and for your offer of assistance in my new effort.

It is my desire to gather some of the tales told by sages and bards, warriors and rulers, and fashion them into something resembling a history of the elven island of Evermeet. Without your aid and introduction, I would not presume to approach the mighty, the famous—and the well-armed. Those who do not know me would surely hesitate to contribute to so ambitious an undertaking. As for those who do know me . . . well, suffice it to say the damage is done. Perhaps the mantel of your fine reputation will enable me to reap credibility where none was sown.

What, you may ask, possesses me to set my hand to so daunting a task as this, a history of Evermeet? My reasons are threefold.

I believe that the lessons taught by elven history have not yet been learned. Though the wondrous island of Evermeet seems inviolate, is it truly so much different from Illefarn, Keltormir, or Cormanthyr? Once, these great centers of elven culture seemed eternal; now they are merely legend. What then may we expect for Evermeet and the elves who have made the island their home and their hope? I pray that my views hold more pessimism than prophecy;

nevertheless, change occurs, often when we are least ready for it. In my short career as a bard, I have observed that facts usually serve only to obscure the truth. Truth, when it can be found at all, is more likely to be heard when it is presented in stories and song.

You are also aware of my long fascination with all things elven. You may recall that you enjoyed a brief respite from my lamentable magical pranks whenever your lessons focused upon the fey folk. Shortly after you retired from your post as my tutor, having expressed your desire to regain your peace of mind and regrow your eyebrows and beard—for which loss I heartily apologize (upon my word, that ink was supposed to glow in the dark, not explode when exposed to candlelight!) I took upon myself the study of Elvish. In the years since, I have achieved a level of fluency that will allow me to read any histories, lorebooks, and letters you can send me. Rest assured I will treat them with far greater care than I showed my mother the Lady Cassandra's lorebooks, and that I shall return them to Candlekeep without the bawdy asides and small charcoal sketches that filled the margins of those books—save of course for those that dealt with elven legend and lore. Even then, I recognized and respected the unique magic of such tales.

My final reason is the most deeply personal. Through the blessings of the gods (which gods, precisely, remains to be ascertained) I am soon to wed an elf woman of royal blood—and mixed race. Her greatest sorrow, and therefore mine, is that she has been denied her elven heritage. While this history cannot restore her birthright to her, it is the only such gift within my power to give. My lady has little use for anything my wealth can purchase. The things she values cannot be found in the bazaars of Waterdeep, and are, alas, in scant supply elsewhere: honor, courage, tradition. As I undertake this work, I keep ever before me an image of this true daughter of Evermeet, whom I love dearly for her elven ways—and despite them.

A contradiction, you think? So would have I, before I came to know Arilyn. My lady is capable of inspiring admiration and exasperation in great and equal measure. I suspect that the story of her ancestors may hold true to this pattern. Yet I will follow the story of Evermeet's elves wheresoever it may lead, as faithfully as lies within my powers. This I swear to you by the Mystery I hold most dear—that the fairest and bravest of these wondrous, frustrating beings could love a man such as I.

I remain respectfully yours in the service of truth, story and song,

Danilo Thann

Prelude: The Edge of Twilight

(1371 DR)

igh above the waters of the Trackless Sea, a silver dragon wheeled, soared, and danced upon the crisp thin air. For many centuries had the dragon lived, and never had she found a pleasure to rival the sheer joy of flight—the rush of the wind and the delightful tingle of ice crystals against her scales.

As she soared over a narrow gap in the cloud cover, she noted that she was not the only creature to take flight on this glorious autumn day. Far below, a flock of white-winged seabirds skimmed over the waves.

Seabirds?

The dragon pulled up, startled. There was no land for many, many miles—how could a flock of such size sustain itself so far out to sea? Curious, she tucked in her wings and went into a stooping dive. Down she hurtled, plunging through the mist and damp of the clouds. Out of habit, the dragon stretched wide her wings just before she broke through the cloud bank, pulling out of the dive and then circling around in the thin mist to slow her momentum. Staying hidden among the clouds was most likely an unnecessary precaution, for even the sharpest-eyed seabird would see the dragon, if he saw her at all, as nothing more than a silver speck. But the dragon was a Guardian; it was her task to see and not be seen.

The dragon peered down at the strange flock. At this height she could see that it comprised not birds after all, but ships. A vast fleet of ships, sailing due west—sailing for Evermeet.

4

"I could attack," the dragon whispered longingly, yet she knew she could not. There were far too many ships, for one thing, and her duty in such matters was clear. She wheeled toward the west, her glittering wings thumping as she climbed back up to the cold, dry air above the clouds. There she could fly more swiftly.

And fly she must, with all the speed that the magic of dragonflight lent her. The dragon had been Evermeet's guardian for nearly as many years as Queen Amlaruil had been its ruler. During her centuries-long vigil the dragon had seen hundreds of ships attempt the passage to Evermeet. Most lay rotting on the ocean floor. But this flock, this fleet, was an invasion force of devastating strength. The dragon could see no other explanation for so many ships—not even during the height of the elven Retreat did so many ships band together at once. If even a tenth of them managed to get past the island's safeguards, they might do considerable damage to Evermeet's defenders.

The dragon sped toward the elven island, her mind reaching out desperately across the miles to search for the mind of her elven partner, so that she might warn him of the approaching danger.

Silence. Darkness.

There was a moment's disbelief—after all, Shonassir Durothil was a formidable warrior, one of the finest Windriders in all Evermeet. Many times had the dragon contacted him, even from so far a distance. If the elf did not answer, it was because he *could* not. Shonassir was dead; of that, the dragon was grimly certain. She did not wish to contemplate the severity of battle, the manner of foe that could send a warrior such as Shonassir Durothil to Arvandor before his time of consent.

The dragon muttered the words of a spell that would speed her flight to the elven homeland. In moments, the cloud mass below her sped by in a white blur. But fast as she was, the dragon had reason to fear that she might already be too late.

When Shonassir Durothil died, he had been on Evermeet itself.

5

* * * * *

High above the deck of *Rightful Place*, unmindful of the dragon sentinel passing swiftly overhead, a young sailor clung to the rail of the crow's nest and peered out over the endless waves.

Kaymid No-Beard, his mates called him, for his visage was indeed as smooth as a newly laid egg. But young though he was, this was his third voyage, and he was proud of his place on this vessel, the flagship of a mighty invasion force. Even better, as watchman Kaymid might be the first to catch a glimpse of Evermeet's fabled defenses.

This thought sent a tingle of excitement racing down the young sailor's spine. He had no thought of fear, for how could they fail? Kaymid knew a secret, a wonderful and dangerous secret that in his mind spelled certain victory. This adventure would climax in a glorious victory, and then he would claim his share of treasure and elven wenches. The battles that lay ahead would only whet his appetite for both.

"Soon," Kaymid murmured eagerly, remembering the tavern-told legends. According to those sailors who had survived such a voyage—which is to say, those who had turned back—the elven defenses began in earnest a fortnight's sail west of Nimbral. This time was nearly up.

Kaymid intently scanned the sea, his eyes seizing every detail: the long, flickering shadow that the ship's mast cast over the waves behind them, the leap and splash of a pair of dolphins at play, the sailor asleep on the deck below, his bald head pillowed on a coil of rope. Kaymid would see everything, miss nothing.

As if to mock his proud thoughts, an island leaped into view, appearing as suddenly as if it had been pulled from a wizard's bag. Beyond he saw a second island, and then another—there was a vast archipelago of them! And between the islands, jagged rocks thrust out of the sea like the tombstones of a thousand unwary ships.

"Danger! Danger, straight ahead!" Kaymid shouted

down in a voice made shrill by sudden fear. "Land, rocky shoals!"

On the deck below, the captain waved acknowledgment and untied his spyglass from his belt, although more for protocol's sake than from any faith in young Kaymid's enthusiasms. Captain Blethis was the son of a sailor and grandson of a pirate. The sea sang in his blood; it had been his home for nearly all of his forty-odd years. He could read the patterns in the stars and the winds as well as any man alive. No, by his reckoning *Rightful Place* was hard out to sea and days from any shore. He'd stake his share of elven treasure on that.

Blethis raised the glass. He recoiled, blinked, then squinted intently at the image it revealed. Sure enough, there *was* land ahead, a barrier even more dangerous than young Kaymid's warning suggested. The slanting rays of the afternoon sun set the islands aflame: The patches of sand were the color of pale roses, the rocks a deadly garden of sunset reds and oranges.

"A coral reef so far north?" Blethis muttered in disbelief. Spinning on his heel, he roared to his crew to turn hard to the north.

"Belay those orders."

The words were softly spoken, yet some fey magic carried them to every corner of the ship. The deckhands hesitated at their work, torn between the danger ahead—now visible to them all—and their awe of the speaker.

A lithe, slender figure emerged from the hold, draped in a cloak against the chill winds and the sting of the sea spray. "Sail on," he said calmly, addressing the helmsman who stood frozen at the wheel. "There is no need to alter our course."

"No need?" Blethis echoed incredulously. "That coral can shear through ships faster than dwarven axes could slice cheese!"

"You yourself have pointed out the unlikelihood of such a coral reef in these cold waters," the cloaked figure replied. "It is merely an illusion."

7

The captain raised his glass for another look at the formidable barrier. "Looks solid enough. You're certain it's not?"

"Entirely certain. We sail on. Have the bosun relay the message to the other ships."

Captain Blethis balked, then shrugged and did as he was told. In doing so he risked all that he had—his position, his share of the plunder, his very life—but he suspected his imperious passenger had as much at stake and more.

Although captain of the vessel, Blethis was little more than a hired hand. The ship he commanded belonged to the elf—in fact, as far as Blethis could figure, *all* the ships in the fleet belonged to him.

The elf. It still amazed Blethis that an elf would lead an invasion force against his own kin. Although, come to think of it, men were quick enough to fight amongst themselves. It shouldn't surprise him to learn that elves weren't much different, but it did. There were several elves on this ship, for that matter, and more on several of the others. As far as Blethis could tell, they were all dead set upon overthrowing the ruling queen and taking over the island themselves. Which was fine with Blethis, since these particular elves were willing to share the spoils of war—and the glory of conquest—with their human allies.

Provided, of course, that any of them survived the voyage.

The captain strode to the bow and watched in silence as the ship closed in on the coral reef. Some of the crew, trusting the evidence of their own eyes over the assurances of the mysterious elf lord, leaped over the rail to take their chances swimming ashore.

"Leave them," the elf commanded. "They will understand their folly soon enough, and the other ships will pick them up as they pass through."

Blethis nodded absently, his eyes fixed on the swiftly approaching rocks. Instinctively he braced himself for the first grating jolt of contact with the unseen coral shelf, but it did not come. Scarcely breathing, he stood tense and watchful as the helmsman steered the ship in a weaving

course between the blood-colored rocks, touching none.
Touching nothing. It was a feat of seamanship that Blethis
would not have believed possible had he not witnessed it.

It was also effort wasted. In moments the first of the
islands lay directly before them, a hopelessly rocky shore
above which loomed a thick tangle of foliage. They were
close enough to smell the thick, earthy scent of the loamy
soil and the deep, complex perfume of growing things. A
large insect flew soundlessly by. Blethis instinctively
swatted and missed.

Suddenly a weird, undulating hoot pierced the tense
silence, rolling out of the dense forest toward them in chilling waves. The call was quickly echoed by other creatures—large creatures, judging from the sound—whose
trumpeting roars seemed thick with hungry anticipation.

Blethis shuddered. He'd heard such cries before, long
ago, when his ship sailed too near the shores of Chult's
jungles. If the elf was wrong, if the ship went aground on
this brutal coastline, all of them were deader than day-old
mackerel.

To the captain's astonishment and utter relief the ship
passed through the cove and the rocks, flowing right into
the "forest" beyond as easily as it might slice through mist.
The colors of the coral formations and the lush green
foliage played over the ship and the stunned sailors as
they glided through the illusion.

Blethis held up one hand and regarded the shifting patterns upon it. He remembered a long-ago moment when as
a child he had stood in the base of a rainbow and watched
the colors splash over his bare feet. This barrier reef, for all
its formidable appearance, was no more substantial than
that rainbow.

"So much for Evermeet's defenses," he murmured.

The elf's only response was a thin smile.

"Storm ahead!" sang down the young watchman.
"Coming this way, and coming fast!"

This time Blethis had no need to raise his glass. The
storm swept toward them with preternatural speed. Scant

moments after Kaymid sounded the alarm, angry purple clouds filled the sky and hurled lightning bolts at suddenly skittish waves.

A whirling cone descended from the clouds. More followed, until a score of them had touched down upon the sea. The water churned wildly as hungry clouds plundered the waves, and the funnels swiftly became darker and more powerful with the force of the swirling waters within. Like a pack of hunting wolves, the waterspouts began to circle the fleet.

"Tell me this is another illusion, elf," Blethis implored.

"The storm is all too real," the elf said, pulling the folds of his cloak tighter about him. "Sail on."

The ship's mate, a burly pirate whose face had taken on a pale, greenish hue that belied his Calishite heritage, lurched over to clutch the captain's arm. "We've had enough, Blethis. All of us. Give the order to turn about!"

Blethis read certain mutiny in the pirate's eyes. "Remember the treasure!" he exhorted. The mate, he knew, gambled at cards, dice, gaming cocks, and the gods only knew what else. His luck with all of them was monumentally bad; he owed ruinous amounts to people who spared no means to collect debts owed them. This voyage, Blethis knew, was nothing less than the man's last chance at survival.

"Treasure's of little use to a dead man," the mate replied flatly, his words not only an admission of his own predicament, but a deadly threat. He released the captain's arm, drew a curved knife from his sash, and raised it high.

As the blade slashed toward the captain's throat, the elf spoke a strange syllable and moved one golden hand in a flickering gesture. Instantly the knife glowed from tip to hilt with fierce red heat. The mate jerked back, his aim spoiled. Then, howling with pain, he dropped the ensorcelled weapon and shook his singed fingers.

Blethis drove his fist into the traitorous sailor's face, and was rewarded with a satisfying crunch of bone. He hit him again, lower this time, with a sweeping upward hook that drove the broken bones of the mate's nose deep into his skull.

Instantly dead, the man dropped to the deck. Blethis was tempted to kick him a couple of times for good measure, but the ship was starting to pitch and roll, and he wasn't certain he could do so without falling on his backside.

"The storm will not harm us," the elf said, as calmly as if the mutinous confrontation had not occurred. "This is the hand of a goddess, a manifestation of Aerdrie Faenya, Lady of Air and Wind. Elven ships may pass through unharmed."

As if to belie these assurances, lightning seared the sky, and a booming crash rumbled over the roar of the gathering winds. Blethis raised his glass in time to see the mast of a distant ship splinter and fall. The oiled sails, which had been dropped at first sign of the approaching storm, were already smoldering. In moments the ship would be a torch. Blethis shot an inquiring glare at the ship's owner.

The elf lifted one shoulder in a careless shrug. "The human-made vessels were useful in bringing us this far— not even the most voracious of Nimbral's pirates would attack a fleet of such size. Some of the humans have fed the hungry creatures of the sea; some ships were given as Umberlee's toll. But we near our goal; it is time to cull the fleet. Most of the human ships will be destroyed long before we reach Evermeet."

Blethis clung to the rail and struggled to absorb this callous pronouncement, and the fact that the vast fleet would be cut nearly in half. "But nearly threescore elven ships will remain," the captain persisted, raising his voice to be heard over the gathering tempest. "That's an invasion force! Whether the ships are elven or not, Evermeet's elves will figure out your intent. Suddenly, our chances look about half as good as they did when I signed on!"

The elf's oddly cold smile returned. "You are more cunning than you appear, Captain Blethis. But do not concern yourself. Not all ships sail to one port; *Rightful Place* will be one of three ships docking at Leuthilspar. And I assure you, Queen Amlaruil will receive us."

"This fool was not far wrong," Blethis said hotly,

11

nudging the downed first mate with his boot. "And he won't be the last to take up arms to end this trip. If you've got some good news, this is the time to speak."

"Listen, then, so you can calm your crew's fears and set your own mind fully to the task ahead," the elf conceded. "One of the elves aboard this ship is Lamruil, youngest son of Queen Amlaruil and the late King Zaor. The *only surviving* royal offspring, if all has gone as our allies planned, and therefore sole heir to the throne of Evermeet." The elf paused, and a flicker of distaste crossed his golden face. "Though Prince Lamruil himself is not particularly impressive, his presence on this ship gives us tremendous power.

"And so," the elf concluded with grim satisfaction, "the queen has little choice but to receive us. Evermeet's future, one way or another, is in the hands of her worthless brat."

* * * * *

"Your advisors have assembled in the throne room, Your Majesty."

Queen Amlaruil nodded, not lifting her gaze from the too-still face of her firstborn daughter. "I shall be along directly," she said in a voice that bore no hint of her weariness or her grief.

The courtier bowed deeply and left the queen alone with the fallen princess.

Ilyrana—that was the name Amlaruil had given her daughter those many years ago, a name taken from the High Elven word meaning "an opal of rare beauty." Ilyrana had been so lovely as a babe, so like the precious stone for which she was named: milky white hair highlighted with the palest of greens, luminous skin so white that it blushed blue tints, and large grave eyes that could change with light and mood from the color of spring leaves to the deep blue of a summer sea. Ilyrana was lovely still, Amlaruil noted wistfully, even in the deathlike slumber that had claimed her since the battle two nights past.

Like most of the Seldarine's clerics, Ilyrana had gone to do battle against the fearful creature unleashed upon the elven island by the evil god Malar, the Beastlord. By battle's end, many priests and priestesses had fallen: Ilyrana was simply gone, although her body remained behind. Amlaruil had not been surprised by this, for there had always been something otherworldly about her oldest child. Knowing Ilyrana's utter dedication to Angharradh, the goddess she served, Amlaruil suspected that her daughter had followed the fight to its ultimate source and was even now standing firm at Angharradh's side. If that were so, then the goddess was well served indeed.

And if it were so, then Ilyrana was unlikely to return. Few elves who glimpsed the wonders of Arvandor, even in such dire circumstances, could ever reconcile themselves to the mortal world.

Amlaruil whispered a prayer—and a farewell—and then rose from her daughter's bedside. All of Evermeet awaited her. There was little time to spare for her own personal tragedies.

The queen swiftly made her way to the throne room. A large assembly awaited her: the surviving members of the Council of Matrons, representatives from each of the noble clans, leaders from among the elven warriors, even a few of the other fey creatures who made Evermeet their home and who fought alongside the elves. As one, they knelt in the presence of the elven queen.

As was her custom, Amlaruil bowed deeply to the People she served, then bade them all rise to tend to the matter at hand. She took the throne and called upon Keryth Blackhelm, the Moon-elven warrior who commanded the island's defenses, to give his report.

But Keryth was not fated to speak this day.

The explosion was sudden, silent—and utterly devastating. There was no thrumming crash, no vibration to set the crystal towers of the city keening in sympathy, not even a tremor to shake the gemstone mosaic floor beneath their feet. Yet there was not an elf in that chamber—not an elf upon all of Evermeet—who did not feel it or who failed to understand what it meant.

The Circles had been shattered. Evermeet's unique magic was gone.

For nearly five days the battle for the elven homeland had raged. Armies of monsters had arisen from the sea and descended from the skies, human wizards of unspeakable power had challenged the Weave of elven magic, ships bearing mounted warriors had swept in upon the island from every side. Worse, creatures from Below had found a path to the island, had sullied the haven that was Evermeet, and had slain many of the island's best defenders. Although the besieged People were unspeakably weary, they had not grown dispirited.

But this blow was surely more than they could bear.

Moving as if in a dream, Queen Amlaruil rose from her throne and made her way over to the open window. Below her was laid out a strange tableau: The teeming streets of Leuthilspar, which moments before had been alive with elven warriors rallying in response to yet another threat from the coast, were utterly silent. The elves stood motionless, frozen in a paroxysm of anguish.

Amlaruil lifted her eyes toward the north. Far away, in the deepest and most ancient forests of Evermeet, the twin spires of the Towers of the Sun and the Moon had reached to the sky. Now they were gone, and the High Magi of Evermeet with them. Amlaruil allowed herself a moment's grief for the loss of friends she had cherished for centuries.

The queen turned to her advisors, who for once were beyond speech. All of them knew what this meant. The only thing that could possibly destroy the Towers was another powerful circle of High Magi. And in these days of diminished power and fading magic, only on Evermeet could such magic be cast. Beset on all sides by invaders, they had nevertheless stood firm. The devastating blow, the only one for which they had not prepared, was this betrayal from within.

Finally Zaltarish, the queen's ancient scribe, gave words to the tragedy.

"Evermeet is lost, your Majesty," he whispered. "The twilight of the elves has come."

Book One

The Fabric of Legend

"If ye ask my advice—and ye have—I'd say to give over this task to thine Uncle Khelben. Of the two of ye, he's the more deserving of it. But since ye don't seem the vengeful sort, ye might as well start this tale at the beginning. It seems to me ye can not tell the story of the elven People without speaking of the gods. Indeed, I've known many the elf who'd have ye believe there's little difference between him and them."

—excerpt from a letter from Elminster of Shadowdale

1

The Godswars

efore time began, before the fabled realm known as Faerie began its descent toward twilight, there was Olympus.

Home of the gods, Olympus was a vast and wondrous place. Here were limpid seas from whose depths sprang new life—beings who would in time find homes upon the infant worlds awakening beneath a thousand suns. Here lay verdant meadows as whimsically fertile as the minds of the gods who walked upon them, and gardens like vast and glorious sunsets. Here was Arvandor, the forest home of the elven gods.

It was to Arvandor that he fled now, wounded and heartsick, and as near to death as ever an elven god had come.

He was Corellon Larethian, the leader of the elven pantheon. Lithe and golden was he, and beautiful despite the ravages of battle. Though gravely wounded, he ran with a grace and speed that a mountain cat might envy. But the elf lord's face was taut with frustration, and one hand was clenched around the empty scabbard on his hip.

Corellon was a warrior—the father of all elven warriors—and he wanted nothing more than to stand and see the battle through to its conclusion. But his weapon was shattered, and he was bound by honor not to use his godly magic against his foe. There was no choice but retreat, for if Corellon fell—Corellon, the essence of elven strength and magic and beauty—then the destruction of the elven People seemed assured.

He took some comfort from the knowledge that for

each drop of blood he spilled an elven child would be born. Thus had it been many times before: This was not his first battle with Gruumsh. He suspected that it would not be his last.

Since dawn had the battle raged, and now dusk was drawing near. All but deafened by the pounding of his own heart, the elf lord faltered to a stop and looked about for a place where he might take a moment's rest and shelter. Such places were scarce on the Moor, a place of endlessly rolling hills, shallow seas of peat, and a few stubborn trees. One tree huddled nearby—a low, gnarled cypress whose twisted and thinly leaved branches swept down to touch the ground.

Corellon ducked into the meager shade and sank down to rest. Even as he did so, his eyes swept the hills and he mapped out plans for a battle that might yet overtake him. He acknowledged that the Moor was not without a certain austere beauty; even so, it was hardly the place for an elven god. Corellon was outside his element, and well he knew it.

Olympus knew no finite boundaries, and within it were lands that defined paradise for many, many peoples. This place had been chosen as a courtesy to another god, one with whom Corellon had sought parlay: Gruumsh, the First Power of the orcish gods.

Gruumsh was at home in the wild moors, hills, and mountains of a hundred worlds. Although the orc lord could never have defeated his elven counterpart amid the trees of Arvandor, here the advantage was his. The familiar setting had apparently emboldened him. From his first strike, Gruumsh had seemed more confident, more grimly determined, than ever before. He came on still in swift and dogged pursuit of the elven god.

Corellon's sharp eyes caught a glimpse of his foe cresting a distant hill. Taller by half than any of the Moor's gnarled trees, Gruumsh was corded with muscle and armored with a gray hide nearly as tough as elven mail. His bearlike snout twitched as he scented the air for the passing of the elf lord, and his iron spear bounced on his shoulder as he strode along. The bestial god bled nearly as profusely as did Corellon, for the battle between them had been long and fierce. The difference between them was that the orc lord still held his weapons, while Corellon's sword lay in scattered shards among the heather.

As he watched the orcish god's approach, Corellon understood for the first time the depth of his own folly. He had asked Gruumsh to come to Olympus so that they might discuss an end to the destructive war between Gruumsh's orcs and the elven children of Corellon—a war that was threatening to shred the very fabric of the ancient realm of Faerie. Corellon had invited, and Gruumsh had accepted.

Accepted, and then betrayed.

The elf lord blamed himself. Although he would have liked to claim that he'd treated Gruumsh as an honorable foe, offering good faith and expecting it in return, he had not been particularly surprised when the orc lord broke truce. In truth, Corellon had been willing to surrender nearly every advantage because it had never occurred to him that he might lose a fight.

He was proud, perhaps too proud, as were his elven children. Corellon had reason to know the cunning and battle fury of his orcish adversary, but he had trusted in his superior agility and in Sahandrian, his marvelous sword. Even now he could not fathom how the orcish god had managed to shear through Sahandrian's magic and metal with naught but a rusty, one-handed axe.

Treachery, Corellon concluded grimly. There was no other explanation, for Sahandrian was far more than a common sword. It was Corellon's own work—he had lavished untold centuries upon the crafting and enchanting of it. Nor was he the only god who'd had a hand in its creation. Sehanine Moonbow, the elven goddess of moonlight and mysteries, had bound moon magic into the shining blade. Since beauty has a power of its own, Hanali Celanil had made of the sword's hilt a work of art replete with gems and intricate carvings. Upon the blade she had etched runes that portrayed—and perhaps captured—the enduring strength of elven love. His beloved Araushnee, the patron goddess of artisans and the goddess of elven destiny, had woven with her own hands the intricately designed silken sheath that padded Corellon's scabbard and warded him with a web of magic.

All of these goddesses had worshipers among the People; it was possible that a high cleric had caught a glimpse of his Mistress's magical essence, and had somehow turned this knowledge against the elf lord.

But why? For what purpose would any elf turn against his own gods? This question, a question that Corellon had never before thought or needed to ask, haunted him as he watched twilight purple the sky and Gruumsh draw ever closer.

The single moon of Olympus crested the distant hills, an amber orb that paled to silver as it rose. Its light sent a hulking, moon-cast shadow stretching out before the orc lord. Noting this, Gruumsh bared his fangs in a savage grin. The bright moonlight was as much his ally as the open terrain, for it made tracking all the easier.

A slight movement on the horizon caught the orc lord's eye. It was little more than a shimmer, rather like the colored lights that danced in the cold northern skies on one of Gruumsh's favorite worlds. But he recognized its source, and grimaced.

Sehanine.

Gruumsh hated all the elven deities and loathed their not-quite-mortal children, but he reserved a special enmity for this wench. A wisp of a female, pale as moonlight and insipid as a bloodless meal, the goddess Sehanine was nonetheless a potent adversary. This offended Gruumsh. Female orcs were generally smaller and weaker than males, and as a result, they held considerably less power. Orcish young learned the precept: "If Gruumsh had intended females to lead, he would have given them bigger muscles." He certainly wouldn't have equipped them with Sehanine's fey magic, or that subtle mind whose depths no orcish warrior could fathom. Corellon was bad enough, but at least Gruumsh knew what to expect from the elven god: battle—straightforward, bloody, and invigorating. That he could understand and respect.

The orc watched with apprehension as the dancing lights coalesced into a slender, feminine form. Like a luminous cloud, Sehanine walked toward him, rapidly taking on substance as she came. Night was her time, and she seemed to draw sustenance and power from the moonlight. In her hands was a shining sword, held point-up before her.

Gruumsh knew at once that this was no common weapon, even as gods reckon such things. No, this sword was a living thing. It was as alive—and as troublesome—as any elven world and all the beings that walked upon it, as vast in power as the sun that warmed that world and the skies that cradled it. The stunned orc noted the thousands of tiny stars that swirled within the wondrous blade and sensed the magic that pulsed through it like an ocean's tides.

It was *Sahandrian,* the sword of Corellon, made whole and new!

Surprise turned swiftly to rage, and Gruumsh let out a furious bellow that rumbled like thunder over the Moor. The proudest moment of the orc lord's godhood had been shattering that sword, watching the glowing fragments fade and disappear. Somehow, this great triumph had been undone by a scrawny elven wench. The orc's hatred of the moon goddess increased a thousandfold, and he howled out a fearsome oath of vengeance upon her and all creatures elven.

But Sehanine walked on, not sparing the furious Gruumsh so much as a glance. She crested the hill on which he stood and began to pass down into the valley, moving within easy range of a spear's toss.

The orc lord's brow beetled at this tacit insult. He whipped his spear from his shoulder and hauled it back for the throw.

The faint sound must have alerted his target, for Sehanine turned to him at last, an expression of faint disdain on her face. Too fast—impossibly fast—she leveled the elven sword at the orc lord as if it were a wizard's staff. A single pulse of silver light burst from the weapon and engulfed him in a shimmering sphere. Blinded and snarling with rage, Gruumsh fisted his free hand and dug furiously at his eyes in an attempt to banish the stars that swam and spun behind his eyelids.

By the time the orc lord's vision returned, the goddess had moved far beyond the range of his spear. She stood beside a gnarled cypress that clung to the top of the hill beyond. To the orc's dismay, Sehanine was not alone—a familiar, golden warrior came eagerly toward her. She knelt to him, Sahandrian held out before her. The lights that whirled within the elven weapon flared and leaped as the rightful owner reclaimed his sword.

Gruumsh shook his now-useless spear and fairly danced with rage. "Knave! Coward!" he howled at Corellon Larethian. "Bested in single combat, you hide behind a female's skirts! And what of your oath? You swore that no elven magic would be brought against me, yet you suffer this witch to undo my victory!"

"Not so," Sehanine said firmly, her silvery voice floating out over the valley that lay between them. She rose and faced down the angry god. "You have broken the truce, Gruumsh of the Orcs, and thus it will be remembered for all time. Corellon holds to the contract he has made with you and to all the tenets of honorable battle. He was never bested. Destroying his sword was no victory of yours. By an elf was Sahandrian undone, and thus it falls to the Seldarine to restore their own."

With these cryptic words, the goddess turned back to Corellon. Her silver eyes swept over him; tears sprang into them as she took note of his many wounds. Sehanine wiped the tears from her cheek and reached out with gentle fingers to touch the god's bleeding face. Instantly the mingled droplets on her hand took on a mystic glow.

"Children of the moon and the sun," she whispered. "Behold, my lord, the souls of elves yet unborn. Even battle with a dishonorable foe cannot diminish the magic we share."

She started to say more, but the bright moonlight that sustained her suddenly dimmed, and the rising wind chased a welter of black clouds across the moon. Sehanine cast a glance over her shoulder. The orc, as she expected, had kicked into a running charge, seizing what must have seemed to him a moment of elven weakness.

The goddess's face hardened. "Kill him, my lord," she whispered fiercely, and touched her fingers to Corellon's scabbard as if in grim benediction. When the dark clouds parted, she was gone.

Corellon bit back the words of thanks and tamped down the questions burning within him. Later, he vowed, he would seek out the moon goddess and have from her an explanation concerning the magic she had done, and the elven treachery to which she'd alluded.

But for now it was enough just to hold Sahandrian again. The elven god raised his sword high, exulting in the feel of the wondrous weapon in his hand and the prospect of renewed battle. With a ringing shout, he raced down the hillside to meet the orc's charge.

They met in the valley below with a thunderous clash. Sparks flew like shooting stars as the elven blade struck the iron haft of the orc lord's spear. Corellon deliberately allowed his blade to glance off the spear; he knew he could not equal or even counter the force of the orc's attack. His advantage was agility. Never once slowing his momentum, the elf ducked beneath the crossed weapons. Metal screeched over metal as his sword slid up the spear's haft with deadly intent.

Gruumsh twisted his spear sharply to one side, flinging the oncoming blade wide. He spun, stepping back to move himself beyond the elf's reach. As he turned back toward his foe, Gruumsh brought the blunt end of his spear down, swinging in hard and low at the elf lord's booted feet.

Corellon danced nimbly back—exactly as the orc hoped he would. Gruumsh's primary weapon was considerably longer than the elf's: Not even Sahandrian could cut what it could not reach.

25

Elaine Cunningham

With a fierce smile, the orc completed the sweeping arc, swinging his weapon up so that the shaft was level, the iron tip aimed at the elf lord's throat. With all his strength he lunged forward, thrusting as he went.

Corellon made no attempt to parry the mighty blow. He ducked under the rushing spear, then pivoted back to face his foe, using his speed to lend power to Sahandrian's swing. The sword scored a stinging blow to the orc lord's hip. Gruumsh whirled at the elf, his spear out full length before him. But the elf stepped in close, too close for the sharp tip to find him. His sword darted in and ripped yet another gash in the orc lord's hide before the shaft of the spear smashed into his ribs.

The elf rolled with the blow, coming up on his feet and once again lunging in close. But Gruumsh had tossed aside his spear. In one massive hand he held a dagger, in the other, the axe that had somehow destroyed Sahandrian earlier that day.

For many moments the foes stood nearly toe to toe, and the clash and shriek of metal upon metal rang out over the watchful Moor. In the hands of the elven god, Sahandrian whirled and thrust and danced, moving so fast that it left ribbons of light in its path. But this time, Corellon's sword held firm, turning aside the orcish god's axe again and again without taking so much as a pit along its gleaming edge.

The enjoined shadows of the battling gods grew shorter as the moon rose high in the sky. Gruumsh's breath was coming hard now, and his ears buzzed as if a swarm of angry insects had taken up residence in his skull. The orc was the stronger by far, but try as he might, he could not get past the elf's guard to strike with his full power. Nor was Gruumsh as agile as the elf, and though he had two weapons to Corellon's one, the elven blade slipped through his defenses again and again. His hide was crisscrossed with garish stripes, and the grip of his axe was slippery with his own blood. It began to come to Gruumsh that the battle he'd thought already won, the victory he'd purchased from a traitor's hand, would once again belong to the elven god.

As if he, too, sensed the turn of battle, Corellon surged forward, ducking under the orc's lumbering swing to leap, sword leading, at the orc lord's throat.

Gruumsh knew at once he had no hope of parrying the elf's attack. Instinctively he ducked and flung his dagger hand up to block the killing thrust. The elven blade bit deep into the orc lord's forearm, sinking between the twin bones—and driving his arm up into his face.

Too late, the orc realized that he still clenched his dagger. His own blade stuck him hard, parting the hide on his meager forehead. Gruumsh heard the horrid sound of metal sliding wetly over bone, felt the sudden easing of resistance as the blade slipped down. Then all other sensation vanished in a white-hot explosion of pain.

Corellon leaped back, tugging his sword free of the orc's arm before the god's fall could bring him down, too. For a long moment he stood and regarded his fallen adversary. On the battle-sodden ground, the orc lord rolled and tossed in immortal agony, his hands clutching at his eyes—one of which was blinded by the copious flow of blood from the gaping head wound, the other blinded for all time. Other than the ruined eye, most of Gruumsh's wounds would heal—too quickly for Corellon's peace of mind—but there would be no more fighting this night.

The elf lord slid Sahandrian back into its scabbard. His fingers touched leather, and a pang of sadness filtered through his elation. Though victory was his, the wondrous padded sheath his Araushnee had woven for him—which he had carried into battle as her token—had been lost during the horrendous fight.

"You are forsworn, blinded, and utterly defeated," Corellon said coldly. "Yet I find these things little enough payment for what I have lost this day."

The orc dashed blood from his face and squinted at his foe with his one remaining eye. "You don't know the half of it, elf," he growled. "And you can't begin to understand what you've lost—you don't even know the names of your foes! As for defeat, I admit none! Kill me now, if you can, and your

27

own silver whore will bear witness that you struck down a wounded and unarmed foe!"

Corellon glanced moonward, and knew that, at least in this much, the orc spoke truth. The goddess of moonlight and mystery would see all and would be compelled by honor to speak of such dishonor before the Seldarine Counsel. Even if Corellon wished to do so, he could not slay the downed orcish god. Nor, by the terms of their agreement, could he banish Gruumsh from Olympus before the orc chose to go.

"You spoke of others," the elf lord said, glancing over the silent hills, "but I see no one ready to take up your fallen weapons."

The orc smirked. "As long as you're on the open Moor, I need no help from anyone. It's a long walk to Arvandor, elf, and you're swaying on your feet like a sapling in a strong wind. Go if you can—I'll not be far behind you. One eye is more than I need to follow a trail through these hills. If you're still standing when I find you, we will fight again. If not, I will kill you where you lie!"

Corellon found that he could not scoff at this grim promise. The heat of his battle fever was fast slipping away, and the weight of his wounds pressed heavily upon him. It was possible that the orc, grievously wounded though he was, could do exactly as he promised. Without another word, Corellon turned once more toward Arvandor.

* * * * *

Dense and deep was the forest curtain that surrounded Arvandor. Lost beings could wander in the woodlands beyond its borders for many days, never once passing over the invisible boundary, perhaps never even realizing that their way was barred. Ancient trees shifted to confound the passerby, paths appeared seemingly at random only to disappear into a forest pool or a bed of ferns; brooks suddenly widened into vast yawning chasms; thick tangles of vines suddenly sprouted thorns or simply refused to part. Arvandor was a haven and a fortress.

Hidden among the green shadows that surrounded and protected Arvandor, an elven goddess clung to the uppermost branches of a tree and peered out over the woodlands. Her slender black fingers clenched tightly around her handhold, and her beautiful face was taut with foreboding.

Three long days had passed since Corellon Larethian, her lover and her lord, had gone to meet with the orcish god. Araushnee awaited the outcome with tense anticipation. She had much at stake. There was no telling what might happen among the Seldarine if Corellon did not return. Although none among the elven gods could truly replace Corellon, many would certainly try.

Araushnee's relationship with the Seldarine's leader was unique. Corellon Larethian was all things elven: warrior and poet, mage and bard, even male and female. But since the coming of Araushnee, the deity had settled into a single aspect: that of a Gold elven male. In Araushnee, he had seen his perfect counterpart: female to his male, artist to his warrior, the mysteries of midnight to balance the brightness of day. Though Araushnee was but a minor goddess, Corellon had been utterly enchanted with her beauty and had made her his consort. She had borne him children—twin godlings as darkly beautiful as herself. As the beloved of Corellon, Araushnee held a place of honor among the Seldarine, as well as new powers that the elven god had bestowed upon her. By Corellon's decree, the destiny of the mortal elves who shared her dark beauty was in her keeping. She had learned to enjoy that power, and she feared its loss at least as much as she feared the battle's outcome.

Her sharp ears caught a faint sound—the distant hiss and rustle of underbrush trampled underfoot. No elven god would make such a clamor. Araushnee had her answer, at last.

The goddess slipped down from her perch on a thread of magic. Her slippers touched the forest floor without a sound, but before she could take a single step toward the victorious orc, her eyes fell upon a most unexpected sight.

Corellon.

The elf lord was but a few dozen paces away. His progress was slow, and he looked as battered as a trod-upon flower, but still he moved through the woodlands like a breath of wind. Araushnee's gaze dropped to his hip. The sheath she had woven and enchanted was gone, and the sword Sahandrian was whole. An invisible aura clung to the sword—the unmistakable touch of Sehanine's moon magic.

Araushnee's crimson eyes flamed at this new evidence of her rival's hand in her personal affairs. Dizzy with rage, the goddess flung out one hand as if to erase Sehanine's handiwork. Magic burst unbidden from her ebony fingertips, spinning out into a vast curtain that blocked the forest in either direction, as far as her eyes could discern.

Corellon stopped, clearly puzzled by the glistening barrier that presumed to bar Arvandor to *him.*

Chagrin tore through Araushnee. Surely the god would know whose hand this was. Even as besotted as he was with her, he would certainly see this act as treachery. And even as weakened as he obviously was, he could easily overshadow the magic of a minor goddess. Then where would she be? Damned by a single impulse, all her work undone.

Thinking quickly, Araushnee began to weave another sort of web. She stepped out of the shadows into plain sight, her face alight with feigned relief and welcome.

Pass through, my love, she said silently, willing her words into Corellon's mind. *The web will not hinder you but will bar the orc. Go, and find healing.*

She felt the answering surge of Corellon's gratitude and love—and was buffeted by a nearly overwhelming wave of exhaustion. As if he sensed this, Corellon quickly withdrew his painful touch. The elven god slipped through Araushnee's net as easily as a falcon pierces a cloud. He kissed his fingers to her in a salute, then disappeared into the forest to seek the trees of Arvandor.

Araushnee stayed where she was. Distasteful though the prospect might be, she had to speak with Gruumsh, for she had questions that only the orc could answer.

She did not have long to wait. Gruumsh apparently had caught an elven scent—whether hers or Corellon's she did not know or care—and he came crashing wildly through the forest toward her.

Toward the web.

The orc blundered right into it. Flailing wildly, he roared and cursed and accomplished nothing but getting himself hopelessly entangled. From the forest beyond, Corellon's laughter floated back toward him like golden bells—beautiful even in mockery.

The orc lord's struggles redoubled, but he was well and truly stopped. Of course, Araushnee mused with a wry smile, the natural defenses of Arvandor would have accomplished that with or without her "intervention." Apparently that thought had not occurred to Corellon. He was too much entangled in Araushnee's charms to see any tapestry but that of her own weaving.

"Fool," she hissed as she regarded one captive and contemplated the other. And as she spoke the epithet, Araushnee wondered whether orc or elf deserved it better.

2

Master of the Hunt

t was no simple undertaking to slip away from the plane of the gods, to take on avatar form and to seek a godly ally in the unfamiliar forests of a mortal world. Not easy, but then, nothing about the task to which Araushnee had set her hand would come without price.

The elven goddess slipped silently through the forest, following unseen threads of magic to a place of unusual power. The Weave was strong on this world. It was a singularly beautiful place, with its single vast expanse of land set like polished jade upon a sea of lapis blue. Dragons roamed the forests and ruled the skies, but other magical races were drawn to this land as bees to clover. New races were rising, as well, increasing their numbers rapidly. Even gods saw promise in the burgeoning world—of late, there had been a veritable migration of powers both great and minor. Araushnee hoped to find an ally among these gods, one powerful enough—and malleable enough—to replace the recalcitrant Gruumsh.

After his battle with Corellon Larethian—not to mention the adventure's ignominious end as a orcish fly in the web of an elven goddess—Gruumsh had adamantly refused to have anything more to do with Araushnee and her ambitions. She was an elf and therefore his immortal enemy, and there the matter lay.

So be it. Araushnee was just as happy to rid her nose of the orc god's stench. There were other beings who could be tricked, cajoled, or seduced into doing her bidding. So she focused on the lines of magic, following them into the very heart of the land. In time they converged into a dense net over a certain ancient wood.

It was a forest as dense and deep as any in Arvandor, and nearly as fey. Enormous treants, almost indistinguishable from the venerable trees around them, observed the goddess's passage with the apparent disinterest common to long-lived beings who measure such events against the passage of eons. Small graces of unicorns scattered and fled before her like startled, silvery deer. Darting pinpricks of light suggested the presence of sprites or faerie dragons—or perhaps the more malevolent but still intriguing creatures known as will o'wisps. But for all the forest's wonders, there was ample evidence of danger: the distant roar of a hunting dragon, a feather fallen from the wings of a molting griffin, trail signs that spoke of manticores, footprints of a passing orcish war band.

It was the last of these that interested Araushnee most, for on every world that she knew, orcs were the bitter enemies of all elves. Surely this tribe's god, whoever he or she might be, would listen with interest to her proposal—provided that she, an elven goddess, could gain the ear of such a god.

While the morning was still young, Araushnee's sharp ears caught the sounds of battle away to the north, where mountain peaks rose far above the tree line to disappear into gathering clouds. As she drew near, she made out the sounds of orcish voices raised in war cries. But there was none of the clash and clamor of weapons that signaled the usual manner of warfare among Gruumsh's children. Indeed, the battle seemed to be coming from the mountains far above the orcs, and it sounded more like a contest between two preternaturally strong bears than any orcish duel. The titanic fighters were lost in the dark clouds, but their roars resounded like thunder, and their clashing shook the very ground beneath Araushnee's feet.

The goddess noticed the orcs gathered at the foot of the mountain, dancing and howling and hooting in what appeared to be a religious frenzy. She wondered if the stupid creatures carried on so whenever thunderstorms gathered over the mountain. Perhaps it was just a coincidence that this particular manifestation truly came from the hands of the gods. From what Araushnee knew of orcs, she doubted they could tell the difference between the two phenomena.

The goddess moved swiftly up the mountain, silent and invisible, aided in no small part by the things she had taken from her daughter's chamber. Young Eilistraee, known among the Seldarine as the Dark Maiden, was already an acclaimed huntress. Araushnee favored flowing gowns and delicate slippers, but these were not suited to her present task or to the wild terrain of this word's heartland. And so, clad in leathers of deep brown, shod in boots that seemed to absorb sound, and wrapped in a dappled green cloak that shifted its colors to match the foliage around it, Araushnee crept up to the battleground. It is doubtful that the combatants would have noted her approach regardless of these precautions, so furious was their battle.

She was too late to see the fighting itself, but she nodded with approval as she gazed upon the victor.

Malar, the Great Hunter, stood over the rapidly fading body of a creature much like himself. Well over twelve feet tall he was, with fur like that of a black bear covering a powerful, thick-muscled body shaped roughly like that of an orcish warrior. Malar lacked prominent fangs to seize and rend his opponents; in fact, he had no snout at all, merely a flesh-draped cavity in the center of his face that served as both nose and mouth. He did not seem to suffer from this lack. From his massive head sprouted a rack of antlers, each point dagger-sharp. The curving claws on his hands were each fully the size of Araushnee's hand. Yet victory had not come easily to Malar: His huge chest rose and fell like waves on a frenzied sea, and the breath that rasped through his oral cavity was harsh and labored.

Araushnee took her daughter's bow from her shoulder

and fitted to it one of Eilistraee's enchanted arrows. She sighted down her target and readied the weapon. Although she fully intended to make a deal with the god, she knew the value of negotiating from a position of apparent strength.

"Hail, Beastlord, Master of the Hunt!" Araushnee called out to him.

Malar whirled toward the musical sound of an elven voice and dropped into battle stance: knees bent and muscles bunched in preparation for a quick spring, arms spread in a parody of an embrace, claws hooked into terrible rending weapons. His eyes narrowed into malevolent slits as he regarded the armed goddess.

"What do you here, elf?" he growled out in a thunderous rumble. "This place is none of yours!"

"No, it is yours by right of conquest," the goddess agreed, nodding toward the fallen god. By now, little remained of the bestial avatar but a dim gray outline. "That was Herne, was it not? I have caught glimpses of him before, on other worlds. A pale copy of Malar, to my thinking."

The Beastlord's arms dropped just a bit. He was obviously wary of the elf but willing to hear more of her flattery. "This orc tribe now follows me," he boasted.

"As they should," Araushnee said, carefully hiding her elation. This Malar was precisely what she needed! An ambitious minor god, almost pitifully eager to expand his influence and power. And most important, a hunter.

She nodded to the shadowy remains of Herne and sighed. "All the same, it is a waste. Not that Herne should fall—never that," she added hastily when a growl started deep in Malar's throat. "A shame only that a hunter as mighty as the Beastlord should waste his talent on easy quarry."

When the god did not seem to take offense, Araushnee lowered her bow just a bit and took a cautious step closer. "I have an offer for you, great Malar, an opportunity such as might never come again to a hunter."

"There is much game in these forests," the Beastlord observed, watching her closely.

"Ah, but is there any challenge that could compare to tracking an elven god through his own sacred forest? That is a challenge only the greatest of hunters would dare take up."

Malar seemed to ponder this, his red eyes glowing intently. "An elven forest, you say? A wise hunter does not lay aside his knife and then walk into the embrace of a bear."

"A wounded bear," she stressed.

"That is even worse."

"As to that, look, and then judge for yourself," Araushnee said. With a quick gesture of one ebony hand, the goddess conjured a shining, multicolored orb and bade the Beastlord look within. Inside the globe was a tiny image of Corellon Larethian, looking (but for his size) as real as if he stood before them. It was clear that the elven god was gravely wounded; the golden light had drained from his skin, leaving him gray and haggard. His steps wove a slow, unsteady path through the trees.

The Beastlord studied the elven god, estimating his size against a stand of golden ferns. "He is small," Malar allowed.

"And weak! See his bandages, already wet and crimson."

The hunter squinted into the orb. "Strange. So much blood, but he leaves no trail."

"You expected anything less of an elven god?" Araushnee retorted. "Even so, surely Malar, the Master of the Hunt, can track him down. Think on it—what renown will be yours when you slay the head of the elven pantheon!"

Malar whuffled thoughtfully. "This forest you show me is elven. Never have I hunted so close to Arvandor."

"What wild place is not your rightful hunting ground?" she wheedled, sensing that the god was sorely tempted. The goddess gestured at the globe. In response, it grew in size until it nearly filled the battle-trampled clearing. "This is a gate to Olympus, great Malar. All you need do is step through."

The Beastlord eyed with great interest the scene within the globe, but he was still not convinced. "You are elven. What has this elf lord done that you want him dead?"

Araushnee thought she knew what answer might best please Malar. "He is weak," she said stoutly. "That offends me."

"If he is so weak, then kill him yourself."

The goddess shrugged. "I would, except that the other gods of the Seldarine love Corellon. They would not accept as their ruler anyone who killed him. And I wish to rule."

"Strange, these elven gods," mused Malar. "It is ever the way of nature that the strongest should rule. Anyone able to kill this god deserves to supplant him. If elves think otherwise, they are weak indeed."

"Not all think so," Araushnee corrected him.

The hunter's crimson eyes met hers, taking her measure. "Perhaps I should kill Corellon Larethian, and you, too, and then take my own chances among your pantheon!"

Araushnee laughed scornfully. "One wounded elven god you could surely slay, but all at once? No, content yourself with the trophy you see before you. Corellon is a far greater prize than any you have won this day."

Malar nodded toward the foot of the mountain, where the orcs' celebration had reached what sounded like a death-dealing frenzy. "A god needs worshipers."

"And so you shall have them," said Araushnee, certain that she knew at last what bait would lure Malar into her web. "The orcs value strength: That tribe will follow you because you defeated their god. How many more orcs will join their ranks when they learn that you have succeeded where Gruumsh One-Eye could not?"

"That elf blinded Gruumsh?" the Beastlord asked, caution creeping into his voice as he regarded the image of Corellon with new respect. Malar knew all too well that Gruumsh, the First Power of the orcs, was a force with which to reckon.

"Yet another sign of Corellon's weakness," Araushnee said hastily. "He should have slain the orc when he had the chance. *I* would have. Or, at the very least, I would have gelded him!"

A low chuckle grated from the hunter. "It is not my way to humiliate my quarry, but to destroy it. Your ways are not mine, elf, yet I cannot deny the appeal in the picture you paint. A gelded Gruumsh! I am not a subtle god, but *there* is irony even I can appreciate!"

Araushnee seized upon the moment of grim camaraderie. "Then go, destroy, and claim your trophy. And when it is done, you will have what you most desire," she said in a voice that was all silk and temptation.

"Which is?"

"Quarry—quarry that will tempt the finest hunters of this world and win you many new followers. Elves," she said, spelling it out at last. "When I rule in Arvandor, I will send tribes of elves to this world. Orcs will hunt them, and in doing so they will follow Malar, the greatest elf-hunter of all."

"Elves!" Malar snorted. "There are elves here already. The Weave is strong: Where there is magic, there are always elves."

The goddess quickly covered her surprise. She had not sensed the presence of elven people upon this world, something that any member of the Seldarine could easily do. Perhaps she had been too absorbed in her quest to be attuned to their presence.

"But the elves here are few and of no real power," she said, hoping that this was indeed the case. "I will send entire clans. Elves who will build cities and craft weapons of magic. Your primitive orcs will rally to you in hope of seizing such prizes. You will become a great power—the god of all those people who hate and hunt Corellon's children!"

At last the Beastlord nodded. "I go," he said simply, and then he leaped into the shining globe.

The vision that Araushnee had conjured dissipated with a faint crackle. When it was gone, so was the Master of the Hunt.

A triumphant chuckle started in Araushnee's throat. Her laughter deepened to shake her flat belly and grew in power as it rolled out in peal after peal over the mountains. On and on it went, growing higher and more uncanny until it seemed to meld with the shrieking of the wind.

And in the valley below, the fierce orcs paused their orgy of slaughter and celebration to listen to the ungodly sound. For the first time that day, they knew true fear.

* * * * *

The long night of battle was a memory now, and the morning sunlight that filtered through the forest canopy brought warmth and strength to the wearied elf lord. Corellon was almost home—he could sense the change in the air, feel the power in the ground beneath his feat. Already he could feel the magic of Arvandor flowing through him. He picked up his pace; the battle with Gruumsh was over, but it had raised many questions that demanded resolution.

A low, bestial growl came from a cluster of scarlet sumac bushes behind him. Corellon stiffened, doubly startled. He'd heard no animal's approach, and he knew no animal in the forest as enemy. He turned cautiously to the sound, hand on the hilt of his sword, just as the foliage seemed to explode from the force of a running charge.

A monstrous, fur-clad being leaped at him, arms out wide and claws curved into grasping hooks. Corellon struck out, slicing across one of the creature's leathery palms. Before the bestial thing could react, the elf had skipped well away.

"Malar!" he called out sternly, for he knew of the Beastlord—albeit, nothing good. "How do you dare to hunt in an elven forest?"

"I hunt wherever I want," the god growled, "and *whomever* I want."

So saying, Malar lowered his head and came at the elf lord like a charging stag. As he came, antlers sprang from

39

his head, each instantly branching out into a score of lethal, bladelike tips.

Corellon stood his ground. Holding his sword firmly with both hands, he thrust up into the rack of antlers. Instantly he twisted so that his back was to Malar, then he bent quickly forward, heaving his entangled sword forward and down with all his strength.

The incredible speed of the elf's maneuver, combined with the momentum of Malar's charge, sent the Beastlord hurtling up and over the much smaller elf. He landed on his back, hard enough to bounce and even skid forward a pace or two. Corellon nimbly leaped forward. With one booted foot he pinned one of Malar's forearms to the ground, and he pressed the point of his sword tightly to the black-furred throat.

"Yield," the elf lord demanded. "Do so, and you will depart this place unharmed."

Malar let loose a defiant snarl. With his unfettered arm, he took a mighty swipe at the elf's legs. Corellon's blade flashed forward to parry. He batted the arm aside—and sheared off a couple of the god's claws for good measure. Quickly Corellon reversed the direction of his swing, slashing back at the Beastlord's throat.

But Malar had simply disappeared.

The point of Corellon's sword sliced into the flattened grass and carved a deep furrow into the ground below. For the briefest of moments, Corellon teetered, off-balance. Before he could get his feet solidly beneath him, a blow struck him from behind and sent him flying. A low, grating chuckled rumbled through the forest as the nimble elf lord tucked and rolled.

Corellon was angry now. It was one thing for *Gruumsh* to challenge him on this, his home plane: Gruumsh was First Power of his pantheon, a mighty god and a worthy, if treacherous, adversary. Malar, on the other hand, was a minor god who scavenged for worshipers among a hundred worlds and as many races of predatory beings. That such a god would challenge Corellon was beyond insult.

The elf rose and whirled, sword in hand. Hanging in the air before him was an enormous, disembodied limb that looked like the foreleg of a titanic panther. The claws were velveted; Malar had batted at Corellon like a malicious kitten playing with a mouse.

Corellon's fist tightened around the grip of his sword. The lights within Sahandrian's lights whirled and sparked in concert with the wrath of the sword's wielder.

With a rush, Corellon advanced upon his strange foe. His sword whirled and darted and spun, carving deep lines onto the catlike limb and sending tufts of black fur flying. Malar's laughter soon turned to growls of anger and pain. The pantherlike claws darted and slashed in return, but never once did they touch the elven god. Corellon danced around the Limb of Malar, taunting, offering an opening where there was none, luring the Beastlord into another attack and then yet another—each time dealing swift and terrible reprisals.

Malar's rage, his overwhelming instinct for the kill, drove him to fight on and on, until his panther fur was sticky with blood, the hide torn to expose sinew and even bone. Many long moments passed before it occurred to the Beastlord that his tactics were driven more by bloodlust than sound strategy. Again the god changed form. As a shroud of utter blackness, he enveloped his elven foe.

Corellon froze in mid-swing. Not because he was startled by the sudden midnight that had fallen around him—he knew of Malar's manifestations and he had expected this—but because of the suffocating sense of evil in the miasma that surrounded him. Corellon instinctively darted to one side; the cloud that was Malar simply moved with him. Deep, snarling laughter resounded through the blackness, deepening the smothering pall of evil.

An eerie red glow fell upon the elf lord. Corellon looked up into the enormous red eyes that floated near the top of the cloud. Without hesitation, the elf lord hauled his sword high overhead and threw it up with all his strength. Sahandrian flipped end over end, twice, forming a spiral of

41

pure light as it carved through the pervasive evil. The tip of the sword sank deep between Malar's crimson eyes.

With a roar of anguish and rage that shook the surrounding trees, Malar disappeared.

Corellon blinked in the sudden brightness and sidestepped the whir that announced Sahandrian's triumphant descent. The sword thudded point-down into the ground before him.

As the elf lord wiped his sword free of the blood and ichor and clinging soil, his thoughts lingered on the battles he had won. Gruumsh had been dealt a grave and lasting injury, Malar utterly vanquished and banished—at least for a time. These were feats that would be remembered in song, and woven into the fabric of a thousand legends.

Yet Corellon found little pride in these victories and nothing of joy. Pressing hard upon him was the presentiment that what he had truly won this day was not glory but new and deadly enemies for his brother and sister gods and for their elven children.

3

Dark Tapestry

raushnee made her way swiftly back to the heart of Arvandor, to the forest home she shared with her children by Corellon Larethian. Though she was returning home, the goddess was not in good spirits.

She had witnessed the battle between Malar and Corellon through another of her magical globes. In the space of a single day, two of her chosen agents had failed to do away with the elven god. Once again Corellon had unwittingly blocked her progress toward her rightful place at the head of the elven pantheon.

Disgruntled as she was, Araushnee felt somewhat relieved once she had shed her borrowed hunter's garb and dressed herself in a filmy gown and dainty slippers, both crafted by her own hands of finest spider silk. She entered her daughter's private chamber without knocking and dumped the borrowed gear onto the floor.

Eilistraee was at home—a rare event—preparing herself for some woodland revel. She looked up from the boots she was lacing, clearly startled by the interruption. Her silver eyes shifted from her tumbled belongings to her mother's face, then warmed with pleasure and excitement.

"Oh, mother! You have been hunting! Why did you not tell me you wished to go? We might have gone together, and made merry sport of it!"

"We might indeed," Araushnee mused aloud as her mind raced over the possibilities. She needed allies, and she would be unwise to overlook those closest to hand.

Certainly Eilistraee would not have been her first choice. The girl was given to quicksilver moods, and she possessed an uncertain temper. One moment she was a carefree child dancing like a moonbeam or running like a silver wolf through the forest; the next moment, she was either as seductive as a siren or as serious as a dwarven god. Well, the girl was of an age when such swings were common, Araushnee noted as she observed her daughter. Eilistraee was no longer a child, and she was far too beautiful to suit Araushnee, who didn't care for competition from any quarter. The fledgling goddess had inherited her mother's face, but her hair and eyes were of a silvery shade that always brought to Araushnee's mind her hated rival, Sehanine Moonbow. Eilistraee was also exceedingly tall, which further annoyed her dainty mother, but Araushnee had to admire the strength and grace in her daughter's long limbs. None in the Seldarine could outrun the Dark Maiden, and few could match her skill with the bow.

Yes, there were definite possibilities in Eilistraee, concluded Araushnee slyly. She doubted the girl could be induced to strike openly against Corellon, for Eilistraee adored her father. But she was young, and her very naivete could be turned into a potent weapon against the elf lord. And although Araushnee needed allies, she also needed scapegoats. One way or another, Eilistraee would serve.

The goddess slipped an arm around her daughter's waist. "You are right, my little raven," she said with rare warmth. "It is far past time that we hunted together. I have a plan. Listen, and tell me if it pleases you. . . ."

* * * * *

Days are long in Olympus, longer than the turning of years upon some worlds, but to Araushnee this one seemed far too short. The morning passed in a blur of activity. First came the drudgery of traipsing through the forest with Eilistraee, learning her daughter's skills and habits—and plotting ways to turn this knowledge against the girl.

Her other child, her son Vhaeraun, also had a part to play, and Araushnee spent no little time schooling him in his role. This proved to be a difficult task, considering that the entire Seldarine was celebrating the dual victories of Corellon Larethian. Avoiding several score of celebrating elven deities, even in a place as vast as Arvandor, proved to be no easy matter. Nor was it easy to hold Vhaeraun's attention: Many a young goddess—and one or two of the elder powers as well—urged the handsome young god to join in the merriment.

At highsun, Araushnee finally left Vhaeraun to his revels. She sought out Corellon, for he might wonder if she did not, and spent the brightest hours of the day in conversation and dalliance. But the time she passed in the elf lord's presence sorely taxed her. Playing the loving consort had never before been a burden to Araushnee, but there was much yet undone, and it was difficult for her to speak sweet blandishments and tell witty stories while her mind whirled with the details of her plot. Finally she was able to slip away, laughingly claiming that she had been greedy in taking so much of his time as her own—subtly reminding him that others waited to celebrate with him. It was a powerful ploy, for all the elves save perhaps Araushnee herself valued the community of their sister and brother gods above all other things. She had places to go, and deeds best done when there were no eyes to witness them.

Seldom did the gods of the Seldarine travel from Arvandor, except to tend the needs and nurture the arts of their elven children. But on this long afternoon Araushnee traveled to many strange and dire places, seeking out warriors for the battle that would come all too soon. The elves were an ancient people, nearly as old as the gods from whom they had sprung, and many creatures envied and hated them. To the gods of all these folk—the orcs and ogres, the goblinkin, hobgoblins, bugbears, the evil dragons, creatures of the sky and the deepest seas, even beings from the elemental planes—Araushnee carried her seeds of war. She did not appear as herself, for to travel in elven form would be courting instant death, or, at the very least, almost ensuring the eventual discovery of her plot by the Seldarine. For this day's purpose, Araushnee took on a new and lethal form, one suited to her talents, yet one that dire gods and denizens could appreciate.

The sun was setting upon the elven forest when Araushnee returned to Olympus, well satisfied with her efforts. Her contentment vanished, however, when she found a visitor awaiting her in her own home.

The translucent form of Sehanine Moonbow strode about the entrance hall in great agitation. She stopped her pacing when Araushnee entered, and stabbed a still-hazy finger in the dark goddess's direction.

"I name you, Araushnee, traitor to the Seldarine, conspirator with orcs and worse," she proclaimed in her silvery voice.

A tendril of worry snaked into Araushnee's mind. What did the moon goddess know? And more importantly, was Sehanine merely speaking jealousy-induced suspicions, or did she possess damaging proof of Araushnee's perfidy?

She folded her arms and regarded the shadowy goddess. "That is a serious accusation," she said coldly. "A dangerous one, too, considering that you are, shall we say, not quite yourself?"

The goddess of moon magic ignored the threat. From the folds of her gown she produced a familiar object—a padded sheath, made from finest silk and worked with brilliantly colored threads. Upon it was an intricate tapestry that depicted the gods at play in their elven forest. A matchless example of the weaver's art, the scene was barded about with runes of warding and protection such as only an elven goddess might fashion. Araushnee's heart thudded painfully as she recognized the enchanted sheath.

"This is your work, is it not? No one else in all of Arvandor could create so wondrous a weave," Sehanine said, with no thought of flattery.

Araushnee tossed back her head. "That makes me an

artist, not a traitor. If you have something else to say, speak quickly and then get you gone."

"When did you weave this tapestry? When were the magic of these runes released?"

The dark goddess brow furrowed as she pondered the strange questions. The runes and wardings were similar to those that gave protection from attack. Corellon, of course, had fought Gruumsh throughout the previous night. And come to think of it, Araushnee did most of the work during the cool hours after midnight, when the moon was bright . . .

Her scarlet eyes widened as understanding came. She had worked when the moon was bright and when Sehanine's power was at its height.

"You sensed the magic in the tapestry was wrong. You knew it—certainly you knew it, for I swear that the very moonlight carries night-born secrets to you—yet you let your lord go into battle wearing a token that condemned him to failure. If I am traitor, then so also are you!"

Sehanine shook her head. "I felt your animosity, that much is true, but I thought it was for me alone. Only when Gruumsh's attack unleashed your curse did I understand. Before the moon rose, when I was too weak to act, the orc shattered my lord's sword and gravely wounded him."

"And you, meddling bitch that you are, simply had to pick up the pieces," Araushnee said angrily. "You took the sheath from him, didn't you?"

"If I had not, would he even now be safe in Arvandor?"

Araushnee hissed with rage and frustration. The goddess of moonlight was also the goddess of mysteries. It seemed she was as good at unraveling them as she was at creating them. And Sehanine was powerful—far more powerful than Araushnee. Or, more precisely, she *would* be, when the moon was high. Even now, with sunset still staining the skies over Arvandor, Sehanine's glassy form was swiftly taking on substance and power. Araushnee had to act now or all would be lost.

Flinging out both hands, the dark goddess let the full force of her wrath and jealousy fuel the magic that poured from her fingertips. Malevolent power spun at the moon goddess in silky threads. Instantly Sehanine was enmeshed in a web far stronger than that which had stopped the charge of mighty Gruumsh One-Eye.

But this was not enough for Araushnee. Her rage stirred a miniature tempest, a wind that howled and raced along the walls of the hall until it formed a whirling cloud. The whirlwind caught the struggling moon goddess and tossed her into the very heart of the tiny maelstrom.

This was precisely what Araushnee needed. Again she lifted her hands, and again threads of magic darted toward her rival. The wind seized them, spun them, wrapped them tightly around Sehanine until the goddess was as tightly and thoroughly cocooned as an unawakened butterfly.

When she was satisfied, Araushnee dismissed the tempest. A smile curved her lips as she regarded the captive goddess. Sehanine was clearly visible through the layers of gossamer magic, but she could not move or speak. As a precaution, Araushnee sent a silent, gloating insult to the goddess's mind. It was like speaking to stone—not even the mind-to-mind community shared by members of the elven pantheon could penetrate that web of magic. Sehanine's capture was complete. It was also, unfortunately, temporary. Moonrise would grant Sehanine power far beyond anything Araushnee could command.

The dark goddess sent forth another silent summons—one that spoke to Vhaeraun's mind alone and that told him, in terms that left no room for argument, he was to cease whatever he was doing and hasten home.

In remarkably short order (for Araushnee had intimated what might occur if he should dally), the young god burst into the hall. His eyes went wide as he regarded the moon goddess—and contemplated the price they might pay for an attack upon one of the most powerful elven deities.

"Mother, what have you done?" he said in great consternation.

"It could not be helped. She knows—or at least suspects—that the sheath I wove for Corellon stole his sword's magic. But being an honorable sister," Araushnee sneered, "she came to confront me with her suspicions before going to the Seldarine Council. The only way she'll get there now is to drop to the ground and slither like a snake. I would almost welcome the council's intrusion into my affairs for the pleasure of witnessing such a thing!"

Vhaeraun peered closely at the magical web that bound Sehanine. "Will it hold, at least until the battle is done?"

"No," Araushnee admitted. "It would not hold at all if she had not been such a fool as to come to me—*me*, her bitterest rival—when her power was next to nothing. But the moon will soon rise. You must take her to a place where there is no moonlight and see that she stays there until the battle is past."

"And then what?" he countered in a tone that approximated his mother's sneer. "How can you hope to rule, with a goddess of Sehanine's power to oppose you? You should kill her now, when she is still helpless."

Araushnee's hand flashed forward and dealt a ringing slap to her son's face. "Do not presume to question me," she said in a voice that bubbled with rage. "If you are so ignorant that you believe one god can easily kill another, perhaps I was wrong to make you my confidante and partner!"

"But what of Herne?" pressed Vhaeraun, eager to salvage something of his dignity even it that only meant winning some small point of argument. "You told me that Malar killed him. And for that matter, why would you set Gruumsh and Malar against Corellon, if neither had hope of success?"

"Don't be more of a fool than you must," snapped the goddess. "It is one thing to destroy a god from another place and another pantheon—even among the gods, there are hunters and hunted, predators and prey. But to kill a member of one's own pantheon is another matter. If it were so easy, would I not already rule Arvandor?"

The young god regarded his mother for several moments, his eyes thoughtful and his fingertips gingerly stroking his stinging cheek. "If it is as you say," he said slowly, "then perhaps you should leave the Seldarine."

"Have you not heard a word I have said this day? I wish to *rule* the Seldarine!"

"Then do so by conquest, rather than intrigue," Vhaeraun suggested. "You have been amassing an army to do your will. Leave the Seldarine, and lead that army yourself! Imagine Araushnee at the head of a mighty force, the leader of the anti-Seldarine!" he concluded, his voice ringing with the drama of it and the pride of one who admires his own visions.

Araushnee stared at him for a moment, then she shook her head in despair. "How did I give birth to two such idiots? Think, boy! List in your mind the great and glorious generals I have enlisted!"

She was silent for a moment, letting the names of the Seldarine's enemies hang silent in the air between them. There was Maglubiyet, leader of the goblinkin's gods. Hruggek, who led bugbears into the hunt and into battle. Kurtulmak, the head of the kobold pantheon—it still amazed Araushnee that kobolds *had* a pantheon. By any measure of elvenkind, these gods were unimpressive foes. Some of the other gods who'd enlisted in the coming battle were considerably more powerful than these, and the list went on at length—but the army that resulted was far less than the sum of its parts. Many of them were enemies, or, at best, held each other in contempt. It was a volatile alliance, and far too much of the gods' ire and energy would be spent on each other. If Vhaeraun was too stupid to see that, Araushnee would do well to rid herself of him at once.

To her relief, a look of uncertainty crept across the young god's face as he contemplated their collective allies. "This army—it can win?"

"Of course not," the goddess stated baldly. "But these gods are strong enough and numerous enough to do considerable damage. And most important, it is an army that none in Arvandor will see as anything other than a coalition of elven enemies. The Seldarine will prevail, but the battle will be long and there will be losses on both sides. We will see to it, you and I, that one of those is Corellon Larethian."

"Our grief, of course, will be heartbreaking," added Vhaeraun with a sly grin.

"Naturally. And all the gods of the Seldarine, stunned by the loss of their beloved Corellon, will rally behind his consort and her heroic son. Once we have this ultimate power, doing away with Sehanine will be a small matter." She shot a sidelong, measuring look at the young god. "You are still willing to do these things?"

When Vhaeraun regarded her blankly, she pointed out, "After all, he *is* your father."

"And he is your lord husband. If there is a difference, please explain it to me. Otherwise, we will say that I am your son and leave the matter as settled," Vhaeraun said. His words were blunt and the implications harsh; instinctively he braced himself for another display of his mother's ready temper.

To his surprise, she laughed delightedly. "You are my son indeed. Your role in this will be carried out well, of that I have little doubt. Nor do I doubt your desire to rule with me when this is done. Go now—be rid of Sehanine and then return as quickly as you can. Time is short. I need you to take this sheath to the Moor, so that Eilistraee can 'find' it this night. The battle begins with the coming of new light."

She held her smile as Vhaeraun kissed her cheek, kept it firmly in place as he cast the minor magic that reduced the trapped moon goddess to manageable size and then bore her off through a newly conjured portal, a magical gate that glistened like black opal.

Perhaps, Araushnee mused, the portal led to some mortal world where the sun-bright days lasted nearly as long as a day on Olympus, perhaps to some deeply buried crypt where Sehanine might lie, helpless and deprived of moonlight until long after the battle for Arvandor was won. Araushnee did not know, but she trusted in Vhaeraun to come up with a suitable exile for her rival. After all, he was her son.

And because Vhaeraun was so truly her own, Araushnee's smile faded to a frown of worry the moment he was no longer there to see. It occurred to her with frightening clarity that he who would so willingly betray his father was likely to turn against the mother with whom he now plotted.

For the first time, Araushnee realized how truly alone she was on the path she had chosen. With this realization came a moment's regret. But the emotion did not linger, and when it passed, something else went with it—a part of Araushnee's heart that had slowly been dying, unnoticed and unmourned. The slender thread of magic that connected her to the other gods of the Seldarine and to their elven children had finally snapped. Whatever else Araushnee had become, she was no longer truly elven.

So be it, the goddess thought. She would still be the undisputed queen of Arvandor, for all that.

And if this could not come to pass, Araushnee realized with suddenly clarity, then she would simply have to seek out a place where she *could* rule. She was what she was, and there was no other course for her.

4

The Trees of Arvandor

n the long, silent hour just before dawn, the gods of the Anti-Seldarine coalition crept through the forest that surrounded Arvandor. Their passage was unhindered. The playful illusions that led passersby astray were quiet, the magical shields were down. Even the sentinels of the forest had been silenced. The treants were deep in an enchanted slumber, the very birds were hushed.

Not far away, in a forest grove where she came each day to welcome the dawn with music and dance, the goddess Eilistraee noted the silence with puzzlement. At this hour, the birds should have been singing their morning summons to the sun and the deer grazing upon the still-damp grasses.

She put away her flute unplayed and took her bow from her shoulder. Although she had never met with danger in this forest, she sensed that something was amiss. There was something wrong in the air—an intangible miasma so strong it was almost like a scent. Instinctively, Eilistraee lifted her head into the wind and sniffed like a wolf.

There *was* a scent, one very familiar to the young goddess. Though some of the elven gods abhorred the death of any forest creature, some of them, like Eilistraee, lived in concert with the ways of Nature. From time to time, she hunted as a hawk hunted, or a wolf. She hunted because she was part of the forest, and because the forest elves of a hundred worlds, whom she saw as her particular charges among the elven children of Corellon, hunted for their food. Many a time her unseen hand had guided an elven archer's aim, or her footsteps had marked a trail to waiting prey. Eilistraee knew well the smell of blood.

She hurried toward the scent, which grew stronger and ranker and more complex until it threatened to steal her breath and twist her stomach. Other odors mingled with the blood and hung heavy in the moist morning air: the musty stench of creatures Eilistraee had never seen, and the faint and lingering scent of terror.

In moments the young goddess stood over the scattered remains of some of the forest's most gentle creatures. Through eyes bright with unshed tears, she made out the bodies of a doe and her two newborn fawns. By the look of things, all three deer had died slowly. The tawny hides were marked with many small, malicious wounds. Most were punctures, such as might be made with sword or spear, but the work of claws and teeth was also in evidence. But this was not the doing of an animal, of that Eilistraee was certain. No animal in the forest would kill, except for food. This senseless carnage was something else entirely, something horrible beyond her imagining. Whoever had done this thing had killed for the sheer joy of it.

Suddenly Eilistraee knew what name to call that miasma that hung in the forest air like foul mist. It was something she had never encountered, but she recognized it for what it was: Evil walked among the trees of Arvandor.

The goddess turned away from the grim site, her silver eyes scanning the trampled, blood-soaked foliage. She would track down whoever had done this, and then she would bring him before the Seldarine Council for judgment. The killer's path would be easy to follow; the feet that had made it were careless and clumsy. But before she began, she lifted her voice in a raven's haunting call. The deer were part of Nature's circle, and by summoning the ravens she would at least give some small measure of meaning to their deaths.

Eilistraee had not walked far before she realized that

this particular evil walked in more than one pair of boots. One creature had slain the deer, but his path soon converged with that of another. And soon after, the pair of footprints was swallowed in a broad swath of bruised and trampled foliage.

The young huntress dropped to one knee to study the trail. Many had passed by, too many for her to make out the individual marks. Frightened now, she put an ear to the ground. The sound that came to her was like that of distant thunder.

The girl leaped to her feet and climbed nimbly into the arms of an ancient oak. From this tree she moved to another, and then another, tracking the invaders from above. Her eyes were keen, and she moved nearly as fast among the trees as she could while on the ground. Soon she had the invaders in her sight.

There were a hundred of them, perhaps more, and all of them were gods. Eilistraee could not give names to many of them, but she recognized a few: the hulking red-furred creature was Hruggek, the god of bugbears; the goblinoid deity was one whose name she had heard but could not recall. They were led by a limping, battle-scarred Malar, who was so battered that he seemed to be driven onward by nothing but sheer malice. All of them were armed far past the demands of a hunt, and they plodded on with grim determination on a direct path toward Arvandor.

How this was possible, Eilistraee did not know—the way to Arvandor was known only to the elves and other forest folk. Nor could she say how it was that this motley army trampled through the forest, snarling and pushing and jostling at each other, without sending a breath of sound traveling through the air to herald their coming.

Desperately the young goddess wished for moonlight, for Sehanine had showed her how to travel the gossamer strands of its magic with no more than a thought. Eilistraee's own magic was no great thing, and it focused mostly upon simple matters: a knowledge of herbs and healing, a special communion with the forest's creatures, a love of music and dance. None of these things would serve now, except, perhaps, her skill for the hunt.

The goddess was tempted to send a small storm of arrows down upon the army. She had a quiver full of fine arrows, and an aim that was second to none. Surely she could bring down a score or more of them before they managed to pull her from her perch.

But then—what? And what would become of the other elven gods when this army came upon them unannounced? With difficulty Eilistraee stayed her hand. She was Corellon Larethian's daughter, and her first duty was to the elven pantheon.

Setting her jaw in determination, Eilistraee sped lightly through the treetops to do as duty bid. Yet there was in her heart a certain pride that it was she who would sound the alarm. And speeding her on was the hope that Corellon, the ultimate elven warrior, would reward her diligence by granting her a place by his side during the battle to come.

She was certain that he would do so, and not just for her sharp eye and quick report. Eilistraee had spent much of the previous night searching the Moor for her father's lost sheath. Corellon treasured it because Araushnee had made it, and he wore it always into battle as a token of his beloved. Wistfully, Eilistraee wondered if he might not also love *her* just a bit more when she returned such a treasure to him.

And so it was that Eilistraee's spirits were bright with hope and excitement, despite the danger that trod grimly toward her forest home.

*   *   *   *   *

The gods of the Seldarine swiftly gathered to meet the approaching threat. From a hundred worlds and from every corner of the sacred elven forest they came, and with them stood the gods of other faerie folk: the pixies, the sprites—even the gods of the ancient Fairy Court had donned armor for battle. The deities of the woodland folk came as well: immortal unicorns, centaurs, and wild-eyed fauns marched alongside the elves. All the powers of Arvandor rallied in uncommon unity against the threat. They gathered, secure within Arvandor's sheltering curtain of magic, and awaited Corellon Larethian's command to attack.

First to strike was Aerdrie Faenya, goddess of the air. The Anti-Seldarine forces pulled up sharply when she appeared; they stared open-mouthed at the apparition before them. From head to waist, Aerdrie appeared to be a beautiful elven woman with pale blue skin, flowing white hair, and feathery wings the color of summer clouds. She moved not on legs, but in a cloud of swirling mist, and with an ethereal grace and speed such as none of them had ever beheld. To the awestruck invaders, it appeared as if the very sky had suddenly descended and taken on elven form.

But Aerdrie was not nearly so delicate as she looked. From her outstretched hand came buffeting winds and fierce lightning strikes that sent the attacking army staggering back, grasping frantically at the whipping branches for handholds. For a brief time it appeared that the invaders might be swept from the forest by Aerdrie's wrath alone.

But other gods were eager to test their powers against the elves. An icy wind swept from the north like a war chariot, bearing upon it the goddess Auril. In her wake came winter storms that made the worst of Aerdrie's attacks seem like gentle zephyrs. Where Auril passed, the trees shivered, and their leaves turned hard and curled inward as if seeking the warmth that lingered within the wood.

Desperate to protect the elven forest from Auril's killing frosts, Aerdrie spread her wings and climbed high above the trees of Arvandor, then tucked and came at the invading goddess like a stooping falcon. The two goddesses of wind and weather met in a clash of lightning and a rumble of thunder that shook the blasted leaves from the trees below.

Grappling in midair like a pair of she-panthers, the goddesses were borne swiftly away on the maelstrom of their own battle. Soon there was nothing to be seen of them but the swirling clouds of dense purple and livid white in the distant sky, and the flashes of lightning that they hurled at each other like insults.

The Anti-Seldarine horde, suddenly freed from the unseen fetters of Aerdrie's winds, rallied and came on. To the utter horror of the elven gods, they passed easily through Arvandor's wall of protective magic. Their pace quickened to a rush as they closed the distance between themselves and the astonished elven defenders.

As he witnessed this defilement of the sacred forest, Corellon Larethian remembered what Sehanine had said of his sword: Sahandrian had been destroyed through elven treachery. It was clear that the goddess had spoken truth and that this same traitor was even now at work. Only an elven god could alter the magic that protected Arvandor. This same traitor, Corellon thought grimly, was most likely among the elven host that stood with him.

But who was it? Sehanine knew, or at least suspected, but she was nowhere to be found. There was no choice but to fight, and this he must do without knowing the name of his most dangerous enemy. Or was it possible, he thought with sudden horror, that Sehanine herself was the traitor? She had witnessed his near-defeat at Gruumsh's hand, she had given him the sword so that he would fight on rather than flee for Arvandor. And, as he had noted before, she was not standing among the forces of Arvandor.

Corellon took a long, steadying breath and turned his eyes to the enemy he *could* see. The elf lord lifted Sahandrian high. "For Arvandor," he shouted as he led the charge toward the onrushing throng.

The elven gods and their cohorts followed Corellon. But the place of honor at his side went to his swift and beautiful daughter. He was proud of Eilistraee for her part in alerting the elves and delighted that she had thought to search the Moor for Araushnee's token. He wore the wondrous sheath now and took comfort from the knowledge that his beloved Araushnee stood back in relative safety, casting magic with other gods whose strengths were more mystic than military.

Corellon stole a glance over his shoulder. Araushnee stood somewhat apart from the other gods of magic, her hands outstretched and her crimson eyes intense with gathered power. Their son, Vhaeraun, stood guard over his mother as she chanted her incantations.

Then the invaders were upon the elven gods, and there was no more time for thought. Corellon slashed and darted and danced, his mighty sword turning aside the axes and pikes of their foes. Many of the elven gods took a stand near him, for the invaders all but fell over each other in their efforts to get at their most powerful foe. Eilistraee fought at his side with a silvery sword and with chilling ferocity, but she was soon swept away by the battle. Corellon lost sight of her in the crush and turmoil.

A piercing, nasal wail that could only be Kurtulmak caught Corellon's attention. He glanced toward the shriek to see the kobold god pluck a shining black arrow from his backside. Corellon noted the odd, almost vertical angle of the arrow and glanced up—instinctively parrying a dagger's thrust as he did so. Eilistraee had found a perch in the trees overhead, and she had another black arrow already nocked and ready. She sent her father a grin that managed to be both impish and fierce, then she sent her next arrow hurtling down into the thickest part of battle.

Her target was a minor goblin deity who was attempting to sneak up on Corellon. Dagger clenched between his teeth, the goblin crawled on hands and knees between the legs of a hobgoblin who fought near the elven lord, standing nearly toe-to-hoof with a centaur and battling with staves. Eilistraee's arrow caught the goblin in the rump; he jerked up, and his head struck squarely between the hobgoblin's legs. The hobgoblin let out a high-pitched scream of pain and outrage. Incensed, he forgot his centaur foe entirely and began to beat his goblin ally with his staff.

The centaur snorted in disgust and trotted off in search of a more worthy opponent.

Corellon chuckled, but all thoughts of mirth vanished as a rust-pitted sword thrust toward him—through the back of the fairy god who fought at his left side.

Faster almost than eyes could follow, Corellon seized his fey brother and tore him off the blade—an action that would bring certain death even to most gods, but which was the fairy's only hope of survival. The sword that had impaled him was iron, as deadly to a fairy as was poison to a mortal.

Corellon registered the enraged whinny close behind him, heard the thud and crunch of thick bones giving way to flailing hooves. He turned and flung his wounded ally over the back of the pegasus goddess. Without stopping for breath or thought, he sidestepped the fall of the orcish god whose skull had been crushed by the winged horse, spun and ducked, then thrust up under the swing of the ogre's iron sword. He yanked the weapon free of the ogre's belly and on the backswing parried the jab of a hobgoblin's spear. And so it went, on and on, long into the morning.

Beset on all sides, Corellon fought on, as did all who defended the sacred forest. Here and there a form faded away—gods did not die easily, but seldom was there fighting such as this among them. There were losses on both sides, and for many long hours it was not clear who would prevail.

But a time came at last when Corellon swung around, looking for the next attacker, and found that there was none to hand. A few stray clangs resonated through the trees, speaking of hand-to-hand skirmishes. Nearby, an angry faun leaped up and down on a fallen goblin, no doubt leaving a tattoo of hoofprints on the defeated god's backside. An ogre stumbled wildly through the nearby forest, swatting and clawing at the small bright lights that clung to him like a swarm of enraged bees. Sprites, Corellon noted, fierce and fearless as usual. Despite their losses—for more than one light flickered and dimmed as the ogre struck wildly at his tormenters—the sprites kept fighting, their tiny swords darting and thrusting as they stung the ogre again and again.

The battle was nearly over; Arvandor was secure. Corellon nodded in satisfaction and thrust his sword back into its scabbard.

An odd, tingling feeling sizzled up his hand as his fingers brushed the weave of the tapestry sheath. Suddenly he was struck by an overwhelming sense of evil, a malevolence more terrible than Malar's cloud of darkness.

Corellon instinctively tried to shy away, and found that he could not. He looked down at his boots. A viscous, sickly green substance had oozed from the ground, and was holding him fast.

"Ghaunadar," the elf lord murmured in horror. Ghaunadar was an ancient, elemental evil, one that had never before been seen anywhere on Olympus. Only the presence of true evil could open the door of Arvandor to such a power. Corellon knew a moment of despair as he realized the extent of the treachery within the Seldarine.

At that moment the ogrish god who fled the avenging sprites careened past Corellon. The ogre's yellow eyes widened at the sight of the trapped elven god, then darkened with bloodlust and dreams of glory. Ignoring the stinging swords of the sprites, the ogre lifted high his flail—a length of thick chain that ended in a spiked ball—and began to swing it in circles as he came at the elven god.

Corellon reached for Sahandrian. The sword would not come free; the tapestry sheath clenched around it like a malevolent fist.

Startled, Corellon glanced toward the place where Araushnee stood. The naked triumph on her face chilled him as even the cloud of Malar or the creeping horror of Ghaunadar could not do.

Before he could absorb this shock, Eilistraee's shriek torn his gaze from Araushnee's gloating face. Corellon glanced up as his daughter loosed an arrow that took the attacking ogre through the throat.

The bestial god stopped; his whirling flail did not. The

chain wrapped, once, twice, around his neck before the spiked balls slammed into his chest. His outline began to fade, but not before two more of Eilistraee's arrows bristled from his throat.

A fourth arrow was already in flight. Corellon felt again the tingle running from the scabbard, saw the arrow subtly change course. As his daughter's arrow spun toward him, Corellon realized why his sword had shattered during the battle with Gruumsh One-Eye.

The pain of Araushnee's treachery swept through him in great, crushing waves. Corellon did not even feel his daughter's arrow pierce his breast.

5

End of Battle,
Declaration of War

unset had faded from the forest, and the moon was just beginning to rise when Aerdrie Faenya, battered but triumphant, flew back to the battlefields of Arvandor. The day had been long, but it had seen Auril Storm-bringer soundly defeated. The price of this defeat had been Auril's eternal banishment from Olympus; henceforth, the goddess of ill weather would have to content herself with bringing winter to mortal worlds. This, of course, would add considerably to Aerdrie's responsibilities—she would have to ensure that the vanquished goddess did not focus her icy wrath upon the elven People. She suspected that many of the defeated and banished gods would take their revenge upon the mortal elves.

As she soared over the battle site, Aerdrie was relieved to note that her brother and sister deities had also triumphed. Most of the invaders had been banished, and the battlefield, though much trampled and bloodied, was nearly quiet. The trees of Arvandor would bear the scars of Auril's storms for some time to come, but all the forest deities would join in healing and cleansing the forest. Already the huntress daughter of Corellon was perched high in one such tree, no doubt saying healing magic over the blasted limbs.

The goddess swooped down toward the soon-to-be-victorious Seldarine, her thoughts already upon the celebration ahead. Her gaze fell upon young Eilistraee just as the grim-faced huntress loosed a black arrow. With horror, Aerdrie saw the arrow streak toward Corellon Larethian. It pierced the shining mail that covered the elf lord's chest and sent him hurtling backward.

A shriek like that of a rising wind tore from Aerdrie's throat. It did not occur to her that Eilistraee's act could be anything other than treachery, for all the Seldarine knew of the Dark Maiden's skill with the bow.

The goddess of air flung out both hands. From her fingers burst a tempest whose fury would have shamed Auril. The blast of wind struck the young huntress with a force that hurled her from the tree. Eilistraee plummeted down, winter-dry branches snapping beneath her as she fell. She hit the ground hard and lay still.

Sparing the fallen goddess not so much as a glance, Aerdrie alighted and hurried over to join the surviving members of the Seldarine, who were clustering around their fallen leader. They all fell back, however, to allow Araushnee passage, and watched in respectful silence as the goddess knelt at Corellon's side to mourn her fallen love.

"He is not dead," Hanali Celanil said suddenly.

Araushnee lifted her tear-streaked face from her hands and affixed an accusing gaze upon the goddess of love and beauty. "How can you, of all the gods, mock my grief? My beloved is gone!"

"The Dark Maiden's arrows could not slay him," said Hanali, this time more emphatically.

"I do not know why Eilistraee would do such a thing, but I do know that her aim is certain. Never once has she missed her mark," Araushnee countered.

Without wasting time in further speech, Hanali pushed aside the elf lord's consort and knelt in her place. Corellon's protective mail parted instantly before her touch. "It is as I thought," she murmured, studying the large arrowhead partially lodged in the elf lord's chest. "Eilistraee was hunting ogres—this arrow is big enough and strong enough to punch through the beasts' hides, but it's too large to slip between Corellon's ribs. It is lodged there. Help me," she said, turning to Aerdrie.

Between the two of them, the goddesses removed the arrow from the elven god and tended his wounds. But Corellon did not revive. There was about him an aura of immobilizing despair, as if the evil that he'd fought throughout that long day had chilled him deeply, leaving him frozen within himself. The other deities began to chant softly, speeding the elf lord's healing with their gathered power. Even Araushnee rallied from her grief to produce a shining vial from the folds of her gown.

"Water from Elysium, infused with healing herbs from the heart of Arvandor. It will help restore him," she said, and lifted the vial to Corellon's lips.

In truth, Araushnee had prepared for this eventuality. She'd had ample evidence of late of how tenaciously her "love" clung to his immortal life. The potion in her vial might not be deadly enough to kill the wounded god, but it would certainly slide him deeper into slumber. With a little luck—and perhaps some repeated doses—Corellon would never awaken. And if the nature of his deathlike slumber should ever be discovered, Araushnee would disclose a simple but devastating truth: It was Eilistraee who had gathered the herbs and brewed the potion. The young huntress had prepared the deadly poison not for her use, but for the war arrows of mortal elves; however, none but she and Araushnee knew this. Since Eilistraee was beyond speech and would be for some time to come—if not for all time—Araushnee felt confident that this particular aspect of her plot was beyond discovery. And then, once Corellon's power was hers to command, she would—

A ray of moonlight, sharp as a stiletto, struck with lightning speed, shattering the goddess's dream of victory and dashing the vial from her ebony fingers. Startled, Araushnee fell back from Corellon and shrieked out a curse, one so vile that it shocked the chanting elven deities into silence.

The attacking moonlight backed away, softened, and spread into a mist—and then took on a form that by now was all too familiar to Araushnee.

"Sehanine!" shrieked the dark goddess. She rose and rounded on her son, who'd been standing at her shoulder like a hovering raven awaiting a chance to feed. Vhaeraun took an instinctive step backward.

"You idiot!" she screamed, her face contorted with rage and frustration. "It is too soon, too soon! Another day, and I would have had so much power that Sehanine could have done nothing. But you—you have destroyed us both!"

She raised one hand to strike the youth, but Hanali Celanil seized her wrist with a strength astonishing for one so delicate. "Enough! Your own words raise grave questions, Araushnee, and be sure that we will find answers. Be mindful that the council that will consider these questions stands here in witness to what you have said and what you do," the goddess said sternly.

Araushnee spun away from her son, violently shaking off the goddess's restraining hand. She glared up into Hanali's exquisite face. "And who will call this council?" she sneered. "No elven god is Corellon's equal in power—and none but he can convene the council. Wake him if you can—or hold your accusing tongue!"

In response, Sehanine Moonbow and Aerdrie Faenya came to flank Hanali. From them all rose a luminous mist, one that coalesced into a single goddess of impossible beauty and daunting power. Araushnee, beholding her, knew with certainty that she beheld her own successor.

"I am Angharradh," the new goddess said in a voice that was wind, moonlight, and music. "From the essence of the three greatest elven goddesses am I born. I am three and I am one—three to ensure that treachery never again enters the heart of a goddess of Arvandor, and one to stand at Corellon's side."

Angharradh stooped and touched her hand lightly to Corellon's forehead, and again to his heart. The wounds closed, and the dark aura that clung to him seemed to part. The elf lord opened his eyes at last. They settled, not on the wondrous Angharradh, but upon Araushnee. His gaze held terrible heartbreak and equally strong resolve.

"A great evil has entered our midst," he said in a dry whisper. "We must confront it now, for the sake of the Seldarine and all our elven children. The Council is convened. Let any who would, speak freely."

And so Sehanine stepped forward and told her story, starting with her suspicions of Araushnee's enchanted tapestry. She spoke of witnessing the battle with Gruumsh, and the shattering of Corellon's sword. She told of her own foolishness in approaching Araushnee, of her capture by the dark goddess's web and her imprisonment at Vhaeraun's hands. In a few terse words she confessed to them how she had escaped and the power she had given up to do so.

The members of the Seldarine were silent as they absorbed Sehanine's dreadful tale. Finally Corellon spoke. "You all have heard the accusations, and you have witnessed disturbing things. You must decide what fate Araushnee has earned."

. "Banishment." The word came as if from a single throat.

Corellon looked into Araushnee's malevolent crimson eyes, marveling that he had never truly seen her before. She stood taut and defiant, her fists balled at her sides and her entire slender form quivering from the effort it took her to keep from striking out at him. Where did it come from—this rage, this terrible ambition?

"What is this that you have done?" he said softly. "What could you possibly hope to gain by such actions? If there is anything that you lacked, you had only to speak and I would have given it to you with joy."

"Exactly," snarled Araushnee. "You would have *given*. True power is not given, but seized! As to your 'great gifts,' I held in my hands the destinies of mortal beings—but was my own ever mine to command? You treated me like some cherished and cosseted possession, while standing in the way of everything I desired!"

"Not so," Corellon told her gently. "Never did I show you such disrespect. I loved you."

"And you will yet live to regret it," she hissed.

The elf lord shook his head in bewilderment and turned

67

to face his son. "And you, Vhaeraun," he added sadly, "though you also have betrayed, you have earned a different fate. You are young, and you merely followed your mother's bidding. It is tragic that this path led you into evil. You must learn to think and live on your own. In time, perhaps, you can redeem yourself and return to the fellowship of Arvandor. But for now, you must find a place on a mortal world alone."

"Not alone," Vhaeraun said firmly. "Eilistraee plotted with us. She deserves to share my fate."

"Eilistraee? I cannot believe this of the girl—" began Sehanine.

"You were not here!" Aerdrie broke in fiercely. "I saw her shoot the arrow that struck down Corellon! And as her own mother points out, the girl has never missed her mark!"

Corellon shook his head. "I cannot believe she would do such a thing!"

"Believe!" hissed Vhaeraun, enraged that Corellon suffered such doubt and anguish at the thought that his precious Eilistraee might have turned against him. He was willing enough to name his son a traitor! Vhaeraun had always hated his younger, favored twin. Now he would have his vengeance.

The young god turned to his mother, his eyes burning with an enmity that set even one such as Araushnee back on her heels.

"You promised me power and honor," he said in a voice meant only for his mother's ears. "But instead, your ambitions have cost me everything. Give me Eilistraee, and I will consider this day's bargain well made."

Araushnee gazed into Vhaeraun's eyes as if into a mirror. After a moment, she gave a barely perceptible nod. "What he says is true," she said loudly. "My children were loyal to me. Whatever fate you assign Vhaeraun should rightfully be shared by Eilistraee. Was it not she who returned to you my enchanted sheath?"

"Where is Eilistraee?" Corellon asked suddenly.

Aerdrie colored deeply, a blue flush that swept over the high sharp bones of her face in a wave of embarrassment and shame. "I was certain she attacked you, my lord, and I struck back. She fell from the tree. She may yet live; I do not know."

"Find her! Tend her," Corellon insisted.

He watched as several of the gods hurried to the tangle of trampled underbrush and fallen limbs. They pulled the girl from the pile and cast healing magic over her limp form.

As soon as her silver eyes opened, they frantically sought for her father. Weak though she was, none of the gods could deter her from going to his side.

Eilistraee stumbled to her knees beside her father. She took the hand he offered her with both of hers and held it to her dark, bloodied cheek. "My arrow—" she choked, unable to say more.

"There is no fault in you, my child," the god said softly. "You did not know what was in the heart of your mother and her son."

Eilistraee's eyes went wide with shock and horror, and lifted to the dark faces of her family. A small cry of pain escaped her as she gazed into their hate-filled eyes.

"What will become of them?" she said at last.

"They are banished, each according to the place they have earned."

The dark goddess nodded and stood. "I will go with my brother."

"It is not needed," Corellon began.

"It *is* needed," Eilistraee insisted, though tears spilled from her silver eyes. "I am young and my powers are small, but sometimes I can see the shape of things that will come. In some small way, I will provide a balance. This is all I see. . . ." The girl's voice trailed off, and she slumped senseless to the ground by Corellon's side.

For a moment, the god stroked his daughter's bright hair and regarded her still face with a mixture of sorrow and pride. Finally he looked to Vhaeraun. "Eilistraee has chosen. Go now, and take her with you. But know that the day your hand is lifted against her will be the last of your life. This I swear, by all the trees of Arvandor."

Vhaeraun's face twisted with hatred and rage, but he had little choice but to comply. Corellon stood silent as the young god shouldered his unconscious twin and disappeared. Finally he rose to his feet and faced his fallen love.

"Araushnee, your sentence has been spoken by the Seldarine. For what you have done, for what you have become, you are declared *tanar'ri*. Be what you are, and go where you must."

Before the horrified eyes of the elven gods, Araushnee began to change shape. Her slender body grew to monstrous size, and her limbs lengthened, divided, and divided again. Araushnee, the cunning weaver and treacherous lover, had become a spider-shaped monster. Most terrible of all was her face, for although her beauty was not altered, her visage was now stripped of artifice and twisted in hatred.

Shrieking like the damned creature she was, Araushnee advanced upon her former love. The elven gods drew swords and moved forward to stand with their lord.

"Hold!" Corellon ordered in a voice so terrible that it froze the gods where they stood. Slowly, regretfully, he stripped the accursed tapestry from his scabbard and then drew Sahandrian. Sword in hand, he faced Araushnee, alone.

The spider elf dropped into a menacing crouch and began to circle her intended prey. Corellon kept his sword up before him, unwilling to make the first strike. His former consort spoke a few sibilant words, and then spat; a stream of luminous venom streaked toward him. He turned the sword slightly and caught the stream with the flat of the blade. There was a horrible hiss and crackle as the venom met and battled the elven blade's magical defenses. But Sahandrian held, and Corellon's defensive swing sent a spray of scattered droplets back upon Araushnee.

The former goddess screamed in agony as the acidlike

poison singed hair from her spidery form and ate deep into the flesh beneath. She reared back on her four hind legs and shrieked out another incantation. Four curved swords appeared, clutched with deadly intent by her four front appendages. The monster came at Corellon in a rush, swords crossing and clashing like two gigantic shears.

Corellon's magical sword flashed and whirled with mesmerizing speed as the elf lord held off the four blades. The face of Araushnee grew hideous with rage as she fought. None of the gods who watched could tell the moment when the last traces of her elven beauty vanished and when she became fully the spider monster. But suddenly she leaped at Corellon's throat, mandibles clacking in hungry anticipation.

The elf lord thrust his sword between the two rending beaks and twisted hard to one side, forcing the spider's attack away from his throat. He leaped back, pulling his sword clear and raising it high to deflect the downward sweep of one of those curving swords. He wanted only to parry the blow, but *Sahandrian* felt strangely heavy, as if the sword suddenly bore the weight of its own opinions and resolve. The magic weapon dipped closer to his foe and sliced cleanly through the hairy appendage.

With a shriek, Araushnee backed off, shaking the dripping stump. Beyond all reason, she came on again in utter frenzy, three swords flailing. Again *Sahandrian* struck, and then again. Twice more the clatter of falling swords and the wails of the wounded tanar'ri rang through the watchful forest.

Even now, Araushnee would not concede her defeat. She cast another spell; a thread of magic rose from her body, suspending itself from some invisible hook high above. She swung back and then came at Corellon, dripping ichor as she came, with her remaining sword held out before her like a lance.

The elf lord easily sidestepped the attack. But as the spider swooped past, she seized him with her hind legs and swept him up from the ground. Corellon swung back with her and hit the trunk of a massive tree with numbing force.

71

The storm-blasted leaves rustled down over the clearing as the monster's beaklike mandible again closed on his throat. But Corellon still held fast to his sword. He brought the weapon up through the tangle of spidery limbs, slicing deep into the bulbous body. Araushnee released him suddenly. With a small, pitiful moan, she swung out of reach on her thread of magic.

Corellon slid along the trunk of the tree and stood on the ground, watching, heartsick, as the creature who had been his love rocked slowly back and forth on her silvery thread, holding her maimed limbs close to her torn body. Despite her horrific form, she looked for all the world like an elven child trying to comfort herself. Just when Corellon thought he could bear no more, the creature's appearance shifted again, and her visage become Araushnee's beautiful, defiant face.

"Kill me," she taunted him in a pain-racked voice. "You will never rid yourself of me, else—even now, my limbs begin to grow anew. But you cannot do it, can you? Even in this you are weak! Kill me if you can, and end it!"

Corellon raised his sword high overhead and hurled it with all his strength. As *Sahandrian* spun end over end toward the former goddess, the elf lord held his breath and hoped that the sword would obey his will, rather than its own. If *Sahandrian* followed its inclinations, Araushnee's taunt would surely become reality.

But the elven sword merely sliced through the thread that suspended Araushnee above the forest floor. She fell, shrieking with rage.

She never hit the ground.

A dark, whirling portal opened on the forest, a gate to another plane. Araushnee spun into the portal, her spidery limbs flailing. For many long moments after she disappeared, the Seldarine listened until her voice—cursing them all and swearing vengeance upon all things elven—faded away and was lost in the howl of the Abyssal wind.

When all was silent, when the dreadful portal had vanished, the new goddess Angharradh came to Corellon's side. "There was nothing more you could do for her," she said quietly. "Araushnee became what she truly was. She is where she belongs. It is over."

But Corellon shook his head. "Not so," he said with deep sorrow. "The battle for control of Arvandor is over, and Araushnee and her cohorts have lost. But I fear that for the elven People, the struggle has just begun."

14th day of Nightal, 1367 DR

To Lord Danilo Thann of Waterdeep, Harper and bard, does Lamruil, Prince of Evermeet, send greetings.

I read your recent missive with great interest. The task you have undertaken, and your reasons for doing so, are even nearer to my heart than you might suspect.

It might surprise you to learn that you are not entirely unknown to me. I remember you from the sentencing of Kymil Nimesin—although admittedly more for the company you kept than for any other reason. At the time, I was struck by the resemblance between your Harper partner, Arilyn, and my sister Amnestria. (Do not trouble your memory—you will not recall my face. I was cloaked and cowled at the time to disguise my identity. My height and size are such that I am not immediately recognized as elven, and my years among the humans have taught me to move and even speak as you do.)

I did not then know or even suspect that Arilyn was Amnestria's half-elven daughter, nor did I sense that my sister's moonblade is now in Arilyn's able hands. Unfortunately, the actual trial of Lord Kymil was private, else I would have learned of my kinswoman's part in bringing this traitor to justice, and could have made myself known to her, and to you.

My mother the queen recently told me of the great service Arilyn did for the elven people of Tethyr. She also spoke of the honor that Arilyn has done me in naming me her blade heir. I have enclosed with this letter a personal note to her, and ask that you give it to her with my highest regards and humble thanks. I hope to meet you both in the near future, to welcome you belatedly to the Moonflower family—although, regrettably, only on my own behalf.

And now, to the business of your letter. You asked me of Kymil Nimesin. There is much I could tell you. He possessed many of the virtues and qualities that define elven nobility: an ancient and honored bloodline, skill in the arts of warcraft and magic, physical beauty and grace, a wide knowledge of lore and history. Few elves can match him with the sword, and I once considered myself fortunate to have studied with him. He was also touted as a far-traveled adventurer. Years ago, I was flattered when he asked me to accompany him to Faerûn for the great work of seeking and recovering artifacts from lost elven lands. At the time, I could not begin to guess what he truly sought.

As a bard, you have surely heard some of the stories told of the lost children of Evermeet. Only two of the thirteen children born to Queen Amnestria and King Zaor are still known to live—this is one of Evermeet's greatest sorrows. It may be that some are yet alive, but Lord Kymil sought to remove all doubt by seeking and destroying all heirs to Evermeet's throne.

Why did he spare me, then? You, Lord Thann, may understand this better than most. Like you, I am the youngest of many children. My reputation among my people is—forgive me—no better than yours. Unlike you, however, I am no thespian who cloaks his talents behind a mask of frivolity. (My mother the queen is kept well informed of the Harpers and their methods, and your work is known to the elves. You, a proven spell-singer, would no doubt find amusing some of the discussion concerning the utter impossibility of a human mage casting elven musical spells.) Unlike you, I am precisely what I appear to be: restless, frivolous, not sufficiently reverential toward tradition, too quick to take action, too fond of feminine charms and ill content to restrict my enjoyment to potential elven princesses, too enamored of the wide world and the many peoples in it—in short, I am hardly a suitable elven prince. Lord Kymil saw in me a moderately useful tool, and no more. No doubt he would have disposed of me, *too, once he thought my usefulness had reached an end.*

What motivated Kymil Nimesin? This question has preyed upon the minds of elven sages and philosophers since the death of my father the king. What would cause an elven noble of great gifts and good family to turn against a royal clan—not to mention a king chosen by the gods themselves?

This is clearer to me than it is to many elves, for I have traveled widely and, like you, I have loved a woman of mixed blood. My heart has become a harp tuned to play melodies not known to the minstrels of Evermeet. My eyes see that pride isolates the elves from the world— and pits them in endless battle against each other.

As a bard and a scholar of elven lore, you know that the elven races have often been in conflict with each other. During the terrible centuries in which the Crown Wars swept in killing waves over the People, Gold elves sought to expand their rule at the expense of Silver and Green elf settlements, Green elves joined with dark elves to combat this aggression, and finally Gold and Silver and Green elves banded together to drive the dark elves Below. The Crown Wars and other battles like them tell but a part of the tale. A subtle, constant battle has been waged between the elven races, a battle that is older than the beginning of elven history. If you would understand Kymil Nimesin and his followers, you must go back as far as lore and legend will take you and observe the ancient conflict between Silver and Gold. From such threads are woven the tapestry of Evermeet.

As you follow the story of Silver and Gold, keep in mind that clan Nimesin is a sept—that is, a minor branch—of the ancient clan Durothil. This fact alone will explain much.

I repeat: Kymil Nimesin represents much of what is valued by elven nobility. By the same token, he illustrates that which is most basically and grievously wrong with the elven People.

Prelude: The Coming of Darkness

10 day of Alturiak, 1369 DR

ymil Nimesin gazed out of the window of his cell into the endless void beyond. Actually, it was not precisely a void, for points of light glimmered like stars in a deep sapphire sky. Starlight was as important to an elf as the air he breathed, and not even Kymil's human captors were so ignorant or so cruel as to deprive him of this.

His other needs had been well met as well. His "prison" was in fact a well-appointed suite of rooms. Kymil had all the basic necessities and many comforts, as well as extras seldom afforded a captive and a traitor. Lorebooks filled a whole wall of shelves, and an elven harp stood on a table alongside a crystal flute. He had parchment and ink in plenty, and even an elegant, golden-eyed cat to accompany him in his eternal banishment. Yes, the Harpers had been generous.

Once again, as he had so often, Kymil relived the day sentence had been passed upon him by the Harper Tribunal, a detestable court comprising humans and half-breeds. He had been found guilty of the murder of twenty-seven Harpers and sentenced to exile to a miniature, magical world on some distant and mysterious plane of existence far from the world known as Aber-toril. The Harpers had decided this was the only way Kymil's life would be safe, for many elves of Aber-toril would otherwise make it a life quest to hunt him down and kill him. His larger crime—treason against the elven crown—was not a matter Harpers could address. Kymil doubted the elves of

Evermeet, given the opportunity to bring him to trial, would have been as merciful as the Harpers.

But there was no gratitude in the elf's heart. The humans who had sent him here were weak, stupid, and shortsighted. He would find a way out of his prison, and then he would complete the task to which he had dedicated his life—the task to which he had been born, bred, and trained.

Kymil envisioned those who had spoken against him at his trial, and then dreamed of the vengeance he would take upon each one. It was an oft-repeated litany, and it had sustained him through his nearly five years of captivity.

First was Arilyn, the half-breed and Harper, who for so long had been Kymil's unwitting tool. A cast-off bastard of the royal Moonflower clan and the heir to a moonblade, she had no knowledge of her royal elven heritage, no place at all in a world where human and elves were not meant to meet, much less mix. When her mother, the princess Amnestria in exile and disguise, was slain at Kymil's instigation, young Arilyn had been left alone and adrift. To Kymil's astonishment, the elven blade had accepted the half-breed child as a worthy heir. He recovered from this insult quickly, however, swiftly enough to make Arilyn part of his plans. It had been an easy matter to woo her, train her, give her a sense of place and purpose—and then to use the powers of her sword to strike against the family that had rejected her. There was a certain justice in this, as well as an irony, that Kymil had found deeply satisfying.

Arilyn, however, had not been of like mind.

Even now, it was incomprehensible to Kymil that a mere half-breed could have bested him. She had ferreted her way through the layers of his plot, she had scattered his Elite Guard and destroyed one of his most talented Circle Singers, she had thwarted his plan to attack the heart of Evermeet, and—perhaps most stinging of all—she had defeated him in single combat.

For all these things, Arilyn would die painfully and slowly. But not, Kymil vowed darkly, before she had been stripped of all her pretensions of elfishness. He would force her into battle against noble elves and see her moonblade turn against her. He would see her utterly outcast by humans and elves alike. He would see the devotion in the eyes of the human mage who so clearly loved her replaced by loathing and rejection. He would see her the plaything of orcs and ogres. And then, he would get nasty.

Once Arilyn was satisfactorily destroyed, Kymil would turn his attention to Elaith Craulnober. This was not merely a matter of vengeance, but principle, for Elaith was not only a Gray elf, but a rogue at that. Lord of a vast business empire that ran the gamut from the shockingly criminal to the merely questionable, Elaith was a power with which to reckon in the great city of Waterdeep. Kymil had employed Elaith's services many times, usually when he needed a task done with which he would not sully his own hand. Yet Elaith had taken Arilyn's side, standing together as Gray elves were wont to do, and had given testimony against Kymil. It was so unusual for one elf to speak against another that Elaith's words had held tremendous weight at Kymil's trial. And there was also the matter of the papers that Elaith had produced—papers that linked Kymil with the evil Zhentarim. The Seldarine be praised, Elaith had not scented the meat of Kymil's dealings with this powerful group!

Then would come Lamruil, prince of Evermeet. Oh, Kymil had seen him at the sentencing, though the fool had taken some care to disguise himself. Even with a cloak muting his elven grace and a cowl covering his telltale ears, there was no mistaking Lamruil for any other. The young prince was strikingly handsome, even as beauty was reckoned among the elves. He had the Moonflower eyes—deep, bright blue eyes flecked with golden lights, and he possessed his father's great height and muscular form. Few elves topped six feet, but Lamruil did so with a handspan to spare. His height alone would fool the less observant, but not only had Kymil made a study of the elven "royal family," he knew Lamruil well. Too well, in fact.

Lamruil had traveled with him for years, unwittingly aiding Kymil in his search for the "lost" Moonflower children. In the process, the prince had fought at Kymil's side, learned from him the art of swordcraft, and uncovered the lost wealth of Kymil's ancestors. It often seemed, however, that the Gray elf pup was more interested in drinking and wenching than he was in their shared adventures. Lamruil certainly showed far too much interest in humans and their affairs, and his gaiety and light-hearted personality was as annoying to Kymil as one of those trite tavern ballads that so delighted humans—and, truth be told, Lamruil as well. It galled Kymil now to think that this spoiled and insipid princeling might try to recover some of the treasure that they'd left in hidden caches throughout the wilds of Faerûn. That treasure Kymil had meant to fund his ambitions against Evermeet.

And yet, perhaps that would be for the best. A smile pulled at the corners of Kymil's tightly set lips. He had warded his troves well, and he doubted that Lamruil, who had scant interest in the art of magic, would be able to survive any attempt to plunder the treasure.

In a way, Kymil would be sorry to see Lamruil die. The young prince had been a useful tool and might again be of some use. Devoted to his sister Amnestria, Lamruil had been blindly determined to find the runaway princess. He was also anxious to see and experience the wide world and eager to link his fortunes with an adventurer of Kymil's renown. The lad had been a fountain of information about the royal family, and a pawn in Kymil's own deadly search for the princess Amnestria and the sword she carried. Lamruil's search for his sister had failed: Kymil's had not.

And he'd gotten away with it for a long time, long enough to give him a confidence that spurred him toward his most cherished goals. After all, Amnestria had been dead for more than twenty-five years, her father for more than forty. This Kymil considered his crowning achievement. All his life—all his life!—he had searched for a means to breach Evermeet's defenses and destroy the Gray elf pretenders to the throne. His family's secret exile from the island had made his task more difficult. Kymil could not set foot upon Evermeet, for fear of alerting the powerful Silver elf who knew his secrets. Yet he had found a way, for the discovery of Princess Amnestria's elfgate had enabled him to send an assassin into the royal city. The elfgate had been his triumph—and his downfall.

Yet Kymil was nothing if not persistent. For five years, he had contemplated a way to turn this failure around. The elfgate had been moved, the silver threads of magic's Weave rearranged in a way that Kymil would have thought impossible. But even that could be turned against the royal elves.

Since the death of Evermeet's king, Kymil had made a special study of magical travel. He understood it as few elves did. In time, he would put this knowledge to work.

Nor was that his only expertise. One of the Elite Guard slain by the half-breed was Filauria Ni'Tessine, Kymil's lover and a Circle Singer of great power. Most elves thought that this ancient gift—a rare type of spell song that could bind disparate magics together—was extinct. But Kymil had sought out Circle Singers, had trained them to weave magic in a manner similar to that done by a Center—a powerful mage who directed a Circle of High Magi. Over the years, the Nimesins and their secret allies had built a Tower of their own upon Evermeet. A circle powerful enough to challenge Evermeet's own and shut the island off from the world—leaving it stranded, imprisoned by its own powerful Weave of magic.

"The elves of Evermeet wished to be isolated from the world. They will get what they wished for—and what they deserve," Kymil murmured.

All that lacked to bring this to fruition was Kymil himself. If only he could free himself from this prison, he could set in motion plans he and his clan had spent centuries putting into place.

83

If only.

The elf's near-delirium faded, and the reality of his imprisonment closed around his heart like the talons of a hunting hawk. A cry of rage and despair escaped his lips— a fearful howl so full of rage that it sent a shimmer of dread down his own spine.

The echoes of his scream lingered long in the chamber, slowly diminishing in a manner than reminded Kymil of the spreading rings sent forth when a pebble is cast into a calm sea.

When all was silent, the incomprehensible happened: Someone—some*thing*—responded to his inchoate call.

A foul scent drifted into the chamber, and the pattern on the fine woolen carpet began to blur as a dark, gelatinous substance oozed up from some mysterious depth below it. Kymil watched, horror-struck, as the entity Ghaunadar took shape before him.

He knew the lore. He knew as well as any elf alive that Ghaunadar was summoned by great and audacious evil. Until this moment, Kymil had never perceived his ambitions as anything but right and proper. The arrival of Ghaunadar was a glimpse into a dark mirror, and the shock of confronting his own image was greater than his dread of the terrible Power before him.

It was not as great, however, as the second stunning surprise dealt Kymil. A large, dark bubble formed on the seething surface of the Elemental God's form, somehow seeming to take on evil power as it grew in size. When the thing burst, Kymil felt that his heart would also shatter, for standing before him was the thing that above all others was anathema to the Gold elves:

Lloth, the dark goddess of the drow.

His horror seemed to amuse the goddess, and the smile on her beautiful face was even more chilling than Ghaunadar's lurking presence.

"Greeting, Lord Kymil," she said in musical, mocking tones. "Your summons has been heard, your methods approved. If you are willing to join hands with those who

84

also plot against Evermeet, we will see you freed from this prison."

Kymil tried to speak and found that he could not. He licked his parchment-dry lips and tried again. The words that emerged, however, were not quite what he'd expected to say.

"You could do this?" he whispered.

Crimson fire flared hot in Lloth's eyes. "Do not doubt my power," she hissed at him. "It would amuse me to see a golden drider—the first! Would you also relish this transformation, Kymil Nimesin?"

Horror clutched at Kymil's heart as he contemplated this threat. Elven sages claimed that Lloth could transform her dark-elven followers into horrific beings that were half-elven, half spider. He did not know, however, which was the more appalling prospect: the transformation itself, or the possibility that he could somehow have fallen within the sphere of Lloth's influence. Never had he contemplated this possibility; nor, apparently, had those who had imprisoned him here. Despite all he had done, there was nothing in Kymil Nimesin's life that so much as suggested the possibility that he might seek any gods but those of the Seldarine. Yet here was Lloth, beautiful beyond telling and filling his room with dark, compelling power.

"I do not doubt you," he managed.

"Good," the goddess purred. "Then listen well. We will set you free of this prison, on the condition that you go where we cannot. The gods of the Seldarine will not suffer us to attack Evermeet directly, but you can gather elves who can and will."

"But how?" Kymil demanded. "There are few elves in all the world who would not kill me on sight."

"There are other worlds, and many are the elves who inhabit them," the goddess said. She laughed at the stunned expression that fell over Kymil's face.

"You faerie elves are so enamored with yourselves, so determined to think you are the only People alive, that you have forgotten your own history," she sneered. "You came to Toril as invaders, more than willing to displace those who came before. Do you think that you are the only elves so minded?"

Kymil struggled with the task of wrapping his mind around this possibility. "Gold elves?" he asked tentatively.

Lloth laughed again, delightedly and derisively. "Ah, but you are priceless—and predictable. Yes, there are Gold elves upon other worlds. I have prepared some for you. Come and see."

Almost against his will, Kymil walked toward the goddess. The seething mass that was Ghaunadar parted to allow him to pass. Kymil gingerly walked through, then peered into the globe that Lloth had conjured from the empty air. The scene within stole his breath.

In a sky whose utter darkness rivaled the obsidian skin of the drow goddess, two strange vessels were locked in mortal combat. One, a graceful winged vessel that looked like a titanic butterfly, was crewed by elves who could have passed as Kymil's near kin. The other was a massive armored ship teaming with well-armed creatures that looked like orcs, but fought with an intelligence and discipline that no orc on Toril could match.

"Scro," Lloth said by way of explanation. "They are a race of clever, powerful orcs from another world, and they fight against the Elven Imperial Navy. As you can see, they will soon prevail against this ship.

"Would you like to know the nature of this butterfly ship, and the elves upon it?" she continued in her faintly mocking tone. "These are survivors of a world in flames. The scro overran their homeland and utterly destroyed it. These elves are desperate for a homeland. They would follow an elven noble who offered them one, and not fret overmuch if they needed to overthrow a kingdom in order to possess it. Thus did your own ancestors, when they fled from a dying world. Thus would you do also, if you were thrust into a new world. Elves such as you believe that rulership is a divine right."

Kymil's thoughts whirled as he stared intently at the life-and-death struggle playing out within the globe. The scope and complexity of the picture the goddess painted, however strange it might seem at first glimpse, fit within the framework of his mind. It was not so very hard to accept.

"What would you have me do?"

Lloth smiled and made a quick, complex gesture with one hand. A burst of fetid smoke filled the room, and from it stepped a second fearsome deity.

Kymil was no coward, but he shrank back before the evil power that was Malar, the Beastlord.

The avatar was enormous—more than twice Kymil's height, and armed with terrible talons and antlers whose prongs looked long and as sharp as elven swords. Malar was armored with a black-furred hide, and he regarded the elf with a derisive expression in his crimson eyes. Although bearlike in general shape, the god lacked a snout or a visible mount. The furred flesh that draped his single oral cavity fluttered as Malar let out a whuffle of obvious scorn.

But the bestial god, unlike his dark-elven ally, wasted no time either greeting or taunting the elf. Towering over the delicate Lloth, Malar bent down and tapped the floating globe with one taloned finger.

"Look here, elf," the god said in a harsh, grating voice. "A second elf ship, taken from Arborianna before it was set aflame. The ship is crewed by a few of my followers—goblins, base born orcs—and powered by a single elven mage. The ship is not big enough or well armed enough to turn the battle, but it has aboard a living weapon that can destroy the scro vessel. A monster that will kill and kill until none remain. You will feed my followers to it, then unleash it upon the scro ship. The elves will hail you as their savior. But be sure to kill the elf mage first, lest he betray you to the others."

Kymil stared at the god. "You would betray those who follow you, and bid me betray one of my own people?"

As soon as he'd spoken the rash words, Kymil feared he'd written his own death order. To his astonishment, both gods broke into long and genuine laughter. Even Ghaunadar joined in after a fashion, for the gelatinous mass bubbled and popped in a grim parody of laughter. Finally the horrible chorus ended, and Lloth wiped her streaming eyes and turned to the bemused elf.

"A few goblins and orcs are a small price to pay for what you will give us. Say the word, and we will set you upon this ship. The rest is yours to do."

"I am to lead an invasion of Evermeet," Kymil said dazedly.

"Was that not your intent? Is that not your dream? With the added strength of the Gold elves of Arborianna, you should have an easy task of supplanting the Moonflower clan and ruling Evermeet."

"If such a plan is to succeed, I will need to contact those few of my followers who remain, both on Evermeet and upon Faerûn," Kymil said hesitantly. "Would this be possible?"

In response, Lloth produced a handful of gems from some hidden pocket in the folds of her silken, ebony gown. These she gave to Kymil. "You will recognize these—these are gems of communication much like those you yourself have used to good effect. Tell me all those whom you wish to contact, and I will see that gems get into their hands."

Kymil nodded thoughtfully. It was a good plan, and it could work. He would gather support from many quarters, then slip down to Toril to lead the sea forces upon Evermeet himself. One question remained, however—an enormous question.

"Why do you support my ambitions?" he asked bluntly. "It seems to me that one elf is much like another in the eyes of Lloth and Malar."

The goddess shrugged. "Evermeet has been denied to me and my children; its queen is Corellon's special pet. The joy of seeing Amlaruil of Evermeet destroyed will be payment enough for the ignominy of any alliance I might have to make. I mean no offense, great Malar."

The bestial god whuffled; Kymil got the impression that Malar was of like mind on the matter.

"That is part, but not all, of my concern," the elf said cautiously. "Once you have begun to destroy Evermeet, will you be content to stop?"

"You are clever," Lloth said approvingly. "The answer, as you suspect, is no. I would love to see the wretched island swallowed by the sea! But that, I fear, must be a pleasure deferred. I do not yet have the power to destroy Evermeet; nonetheless, I will take what pleasure I can."

The grim, naked ambition in the goddess's voice horrified Kymil. He did not know what ambitions the goddess harbored within her dark heart—he did not truly want to know—but somehow he believed that she would do all she offered. He himself had made several improbable alliances in order to reach the goals he had accomplished thus far, and he had honored them insomuch as they advanced his purposes. He saw his own resolve reflected back from the mirror of Lloth's crimson eyes.

"What you say, I will do," he said simply.

Book Two

Silver and Gold

"No one, not even the wisest and most venerable elven sage, can say with assurance when and from whence the first elves came to Toril. But tales are told of a time long past, when elves fled by the thousands from war-torn Faerie, that magical land that exists in the unseen shadows of a thousand worlds.

The songs and stories that tell of those times are as numerous as the stars. No one now living could give a history that would sate those sages who search the ancient lore as a lover studies his beloved's face, or as dreamers who gaze up into the night sky and wonder.

But sometimes a pattern emerges from the telling of small tales, much as the individual bits of tile or stone become a mosaic, or a thousand bright threads interweave to form a tapestry."

—Excerpt from a letter from Kriios Halambar, Master Luthier of New Olamn Barding College, Waterdeep

6

Weaving the Web
(Time of Dragons)

n victory, they were defeated.

The elves of Tintageer—at least, those few who had survived the long siege, the battle that followed, and the horrendous magical cataclysm that ended it—clung to each other and watched as the last few invading ships were torn to driftwood by the raging sea. Not a single enemy remained on their island. All had been shaken into the angry waters by the magical attack whose power went far beyond the expectations of those who'd unleashed it. Even now, violent convulsions shuddered through the elven island, as if the land itself felt a lingering horror—or a premonition of doom.

"The trees!" one of the females cried suddenly, pointing to the line of limber palms that swayed wildly along the shore.

Her fellow survivors looked, and a murmur of consternation rippled through the battered group. Before the battle, those trees had lined the broad street that swept past Angharradh's Temple—a street that once had been hundreds of paces from the ocean. Even as the elves watched, horrified, the crashing surf climbed higher and higher along the diamond-shaped patterns that scored the tree trunks.

"To the dancing hill. Now!" ordered an elven youth. His voice—a fledgling baritone—cracked on the final word and rose into shrill, childlike soprano.

But the elves obeyed him at once. They would have done

Elaine Cunningham

so even if the wisdom in the young elf's reasoning was not so patently obvious. Although Durothil was little more than a child, he was the youngest brother of the king—and all that remained of Tintageer's royal family. More, there was something about the young prince that commanded respect, despite his extreme youth and the uncertain timbre of his voice.

The elves turned away from the ruined city and hurriedly picked their way through the rubble-strewn groves that led to the dancing hill. The highest point of the island, it offered the best hope of a haven until the unnaturally high waters receded.

As they neared the crest of the hill, the elves' footsteps grew lighter and their ravaged countenances eased. This sacred site harbored their brightest memories and their most powerful magic. Here they gathered to celebrate the turning of the seasons, to sing the old songs and dance for the sheer joy of existence, to gather starlight and weave it into wondrous spells that blessed and strengthened the People or lent magic to their artworks.

But the elves' remembered joy was short-lived. The ground beneath their feet began to shiver, then convulsed briefly and violently as if in anguish.

An eerie silence followed the quake, broken by a faint murmur coming from the distant, watery horizon. The elves looked out to sea and understood that the island's tremors had been its death throes. A vast wall of water swept in from the west.

The elves stood watching, stunned and silent, as death raced toward them.

"We must dance," Durothil urged, shaking the elf nearest him as if to waken her. Bonnalurie, the island's only surviving priestess of Angharradh, gazed at him for a moment before his meaning pierced her grief-befogged mind. Her eyes brightened, then flamed with determination. Together they rallied the elves and explained their desperate plan.

Under the priestess's guidance, the elven survivors

formed a circle and began to follow her through the steps
of one of the most powerful of elven spells. All joined in the
dance, even the younglings and the wounded, though they
knew not the High Magic that it cast, although the risks to
themselves and their priestess were enormous.

When her charges had merged fully with the rhythm of
the dance, Bonnalurie began to sing. Her silvery soprano
voice rang out over the island, calling upon the power of
her goddess, gathering the threads of magic that emanated from each elf and weaving them into a single purpose.
The magic she shaped was a Seeking, one powerful
enough to move beyond the veils separating the worlds, to
find a place of power such as the one upon which the elves
now danced—and to open a pathway to this new world.
Under normal circumstances, only the most powerful
elven mages would dare to cast such a spell, and then,
only with the support of a Circle. Though she was no
mage, Bonnalurie knew more of the Art than did most
clergy. She understood the enormity of the task she had
undertaken and the price it would demand of her. And not
from her alone: Only a few of the elves who danced to her
song would travel the silver pathway in safety. As for the
others—well, Bonnalurie needed every breath and pulse
of magic she could muster in order to shape this spell. If
she failed, all would perish.

Caught up in the magic, the elves danced on in near
ecstasy, not knowing what they did but somehow finding a
place within the emerging pattern of the dance. One after
another, they began to sing, taking up the thread of Bonnalurie's song and adding to it the magic of their own life
essence. Some of the elves grew pale, wraith-like, as they
were consumed by the magic they cast. But not one foot
faltered, and their collective song rang out in defiance of
death's approach. They danced and sang long after they
could no longer hear their own voices over the roar of the
surging tide.

A shadow fell over the dancers as the wall of water blotted out the setting sun. Then the sea slammed into the

island, sending the elves spinning off into the silver path their magic had woven. Even there the sea seemed to follow, for the explosion of power that swept them away buffeted them like dark and merciless waves.

After what seemed an eternity, Durothil landed upon an unknown shore with a force that sent agony jolting through every fiber of his body. Ignoring the pain as best he could, the young elf rolled onto his back and came up in a crouch, hand on the hilt of his dagger. His green eyes swept the area for danger. When he perceived none, he forced himself to take measure of those elves who had completed the magical journey.

Durothil did not see Bonnalurie among the dazed survivors. He had not expected to. Although magic was as natural to them as the air they breathed, few elves could survive in the eye of a storm so enormous. Gathering and channeling so much magic required great strength, extensive training, and enormous discipline. A circle of High Magi, working together, could shape and direct these forces without ill effect. But Bonnalurie had acted alone and had channeled the magical tempest through her own being. It had swept her away.

Later, Durothil vowed silently, the survivors of Tintageer would mourn the priestess's passing and sing of her courage and her sacrifice for the People. But not now, nor for many days to come. Durothil's throat felt tight with too many unsung songs of mourning.

Of all the elves of Tintageer, an island that boasted one of the most wondrous and populous civilizations in all of Faerie, fewer than one hundred had lived through the battle to dance upon the sacred hill. Of these, not more than half remained. It was not an auspicious beginning; even so, they had survived, and they would rebuild.

Durothil drew in a long breath and turned his gaze out over his new realm. There was no doubt in his mind that he would rule—the right and the responsibility were his by birth. The well-being of these People, for good or ill, was in his hands. Young though he was, he would ensure that they prospered in this new land.

It was a fair land, he noted, as wild and rugged as the fabled northlands of Faerie. From where he stood—a small, flat plateau atop a soaring mountain—the view was one that stole the breath and quickened the imagination. A host of enormous mountains, so tall that their summits were lost in thick banks of sunset clouds, stood like watchful sentinels as far to the north and west as Durothil's eyes could reach.

The young elf's gaze swept down the rocky slope before him, over the thick pine forest that blanketed most of the mountain. In the valley below, a river wandered through verdant meadow, its placid waters reflecting the brilliant tints of rose and gold cast by the setting sun.

Nodding thoughtfully, Durothil took a deep breath and squared his shoulders for the task ahead. He noted that the air was thin and crisp, quite unlike the sultry, flower-scented winds that caressed his lost island home. Yet the bracing winds felt alive, singing with magic that was not so different from that to which he had been reared. The Weave was strong upon this new world, and already the young elf could glimpse his own place within the magical fabric. Where there was magic, elves could thrive. In time, this land would become a true home.

"Faerûn," Durothil murmured, adding the rising inflection that changed the elven word for his homeland into something new, yet familiar. He turned to face his people, and took heart at seeing his own sense of wonder—and recognition—reflected upon several elven faces.

Under Durothil's direction, the survivors set to work. Several minor priests had survived, as well as a few mages. These began tending the wounded with the salves and spells that remained to them. Those whose store of magic had been depleted offered prayers or simply gave comfort to those who had been shattered by the loss of their homeland, and those who were dazed by the new and unfamiliar world in which they found themselves.

And strange it was, Durothil silently agreed, despite the reassuring tug of the magical Weave. Even the stone beneath their feet was odd. The plateau was remarkably flat, almost as level as a floor, and apparently made of a single rock. The floor was slick and smooth, shiny as polished marble. Yet for all that, there were odd lumps here and there. Ever curious, the young elf wandered to the edge of the flat, then took his dagger from his belt and began to chip at one of these lumps. The stone was as brittle as glass, and it fell away easily to reveal an odd, charred shape. Durothil quickly dug free a slender metal tube from the stone.

He picked it up, noting the silent hum of magic that flowed through it. As soon as he lifted the tube, he caught the glint of a brighter metal beneath—a sword, most likely. A few more blows with his dagger confirmed the nature of this second find. Frowning in puzzlement, Durothil lifted the magical tube to the fading light and turned it this way and that, trying to make sense of it.

"A wrist bracer," announced a male voice in the odd accents of Faerie's far northlands. The speaker—a tall, flame-haired elf—stooped and took the metal tube from Durothil's hand without bothering to ask permission. After a moment's scrutiny, he announced, "Elven make, I'd say. The sword, too."

Durothil shrugged, though he suspected the older elf was right. Sharlario Moonflower was a merchant—a pirate, more likely—who'd had the misfortune to make port at Tintageer days before the invading forces struck. The northerner's appearance was quite different from the golden, elegant beauty of Tintageer's folk. Sharlario's skin was pale as parchment, a stark contrast with his bright red hair and sky-colored eyes. Odd though his appearance was, his ways were stranger still. Blunt to the point of rudeness, Sharlario had little use for the elaborate traditions and protocols of court life. At the moment, however, he seemed to share in full measure the young prince's curiosity about the objects buried in the stone.

"A metal armband, a sword. Now, how did they get there?" mused Sharlario. His blue eyes suddenly went wide, as if the answer had struck him like a blow. With one quick, fluid movement, he rose and whirled to face the others.

"You, priestess—gather those children together," he snapped, his voice crisp with urgency. "All of you, head down the mountain as fast as you dare. Find shelter—small caves if you can, thick trees if there's nothing else. Help the wounded. Hurry!"

Durothil caught the elf's arm. "By what authority do you command here?" he asked indignantly.

Shaking off Durothil's restraining hand, the pale elf brandished the charred metal band. "Think, boy! An elf wore this bracer, held that sword. She died in a blast of heat that turned her into dust and melted rock and soil into soup. What do you know of that can do *that?*"

Despite the speed of Sharlario's words and the urgency of his tone, Durothil regarded him silently for a moment. Elven kings did not speak or act in haste, and the young prince desired to comport himself with appropriate dignity. He also found himself wondering, incongruously, how Sharlario had decided that the bracer's former owner had been female.

"Are you utterly ignorant of magic?" Durothil retorted in due time. "In a spell battle between mages of sufficient power, it is—"

Sharlario cut him off with a curt, exasperated oath. "Stop dithering, boy—there's a dragon about. You give the command to flee, then, but do it while your people yet live!"

Durothil's eyes widened as the truth came to him. "Dragonfire," he murmured, eyeing the glasslike stone and understanding at last the danger into which they had stumbled.

"Do as the pirate said, and hurry!" he shouted to the watchful elves, ignoring Sharlario's insulted glare.

As the elves rushed to do his bidding, Durothil shielded his eyes with one hand and squinted into the west.

There lay the most rugged mountains. Dragons made their lairs in the mountains, or so the old tales said. There were no dragons upon the island that had been Durothil's only home, but legends were plentiful. By all accounts, dragons were creatures of enormous power and magic. It was likely that the creature who had razed this site could sense the spell that had brought the elves to this place. Even now, it might be coming to investigate the intrusion.

Sure enough, a tiny spot against the fading gold of the sky quickly took ominous shape. A dragon, red scales flaming in the dying light, swept toward them.

Durothil thrust aside sudden, paralyzing fear and tried to assess how long it would be before the dragon was upon them. Too soon, he concluded grimly. Before the fleeing elves could descend down past the tree line, the dragon would come, and it would easily pick them off.

The young prince drew his blade. Planting his feet wide, he brandished the sword and shouted a challenge into the rising wind.

No quick burst of flame could melt rock, Durothil reasoned. The blast of dragonfire that had transformed this mountaintop must have lasted a long time. It was his task to ensure that the next blast lasted long enough to drain the dragon's strength and allow the elves time to escape. He would purchase this time for the elves by drawing the dragon's fire upon himself.

It did not occur to the young prince to do otherwise. To die for his People was the final duty of any elven king.

To his surprise, Sharlario Moonflower stood with him, his own sword at the ready. But the older elf's cold blue eyes were fixed not upon the approaching dragon, but on a more immediate threat.

Seven elflike beings flew toward the scarred mountain, borne on wings like those of gigantic eagles. Two of them held a net stretched between them, and they swooped down toward the pair of elven defenders with grim intent.

Before Durothil could react to this second attack, Sharlario shouldered him roughly out of harm's way. The younger elf went reeling and stumbled over the edge of the precipice. He rolled down the steep incline, hands flailing wildly as he sought a hold. But the slope was slick and smooth from the molten stone that had spilled down the mountain after the dragon's last attack.

Down he tumbled, as swiftly as if he were sliding down one of Tintageer's waterfalls. But no soft spray and warm water awaited him at the bottom. When at last the smooth stone gave way, Durothil bounced and rolled over the bruisingly rough terrain. He saw the pile of boulders approaching him in a spinning gray blur, but could not veer away in time.

There was no sensation of stopping, but pain exploded through him like a sudden blinding light. Gradually the brightness dimmed into the gray void of oblivion. The last image Durothil's dazed eyes gathered before he slipped into the haze was that of Sharlario, entangled in nets and struggling like a hooked fish as he was carried away by the winged elves.

* * * * *

The wheel of the seasons turned many times before the young prince was at last restored to his people.

A band of Gold elf hunters came upon Durothil in the deep forest, found him studying the plants that grew in hidden places with a concentration that suggested he had no other thought or care. Though the hunters pressed him with many questions, Durothil could not tell them where he had been those many years. He simply did not remember; the years that had slipped away from him were meaningless to Durothil, who in his heart and mind was the same young prince who had led his people away from dying Tintageer.

Although he was happy to be among the elves once again, Durothil did not like the changes that had taken place in his absence, nor was he entirely comfortable with the new place the People had found for themselves.

The magic that his people had cast on distant Tintageer had been a true Seeking. It had found a place of power, a dancing hill similar to the sacred site on their homeland. For many hundreds of years, a clan of forest-dwelling elves had gathered starlight and magic on the mountaintop plateau. Many of these fey People had perished one midsummer in the fiery breath of the red dragon who called himself Master of the Mountains. Those that remained welcomed the newcomers to their forest home. And the elves of Tintageer, the proud, golden people from the ancient southlands of Faerie, had mingled with these wild folk.

To Durothil's relief, not all took to native ways. Some of the elves kept proudly to themselves and strove to plant the seeds of their magic, arts, and culture in the forest soil. Amazingly enough, one of these elves was Sharlario Moonflower.

The red-headed warrior had survived and had wed a Faerie woman—a devout priestess of Sehanine Moonbow. Between them they had produced a roisterous brood of young elves, most of whom had inherited their father's pale skin and flaming hair. Almost without exception, members of the burgeoning new clan followed their mother in the veneration of the Goddess of Moonlight. Already the others were referring to them as "Moon elves."

As for Sharlario, he often spoke of the avariel, the winged elves who had rescued him, and the wonders of the Aerie, the magical, hidden mountaintop realm to which they had spirited him. He told of the service he had lent the avariel in fighting the red dragon and banishing him from the northern mountains. The avariel were but one of many races of elves in this new land, Sharlario claimed, and they had told him of other clans that peopled the land. There were many elves, scattered throughout the forest, or living in the hot southlands, and even abiding in the depths of the distant sea.

This experience had shaped Sharlario's destiny—or, perhaps, confirmed it. On his native Faerie he had been a merchant who sailed the seas, gathering news and bringing goods to distant elven lands. He was a wanderer still, for the tales told him by the avariel had set his imagination aflame. Nothing would satisfy him until he could see with his own eyes all of Faerûn. He and his children often left to explore their new world, searching for adventure, and seeking out others of their kind. The stories they brought back with them were wondrous tales of the sort that would be passed down from parent to child like titles or treasure.

The elves enjoyed Sharlario's stories, but few believed his account of the avariel. None of the forest folk had ever encountered such beings, and the concept of winged elves seemed too fanciful to credit. Not even Sharlario ever again caught sight of one, except in the remembered dreams of his revery. This did not keep him from claiming that the avariel continued to watch over him.

Of all the elves, only Durothil did not tease the Moon elf adventurer about his fancies. He, too, had seen the winged elves. But by unspoken agreement, he and Sharlario never spoke of that day—or of little else, for that matter.

When Durothil returned after his long and unexplained absence, he found that his people had absorbed the ways of the land and no longer needed or wanted a king to rule them. There was no crown for which to contend; nevertheless, Durothil could never rid himself of the feeling that of all the elves of the forest, Sharlario could have been his most formidable challenger for kingship. This he could never forget.

There was also the matter of his own lost years. Durothil understood the Moon elf's fancies far better than he liked. He never saw Sharlario's guardian avariel, but throughout the seasons that followed, Durothil often caught fleeting glimpses of silvery wolves, unnaturally large in size, following him through the forest like elusive shadows. And for all the years of his life, his revery was haunted by the night song of wolves, and vague memories of the kindliness of the shapeshifting elves who called themselves the lythari. Those fleeting dreams, and the deep scar that, although hidden by his thick golden hair, stretched across the crown of his skull, were the only things that remained to him from his early years upon Faerûn.

As the years went by, Durothil schooled himself to put the shadows of his past behind him. Since he was not called upon to reign, the elf turned his efforts to the pursuit of Art. Despite fierce headaches that continued to plague him, he excelled in magic. The Weave that he sensed that first day in Faerûn came easily to his call, and he grew swiftly in skill and power. He also had a vast, and seemingly instinctual, knowledge of herbs and potions—perhaps a legacy of his lost years—that served him well in this pursuit. Within a few decades, Durothil was accounted the most powerful mage in the northland forests.

Sharlario Moonflower continued to wander, and he often returned to the forest with word of other elves he had encountered. Some of them were refugees from Faerie or from other worlds. Others were strange, primordial beings who inhabited the trees and the waters and who seemed to have sprung from the land itself. But though many of these wild clans were wary of newcomers, they offered no threat.

That was well, for war of a different kind was brewing in Faerûn.

In this land of rich magic and vast wild spaces, dragons ruled the skies and contended with each other for ownership of the forests and mountains. Some of these regarded elves as cattle or vermin, to be eaten or destroyed at whim. Many an elven settlement had been lost to their appetites, destroyed as completely as that long-ago midsummer celebration on the dancing hill. The dragon known to the Green elves only as Master of the Mountain was among the most rapacious. Other dragons were more benign lords, though few gave much thought to the smaller creatures who dwelt upon their hard-won lands. They had other, graver concerns: battle with their own kind.

Fierce and bitter were these wars of conquest, and each

spring fewer dragons made the flight to the cool north-lands. Determined to achieve supremacy—or perhaps desperate for survival—some of these dragons began to consider the wisdom of seeking new ways.

As he came to understand this conflict, Durothil glimpsed a path by which he himself might regain the power that was his lost birthright. He began to spend more and more time on the mountaintop where he and Sharlario had encountered the dreaded Master of the Mountains in that distant past. The red dragon had been vanquished and exiled, that was true—but his time would come again. He would rule these mountains as he had once before, and the combined efforts of the elves and Sharlario's avariel would not prevent his return.

And when that day came, he, Durothil, would climb to power on the wings of a dragonlord.

7

Brother Against Brother

here were some things, Sharlario Moonflower mused, of which one could never tire. The many-colored flames of a driftwood campfire, the pleasure of hearing his firstborn son sing ballads that had been ancient when his ancestors walked upon Faerie, the lure of places not yet seen—such things as these Sharlario counted as blessings from the gods. But though the night was warm and bright with all these blessings, the Moon elf was hard-pressed to keep his mind upon the song that spilled from his son's silver lyre.

Nearly three centuries had passed since Sharlario had been torn from Faerie and cast upon this distant shore. This was a long time, even as elves reckon such things, and yet the years had passed far too swiftly. Sharlario sighed and tossed another twisted gray stick of driftwood onto the fire.

His son, Cornaith, glanced up at the sound. The expression on Sharlario's face stole the song from the young elf's throat. His fingers instinctively muted the strings of his lyre.

"You seem weary, father," Cornaith said. "Shall I stop, that you may seek revery?"

The Moon elf managed a smile. "Weary enough, lad, but I doubt that revery would bring me restful dreams this night. Time grows short—there is too much left undone."

"Yet we have accomplished much this trip," the young elf said earnestly. "We have been gone from the mountains not quite two years, yet we have established diplomatic ties with no fewer than ten Green elven settlements. This is remarkable, even by your standards. Surely we have allies enough to meet any challenge that lies ahead."

"You have never fought a dragon," Sharlario said simply. "I would pray that you never need do so, but that would be akin to praying that winter might not come. Time follows its own course, and the years of the dragon's banishment are nearly spent. The creature will return, of that I have little doubt."

"And we will turn it back, as you did before," his son said confidently.

Sharlario did not answer. He seldom spoke of that long-ago battle, other than to assure the other elves that the red dragon had been ousted and would not soon return. Few of them credited his story of the avariel, so there was little reason to speak in depth and detail of his service to the winged elves. Nor would he, for any reason. The price for that victory had been enormous, and the debt was coming due.

"What credence do you give the tales told of the Ilythiiri?" Cornaith asked as he idly plucked a tune on his lyre. "For my part, I cannot believe that the southern elves are quite as powerful or as ambitious as we've heard tell. Nor can I believe the stories of their supposed atrocities."

"*Believe*," proclaimed a female voice from the shadows beyond the campfire.

Both elves jolted at the sound. Sharlario's hand went instinctively to the dagger at his belt. As he rose cautiously to his feet, he noted the rapt expression in his son's eyes, and understood it well.

There was nothing that Cornaith loved so well as music, and there was more melody in that single spoken word than in many an air or ballad. Like all elves, Sharlario had a keen love for beauty, and he himself was instinctively drawn to the unseen speaker. Even so, he called to mind a spell that would turn aside magical attack, and he kept his hand at the hilt of his dagger.

"If you come in peace, you are welcome at our fire," he said.

The shadows stirred, and an elven female stepped

into the circle of firelight. Despite his centuries-long career as a diplomat, Sharlario felt his jaw go slack with astonishment.

Their visitor was without doubt the most beautiful creature he had ever beheld. Her face was elven, with its sharp angles and delicately molded features, but her skin was the color of a starless night. She stood taller than any elf he knew—well over six feet—and her long limbs were bare beneath the short, filmy black tunic that, other than a hooded black cloak, was her sole garment. But for the large, silvery eyes that regarded him solemnly, she was midnight in elven form. Sharlario had the oddest feeling that he beheld shadow made substance.

"I thank you for your welcome, Sharlario Moonflower," the female said in her low, musical voice. Before the Moon elf recovered from the shock of hearing himself addressed by name, the stranger shrugged back her cloak. Hair the color of starlight spilled over her naked black shoulders in gleaming waves. A silvery aura clung to her hair, a wondrous, magical light that could not be explained solely as reflected firelight.

Cornaith, who had risen with his father to greet their visitor, sank to one knee. His face was suffused with awe, and he gazed at the ebony goddess—for that she certainly was—as if she was the answer to that question which every soul felt, but no words could frame.

"My lady," he said in deeply reverent tones. "What great thing have we done to be so blessed? How may we serve you? May we know your name?"

The goddess turned her gaze to the younger elf, and her somber expression softened. "Your song was lovely, Cornaith Moonflower. It drew me here and gladdened my exile. I will answer all your questions, but first, seat yourself." An impish grin flashed onto her face. "That rock you are kneeling on cannot be comfortable."

When Cornaith hesitated, the goddess sank to the ground and arranged her long limbs in the sort of cross-legged posture that a child might take. She patted the ground beside her in cozy invitation, then quirked a brow at the still-watchful Sharlario.

"I am known as Eilistraee, the Dark Maiden. I require from you neither reverence nor vigilance," she said softly. "I come as a friend, and in need of friends. Put aside both your weapons and your wonder, and let us talk. There are things that you must know if you intend to confront the Ilythiiri."

The sadness in her voice smote Sharlario's heart, and he did as she bid. "You spoke of exile, lady," he commented. "Forgive me, but I have never heard of such a thing. From whence are you exiled, and, if I might ask, why?"

"Most recently, from the southlands," the goddess said. "Many of the elves there worship Vhaeraun. You may not have heard of him—he fell from the Seldarine when Faerie was still young, and few of the People know his name. His followers are like him: proud enough to believe themselves destined for power, and ruthless enough to seize it any way they can. As they grow in number, Vhaeraun grows in might. With each tribe the Ilythiiri enslave, with each city they destroy, Vhaeraun's influence spreads like a bloodstain upon the land. Finally, he became strong enough to achieve that which he most desired."

The goddess was silent for a long moment, staring into the dying campfire. "Vhaeraun hates me. He bids his worshipers harry and destroy all who follow me. He would see *me* destroyed, if such were in his power. It is not—quite. Yet I must leave."

"If it is followers you require, be assured that I do not fear this Vhaeraun," Cornaith began.

"You should." Eilistraee cast a quelling look at the earnest young elf. "Though he is but a young god, Vhaeraun is vain and malicious, quick to attack those who do not give him homage. And that, you must not do."

"I had no thought to," the Moon elf said emphatically. "Until this night, I wished nothing more than to follow my mother in her dedication to Sehanine Moonbow."

Eilistraee shook her head sadly, turning away the worship in the young elf's eyes. "I am honored that you think of me, Cornaith Moonflower, but do not forsake your devotion to Sehanine. No, listen," she said, cutting off his protestations. "The gods experience time in ways you cannot understand. There are some of us who hear echoes of things that have not yet happened in mortal experience. I have foreseen that most of those who follow me will, like me, be exiles, wanderers who will never find their way to the elven homeland."

"Elves, barred from Arvandor?" Sharlario demanded. "Surely not!"

The goddess's silver eyes grew misty, as if they turned away from time and place to gaze upon visions no mortal could see. "No, not Arvandor. There will be another homeland. There *must* be another homeland," she said, her voice becoming more intense. "The storm is coming, Sharlario Moonflower, when the children of one father will become bitter enemies. Thus it was, and thus it will be, again and again. The actions of the gods ripple down through time to touch their People. Soon, mortal elves will know the pain and turmoil that tore the Seldarine asunder."

"This Vhaeraun must be powerful indeed, to inspire his followers to such conflict," Sharlario said in a troubled voice.

Eilistraee's silver eyes snapped back into focus. "Not Vhaeraun," she whispered, her beautiful face deeply troubled. "Other dark gods will come, and soon."

Neither Moonflower elf could think of words to respond to this pronouncement. For a long time the trio sat, their silence colored only by the occasional crackle of the fading embers, the soft chirruping of night creatures, and the murmur of the nearby sea.

"There is one thing more that you must know and fear," the goddess said at last. "High Magic, which brought you to this place, can be a wondrous thing. It can also be used for great evil. You will find this to be true, if you visit Atorrnash. You who have never had reason to fear magic must learn to be wary of it and those who wield it."

"Atorrnash?" ventured Cornaith.

"It is a great city, not quite three days' travel to the

south. There you will find great riches, powerful magic, and those who offer alliance in your battle against the dragons. Consider such gifts carefully—some carry a hidden price."

The goddess rose abruptly, and lifted her eyes to the sky. Overhead the moon shone full, and beams of its light filtered through the canopy of trees that sheltered the elves' camp. Eilistraee reached out and touched a finger to a shaft of light, and her face took on the intense concentration of one who listens to distant voices.

"I have overstayed myself. There is more you should know, but I cannot linger. Beware." With this, she leaped onto the shaft of moonlight and was gone. A faint radiance lingered in the air for a moment and then disappeared like a snuffed candle.

It seemed to Sharlario that never had a darkness seemed so oppressive as the one Eilistraee's departure left behind. Despite the bright moon and the glow of the dying campfire, despite the company of his well-beloved son, the elf felt a desolation more poignant than anything he had ever known.

He glanced at Cornaith, and read in his son's eyes a pain that was like bereavement. All of which explained, he supposed, why the gods seldom appear to their People— they knew the void their absence left behind.

Sharlario rose abruptly and kicked the fading embers into ash. "Come," he said. "We have nearly three days' travel to Atorrnash."

The younger elf looked at him in astonishment. "Did you not hear what the goddess Eilistraee said? She warned us of the evil of this place."

"She also told us of the power. And she did not actually bid us stay away," Sharlario pointed out.

Since he was an honest elf, he knew these words were meant as much to silence his own unease as his son's protest.

* * * * *

Before sunset on the third day after their encounter with the Dark Maiden, the Moonflower elves reached the gates of Atorrnash. Cornaith, who had never seen a city of such size and splendor, gazed at everything with such wide-eyed astonishment that his father had to remind him more than once to mind his mission—and his dignity.

But Sharlario's reproaches were not as sharp as they might have been, for he himself was awestruck by the Ilythiirian city. He had seen on Faerie the wondrous dwellings that elven magic could coax from crystal, or coral, or living trees, the mighty castles that were fashioned of marble and moonstone. Never had he seen anything quite like Atorrnash.

The city was perched at the very edge of the sea, on all three sides of a long, narrow bay that thrust deep into the land. Many of the buildings were fashioned of dark stone—not carved into the rock, as were the cities of the dwarven folk, or made from piles of masonry such as the halflings favored, but stone that had been drawn up from the depths of the ground in the form of finished buildings. Gemstones glittered in precise patterns against the smooth stone, sometimes forming elaborate mosaics that covered entire walls or even paved the walkways. Most wondrous of all, however, was a vast castle of stark black stone whose turrets soared into the sunset clouds. A high wall surrounded the keep, enclosing a vast estate. A similar, lower wall of black granite encircled the entire city, a wall without seam or crack to mar its surface. By all appearances, it was a single expanse of solid rock. This was a mystery to Sharlario, and the wall seemed powerfully evocative of the mysteries that awaited them within.

In the days that followed their arrival to Atorrnash, Sharlario began to suspect how the strange stone walls and dwellings might have come into being.

The first thing Sharlario noticed was that there was something very wrong with the bay. The waters were too turbulent for such a sheltered place, troubled even at low tides and on the calmest of days. When night fell, and

when the winds blew hot and dry from the south, the sea
shrieked like a lost, demented soul. The Bay of the Ban-
shee, the Ilythiiri called it, and probably for good reason.
It was whispered that many elves had died from the force
of the magic that ripped apart the land to fashion the city,
and many more had perished when the sea rushed in to
fill the void. Sharlario felt the uneasy presence of these
restless souls in the voice of the sea.

But there was nothing about the Moonflowers' twilight
arrival to suggest anything of this grim history. The keepers of the gates asked their business and listened with courtesy as Sharlario requested the opportunity to speak with
the leaders of Atorrnash on behalf of the Tintageer elves of
the northern mountains. The guardians sent runners at
once to Ka'Narlist Keep—the black castle that dominated
the city—and before the sunset colors had faded away, the
Moonflowers were settled in the lavish guest quarters of the
city's archmage.

They did not actually see Ka'Narlist for several days. The
archmage sent his apologies, along with assurances that he
would attend them as soon as his work permitted. In the
meanwhile, his servants informed them, they were to enjoy
the guest house and gardens, and explore the city as Ka'-
Narlist's guests. The latter honor, as Sharlario soon learned,
meant that they were given immense deference and unlim-
ited credit wherever they went. In the markets, they quickly learned not to handle any goods, or even linger too long
at a booth—anything and everything they admired was
quickly pressed upon them as a gift. In Sharlario's experience, elven cultures shared the ancient custom of exchanging gifts, and in many places the splendor of the gift was
viewed as a measure of the giver. But this generosity went
beyond anything Sharlario had ever seen. Stranger still,
never once would an Ilythiirian elf accept a return token.

The Moon elf's curiosity grew as the days passed. Many
of the elves of Atorrnash were as dark-skinned as the goddess Eilistraee. These dark elves, he noted, seem to hold
most of the positions of influence in the city, while the

fairer races were gatekeepers, shop owners, and servants. Never had Sharlario seen such starkly drawn divisions among the various elven folk, and it troubled him. So did the plethora of peculiar-looking beings that crowded the markets and the streets. Sharlario had encountered many strange and wondrous creatures in his travels, and he was constantly astonished by the diversity of life upon Faerûn, but this was beyond all his experience. His natural sensitivity to magic led him to suspect that Art had had a hand in shaping these creatures. He also noted the fear that leaped into the eyes of the Ilythiiri when he tried to speak of such matters.

Also odd was the isolation in which Ka'Narlist kept his guests. The guest dwelling was spacious and grand, and the gardens were filled with lush flowers and playing fountains such as Sharlario had not seen since his days on the lost island of Tintageer. A small army of servants was on hand to tend promptly to any request, and luxuries and diversions of all sorts were offered. In no way could the archmage's hospitality be faulted, yet the guest quarters were set well outside of the walls that surrounded Ka'-Narlist Keep. Even the grounds, outbuildings, and paddocks that surrounded the castle were separated from the guests' domain by high black walls.

It did not surprise Sharlario, therefore, that when at last word came that Ka'Narlist would receive his guests, the audience was to be held not in the keep itself, but in the visitors' gardens.

In preparation, Sharlario and Cornaith dressed themselves according to local custom in some of the fine clothing and gems with which the too-generous merchants had gifted them. Cornaith also brought with him a small golden harp—a nearly priceless magical instrument that he had admired before he learned the inevitable result of such courtesy. He would never forget the stricken expression on the owner's face as she insisted with gracious phrases that he take her harp.

When the sundial's shadow fell upon the rune that

marked the appointed hour, Ka'Narlist appeared before
them without warning or fanfare. At his side stood a
watchful male wemic—a centaurlike being with a powerful human torso atop a body like that of an enormous lion.
With his tawny skin, catlike nose, and thick flowing mane
of black hair, the wemic was a most unusual and impressive sight. But after the first startled glance, the Moonflowers turned their attention fully upon the archmage.

Ka'Narlist was a dark elf. Like most of the city's elite
class, he had crimson eyes and stark white hair. Unlike
most of them, he did not flaunt his wealth and status. He
wore a simple white tunic over trousers and boots such as
an adventurer might wear. There were no rings on his
hands, and his hair was plaited back in a single braid and
bound with a leather thong. Much smaller and slighter
than Sharlario, he nonetheless projected an aura of
tremendous power.

The archmage greeted them graciously and asked a
number of questions about the elves to the north. Noting
the harp that Cornaith carried, he asked for a song and
seemed genuinely pleased by the young elf's performance.
More, he listened gravely to Cornaith's request that the
harp be returned to its owner and instructed his wemic servant to see that this was done that very day.

Yet despite all these courtesies, Sharlario felt wary. The
answers he gave his host were more guarded than was his
custom, and he instinctively found himself listening for
hidden layers of meaning in the archmage's words. He
thought he probably would have done so even without
Eilistraee's warning. There was something about the dark
elf that inspired caution.

"That is a very fine dagger you carry," Ka'Narlist
commented, nodding toward the long knife tucked into Sharlario's boot. "I don't believe I've seen one quite like it."

Remembering local custom, the Moon elf slipped the
knife from his boot and handed it, hilt first, to the wizard. "It
is yours, if you will do me the honor of accepting so small a
token."

"With pleasure," the dark elf said. He shifted aside a fold of his tunic to reveal a weapon belt from which hung a jeweled dagger and two small silk bags. He removed a dagger from its sheath to make room for Sharlario's gift, then he offered his to his guest as an exchange.

The weapon was a marvelous thing, with a bright satin sheen to the blade and a large ruby set in a richly engraved hilt.

Sharlario bowed and accepted the fine dagger, wondering as he did why the archmage had pointedly admired a lesser weapon. The dagger in the Moon elf's belt was clearly visible, and nearly as fine as the one Ka'Narlist had just given him. It would have been a nearer exchange. He wondered what the inequity signified.

"In our land, an exchange of weapons is a sign of trust," the archmage said with a faint smile. "In some circumstances, it is also a pledge of service or assistance."

This was something Sharlario had not anticipated, but it made a certain sense. "What service do you require of me?"

Ka'Narlist's crimson eyes lit with amusement. "That was not my intent, I assure you. To the contrary. You have traveled far, no doubt with some purpose in mind to speed your steps. Speak freely, and I will aid you if I can. At the very least, I can answer some of your questions. I suspect you have many," he added shrewdly.

The Moon elf nodded thoughtfully. As a diplomat, he had learned the value of news from far places. What he had just given Ka'Narlist might well be many times the worth of the ruby-hilted dagger. He was also tempted by the offer of information in exchange, and eager to hear what explanations the archmage might give for some of the customs of Atorrnash.

"I have heard that many of the People in this land worship Vhaeraun. Of this god I know little, and would like to learn whatever you can teach."

"Vhaeraun!" The corner of Ka'Narlist's lip lifted in an expression of contempt. "A minor godling, an upstart. His followers are mostly thieves, raiders, rogues of all kinds. I myself have nothing to do with this god."

"Most reassuring," Sharlario murmured.

"For those who seek to understand the source of power, to tap the force of life itself, there is only Ghaunadar, the Ancient One," Ka'Narlist continued. He shot a wry look at the wemic, as if exchanging an unvoiced secret. "You and your son may yet have an opportunity to observe a service to the Elemental God."

Sharlario did not find that reassuring in the slightest, though he had no knowledge of Ghaunadar. "Another thing puzzles me," he said. "I cannot help but notice the division between the dark elves and the fair. In other places, I have seen class distinctions of royal, noble, and common, but these are matters of birth and breeding."

"And the division of Atorrnash is not?" the wizard retorted. "It is a simple matter, really. Nature is governed by certain immutable rules. By virtue of claw and fang, the lion will always triumph over the goat. Given time, the pounding of the sea will wear away the stone. And when dark elves mingle with the lighter races, the offspring invariably take after the dark parent. It is all much the same—that which is greater will prevail. Our numbers increase steadily, both through birth and conquest. The dark elves are the dominant race, so ordained by the gods," Ka'Narlist concluded in a matter-of-fact tone. "By this, I mean no offense."

The apology was so obviously specious that Sharlario declined comment. "Nature is indeed full of wonders," he continued. "The sheer variety of Atorrnash's inhabitants leads the observer to marvel at nature's prodigiousness."

Ka'Narlist's crimson eyes glinted with amusement. "Delicately put. As you surmised, nature has had little enough to do with most of those ridiculous creatures that crowd the streets," the archmage said with a touch of asperity.

"What, then?"

"There are many wizards in this city who experiment with powerful magic, and in the process create twisted beings of all descriptions. There is an art and a science to

117

such things, but most of the wizards go about it as if they were scullery servants tossing bits of herbs and meat into a stew pot. The result is the appalling hodgepodge you witnessed."

"And you do such things, as well?" Cornaith demanded.

"I do such things, my dear young elf, but not 'as well.' Better. Far better. I do them as they should be done. My studies are thorough, my results remarkable."

Ka'Narlist allowed a moment's silence to give weight to this pronouncement. "You might think me prideful in these claims," he continued in a disingenuous voice, "But I mention my work only because rumor has it you are merchants as well as diplomats. I thought you might be interested in acquiring some unusual slaves. There are several intriguing breeds that are unique to my stables."

Sharlario caught his son's eye with a silent warning, commanding the visibly enraged youth to hold his tongue. In truth, he was as appalled by this as was Cornaith, but he understood that speaking of it would do little good and could cause considerable harm. One thing his centuries of travel had taught him was to observe well, ponder long, and speak only after much thought. But even as Sharlario reminded himself to reserve judgment on a culture he understood but little, he began to see how the Dark Maiden's prophecy might well come to pass.

"Despite the class divisions, surely all the People of Atorrnash would stand together against a common threat," Sharlario commented. It was, in his opinion, well past time to turn the conversation to safer matters.

The mage lifted one snowy brow. "Such as?"

"Dragons, for example. Is Atorrnash threatened by their wars?"

"Not really. The use of magic is intense in the city, and most dragons find this uncomfortable and give Atorrnash a wide berth. They do bedevil trade routes from time to time, but except in the savannahs and the forest to the north, dragons are a minor inconvenience at worst. Except, perhaps, for that one," the mage amended, grimacing slightly as he nodded toward a faint red dot in the sky.

Sharlario looked up, and his heart plummeted. "The Master of the Mountains," he murmured in a voice raw with dread.

"You mean Mahatnartorian, I take it. Yes, he is a bit of a nuisance. I have lost considerable cattle to his appetite— my herdsmen's magical defenses are pitifully inadequate against a great wyrm. I will construct better wards when my work permits me the time. But surely, Mahatnartorian is no threat to your homeland, distant as it is."

"The dragon is flying north, and I know where he is bound," the Moon elf said grimly. "We must leave at once."

"Ah." Ka'Narlist nodded in understanding. "You have had dealings with him, I take it?"

"He was conquered and banished by a clan of avariel. I fought with them, as I owed them an honor bond."

"Avariel?"

"Winged elves," Sharlario said grudgingly, wishing for some reason he had not spoken of them.

But Ka'Narlist seemed to take the comment in stride— no doubt he was jaded by exotic beings brought into existence by his own work. "And now the dragon is returning to settle the score. Of course you must go. But if you can tarry an hour's time, my wemic will see that you have a warrior band to take with you. A vengeful dragon is no easy thing to vanquish."

For a moment, Sharlario was tempted. He could not dismiss, however, the casual way that the archmage had spoken of the dark-elven attitude toward conquest and dominance. Instinct told him that accepting Ka'Narlist's offer would almost certainly seal the fate of the forest elves.

"I thank you, but I cannot wait. Not only is my family endangered, but I am bound by oath—" the Moon elf began.

Ka'Narlist cut him off with an upraised hand. "I quite understand. Do as you must, with all possible speed." The wizard turned to the ever-attentive servants who lingered on the garden's perimeters and bade them escort the Moon elves to the northern gate without delay. "Or better yet," he amended to Sharlario, "I will put you well on your way myself. Did you pass close to the white cliffs, some several days' travel to the north? Good. I shall send you there."

The wizard stretched out one hand. He clenched it into a fist, then made a quick sweeping motion to one side. There was a brief flash of light, and the Moon elves were gone.

"Hmph," the wemic grunted, obviously unimpressed by this solution to their visitors' problem. "They're not dressed for the trail."

"They are now. All their original belongings are with them, as well as most of the things they acquired in the city. Except for this harp," Ka'Narlist said, his lip curling as he cast a derisive glance at the instrument. "Dispose of this tinkling horror at the first opportunity."

"As you wish, master. But the elves—you just let them go," the wemic said, a question in his catlike eyes. "You had thought to give them in sacrifice to your god."

Ka'Narlist shrugged. "Fetch me another pair of white elves from the slave market—Ghaunadar will not mind the substitution. I have a different use for the northerners."

He waited for the wemic to ask, but the slave merely gazed at him—or past him. Ka'Narlist chuckled.

"You are stubborn, Mbugua. I see you wish to know, but I could flay your hide from your bones before you would ask. Very well, then. As you know, the dark elves are not the only People wielding powerful High Magic. Our raiders have been perhaps a bit too zealous of late, and conflict between the races of elves escalates. In time, there will be war, and the fair races have much to avenge. As things now stand, the outcome of such a war is in no way certain. And yet, if our visitor speaks the truth—"

Here Ka'Narlist paused and raised an eyebrow in question. The wemic knew what was expected. He had been a shaman among his own people, and he was still well versed in reading the hearts and spirits of those around him.

The slave grudgingly nodded an affirmation. "He speaks truth."

"In that case, I should very much like to acquire some of these winged elves. Sharlario Moonflower is a merchant. Perhaps he could be persuaded to provide me with a few."

The wemic did not need to ask what use his master had for such exotic creatures: The castle dungeons and grounds were teeming with the results of Ka'Narlist's magical tampering. And he knew his master well enough to suspect what in particular he had in mind.

"You would make winged dark elves," Mbugua stated.

"Night flyers," the wizard affirmed, his crimson eyes misted with the vision of future glories. "What an amazing army they would make! Invisible against the night sky, armed with dark-elven weaponcraft and magic!"

The wemic shook his head, not only to express his doubts, but to shake the horrific image from his mind. "But the red-pelt is an honorable elf. He will not bring his winged brothers to you as slaves."

Ka'Narlist only smiled in return. "It is a rare merchant who will not be swayed by enough gold and gems. But say that you are correct about our red-haired friend. Do you forget how *you* came to this keep? Have you forgotten the raid that enslaved your clan and all but destroyed your savannah? Have the scars from my chains faded from your wrists and paws? Has the stench of your dead mate's burning fur been banished from your dreams?"

The wemic did not respond to the dark elf's taunting. He knew better, though his throat ached with the effort of holding back roars of anguish and fury.

"You have sent raiders to follow the red-pelted elves," Mbugua murmured as soon as he could trust himself to speak.

"Nothing so crude as that. I have sent a scrying jewel with him. Why else would I trade a prince's weapon for a peasant's trinket?" the dark elf reasoned. "If Sharlario Moonflower's tales are true, then Mahatnartorian will try to reclaim his mountain kingdom and avenge himself on these avariel, these winged elves. I would like to observe these creatures in battle, learn their strength and their customs. If the winged elves show promise, then I will follow Sharlario to their hidden places. When I have need of these avariel to serve in my own war, I will send raiders to harvest them."

"This war—it is coming soon?"

Try as he might, the wemic could not keep a note of hope from his voice. In such a conflict there was a chance of defeat for his master—and freedom for himself and his kin.

The dark elf's smile mocked these dreams. "Not for many thousands of years, my loyal servant," he said softly. "But do not trouble yourself on my account—I will still be alive and in power, and my people will win the battle handily. And you, my dear wemic, will still be around to witness this victory—in one form or another. This, I promise you!"

* * * * *

As sunrise broke over the eastern hills, Durothil crouched on the blasted plateau that had once been a sacred dancing hill. The elven mage was motionless but for the green eyes that scanned the southern skies. For years now he had spent hours at a time on this mountain, keeping watch and strengthening both his plans and his resolve.

It had taken him a long time to figure out what Sharlario Moonflower was doing. The Moon elf traveled incessantly, seeking out elven communities and enlisting their help for a coming battle. From what Durothil could gather, the great red dragon who had blasted this mountaintop had been bested and sent into exile by the winged elves, with Sharlario's assistance. Dragons, from all accounts, followed certain codes of battle and behavior. Red dragons were treacherous creatures who did so only with great reluctance—and who usually exacted vengeance later. The time of banishment was almost up.

That morning had dawned bright and clear, but the

wind was sharp with the promise of coming winter. Durothil rose and began to move about, swinging his arms to warm himself. He walked over to the edge of the plateau and gazed out over the foothills into the southern sky. There was no sign yet of the approaching red dragon.

A breeze swept up from the steep cliff below, bearing a strange odor to the watchful elf. Puzzled, Durothil wrinkled his nose and tried to place it. There was a powerful scent of musk, with an sweetish note reminiscent of the lemon trees that once had bloomed in the royal gardens of Tintageer.

Suddenly Durothil found himself looking directly into an enormous pair of yellow eyes. The shock froze his feet to the mountain even as his well-trained mind took note of details: those eyes were each as big as his own head, they were slashed with vertical pupils and bright with a malevolent intelligence, and they were set in a terrifying reptilian face armored with platelike scales the color of old blood.

As the stunned elf stared, something like a smile lifted the corners of the creature's maw. Steam wafted from wet and gleaming fangs.

"You have much to learn of dragons, little one," the great creature rumbled, punctuating his comment with a puff of sulfur-scented smoke. "We have wings, yes, but we also have legs! People always expect to be warned by the crash of underbrush and the clanking of scales, when in truth no mountain cat walks in greater silence."

Durothil shook his head in dazed denial. This was not at all how this meeting was supposed to go. All his magic, all his careful preparations, were locked in some inaccessible part of his mind by the paralysis of dragonfear. The elven mage knew better than to look into a dragon's eyes, of course, and he would never have done so had the creature not surprised him. Now, he was as helpless as a trapped mouse awaiting a raptor's strike.

The dragon's wings unfurled with a sound like a

thunderclap and then thumped rhythmically as Mahatnartorian rose into the air. He wheeled slowly about, holding Durothil's eyes with his hypnotic gaze and forcing the elf to turn with him as he circled around and lowered himself onto the center of the plateau. The dragon lifted his horned head and sniffed at the air.

"There is interesting magic about, elf. Yours?"

Durothil nodded, despite all his attempts to resist the creature's power.

The dragon settled, tucking his front paws under his chest and wrapping his tail around his scale-covered body. Something about the posture brought to the elf's mind an incongruous picture of a bored house cat.

"I would like to see what magic you've prepared against me," Mahatnartorian continued, in much the same tone as a king might command a performance from a jester of scant renown. "Do your best, little elf. Oh, don't look so surprised—or so hopeful. The best wizards of the south could do nothing to harm me. My resistance to magic is too powerful," he said complacently.

"Then how did Sharlario Moonflower subdue you?"

The words were out before Durothil could consider the consequences. As he cursed his fear-addled tongue, the dragon's eyes narrowed into slits.

"You are fortunate, elfling, than I am in the mood for diversion," he said in an ominous rumble. "By all means, divert me. I rather hope your magical attack tickles—I have grown unaccustomed to the cool air of these northern lands, and a hearty laugh might be pleasantly warming."

Durothil felt the dragon's hold on his mind slowly slip away. As soon as he could move of his own accord, he tore his gaze from those malice-filled eyes. Then he reached into a moss-lined bag and gently removed a small cube. He took a deep breath and began the chant he had been preparing for years.

The dragon listened, massive head swaying in derisive counterpoint to the rhythm of the elven chant. As the magical forces gathered, however, the dragon's horned brow beetled in puzzlement and consternation. The elf was focusing his efforts not upon the dragon, but upon some object—and on something else that Mahatnartorian could not quite identify.

As Durothil's chant quickened and rose to a swift climax, he hauled back one hand and hurled a small object at the dragon. A small, viscous green glob splatted on the creature's armored side.

Mahatnartorian regarded the mess, one horned brow lifted incredulously. "That is the best you can do? You disappoint me, elfling. At the very least, you could—"

The dragon broke off abruptly as a sudden chill, sharp as a rival's teeth, stabbed through the protective armor of his scales. He glanced down, and noted that the spot of green was beginning to spread. The dragon reached out with the tip of his tail and tried to peel the strange substance off. His tail was caught fast in it—try as he might, he could not pull his tail free of the elastic substance.

Roaring with rage, Mahatnartorian rose onto his haunches and tore at the swiftly spreading goo with his front paws. Not even his massive talons could halt the flow. Frantic now, the dragon beat his wings in an instinctive attempt to fly, to seek the safety of his lair. The buffeting winds sent the elf hurtling back, rolling perilously close to the edge of the flat.

But the effort came too late. The dragon's hind quarters were already stuck firmly to the mountain. In moments Mahatnartorian was completely encased in an enormous cube that claimed nearly the entire plateau.

Durothil scrambled to his feet, his chest heaving and his breath coming in ragged gulps. He walked cautiously around the still-struggling dragon, taking care not to meet its stare. Finally the dragon settled down in apparent resignation, and its massive jaw moved slightly as if in speech. There was a moment's silence as a ripple passed through the cube to the outer edge.

"How did you do that? What magic do you command?"

The dragon's voice was oddly altered by its passage through the cube—muffled and mutated until the wobbly cadences sounded more like the mutter of a drunken dwarf than the great, thrumming bass instrument that was nearly as terrifying as dragonfright. But to Durothil, those words sounded sweeter than a siren's lullaby.

"I do not command such power—I merely entreat. Since elven magic would not serve against so mighty a foe, I sought the power of an ancient god to bring against the great Mahatnartorian." The response was extravagant, but Durothil was in a mood to be generous—and he knew of the legendary vanity of red dragons.

"A god. Hmm." The dragon seemed somewhat mollified by this information. "Very well, then. Now that I'm subdued—although I'll have you know that this is hardly the traditional means of subdual—what service does your god require from me?"

"Information," the elf began. "I have heard rumors of silver dragons to the north."

"Consider them confirmed."

"Your part is not so easy as that. I need to know where the creatures lair. And I need an egg. When I have retrieved and hatched a viable egg, you will be free to go."

The dragon's shoulders abruptly lifted and fell, sending a shiver through the cube. A moment later, his derisive snort broke through the gelatinous barrier.

The next series of ripples came quickly, heralding the force of the words to come. "In that case, elfling fool, I will sit in this ridiculous cube forever. You have no hope of success. Have you ever seen a brooding she-dragon protect her nursery? No, of course you have not, for you are still alive to stand before me with that annoying smirk on your face."

There was more truth in the dragon's words than Durothil liked to admit. The retrieval of a living egg was the weakest part of his plan. "You have another suggestion?"

"I will retrieve this egg for you," the dragon offered. "Loose me now, and I will hunt down and slay the silver she-dragon. That I would do, regardless, for I wish to add the silvers' hunting lands to my own territory. You may consider the egg the fulfillment of the terms of subdual. It is unorthodox, but what about this encounter is not?"

Durothil considered this. "What assurances do I have that you will deliver a viable egg? Or even a dragon's egg—for all I know of such matters, I might find myself saddled with a manticore kitten. And what is to keep you from turning upon me and my people, once the egg is delivered?"

The laughter that emerged from the cube was tinged with genuine respect. "You are learning, elfling. Let us make a bargain then, leaving your part undone until you have bonded with your silver hatchling. Then you will find some ruse to bring Sharlario Moonflower to this mountaintop. Do that, and I will consider this a bargain well made. The rest of the forest elves can live in peace."

"I cannot betray one of my own People to you!" the elf protested.

"Can you not? Yet you demand that I deliver one of mine into your hands. For all I know—or care—you could want the little silver brat to cut up for use in your spells, or to sacrifice to this god of yours. Ghaunadar, isn't it?" the dragon said shrewdly. "Now that I consider the matter, you are precisely the sort of being who would draw the Elder God's attention—ambitious, smarter than most of your kind, perhaps a bit of a rogue. Willing to try new things, to stretch the limits. Strong with the life-force that Ghaunadar reveres—and craves.

"You do know about that particular little requirement, don't you?" the dragon continued. From the corner of one trapped eye, he caught a glimpse of Durothil's puzzled face. A chuckle rumbled through the viscous slime that was a gift of the ancient, evil god.

"You don't! By Tiamat's Talons, you are more a fool than you appear! Did you think that one such as Ghaunadar would grant you such gifts, yet demand nothing in return? Oh, he will demand, upon that you may stake anything you like. He will demand the sacrifice of a life-force—yours or another's. So why not persuade Ghaunadar to consider this Sharlario Moonflower the required sacrifice? Thus can you pay two debts with a single coin. Are we agreed?"

Durothil stood silent, stunned and shamed beyond speech. He had known only that Ghaunadar was an ancient power, one who had sought him out and offered assistance in his quest to aid and rule his People. He should have seen Ghaunadar's evil nature; he should have known what sort of service the god would require of him. He should have, but he did not, so blinded was he by his desire for power. But that desire, in and of itself, was not evil. Surely not.

"I will free you now," Durothil heard himself say, "and all will be as you said, except for one additional condition. I will bring Sharlario Moonflower to you when I have trained the dragon to carry me on its back. Or, if I fail in this endeavor, I will return twenty years from the day of the hatching. And on that day, Ghaunadar will have his elven sacrifice."

"Done." The dragon's voice rumbled with satisfaction.

With a heavy heart, the elf chanted the prayer that would reverse the godly spell and free the dragon from Ghaunadar's grip. At once the dragon leaped into the sky, his wings thundering as they carried him toward the lair of the doomed silver dragon.

Durothil's eyes were dull as he gazed into the sky, for they regarded not the triumphant and fleeing Mahatnartorian, but his own lost honor.

* * * * *

When Sharlario and his son returned to their forest home, they found a settlement ringing with praise for the hero Durothil. The elven mage, it seemed, had entrapped the red dragon in a mighty spell and had once again banished it. Many of the elves had been alerted by the trapped dragon's roars. Some had witnessed the scene, for the morning was clear and the plateau was clearly visible from the forest.

Sharlario was relieved to hear of his people's reprieve, but puzzled. Had not Ka'Narlist, the archmage of mighty Atorrnash, said that this dragon could not be overcome through elven magic? The Moon elf respected Durothil's ability, but he would not have thought the Gold elf's magic greater than that wielded in the southern lands.

Perhaps, Sharlario concluded, Durothil simply used his power with greater restraint and responsibility. After all, the mark of the truly great was not merely having power, but knowing how and when to use it.

The Moon elf was not particularly surprised when Durothil shunned his people's accolades to spend more and more of his time alone. Sharlario knew all about that. He himself had never been the same after his encounter with Mahatnartorian. For every night of the three hundred years that had passed since that day, the dragon had followed him into his dreams. Not a night passed that Sharlario was not visited by visions in which he saw again the beautiful avariel maid who had captured his heart, caught in the dragonfire meant for him, plummeting to the ground in a tangle of ruined wings. Swept up in a fighting rage that went beyond anything he had ever known or witnessed, Sharlario had forced two of the avariel to carry him above the dragon, to drop him onto the creature's back. While the monster flew—leagues above the mountains below—Sharlario had climbed to the dragon's head and lashed himself to one horn. Suspended from the horn, he'd swung down into the dragon's face and pressed his sword— and his own face—against the glossy surface of the dragon's eye. So great had been his rage that not even the dragonfright could pierce it.

The memory of that malevolent eye terrified Sharlario now. So did the dragon's promise of vengeance when the term of his banishment ended. All of this haunted his revery, and tainted what happiness he had found since that day. He had married a woman of Faerie and he loved her well. Their life together had been filled with small quiet joys and shared laughter. Even so, not a night passed, but that in revery Sharlario did not wander again among the bodies of the lost avariel, mourning the loss of so many of these wondrous folk. Even so, not a night passed when he did not see the faces of his own beloved wife and children superimposed upon those charred and broken bodies. Yes, Sharlario understood Durothil's need for solitude and healing.

So he gave the mage a respectful distance for several moons. After a time, however, he thought he might better serve by offering the Gold elf the opportunity to speak to someone who could understand.

He took himself to the mage's tower, and was a little surprised to find Durothil both friendly and welcoming. The Gold elf served him feywine with his own hands and asked many questions about Sharlario's recent travels. He was particularly interested in hearing of the dragon wars, and how such things impacted the elven People.

"You are a diplomat—have you ever considered what might be accomplished by an alliance between the elves and the goodly dragons?" Durothil asked him.

Sharlario blinked, taken aback by this suggestion. "Too dangerous. Not all dragons are evil, that is true, but why would any dragon have anything to do with the People? What sort of benefit could we offer to creatures of such power and might?"

"Elven magic is both powerful and subtle," the mage responded. "Although it is unlike a dragon's attack, it could compliment and augment the creature's natural weapons. Working together, a mage and dragon could be a formidable team. I have long dreamed of starting an army of dragonriders."

"But think of the possible recriminations against elves, should we meddle in the draconian wars!"

"There is that," Durothil admitted. "But if enough elves and goodly dragons are bonded in purpose, perhaps we can work together for mutual survival. The number of dragons diminishes—they cannot afford to fight each other on such a scale for long or they will utterly destroy themselves."

A terrible image came to Sharlario's mind: the dark elf Ka'Narlist mounted upon the back of a great black wyrm. "But if noble elves align with dragons, evil wizards would quickly follow. Where would we be then?"

Durothil jolted as if the Moon elf had struck him. He sat silent for a long moment, searching his visitor's face. "Do you know of a wizard among the People who has turned to evil?" he asked in a hushed voice.

"Oh, yes," Sharlario assured him grimly. He told of the Gold elf of Atorrnash, and his encounter with the dark elf mage Ka'Narlist. Durothil listened in horrified fascination.

"And this dagger he gave you—do you carry it with you now?"

"No. For some reason, I do not like to have it near me, and keep it in a chest in my home. Why?"

The Gold elf did not answer, but sat for many moments, apparently lost in his own thoughts. After a while he stood, and invited his visitor to follow him.

Durothil's home was a tower within the trunk of a living tree. From the forest elves he had learned the magic of coaxing trees to grow in certain ways, and the secrets of how to live in harmony with the needs of his living abode. His was a grand home by the standards of the village, with several rooms stacked atop each other within the massive tree, and others hidden among the branches—although these rooms were more like dimensional portals than anything the forest elves employed. Durothil led his guest to one of these magically constructed towers.

Sharlario followed his host into a vast room that appeared to be an exact duplicate of the mountaintop plateau—with one exception. In an enormous nest, shielded from the extremely realistic illusion of sun and wind by a rocky alcove, was an enormous, speckled, leathery-shelled egg.

Sharlario walked cautiously closer. He raised incredulous eyes to the Gold elf's face. "This is a dragon's egg!"

"A silver dragon," agreed Durothil. "It is near to hatching. I will be the first being that the hatchling sets eyes upon. It will think of me as its parent—at least, for a short time. After that, I will raise the dragon to know its own kind and their ways, but will also teach it elven arts: magic, music and dance, the knowledge of the stars, and the art of warfare. Ultimately, I will teach it to carry me on its back, and how to work with me as a team."

The Gold elf walked over to the shell and patted it fondly. "You see before you Faerûn's first dragonrider. There will be others. For this, I need your help."

Sharlario struggled to take this in. "How?"

"I have heirs, but it seems we have little to say to one another. But you have a way with the young elves, and several restless sons and daughters of your own. Help me train this dragon, and then teach the young ones. Together, we will gain the knowledge—I as a dragonrider, and you as teacher of those who will follow. For many years have I worked to this end," Durothil said earnestly. "It is the best way my mind can fashion to vanquish the evil dragons, for once and all."

For a moment, the image of the slain avariel flashed into Sharlario's mind. He nodded slowly, and then came to stand beside the mage. As if in pledge, he placed his own hand upon the dragon's egg.

* * * * *

The years passed, and Durothil's dragon proved to be all that the mage anticipated—and far more. In a burst of unoriginality—no doubt caused by the excitement of the dragon's birth—Durothil named her Silverywing, and she became so dear to him that at times Sharlario suspected that the mage loved his silver daughter better than his own golden offspring. Certainly, he seemed to have a better understanding of her ways. They spoke mind to mind, in a manner much like elven rapport.

Swiftly the creature grew from an endearing little hatchling to a thoughtful, intelligent being who learned all that the elven partners had to teach her with a pleasure that surpassed even the innate elven love of learning and beauty—and warfare. Silverywing and Durothil learned to work together to create spells and attacks that neither elf nor dragon alone could counter. And as the years slipped by, all three of them learned one more thing that elves and dragons gained from such a bond: friendship.

For nearly twenty years, the dragon practiced flight within the confines of Durothil's magical dimension. She viewed the world beyond through scrying globes that she and her human mentor created together, and she tried to hide her ever-growing restlessness. Finally the day came when Durothil proclaimed her ready to venture into the outside world.

At the Gold elf's request, Sharlario went ahead to the mountain top. Durothil had prepared a spell which could carry dragon and rider from her magical home to the duplicate world beyond, but first he needed information about the winds, for this he could not glean through the scrying globes. Sharlario was to go ahead, and relay the needed information.

The Moon elf left the forest village while it was yet night, for Durothil thought it best that Silverywing try flight in the early morning hours, while the air was relatively calm. Sharlario climbed to the top of the mountain, sure-footed as a cat in the darkness. As he walked, he schooled himself not to think of the battle which had begun here three centuries past.

No sooner had Sharlario reached the summit than a familiar roar thrummed through the air. Nightmare became reality: Mahatnartorian broke free of the sunrise clouds and came at him in a rush of blood-colored wings.

There was no time to flee—already Sharlario could feel the heat of the great wyrm's breath. Since he could do nothing else, Sharlario pulled his sword and waited to earn a warrior's death.

But the dragon was not content with a quick strike—he pulled out of the dive and tossed a large object at the elf. Sharlario dropped and rolled aside as shards of glass and multi-colored magic exploded against the mountain. A round disk rolled toward the elf, a piece of fine green marble small enough to fit within the palm of his hand. Sharlario's eyes widened as he recognized the base of one of the scrying globes that Durothil and Silverywing had created.

The red dragon's mocking laughter rolled out over the mountains as Sharlario knew himself to be betrayed.

Sharlario was not prepared for the intense stab of pain this betrayal brought him. Though the former prince had made no secret of his opinion that Gold elves were innately superior to all others, during the years that he and Sharlario had worked together, they had become partners, even friends—or so Sharlario thought.

The Moon elf rose and walked to the center of the flat. He unwrapped the globe that Durothil had given him so that he could relay the needed information. He placed it there, so that the treacherous Gold elf might see and savor his triumph. Then he drew his sword again, and waited for the dragon, and death.

Mahatnartorian began to circle. Sharlario had learned enough of dragons to understand what was coming. The red was gathering his power, stoking his internal flames in preparation for a blast of terrible magnitude.

The Moon elf watched, resigned to his end. He had lived long, and he was near to the time when Arvandor's call would summon him home. This was not how he wished to present himself before his gods, but the choice was not his to make.

Suddenly Sharlario started, then squinted at the silvery streak that was almost invisible against the clouds. In another heartbeat, there could be no doubt: it was Silverywing diving at his attacker, flying like an arrow toward the much-larger red.

The Moon elf's lips moved in agonized denial as the wondrous creature he had trained and loved plummeted toward the red dragon's back. Before she could slash at the red's leathery wings, the wyrm rolled in flight and seized the young female in his taloned embrace. The two dragons spun together, each grappling for a killing hold.

It was an unequal battle, and over quickly. Silverywing's head fell back, her graceful neck nearly sundered by the red wyrm's teeth. Her glittering wings flapped limply as her body began to fall from the red dragon's talons.

But Silverywing's descent stopped abruptly, and her body seemed to bounce as if it were suspended from Mahatnartorian's talons by a flexible cord. A shriek of rage shook the stone beneath Sharlario's feet as the red dragon strove vainly to rid himself of his kill.

Sharlario watched in astonishment as the great dragon's flight grew sluggish. Finally the crimson wings ceased to move, and the enjoined creatures plummeted down toward the mountains.

Toward his mountain.

The Moon elf turned and fled, half running, half sliding down the slope. When he reached the first of the trees, he braced himself and hung on for dear life. The impact shuddered through the mountain and nearly tore the elf from his hold.

When all was still and silent, Sharlario made his way back up to the top to say his farewells to his dragon friend. To his astonishment, three beings lay shattered on the mountaintop, joined together by an odd, viscous green substance.

Mahatnartorian had hit the mountain first, and his body was crushed under Silverywing's weight. Durothil was still astride her back. He moved slightly, and his swiftly fading gaze fell on Sharlario's face.

"Do not," he cautioned in a hoarse voice as the Moon elf made move to help him. "The bonds of Ghaunadar are not for such as you. Wait—they will fade soon."

It was true—the sticky substance was rapidly disappearing. As soon as the mage was free of its bonds, Sharlario went to him to see what might be done. He slashed open the Gold elf's torn and blood-soaked tunic, and knew that anything he might do would be useless. Every bone in the elf's chest had been shattered—to move him would only speed his end.

A crimson froth began to gather at the corner of Durothil's lips. "Train the others," he muttered. "Swear it!"

"I swear," the Moon elf said, his heart heavy with guilt over his suspicions. "My friend—I am sorry. I thought—"

"I know." Durothil's smile was faint and self-mocking. "Do not concern yourself. All is well, my friend. You see, Ghaunadar has had his sacrifice."

* * * * *

Many more years were to pass before Sharlario came to understand the full meaning of Durothil's final words. He never spoke to the other elves of the mage's involvement with the evil god Ghaunadar, or of his own suspicions concerning how near Durothil had come to bringing the matter to a very different conclusion.

But there was no need to tarnish their hero's luster, or to dim the enthusiasm of the young elves who saw that even a fledgling dragon, elf-trained, could bring down a great and evil wyrm. In the end, Sharlario surmised, what mattered was not only the honorable choices that a person made, but the temptations they overcame to come to that place of decision.

By that measure, Prince Durothil was a hero indeed.

8

From the Abyss

he gray sludge that covered the Abyss suddenly bulged into a large bubble, which popped and sent sulphurous steam and globs of foul-smelling muck spewing into the dank air. The being who had once been the goddess Araushnee dodged the splatter instinctively, not giving the eruption so much as a thought. She was accustomed to such things by now, for the Abyss had been her home for a very long time.

Like most tanar'ri, she had taken a new name. She was now Lloth, Demon Queen of the Abyss. Or, to be more precise, she had conquered a considerable portion of the Abyss, and was considered to be one of the most powerful tanar'ri in that gray world. Entire leagues of the fearful creatures trembled before her and hastened to do her bidding.

Lloth's dominion encompassed not only the denizens of the Abyss, but also some of the gods who had come to this place either by choice or exile. Her struggle with Ghaunadar had been long and bitter.

The Elemental Evil was not one of the gods whom she had recruited in her attempt to oust Corellon; he had come to Olympus unbidden, drawn by Araushnee's ambitions and her vaulting pride, granted entrance by the seething evil within her heart. Her fall from Arvandor had delighted Ghaunadar, for he desired the restless energy that was Araushnee, and wished to assimilate her into himself.

The ancient god had followed her from Olympus into the Abyss, and he had tried to woo and then to conquer—

and he had failed at both. In his rage, Ghaunadar had slain many of his most powerful worshipers, and robbed others of their sentience. Entire species of beings were no more, others were reduced to sluglike creatures without thought or will. And in doing so, Ghaunadar destroyed much of his own power, as well.

This he blamed on Lloth. He was her enemy now, and a rival in all things. Yet even such as he, an ancient god, had to acknowledge Lloth's greater power. Nor was he the only deity to do so—even that wretched Kiaranselee gave homage to the Demon Queen.

Lloth cast a disgusted glance toward the corner of the Abyss where the goddess of the undead held sway. Kiaranselee was a dark elf, like herself, though she called herself "drow." Her followers were pitiful shadows of the creatures they once had been, evil elves from an ancient world whom Kiaranselee had slain and made into unthinking minions. When she was not on distant worlds bedeviling her drow children, Kiaranselee was content to rule in her frigid corner of the Abyss. She demurred to Lloth because she had no choice in the matter. In this place, the former goddess of dark-elven destiny ruled.

And so it was that she who had been Araushnee had come to possess everything that she once thought she wanted: power beyond imagining, a kingdom of her own, gods kneeling before her, mighty creatures trembling at her whims.

Lloth stifled a yawn.

It was all so predictable, the Abyss. She had conquered, and she reigned, and she was so bored that she had once or twice been tempted to try to strike up a conversation with some of Kiaranselee's undead minions. She had power, but found it did not satisfy her cravings.

"I curse you, Corellon, you and yours," Lloth murmured, as she had so often over the many centuries that had passed since her banishment.

The darkly beautiful tanar'ri sank onto a throne which

her minions had carved from a giant, desiccated mushroom. Propping her chin in her hands, she once again pondered her fate.

None of the power that Lloth had gained in the Abyss could amend for her lost status. She was no longer even a goddess, but a tanar'ri. Her form was more comely and her power was greater than most of the creatures that inhabited this place, but she was not what she had been. No amount of power in this gray, mushroom-infested plane would erase Corellon's unpaid debt.

Suddenly Lloth sat upright, her crimson eyes blazing with inspiration. Of course! Now that power was hers, she would reclaim her godhood. The way to this goal had been blazed by Ghaunadar himself; the Ancient One was seeking new worshippers so that he might rebuild his power. Why could she not do the same?

As a tanar'ri, Lloth could never return to Olympus. Even as a goddess, she might never amass the power or find the opportunity to enter Arvandor as a conqueror. But she would strike at the Seldarine where she could.

She would destroy their mortal children.

*   *   *   *   *

Centuries had passed since the death of the great mage Durothil, and the passing of master dragonrider Sharlario Moonflower into Arvandor. Their descendants no longer spoke of Faerie, except as a place of legend. Faerûn was truly their home, and they had built a wondrous culture that owed to all the worlds from which their ancestors had fled.

Some of the forest folk lived as they had for centuries untold, but many elves drew away from the ways of the forest to build themselves cities that rivaled even fabled Atorrnash for splendor. Hidden among the trees and clinging to the mountains were marvelous dwellings of crystal and moonstone, streets paved with precious stones, and communities of artisans, scholars, musicians, mages and warriors. These elves produced marvelous works of beauty, magical weapons, and dazzling skills in the fighting arts.

In these centers of learning, the art of High Magic thrived. The Circles were established—small bands of powerful High Magi who together could cast spells beyond the imagining of any solitary elf. Each Circle was based in a tower, which quickly became the focal point of any elven community. One of the more immediately useful functions of the towers was the ability to send communications swiftly from one elven enclave to another, preventing the communities from becoming isolated. Despite the growing problems with the Ilythiiri in the south, it appeared as if the People of Faerûn would achieve remarkable unity.

But this very wealth and power drew many new dangers upon the elves. Dark-elven raiders from the south foraged northward, attacking trade routes and farming villages. Some of these raiders settled in the far north, hiding in caves by day, and coming out to strike under the cover of darkness.

Dragon attacks continued, though between High Magic and the dragonriders, the elves were showing promise of supplanting the dragons as Faerûn's dominant race. But it was not the powerful magic of the south or the might of dragons that the elves had most to fear: Their most dangerous enemy had become the orcs.

For many years, orcs attacked like the rogue wolves that from time to time stole a goat from a remote pasture. The orcs struck at the elves whenever they happened upon them. Most elven communities, even tiny farm settlements, were more than equipped with arms and magic—and the skills in both—to turn back these occasional attacks.

But orcs were nothing if not prolific. From time to time, their numbers grew so great that their clans spilled out of their highland lairs to form a horde that swept like locusts over the land, devoured everything before them.

In the autumn of the Year of Singing Sirens, the orcs marched in numbers greater than the elves had ever seen. They overran the northland plains and plunged deep into the forests. The city of Occidian—that great center of elven music and dance—was conquered and the orcs pressed on to the very gates of the ancient city Sharlarion.

At that time, Durothil's Keep was held by the archmage Kethryllia. This warrior-mage was also known as Amarillis, the high elven word for "Flame-Flower"—partly for her red-haired beauty, and partly for the searing anger she loosed in battle.

Like many of the elves, Kethryllia studied many arts during her long life, but concentrated her skills upon a single great work. For decades, this work had been the forging and enchanting of a great sword. Just two nights past, in a rite that gathered starlight and magic upon the mountaintop plateau known as Dragonriders' Leap, she had completed her task. For years, the mystics had been predicting that this sword, *Dharasha*—"destiny"—would play an important role in the history of the People.

What better task than this, the protection of their city?

In her tower, Kethryllia heard the desperate murmurs of her people, and their frantic preparation for war. Their skill at arms was their last defense, for the Tower of Magi stood empty and silent. The Circle had bonded with their distant brother and sister magi of Occidian's Tower to aid and support their defense of that city. But the orcs and their unknown allies had inexplicably broken through the magical wards, and the Occidian Tower had been shattered. The magical backlash had slain the High Magi of Sharlarion, as well. Thus it was that the elves were left to depend on their weapons and battle-magic, and upon those whose skills in such matters were proven and renown. Kethryllia Amarillis was chief among these—songs and legends of her exploits followed her like shadows.

In her centuries of life, the Moon elf warrior had helped turn back orc hordes, had battled bands of dark-elven raiders, and helped her people track and slay a green dragon that bedeviled travelers to their forest city. She had even stood against dark sorcery—that which could raise the dead into mindless, nearly unstoppable warriors. Kethryllia had lost her sister, and very nearly her own life, to the tireless swords of a zombie host. Her response to all these evils was the power of the enchantments she placed upon *Dharasha*. It was time to put the weapon's powers to the test.

But it had been many years since Kethryllia had been in battle. Of late she had been thinking that perhaps it was time to settle down, to raise a clan before the call to Arvandor grew too strong for her to ignore.

Kethryllia's lips curved in a smile as she thought of Anarallath, the light-hearted cleric of Labelas Enoreth with whom she shared a bond stronger than friendship or passion, though certainly there were those things between them as well. It was time that they were wed. She was no longer young, even as elves consider matters of youth, though she was still as lithe and flame-haired as she had been as a maiden. It was time and past time that they formalized their love.

As Kethryllia prepared for battle, she gave no thought to the possibility that their bonds of love might be broken this day, and that the clan she hoped to found might die unborn.

The elf woman quickly dressed herself in padded leather armor, over which she placed a long vest fashioned of tiny bronze and silver plates, a wondrous armor that was nearly as flexible as mail, and that paid homage to the bronze and silver dragons who served as guardians of the city. But the dragonriders, Sharlarion's second-strongest defense, were far to the south, where a pair of mated black dragons ravaged the countryside to create new territory for their maturing brood.

The High Magi were dead, the dragonriders gone. This fight belonged to Kethryllia, and she found that she was eager for it. She thrust her sword into its new scabbard and tucked knives into sheathes set into her boots and strapped to her forearms. On impulse, she picked up an ancient dagger—a wonderful jeweled weapon that she had recently discovered wrapped and warded and stored in a chest in a far corner of Durothil Keep. Legend suggested that it was once owned by one of their city's founders. She would carry it now, in defense of the city and the legacy that Sharlario Moonflower had left behind. Thus prepared, she tucked her flaming braids under a winged helmet and strode out into the courtyard.

The city was strangely silent, though nearly every elf who lived within it was ready for battle and in position. They stood in disciplined formation. First, a vast shield-wall of elves formed a barrier beyond the perimeters of the city—Sharlarion had no walls of stone or timber, for it melded with the forest. Behind the first defense stood the archers. The ground before them bristled with ready arrows, and their quivers were as large and full as a farmer's basket at harvestide. Immediately behind the archers were elves armed with swords and spears. This group would quickly dispatch any orcs who managed to break through. The next ring of defenders were wielders of magic—not High Magi, but formidable nonetheless. Clerics stood ready to tend the wounded, and even the children moved with quiet efficiency: bringing buckets of water, crushing herbs for poultices, rolling bandages.

Kethryllia nodded as she surveyed the battle-ready elves. She took her place among the fighters, and with them listened to the rumbling, ominous crescendo of the orc horde's approach.

When the first of the orcs came into sight, a murmur of consternation rippled through the elves. The orcs marched boldly down the trade route in precise and orderly fashion. Keeping pace alongside them were other squadrons, who kept as tight a formation as the thick foliage allowed.

This was unusual behavior for orcs. It was apparent to Kethryllia, who knew firsthand of horde tactics, that some greater intelligence was directing their movements. And since orcs respected brute strength far more than they did intelligence, it was likely that their unknown commanders possessed a formidable amount of both.

For the first time, Kethryllia's confidence in the battle's outcome began to waver.

The orcs came to a sudden stop. There was a flurry of movement back in their ranks, but none of the elves could discern its cause. Suddenly a harsh thud resounded through the trees. With a whine and hiss, an enormous flaming arrow soared up over the heads of the orcs and descended in an arc toward the city.

"A ballista," Kethryllia muttered in disbelief. The orcs were barely beginning to manage the simple long bows they copied from their elven foe. Where did they learn of such weapons?

Fortunately, the elven wizards had expected fire arrows—albeit, a considerably smaller version. A pale-haired female pointed her crystal staff at the oncoming blaze and shrieked a single word. White fire flashed from the staff and leaped up to meet red. The ballista's flame was frozen instantly; the weapon hung in the air for a moment, glowing like a giant magical torch fashioned of amber and ruby. It fell to shatter harmlessly against the paved courtyard of an elven dwelling.

More flaming arrows followed, with the same result. When it became apparent to the attackers that this tactic was availing them nothing, a horrid, rumbling command rolled out over the orc horde. Scores of the bestial creatures broke into a screaming charge.

The elves' shield-wall dipped, and archers sent a storm of arrows into the oncoming ranks. Deadly accurate were their arrows, and the orcs were cut down like grain before a scythe.

Wave after wave of orcs came on, only to be felled by the elven archers. Soon the attackers were climbing over a thick carpet of the slain, only to fall themselves. So vast were the numbers of dead orcs that soon the elves who formed the shield wall were forced to fall back toward the city.

Kethryllia frowned as she watched the continuing slaughter. Despite the number of orcs who lay on the forest floor, many remained to carry on the attack. It occurred to her that the elves might well be defeated by their own success.

The piles of corpses were hemming them in, pushing

the elven defenders back into the city itself. It would not be long before the outer buildings were within the reach of the orcs. Once the invaders captured the outer buildings, they could easily overrun the city, for most of the buildings were connected by intricate walkways that wove a nearly invisible web through the trees.

Moreover, the grisly wall was impeding the archers' effectiveness. The elves could no longer see their targets, but were shooting blind up over the heaps of slain orcs in hope that the falling arrows might find a mark. The clank of arrows against unseen wood and leather shields suggested that this tactic was not meeting with much success.

Suddenly Kethryllia understood the horde's strategy. The orcs were deliberately using their brothers' bodies as a bridge to victory. Soon, they would swarm over the top of the pile in numbers that the elven archers simply could not decimate.

Well, the elves would simply have to beat them to it.

Kethryllia lifted her sword high. "To me!" she shouted. "To me, all who would take the fight into orcish ranks!"

There was a moment of stunned silence as the fighters regarded the apparently suicide-bound warrior. Then Anar-allath shouldered his way through the clerics and came to stand at her side.

She gave her love an incredulous look—he was no coward, but neither was he trained for such fighting. Anar-allath smiled and shrugged.

"Perhaps I grow homesick for Arvandor," he said with forced lightness. Then his face grew deadly serious, and he lifted his voice to carry out over the ranks of the elven war-riors. "If we do not fight, all of us, then Arvandor will be the only home remaining to our People!"

Anarallath's words galvanized the fighters, and they came as one to stand with the Silver elf warrior. If an unarmed cleric had the courage to charge an orc horde, they could do no less. Which, Kethryllia suspected, was precisely what Anarallath intended.

The elven priest cast a smug grin at his love as he accepted a short sword from one of the fighters. "Well, Flame-Flower, will you lead this charge, or shall I?"

"We go together," she said with deep gratitude. Then, because she could not resist teasing him in kind, she added, "But do try to keep up."

Anarallath's laughter was lost in Kethryllia's ringing battle cry. The Moon elf warrior scrambled up the wall of fallen orcs and flung herself into the next wave of attackers.

This development startled the orcs and halted their headlong charge. But it was only for a moment—the creatures' fangs bared in fierce grins as they came at the elven warriors with renewed vigor. Orcs enjoyed killing elves in any number of ways, but few things were as satisfying to them as hand-to-hand combat.

The nimble elves darted and spun amid the churning melee, making several hits for every one the much-slower orcs managed to land. Kethryllia seemed to be everywhere, her great sword flashing as it turned aside the battle-axes of her foe. And where she went, so did Anarallath. He was not as skilled a fighter as she, but the mind-and-soul rapport the lovers shared enabled them to work together as smoothly as if they were Tower-trained magi melded together in the casting of a single spell.

But as the battle raged on and on, Kethryllia began to wonder if this had been a wise strategy, after all. The elven warriors were pinned between the dead orcs and the host of attackers. Fortunately, the orcs' own vast numbers seemed to work against them. So eager were they to engage their elven foes that they all but clambered over the orcs in front of them to get at their preferred opponents. As often as not, their axes and swords bit into orcish flesh—either by accident, or in sheer impatience.

At long last, the battle was over. Most of the elven defenders had fallen, and only a few score of orcs remained of the hundreds who had marched upon Sharlarion. These survivors fled noisily into the forest.

"May you be greeted by the teeth of the lythari," Kethryllia muttered as she sheathed her sword.

It was then that she saw the orcs' commander. A darkness that she had taken to be a forest shadow broke free of the thick foliage and rose to a height twice that of an elf. The creature's horned head had a face that reminded Kethryllia of a slavering, battle-mad wild boar. Its massive body was shaped like that of an orc, but an extra pair of muscled arms erupted from its hairless torso. Wings like those of a gigantic bat sprung from its shoulders. Except for a pair of burning crimson eyes, the creature was the dull and lifeless color of desiccated wood.

A roar more terrible than that of a dragon broke from the Abyssal creature, and it lifted its two pairs of taloned hands in preparation for a magical attack. "You have not yet defeated Haeshkarr!" the creature rumbled.

This, Kethryllia had not anticipated. As the warrior stood in stunned indecision, Anarallath shouted for his brother and sister clerics to join him. He darted forward, brandishing his holy symbol of Labelas Enoreth and chanting the most powerful spell of banishment known to the priests of Sharlarion.

One by one, the priests took up the chant. Under their combined assault, the forest behind the tanar'ri seemed to dissolve into a swirling maelstrom of gray mist. The massive figure of the creature began to waver, then faded into a translucent haze that was sucked inexorably toward the swirling mist.

The tanar'ri Haeshkarr shrieked with fury as it was pulled back into the gate. With a sudden surge, almost too fast even for elven eyes to follow, it lunged forward and seized the priest who had defeated him. Then just as quickly, both fiend and Anarallath were gone.

Without thought or hesitation, Kethryllia exploded into action. She ran like a deer for the fading gate and dived headlong into the Abyss.

The warrior found herself alone in a world of swirling gray mists. Distant cries and groans resounded through the dank air, but there was no sign of life except for the giant mushrooms that squatted in the sludge.

Suddenly the mist parted, revealing the tanar'ri Haeshkarr. With two of its hands, Haeshkarr held the struggling Anarallath slung over its shoulders, as a hunter might carry a slain deer. The creature lifted one of its free hands and pointed at Kethryllia.

"Kill her, then attend me," it snarled to no one that Kethryllia could see. Knowledge of her foe wouldn't have mattered, for the elf was already sprinting toward the tanar'ri. But the dense gray fog snapped shut around the demon and the captive elf like a cloak.

A hollow, hooting cry echoed directly over Kethryllia's head. The warrior ducked as an eagle-sized creature burst from the sheltering mist in a flurry of wings.

She darted aside and squinted up into the foul mist. Six leering, winged creatures flapped overhead, circling her like ravens assessing the repast offered by a recent battlefield. Kethryllia drew her sword, slashing out as another of the imps dived at her. But the creature was agile enough to veer away before she could touch it. They continued like this, harrying her from all sides. It soon became clear to the elf that she could not overcome these creatures while they flew.

Kethryllia deliberately slowed her sword, missing parries and accepting a few hits from the creatures' teeth and talons. As soon as she thought she could convince them she was bested, she crumbled and fell face forward onto the seething ground, her sword lying beside her limply curled fingers.

The imps landed and began circling her cautiously. One of them leaped forward and took an experimental rake at her hand with its talons. Kethryllia forced herself to stay absolutely still. Cackling with evil glee, the imps closed in to feed.

Kethryllia snatched up Dharasha and swung it around hard and low, using the momentum to pull herself into a sitting position. As the mighty sword circled, it cut through two of the startled creatures. The other imps squawked and started to flap away. But the elf continued her spin, coming to her feet as she went. By the time she'd circled three times, spiraling up with her sword as she went, five of the imps lay dead.

She leaped at the sole imp who had succeeded in taking flight, and just barely managed to seize its ankle. The thing was stronger than she'd anticipated and it pulled her sharply forward. They fell together, both of them landing face first in the sludge. But the imp was up in an instant, hobbling along at astonishing speed—and dragging the elf behind.

The warrior tried to bring her sword arm up and to bear, but the heavy sludge through which the imp dragged her kept it pinned to her side. She hooked her boots around a mushroom stem, hoping to slow the imp's headlong flight. The fragile plant gave way immediately, sending a spray of stinging, foul-smelling spores into the air. Kethryllia's eyes burned as painfully as if she'd caught a skunk's blast full in the face.

Blinded, aching in every muscle, the Moon elf refused to let go. There was a chance she could subdue this imp and force it to bring her to its master. At the very least, she could destroy the tanar'ri's minions and hope to draw its wrath upon herself. She was not sure how else she might find the tanar'ri and her love in this vast gray place.

Suddenly her arm jerked upright with a force that pulled it painfully loose from her shoulder. The imp had despaired of shaking her loose, and had once again taken flight.

Kethryllia still couldn't see, but she knew where to swing. She scrambled to her feet, half-dragged upright by the desperately flapping imp, and swung Dharasha in a sweeping arc. There was a brief, terrible scream and then a flood of scalding ichor.

The elven warrior tossed aside the portion of the imp she still clutched and then staggered out of the steaming, foul-smelling puddle. She sheathed her sword rather than plunge it into the ground—for she did not trust the churning sludge beneath her feet not to snatch it from her—and began to tend her hurts.

First she clutched the shoulder with her good hand and forced the bone back into its proper place. The pain was intense, and the shoulder would be very sore for many days to come, but she needed whatever use of that arm she could muster for the battle ahead. That done, she groped in her bag for the healing potion that every elven warrior of Sharlarion carried. She pulled the stopper with her teeth and poured a small amount into one hand, then massaged it over the lids of her burning eyes.

She was aided by the terrible, numbing cold of the Abyss, which oddly seemed to ease the pain and speed the return of her vision. Or perhaps she was just noticing the cold now that her pain was receding. Whatever the case, the dank, vaguely chill air had suddenly taken on a wintry blast—and carried on the cold winds was a stench beyond anything Kethryllia had imagined possible.

Through the haze of her still-aching eyes, the warrior saw standing before her a beautiful, black-skinned elf, taller and more terrible than any mortal being and quivering with barely suppressed rage. Despite the cold, the elflike creature was dressed only in filmy black scarfs and a veritable dragon's hoard of silver jewelry.

Standing in neat formation on either side of the goddess was a squadron of vacant-eyed elves, some of whom were badly rotted. Though all had once been black of skin, most of the creatures' faces had faded to dry and dull gray. Green flesh, even bone, showed through where the dead skin had peeled away.

Kethryllia's throat tightened with horror and dread as she considered these unnatural creatures. All of these undead elves were well armed, and though they would fight without passion, they would fight with all the skill they had known in life. Kethryllia had faced living dark elves before, and she knew just how formidable these skills could be.

The Moon elf turned to the tall dark elf and talked fast. "Great goddess, I have no quarrel with you or your warriors. I will leave your realms at once, if that is your wish—only first tell me where I might find the tanar'ri Haeshkarr."

"Haeshkarr?" the elflike being echoed in a shrill, sulky voice. "He is a minion of Lloth. What business do you have with him?"

"Revenge," Kethryllia said grimly, and was surprised to see the goddess's scarlet eyes light up with insane glee.

Just as quickly, the light snapped out. "A mortal," the dark elf sneered. "What use could you be to the great goddess Kiaranselee? Many desire vengeance, but few have the means or the will to achieve it!"

"Then let me prove myself," the elf said calmly, for a plan was quickly formulating in her mind. "Send any three—any five—of your undead warriors against me. If I prevail against such as these, perhaps I might be of some value to you in your own vengeance against Lloth."

It was a guess, but apparently a good one. The goddess clapped her hands in delight, then swept a pointing finger at several of her dark-elven slaves. "Kill her, kill her, kill her!" she shrilled at them.

Five of the zombies lifted their weapons and advanced on Kethryllia. The Moon elf drew her enchanted sword and lunged at the nearest undead. The creature blocked the strike with a jerky, yet precise parry. Kethryllia flung the enjoined blades high, then pivoted to the side and kicked out hard at the creature's knees. The desiccated bone crumbled, and the undead creature went down. The elf brought Dharasha down in a sweeping backhand. The moment that the enchanted sword touched the undead dark elf, the creature dissolved into dust.

The goddess Kiaranselee shrieked, whether from rage or excitement Kethryllia could not say. Nor did she have time to ponder the matter. The Moon elf warrior blocked the high sweeping cut of another zombie's sword, then spun back to parry the lunge from the undead who crept up behind her. She dropped low to the ground in a crouch, then brought down both of them with a deft leg-sweep. She stabbed first one, then the other creature, before either had the chance to rise.

The remaining pair of zombies rushed Kethryllia while she was down. She rolled aside, then rolled back, bringing the flat of her sword swinging over to smack the nearest undead. This one crumbled instantly, as well. The Moon elf leaped to her feet and faced off against the remaining dark-elven slave. In moments, it too lay at rest—if a drifting pile of foul-smelling dust could be considered eternal peace.

Breathing hard, Kethryllia faced down the dark-elven goddess. She knew that even at her best—rested and unhurt—she could never overcome five dark-elven fighters. But Dharasha had been enchanted to destroy undead creatures with a mere touch. It held no such power over the denizens of the Abyss. Kethryllia figured that the goddess didn't need to know any of this.

The goddess of vengeance and the undead applauded. "Oh, well done, mortal! Not even the tanar'ri can overcome the best of my servants with such ease!"

Kethryllia lifted her sword to her forehead in a gesture of respect. "Then command me, and tell me how I might serve both your vengeance and my own."

With a lightning change of mood, the goddess drew herself up into a regal pose. "Swear allegiance to me, first," she demanded. "Follow me in life and beyond, and you will ever be first among my servants."

The Moon elf hesitated—after all, Anarallath's life was at stake. Though her first instinct was to agree to anything the obviously insane and undoubtedly evil goddess demanded, Kethryllia found that she could not.

"I am sworn to Corellon Larethian, the master of both magic and the fighting arts," she said stoutly. "I will serve you as best I can in this matter alone, but I can swear allegiance to no other god."

Amazingly enough, the flicker of temper in the goddess's eyes did not erupt into full-scale wrath. "Corellon Larethian," she repeated slyly. "Oh, how that will sting! Very well, mortal, I will tell you where Haeshkarr might be found. All that you need do in payment is this: with each tanar'ri you slay, proclaim that you do so in the name of your god!"

* * * * *

Lloth clutched at the armrests of her mushroom throne and gazed down into a scrying pool she had fashioned from black slime. She watched in rage and disbelief as a mortal elf cut her way through a horde of powerful tanar'ri. With each creature that fell, the elf woman proclaimed a victory for Corellon Larethian. And each victory was a dagger-thrust at Lloth's pride.

Without noticing what she did, the beautiful tanar'ri slipped down from her throne to kneel at the edge of the pool, watching in disbelief as the flame-haired elf brought a single sword against the four matched weapons wielded by the mighty Haeshkarr—a tanar'ri that even Lloth herself did not command without a certain degree of diplomacy. Her nails dug deep into the muck as she watched the powerful creature fall—and the victorious elf woman fall into the arms of a mortal being whose golden beauty was far too reminiscent of Corellon himself.

Lloth's first impulse was to seek out and slay the mortals who presumed to enter her realm. The desire to destroy this knight of Corellon was like a fever in her soul—the first true heat she had felt in this world of halflight and eternal despair for many, many years. But enough remained of the wily Araushnee to stay the tanar'ri's hand—at least until she could ascertain how best to serve her own purposes.

Thoughtfully, Lloth watched as the elven lovers struck out in the direction from which the female had come. In time, they would find a gate back to their mortal home. If she did not hinder them, they would probably escape the Abyss. But, Lloth reasoned, they need not escape *her.*

The tanar'ri's heart quickened as she considered the possibilities. She would follow this formidable champion of Corellon Larethian, and the male cleric whose purity of heart was an offending blot of light on the Abyssal landscape. If these elves were representative of the People they left behind, what better place to begin her vengeance against Corellon and his precious children?

Lloth's lips curved in a smile. And where there were elves, there were potential worshipers. She had little hope of corrupting such elves as these she had seen this day, but did not even the evil and insane Kiaranselee have her followers? Lloth would follow the elven lovers to whatever world they called home, and see if she might stake out a claim there.

The goddess once again consulted the scrying pool. In it she conjured the image of the red-haired warrior and the golden male she had rescued. Lloth watched as the pair emerged triumphant into a ravaged forest, as they waded through the carnage left in the wake of the tanar'ri Haeshkarr. Lloth was intrigued—she had not known that her minion demon had such interesting toys at his disposal as rampaging orc hordes. The destruction they had visited upon the elves was most gratifying. Lloth remembered Malar, and the Great Hunter's desire to gather to him orcish worshipers. She wondered how he'd fared, and whether it might not be time to visit him once again.

As she viewed the world, Lloth felt the tug of a familiar presence. Dimly, she recognized it as the one elven god from whom she was not entirely estranged by her new nature as tanar'ri—her son, Vhaeraun. Curious now, she commanded the scrying globe to seek out the young god's territory.

The scene changed from the trampled elven forest to a city that surrounded a long, narrow bay. Here also was war, but war at its beginning rather than its grim conclusion. The goddess watched with intense interest as hordes of dark-skinned elves readied for battle. A delicious tang of evil was in the air, a weave of dark magic that centered on a single elven male.

Lloth gazed with interest upon the leader of the ready army, a dark elf called Ka'Narlist. Though he looked young and vital, Lloth sensed that he was an ancient being, sustained long past the normal years of an elf by the force of his magic. The source of this incredible power fascinated Lloth: The wizard wore a cunningly woven vest fashioned of chain mail and dark pearls—each of which contained the essence and magic of a slain Sea elf. Delightful, this elf!

The goddess eased her way into his thoughts, and found that his mind was not barricaded against such as she. What she read there was grim enough: Ka'Narlist was utterly rapacious and powerful enough to feel himself able to indulge his desires without qualm or restraint. What he wanted now was power—magical power, and the power that came with conquering and subjugating the fair races of elves—but his ultimate goal required nearly the power of a god. He was vain enough to believe it within his grasp.

Lloth rather liked him.

She smiled as she beheld the ancient, resourceful wizard. She approved of his ambitions, and she eyed with interest the things he offered: a powerful army ready and eager to crush the fair elves, magic that fell just short of godhood, followers that might well become hers. That she would snatch him from his current devotion to Ghaunadar added hugely to his appeal.

A shimmer of anger passed through the dark goddess at the thought of the Elemental Evil, but this time her ire was directed at herself rather than some other being. While she had busied herself carving a vast domain from the Abyss, her conquered subjects had found more interesting things to do elsewhere.

No more. Before her, Lloth saw possibilities far more to her liking than tormenting the creatures of the Abyss. The dark elf Ka'Narlist was a being she could truly enjoy. Perhaps it was time that she take a new consort. She had no doubt that he would accept her joyfully—they were as like each other as two dark pearls. She might even bear children to him, and why not? She would not be the first god to be tempted by a mortal, nor was she likely to be the last. And the children they might spawn—ah, the possibilities of breeding such delicious evil into a race of elves! Such elves would trample Corellon's children, conquering the world and breeding worshipers for Lloth, followers she could claim with pride!

Ka'Narlist's dark and vaulting ambitions set new flame to her own. Lloth would be a goddess once again. She who once had spun the thread of the dark elves' destiny felt that her hands were set once again to the loom of fate.

The scene in her scrying globe changed again, returning to the forest and the pair of elven lovers. With a cynical smile, Lloth observed as the survivors of the elven settlement lauded the warrior and her lover as heroes.

There was little that Lloth enjoyed more than dark irony. More satisfying than hatred, more subtle than vengeance, here it was before her, and in plenty! What would these elves think, she wondered, if they knew what eyes had followed their beloved Kethryllia to their forest home? If they knew what evil the flame-haired warrior's courage and devotion had unleashed among them?

Even as the thought formed, Lloth felt a familiar pulse of evil emanate from the scrying pool. She reached out for it, seeking the source. An ancient dagger in Kethryllia's weapon belt pulsed with subtle, malevolent energy.

After a startled moment, the goddess recognized the source of that evil: the dagger had been sent north by Ka'-Narlist himself, several centuries past. He had waited with rare patience until someone had found the hidden dagger, and had worn it in respect for the honorable elf who once owned it. And Ka'Narlist, sensing the energy, prepared his warriors to march in conquest. Irony upon irony!

Lloth threw back her head and laughed with dark delight. Ah, but she had chosen her new consort well! For once, she did not begrudge Sehanine Moonbow or Angharradh their place at Corellon Larethian's side. She, Lloth, had found a mate much more to her liking!

9

The Sundering

enturies passed, centuries during which the children of Lloth preyed with increasing strength and ferocity upon the children of Corellon. Such was the force of their enmity that the fair races of elves, Gold and Silver and Green, set aside their constant rivalries to seek a combined deliverance from their dark elven foes.

They gathered in the very heartland of Faerûn by the hundreds, the High Magi of the elven people. All the fair races of elves—except for the sea folk, whose magic had long ago dwindled almost to nothing—sent the best and most powerful of their mages to the Gathering Place.

Upon a broad plain, a place set aside long ago for this use, the elven mages met to prepare for the greatest spellcasting any of them had ever known. On the land surrounding this place, farm villages and a trading community had grown with the sole purpose of preparing for and supporting this event. The elves of Gathering Place—for so it had been known since the childhood of the most ancient elves still walking in mortal form—had made this day their life's work. Though there were hundreds of magi, each found a carefully-prepared welcome that would do honor to a Seldarine avatar.

For centuries the elves who made Gathering Place their home had labored to build a Tower greater than any their world had seen before. Fashioned from white granite that reflected the elusive colors of the sky, it stood taller than the most venerable oak. A large, curving stairway wound its way up the entire inner wall of the Tower, and onto each stair was carved a stone seat, and the name of the mage who would occupy it. Together, these mages would cast a single spell.

Never before had so many High Magi gathered in one place. Together they had the power to destroy worlds—or to create one.

From the fabric of magic, from the very Weave itself, the elves had planned to fashion a new and wondrous homeland, a place that was theirs alone.

Not every elf on Faerûn applauded this vision. Tensions between the Ilythiiri and the fair elves of the north were increasing with each season that passed. The decision to exclude the dark-elven mages from this great spell-tapestry only served to increase the animosity between the races. Yet the Gold elves, in particular, were adamant. They would create an island kingdom. This place, which the oracles had named Evermeet, was to be a place where no dark elf might follow, a haven for the children of Corellon Larethian. The dark-elven followers of the goddess Eilistraee found in this a particularly poignant irony, but their voices were drowned by the insistent chorus of Gold elves seeking a return to the glories of Faerie.

There were also protests from those who studied the ancient lore, for they were made uneasy by the tales their ancestors had passed down through the centuries. The story of lost Tintageer, destroyed by a spell so powerful that its wake could swallow a mighty island, was told as a cautionary tale in every village. But most of the elves thought of this as little more than a legend. And even if it were true, what had that to do with them? They had complete confidence in their magic, and in the visions of the elders who saw an island homeland as the People's true destiny.

Finally the day came for the spell to be cast. In the quiet hours before dawn, the magi came in silence to the tower and took their appointed places to await the arrival of the elf who would channel and shape the casting.

Long ago, lots had been cast under the prayerful guidance of a similar gathering of elven priests. They had chosen an elf to act as Center—the mage who would gather the threads of magic from all parts of the circle and focus it into a single purpose.

Oddly enough, the person chosen for this task was not at the time a mage at all, but a slip of a girl, a wild elf maiden known only as Starleaf. She accepted her destiny willingly enough, and though it saddened her to leave the forest behind, she was a diligent student and she took well to her training by the Magi. There was not an elf among the gathering who would not admit, however grudgingly, that Starleaf was the best and most powerful Center they had ever known.

The forest elf took her place in the middle of the tower floor and began the long, slow meditation that enabled her to reach out to and find the place on the Weave that belonged to each of the magi in the Tower. Eyes closed, she turned slowly as she gathered each thread of magic and let it flow through her into a single place of power. In her mind's vision, she could see the shimmering weave as clearly as if it were etched in the night sky. When all the elves were fully attuned, Starleaf began the great chant.

Like the wave of a mighty ocean, the cadence of the chant rose and fell as the elves gathered in the power of the Weave and shaped it to their will. On and on they chanted, throughout that day and into the long night. As the Day of Birthing dawned, the spell began to approach its apex. The very Tower shuddered as the force of the magic drawn from the Weave itself flowed through the gathered magi. Utterly caught up in the casting, the magi did not at first notice that the flow of power was taking on a momentum of its own.

Starleaf felt it first. The elves did not merely use the Weave, they were part of it—and she felt the souls of the High Magi begin to rip perilously free of the fabric of life.

At that moment, the casting was completed. Yet the flood of magic power went on and on, and the elves could not come free of it.

The Tower shook as if it were being tossed like a toy between two titanic gods, and the roar and shriek of the unleashed spell melded with the cacophony outside the Tower. With her heightened senses, Starleaf felt the agony of the land as tremor after tremor ripped through it. She saw the one land of Faerûn sundered, and vast portions of it swept away, tearing again and again as they went to leave scatterings of islands upon the once-pristine ocean. She saw the destruction of great cities, the collapse of mountain ranges into the sea, the flooding tides that swept away terrified People and creatures on a hundred newborn shores. All this she saw, for at this moment Starleaf was utterly one with the Weave.

And yet, she stood alone. The mortal forms of the magi had been consumed by the magic, and their life essence was caught up in it, lending fuel to the cataclysm they had unleashed.

But Starleaf could still envision the faint, glowing lines of the web of magic they had fashioned. She cupped her hands before her, summoning the power that once had been the High Magi of Faerûn. She called to them, pleaded, entreated, and demanded, using all the Art to which she had devoted her life. She clung to them as they faded inexorably away.

But as the final glimmer of their collective light faded from her mind, as darkness blotted out even the bright pattern of the Weave, Starleaf's last thought was of the ancient forest, the homeland that she had left behind in her duty to create another.

* * * * *

When Starleaf awoke, she was lying on the cold floor of the dark and silent Tower. She dragged herself up, trying vainly to push through the haze of pain and utter exhaustion that gripped her. The first thought that came to her was that the Gathering had failed.

As the dull roar faded from her head, she caught a sound that no ear could hear—a silent hum beside her.

Starleaf blinked away the spinning lights that whirled before her eyes and focused on the object.

In a shallow bowl that looked as if it had been carved from a single blue-green gem was planted a small tree—a tiny mature oak, perfect in miniature and glimmering with tiny green and gold leaves. Wonderingly, Starleaf touched a finger to the silvery bark, and felt a nearly overwhelming surge of love and recognition. She instinctively knew that within the tree dwelt the souls of the High Magi, and they were content.

"But how can that be?" she murmured. "Contentment, when we have failed?"

"Not so," said a gentle voice behind her. "At least, not utterly."

Starleaf turned, and her eyes widened in awe and terror. Standing before her were two golden-haired elves, too beautiful to be mortal beings. The male was dressed in armor, and lights swirled like dizzy stars within the wondrous sword that hung at his side. His female counterpart, gloriously gowned and shining with gems the color of starlight, stepped forward and lifted the stunned forest elf to her feet.

Starleaf knew without doubt that she beheld the most powerful of the elven gods, and she sank into a deep reverence.

"Rise, and listen to what we have come to say. You were chosen for this task under our guidance," the goddess Angharradh told her. "Once, in a land devoted to my worship, the priest and mages cast a spell that nearly destroyed them all. There are some things the gods cannot prevent, for to do so would be to take all choice from the hands of their mortal children. Yet this time, we did what we could. With your help."

The elf looked to the tiny tree. "What is this?"

"The Tree of Souls," Corellon Larethian told her soberly. "Guard it well, for it will play an important part in ensuring that the People have a home upon this world. Keep it safe on Evermeet, in a hidden place."

Hope brightened Starleaf's eyes. "Evermeet? It exists? Where is it?"

Corellon touched a finger to the elf's forehead. Instantly she saw in her mind's eye a spinning world, upon which she recognized the torn and scattered remnants of what had been Faerûn, the one land. Glowing like an emerald in the sea was a small island, separated from land masses on either side by vast expanses of water. And even as she watched, the tattered Weave began to repair itself—dimmer over much of the world, true, but bright and fair upon the island.

Then Starleaf was on the island itself. Its beauty brought tears to her eyes, for here was everything an elf could desire: deep and ancient forests, rich glades, laughing rivers, pristine white shores, the company of both forest creatures and magical beings, and a joyful, vibrant magic that filled the air like sunlight.

Starleaf touched the Tree of Souls, wishing to share this vision with the elves who died to bring it into being.

"We succeeded, after all," she murmured joyfully.

"As to that, I am not so certain," Angharradh said sternly. "When you go from this tower, you will quickly see what I mean. Have you any concept how many of the People lie dead? How utterly changed is the world?

"It is true that Evermeet is in part the result of the magic you and yours tore from the Weave of Life. But that alone would have not availed—too much of the power of the casting was drawn off by the destruction that resulted. For lack of a better explanation, you might say that Evermeet is a piece of Arvandor, a bridge between the worlds—and the combined work of mortal elves and their gods. Do not take too much of the credit upon yourself—and neither should you take all the blame," the goddess added in a softer tone. "What was done, was destined. It is your part to see that the People find their way to this hard-won homeland."

Starleaf nodded. "I will plant the Tree of Souls on Evermeet with my own hands," she vowed.

"Not so," Corellon cautioned her. "Guard it and protect it, yes. But the Tree of Souls has another purpose. A time may come when elves wish to return to the mainland, or perhaps, they may have no choice but to return. Within this tree lies the power of High Magic, a power that even now is fading from the land. In time, only on Evermeet will such magic be cast. The souls within this tree, and those of the elves yet unborn who will yet chose to enter it rather than return to Arvandor, will grant the People a second chance upon Faerûn. Once this tree is planted it will never be moved again. The power within will enable the elves to cast High Magic within the shadow of the tree, which will grow in size and power with each year that passes.

"Remember what I have told you, and pass on my words to he who takes the guardianship of the tree from your hands," Corellon told her sternly. "The Tree of Souls must not be taken lightly, or planted on a whim."

"I will remember," the elf promised. And as she did, she silently prayed that the need to plant the Tree of Souls would never come at all. Her heart and soul sang with the vision that was Evermeet, and the sure knowledge that nothing this side of Arvandor could take its place in the hearts of the People.

10

Returning Home

espite the ravages that occurred during the Sundering, the elven People slowly rebuilt. In time, they once again thrived upon the many and varied lands of what had once been Faerûn. The old name remained, but it came to describe only one expanse of land.

Hundreds of elven communities were lost in the chaos and destruction of the Sundering; others were changed forever. The forest community of Sharlarion, however, was one of the few that survived nearly complete. These fortunate elves increased their number and spread into the surrounding forests and hills and lowlands, in time creating a kingdom which was known as Aryvandaar.

It was an age of powerful magic, and throughout Aryvandaar the towers of the High Magi dotted the land like buttercups upon a summer meadow. Many were the great works of magic that these mighty Circles created: weapons of war, statues of the gods that sang to greet the dawn or that danced in the starlight, gems that stored mighty spells. Perhaps the most powerful of all these works were the magical gates that linked the mainland communities to Evermeet.

Although most of the elves were content with their homes, Evermeet was always on their minds. The island homeland formed an enormous part of their elven identity, as well as each elf's personal destiny. "May you see Evermeet," was an oft-spoken blessing, for it wished the recipient a long mortal life which would end at a time and place of that elf's choice. Indeed, many elves made a pilgrimage to the elven island before answering the call to Arvandor.

Despite the importance of Evermeet in the hearts and minds of the People, the Council of Elders decreed that the time for actual settlement of the island had not yet come. There were other concerns that kept the elves fully occupied on the mainland.

At this time, the Gold elves wielded most of the power in Aryvandaar, though seats on the Council of Elders were held by worthy members of all the fair races of elves. These Gold rulers were proud of their kingdom's accomplishments, and eager to expand their territory so that the wonders of Aryvandaar could be increased and shared. What began as a grand vision, however, slowly degenerated into waves of brutal and bitter warfare.

For centuries, the Crown Wars ravaged the land from the northernmost forests to the sun-baked southlands. So vast and widespread was the destruction that Aryvandaar's continued glory—indeed, her very existence—began to seem less than certain.

Compounding the elves' woes, a new and powerful goddess had risen to power in the south, a dark goddess who seemed intent upon the utter destruction of the fair races of elves. On her command, the Ilythiiri began to press north in large numbers, creeping through tunnels and fissures that the Sundering had created in the depths beneath the surface world.

As the Ilythiiri moved into the heart of the hills and mountains, they were met with resistance by many of the dwarven clans who for untold centuries had labored to create order out of the chaos of their underground world. Long and bitter were the battles between these races, and many of the dwarves were slain. Some of the stout folk fled north, and sought a new home in the hills of Aryvandaar. These the elves welcomed, albeit cautiously. Aryvandaar had been badly weakened, and even dwarven allies were preferred to the fate that many of the Elders feared—the utter destruction of the ancient kingdom.

The time was ripe for Evermeet to become a realm, one to which the elves could escape if need be, a haven that they could readily defend. And so the Council chose several noble clans to begin the settlement of their elven homeland.

As all anticipated, House Durothil was the first to be selected. The lot fell also to two other powerful Gold elf clans, Evanara and Alenuath. Of the Moon elf houses, Amarillis, Moonflower, and Le'Quelle were chosen. It was the task of each individual house so honored to select those members who would go to Evermeet and those who would remain behind. Nor were these nobles the only elves so chosen: Each family brought servants from among the common folk, warriors taken for the most part from less-powerful clans who owed fealty to the great noble families, and a number of elves who possessed skills in various necessary crafts. Cobblers, coopers, gem smiths and hawk masters were as important to the island kingdom as the nobles who would govern and protect them.

After much debate, it was decided that Evermeet would be governed by its own Council of Elders. Each of the noble clans would have two seats. The head of the council was to be Keishara Amarillis, a High Mage who was accounted a worthy descendant of the famous Silver elf hero. Although many of the Gold elf families were disappointed that this honor did not fall to their house, most agreed that Keishara was the most suitable choice for the role of High Counselor—and the one most likely to be accepted by Gold and Silver elves alike.

On the appointed day, a large band of settlers—some two hundred elves—headed westward. They traveled lightly, taking necessities for the journey, as well as a number of unique, inherited items such as lore books, magical weapons, and fine musical instruments. The resources of Evermeet would provide that which they needed, and the elves were confident that they would soon build a city to rival any in Aryvandaar. Indeed, the island was not utterly devoid of elven presence. Wild elves had lived on Evermeet since the day of its creation, many centuries past. According to the priests of the Seldarine, the gods had ordained that it should be so. The forest elves would live in harmony with the land—and also attune the Weave to a uniquely elven cadence. The island required the presence of Gold and Silver elves to refine and structure that magic.

From one new moon to the next, the chosen elves traveled westward. Finally they heard the murmur of the sea, and they made their way south along a high and rock-strewn coast until a single enormous mountain loomed before them.

In this place, a plain nestled between two forests, was a fine deep water harbor. Sea-going elves often put in to land here, mooring their ships to undersea piers with the help of the merfolk and the Sea elves that lived along the coast.

The Aryvandaar elves looked with great interest upon the seaport. Unlike the cities of Aryvandaar, there was little to distinguish this place from the wilderness surrounding it. Indeed, for a wanderer who happened upon this place, there was nothing to see at all. But among the elves there were some who had traveled to the spring faire, and who knew how quickly a teeming marketplace could spring up in the shadow of the mountain. An ancient dwarven kingdom honeycombed the mountain, and halflings lived in the hills and forests beyond. Even a few human traders from the primitive tribes to the far north ventured down to the harbor marketplace when the worst of the ice flows melted from the sea. But it was high summer now, and even the ships that would carry them to Evermeet were hidden away in the sea caves to the south.

* * * * *

The elves didn't have to wait long for the first vessel to break the endless blue of sea and sky. Rolim Durothil watched with awe as the elven ship swept into the harbor. It was a graceful vessel fashioned of light wood, with a prow shaped like the head of a gigantic swan. The twin sails rose like wings over the curve of the rail; indeed the entire ship seemed poised as if to take flight.

Rolim's heart quickened with excitement. This was the adventure, the opportunity, for which he had waited his entire life. He was the third son of the Durothil patriarch, and as such did not stand to inherit position and power in Aryvandaar. What he possessed, he had earned for himself with his sword and by his wits. As a warrior, a survivor of the terrible Crown Wars, he was not without wealth and honor of his own. And now he who had fought to expand the kingdom of Aryvandaar was on his way to carving his own place from the wilderness of Evermeet.

Ever since the choice for High Councilor had been announced, Rolim had been quietly furious that this honor had fallen to a Silver elf. This title should have been his by right of birth and by virtue of his talents and accomplishments. A Durothil should rule in Evermeet. In Rolim's mind, it was that simple.

He cast a sidelong glance at Keishara Amarillis, who stood with her hands on her narrow hips and her eyes fixed on the approaching ship. She was not young—perhaps in her fifth or sixth century of life—but she was comely enough: slender and tall, with a direct gray-eyed gaze and the fiery locks characteristic of her clan. Hers were cropped short, and they clustered about her finely molded head in a tight cap of bright curls.

As he appraised the High Councilor, Rolim began to consider a possible side route to power. He had enjoyed in his travels the company of an impressive number of fair maidens, and he prided himself upon his skill in the fine art of wenching. This over-ripe beauty would fall into his hand all the faster for the time she'd spent upon the vine. She would be easy enough to conquer, and then to influence . . .

As if drawn by his musings, Keishara turned and looked directly into his intense and unguarded stare. Rolim suspected that his thoughts were written all too clearly upon his face. Well, little harm done, he thought, brushing aside his momentary touch of embarrassment. Although he had not meant to start his campaign for Keishara's favor in so blunt a manner, perhaps it was well to give her something to ponder during the sea voyage.

But Keishara did not flush or simper, as did the village maids whom Rolim had charmed by the score. If anything, she looked mildly amused.

Amused!

At that moment, Rolim Durothil declared war—a private and hidden war, but none the less serious. No elf of the Amarillis clan would lord it over him with impunity. He had thought to allow Keishara to retain her place of honor; that was simply out of the question now. He would rule, by whatever means came most readily to hand.

A tentative hand upon his sleeve shattered his dark thoughts. Rolim spun and stared down at his espoused wife, a nondescript, mouse-colored creature from some lesser branch of the Moonflower clan. She was a High Mage, supposedly, and since Rolim had little magical aptitude of his own to pass down to his children, his father had suggested that he take a wife whose strengths complimented his own. Even though she was not of the Gold elf people, Rolim had agreed because there was a certain wisdom in what his father suggested. If the Durothils of Evermeet were to grow in power and influence, they would need to breed magic into the line. Even so, if Rolim had seen the wench before he signed the papers of betrothal, he might not have been so quick to reach for the quill.

"My lord Rolim," she began in an apologetic tone.

"What is it, my lady—" He broke off suddenly, for his future wife's name nimbly avoided his tongue, so absorbed was he with his ambitions.

The elf woman flushed but did not comment on this lack. "Our escort is ready to ferry us to the ship," she said, gesturing to a small boat and the two Sea elves who awaited them at the oars.

Rolim's future wife smiled at the strange-looking elf who helped them aboard. "Our thanks, brother. You and your kinfolk are kind to see the People of Aryvandaar to our new home. If ever there comes a time when you require the services of a land-dwelling elf, please call upon our family. This is Rolim Durothil, who is to be my lord husband. And I," she said with a pointed glance at the Gold elf, "am the mage Ava Moonflower."

A smile twitched at the corner of Rolim's lips. Perhaps the wife foisted upon him by clan and council was not quite the mouse she appeared to be. Certainly she seemed to charm the Sea-elven servants. And she was not entirely without appeal, with her enormous grave, gray eyes and the abundant hair that was not quite silver, but rather the soft gray hue of a kitten's fur. Nor did she appear quite so colorless, with that slight flush of pique resting upon her cheeks.

Perhaps, mused Rolim Durothil as he gazed upon his future wife, this sea journey would be more interesting than he had anticipated.

* * * * *

The voyage to Evermeet was long, but the first handful of days passed by without incident. In fact, the elves of Aryvandaar had little to do. The ship was ably crewed by a large number of Sea elves who took turns tending the onboard duties and scouting ahead for danger in the sea below. Only the ship's captain was a land-dwelling elf, a Moon elf commoner whose name Rolim never bothered to learn.

For the most part, the future patriarch of Evermeet's Durothil clan spent his time making subtle liaisons with the other Gold elven families. These nobles devoted endless hours to drawing up plans for the city that they would build. Since Rolim's clan was the most prominent house among them, the others seemed willing enough to accept his lead and fall in line with his suggestions.

What Ava Moonflower did during the day, Rolim did not know or particularly care. At night, she took her revery belowdecks, in the company of the female travelers. There

was little privacy aboard the ship, and Durothil knew that
their time as husband and wife would not begin until they
reached the elven homeland. What he did not expect, however, was the impatience he was beginning to feel whenever he caught a glimpse of his future wife's tiny form. Nor
did he expect Ava's pale, serious face to intrude upon his
revery and sweeten to find its way into his dreams of ambition and glory.

Late one night, Rolim was pulled from his revery by an
unusual break in the lulling rhythm of the ship's movement. He sat upright, noting that although the ship
pitched restlessly, there were no sounds of rain or wind.

Curious, he snatched up his cloak and sword belt, then
climbed the ladder to the deck. A few tense and watchful
deckhands stood at the rails, their faces grave and their
webbed hands clutching ready weapons. A few of the Aryvandaar elves, still heavy-eyed from sleep, clustered
together. It occurred to Rolim that these represented all
the High Magi aboard ship. Among them was Ava, her
mass of pale hair untied and blowing about her like a
small storm cloud.

Rolim hurried over to the mages. He took his future
wife's arm and drew her away from the others. "What is
happening?" he demanded.

"The ship is under attack," she murmured, paying him
scant heed. Her troubled gaze lingered upon the grim-faced
spellcasters. "We stand ready to form a Circle if need be. You
must let me return to the others—I am Center."

"You?"

The disbelief in his voice brought a flame to Ava's cheeks.
Her chin lifted as she met his eyes. "Yes, I. This would not
be my first battle, though I am certain that also surprises
you." Her ire faded instantly and her attention returned to
the cluster of mages. "Alas, the magi can attack only if the
enemy breaks though our defenses and strikes the ship
itself! I only wish there was something we could do now to
aid the sea folk who fight for us!"

"They are paid well for their efforts," Rolim noted. "And

it seems to me there is little you could do to affect a battle you cannot see. Save your magic to aid those for whom it was intended, Lady Mage, and don't waste time or thought upon those two-legged fish."

Ava's eyes kindled with wrath. Her hand flashed forward and slapped Rolim squarely in the face with a force that snapped his head painfully to one side. Before he could think better of it, Rolim's warrior instincts took over and he struck back.

He never got close. The tiny female caught his wrist with both hands and spoke a single terse word. The next instant, Rolim, a seasoned Gold elf warrior, was flat on his back on the hard wood of the deck and his future wife's knee was pressed hard at his throat.

"The next words you say against any of the People will be the last you utter," Ava informed him in a soft, even tone. "All of those upon this ship were chosen by lot, under the eyes of the gods, and we each have a purpose and a destiny. But you will not bring the turmoil and destruction of the Crown Wars to this new land, this I swear before all the gods! If you try, I will fight you at every turn, my lord."

And then she was gone. Rolim scrambled to his feet and scanned the deck with furtive eyes. No one, it seemed, had noticed his humiliation at the hands of his as-yet unclaimed wife. All were intent upon dragging aboard the wounded Sea elves who had floated to the moonlit surface.

Near the far rail, Ava knelt at the side of a dying female warrior, her pale hands trying in vain to hold together the gaping folds of the sea woman's death wound. Tears spilled down the mage's cheeks, but her voice was strong and calming as she sang the ancient prayers that guided the warrior's soul to Arvandor, the hone of all elves, just as Evermeet must be.

As Rolim watched the Silver elf mage at her selfless, heartfelt labors, he felt a sudden wrenching pain, as if something broke free from around his heart. Warmth and light flowed in, bringing a peace that he had never known he lacked.

Without hesitation, Rolim reached into his bag for the healing potion that every warrior of Aryvandaar carried, his last and personal salvation in the event of battle gone awry. He went to Ava and handed her the priceless vial.

"For our people," he said softly.

For just an instant, her gaze clung to his, but in that brief time Rolim saw in her gray eyes the measure of what he might become. It was a very different image from that which his ambitions had fashioned, but he was nonetheless content.

And at that moment, though many days would yet pass before he walked upon its shores, Rolim Durothil truly came home to Evermeet.

* * * * *

The goddess Lloth was in a quandary. For centuries she had preyed upon the elves of Aber-toril, and had found it to be an occupation much to her liking.

Lloth seldom remembered that she had once called the god Vhaeraun her son. Now he was merely a rival. As for Eilistraee, Lloth never wasted a thought upon the girl one way or another. The Dark Maiden lived much as she had in long-ago Arvandor: She'd taken to the forest, where by all accounts she squandered her scant store of godly magic in aid of lost travelers and elven hunters.

Lloth preferred the burgeoning cities of southern Faerûn, where turmoil and intrigue bred like lice. She was also growing fond of the dark and twisted tunnels that seemed fashioned for the express purpose of hoarding treasure, staging ambush, and engaging in other delightful clandestine activities. After the dulling sameness of the Abyss, the simmering conflict between the Ilythiiri and Corellon's fair-skinned children was a bracing tonic. The Crown Wars had been a source of dark joy. All things considered, Lloth had not been as happy for millennia.

She was of mixed mind, however, concerning the

matter of the Sundering. The mortal body of Ka'Narlist had been swept away by the terrible floods, and the wondrous city of Atorrnash reduced to legend. Lloth did not mourn the loss of her consort, for she had long ago tired of him. Males, she concluded, were not worth the bother. She did not regret the loss of Ka'Narlist's person, though she rued the loss of that wondrous vest of Sea elven magic. There was the possibility that Ka'Narlist had managed to capture his own essence in one of his dark pearls. Lloth did not like the idea that the final fate of the malevolent, ambitious entity was not altogether certain.

Other effects of the Sundering also brought mixed emotions to the goddess. On the one hand, it had destroyed many of her worshipers. Yet for each of her elves that had tumbled into the sea or been crushed by falling stone, at least three of Vhaeraun's followers had perished. Lloth reigned supreme among the dark elves' gods.

Thus was victory won on any battlefield, as Lloth knew well. The last few centuries had left her with considerable expertise in the art and practice of elven warfare.

So intriguing was this new hobby that she had abandoned altogether her ancient craft of weaving enchanted tapestries. Living beings made more interesting threads for her looms, and the ever changing webs they wove were infinitely more appealing to the dark goddess than the well-ordered destinies she had once fashioned and fostered for her dark elven charges. Her time in the Abyss had given her a taste for chaos.

She was not pleased, however, about this matter of an elven homeland. Lloth might be barred from Arvandor, but there was no place upon this world that she would suffer to remain beyond the grasping hands of her dark followers.

Yet try as she might, Lloth could devise no way to strike against the island. She herself was barred from Evermeet as surely as she was from Arvandor; the same magical barriers that protected the Sacred Forest of Olympus from evil gods also warded the elven island.

This angered Lloth, for it was but one more insult to come from the hands of Corellon Larethian. The dark goddess vowed that, in time, she would find a way to destroy Evermeet. This goal became a focus, a receptacle for all her ancient animosity toward the elven god.

There were, however, other matters that absorbed Lloth's immediate attention. The dark elves had been driven below ground. There was new territory to conquer, new magic to learn. The descendants of Ka'Narlist and Lloth were now called drow, and they were as evil and fearsome a people as Lloth could have desired. In time, they would become powerful enough to emerge from their dark world and reclaim the whole of Aber-toril. In time, the drow would bring about the utter destruction of Corellon's children upon the mainland. When that was accomplished, when the elves of Evermeet stood utterly alone, it would be a small matter for her followers to invade and overtake the island, no matter how enchanted it might be. Yes, Lloth had much to accomplish in the warrens and caverns of the great Underdark.

In the meanwhile, Lloth needed an agent to work on her behalf on the surface world. The Ilythiiri raiders who had pressed into the far north often brought back tales of barbarian tribes of humans—fearful warriors who worshiped totem beasts—and oftentimes of the Beast Lord who commanded them. It seemed that Malar, her old acquaintance, was beginning to enjoy a bright turn of fortune.

Perhaps, Lloth mused, it was time to pay a visit to the Great Hunter, and to light once again the fire of vengeance in his heart. Let him spend his strength and his efforts on bedeviling the "elven homeland" while she occupied herself elsewhere.

And why not? Provided that she prodded him in the right direction, Malar was resourceful enough to do justice to the task. Lloth had little fear that the Beast Lord would complete the task and steal her moment of vengeance, for though he had grown in cunning and strength since his attack upon Corellon, Malar definitely lacked the power to challenge alone the forces of the Seldarine.

Even so, a few centuries of torment at the hands of the Beast Lord would make the eventual conquest of Evermeet all the easier.

3rd day of Ches, 1368 DR

To Danilo Thann, beloved nephew of my beloved Khelben, does Laeral Silverhand Arunsun send fond greetings.

Dan, my love! Thank you for your letter, and for the wonderfully silly ballad you composed for me. You will never know how gladly I welcomed every foolish line, for my visit to Evermeet has not otherwise been filled with mirth.

Do not misunderstand me—I consider myself fortunate to be among the handful of humans allowed on Evermeet. You know, of course, of my long-standing friendship with Evermeet's queen. Nor am I the only one of the Seven Sisters who has had dealings with Queen Amlaruil. My sister Dove's son was fostered here, kept safe from the many who would harm him to strike at Dove. He was raised in the ways of the elven folk, and is now living in peace and honor as a ranger in the wilds near Shadowdale. What you do not know is that my own child also found a haven on the elven island.

I wish I could have seen your face as you read that last line. You did not know I had a child, I suppose. Very few people do. I thought it would be better so. What I did not anticipate—and should have—was that my wild and beautiful Maura would find a way to thrust herself into general knowledge. That she did so unwittingly makes the situation all the more difficult.

But I am putting the tail before the teeth. I shall start again, this time at the beginning.

You know my story better than most. For many years I traveled with the adventuring party known as the Nine. We found an artifact, the Crown of Horns, and I in my pride decided

*that my powers of will and magic were sufficient to counter
the evil I sensed within it. I wore the Crown, and it claimed
me as its own. Years went by, terrible years during which I lost
Laeral and became the Wild Woman, the Witch of the North. I
remember little of those years, which in many ways is a blessing. But there were things lost to me that I would give centuries of my life to recall. One of these is Maura.*

*I do not remember her begetting. I cannot tell you who
her father was, nor do I remember the months that I carried her. Of her birth, I can tell you little more. All I recall
is a terrible storm outside my cave, a soothing voice
nearby, and the fierce piping cries of a baby whose face I
cannot recall. My sister Dove found me in travail and
tended me, and then took the babe to Evermeet for protection and fosterage. In my terrible madness, I could not
care for her, and no one on Faerûn dared to do so. No one
knew what influence the Crown of Horns might have had
on this poor babe. Such was the legacy I gave my child.*

*But Maura thrived on Evermeet. Any taint she might
have taken from the evil artifact was cleansed by the healing magic of that fair land. She grew up fierce and wild
as any forest elf, yet always and entirely her own person.
Among the elves, she stands out like a scarlet rose among
snowdrops—vivid and startling in her bright beauty. She
did not inherit the silver hair common to me and my sisters; she is as dark as I am fair, and even more exotic in
appearance. There is no telling what Maura's sire might
have been. Her pale bronze skin and lavish curves suggest
southern blood, her sharp cheekbones and almond-
shaped eyes hint at elven ancestry—although that she
might as well have gotten from me. She has, I blush to
confess, a bit of my own vanity and love of drama. Maura
is often flamboyant in her ways and her dress. Other than
her love of swordcraft—she is a notable fighter—she has
little in common with the elves. In fact, I had traveled to
Evermeet this time with the thought to bring her home at
last, now that she is a woman grown.*

To my dismay, I found that my restless and impatient

*Maura no longer wished to leave. She has fallen in love
with an elf—an elf whose name and rank decree that
nothing but grief can come of their union. You have come
to know this elf of late through your letters: Lamruil,
Prince of Evermeet.*

*I need not tell you how ill content Queen Amlaruil is
with this news. You know full well that she lost her best-
loved daughter, Amnestria, to the love of a human. For
many years, the queen refused to acknowledge the existence of Amnestria's half-elven daughter. Even now, while
she privately speaks well of Arilyn, she does not and
cannot acknowledge your wife as her kin, nor can she
allow her upon the elven island. The elves of Evermeet,
particularly the Gold elves, would see Arilyn's presence as
a terrible threat to all they hold dear—all the more so, for
her royal blood. Do not for a moment think that my personal friendship with the queen, or my status as Elf-
friend, or even the fact that I am numbered among the
Chosen of Mystra make my daughter an acceptable mate
for a prince of Evermeet. Maura would bear him half-
elven children, and that would be accounted a tragedy.*

*In your letter, you asked me to give you some insight
into why the elves shun those of mixed blood. This is a difficult question, but the answer says much about the
nature and the minds of Evermeet's elves.*

*You love a half-elf, so you have seen something of the
grief common to these beings who live between two
worlds. So also have I, for my mother was half-elven. So
desperate was she for a place of her own, that she joyfully surrendered herself as avatar to Mystra that her children might become—like herself—something both more
and less than human.*

*I am accepted on Evermeet, but only because my elven
heritage is not apparent—lost, perhaps, beneath the
mantle of Chosen of Mystra. For love of me, Amlaruil
accepted Dove's child and mine in fosterage, but only with
the understanding that their elven blood would be a
matter of deepest secrecy.*

Elaine Cunningham

Let me tell you the story of how Amlaruil and I first met. It was in revery—that elven state of wakeful dreaming that is more restful than sleep. As a child, I often went into revery. It was not so much a nap for me as an adventure. Even then, the silver fires of Mystra burned bright within me, and I was able to do things that no fully human mage can accomplish. In revery, I often slipped into the Weave itself, and I sensed the beings who make up its warp and weft. Most of these were elven, of course— human mages use the Weave, but elves are a part of it in ways that no human can fully understand.

On one such journey, I met Amlaruil. Now, understand that Amlaruil's tie to the Seldarine is as strong as mine to Mystra. She was surprised to meet a child in revery, astonished that one so young possessed so much power. We met often after that first time, and became closer than sisters before ever we set eyes upon each other.

I remember my first trip to Evermeet. Amlaruil sent me an elfrune, a ring that would enable me to travel to Evermeet with a thought. I will never forget the look of utter befuddlement on her face when she beheld me for the first time.

You know what she saw—a girl taller than most men but slight of form, with silver-green eyes and an abundance of silver hair. I am different from most women, perhaps, but I am recognizably a human woman. For the first and last time, I saw the future Queen of All Elves utterly lose her composure.

"You are N'Tel-Quess!" she blurted out, charmingly referring to me as a "Not Person."

"I am Laeral," I responded. In my mind, that was all and enough. I am as I am, and cannot be otherwise.

She nodded as if she heard and dimly followed my unspoken reasoning. "But you travel the Weave. You speak Elvish!"

"My mother was half-elven," I told her, by way of explanation for the latter feat.

Her face immediately arranged itself into a polite mask. "Oh, I'm so sorry," she said with great feeling.

I burst out laughing—I could not help it. Her tone was precisely that used by any well-bred person when told of some personal tragedy or family disgrace. Thus did Amlaruil regard half-elves. She still does, I suppose, and in this she is typical of Evermeet's elves.

What, then, am I to do with my Maura? She is as stubborn and headstrong as I am, which does not bode well for her—or for that matter, for Evermeet. What will occur if Lamruil should be called upon to take the throne? None of the elves, especially the Gold elf clans, would accept Maura as queen. In truth, they would be unlikely to accept Lamruil with or without Maura. Like his love, he is "too human."

Dan, my friend, I fear greatly for the People of Evermeet. Their splendid isolation is a delicate and fragile thing. Like you, I fear that it cannot long endure. Change is inexorable, inevitable. Given time, the waves will wear away the strongest rock. The elves, for all their wisdom and despite their long lives, do not fully understand this. Perhaps a union between Lamruil and Maura would force them to see what is all around them.

Or perhaps it will only speed what many elves fear most of all—the end of Evermeet, the twilight of the elves.

Oh, Dan, I wish I knew. And while I'm in the business of wishing, I wish I could have kept my baby Maura, I wish I had raised her myself away from this seemingly inviolate but fragile island. I wish that I had taken her away sooner, before her wild beauty caught Lamruil's eye. And I wish you were here, to tell me stories and sing me silly songs and make me laugh as you always do.

I fear that my letter has done little to answer your questions. But perhaps my story has cast some light on the character of Evermeet. The elves created Evermeet because they wish to remain what they are. But their history is a constant struggle between those who cling to ancient traditions, and those whose bold innovations have shaped Evermeet. Even the monarchy was once a radical idea. There are still those who consider it so, and

Elaine Cunningham

who secretly long for the return of the ancient council. Thus it continues—the battle between constancy and change.

You will see this thread running through all of elven history. Nowhere is it more apparent than on Evermeet. And nowhere is it more flagrantly confronted than in the person of a half-elf. Start there, then, to understand the nature of this land.

I will return to Waterdeep soon—without Maura, I fear. In the meanwhile, kiss your uncle Khelben for me. It will irritate him, and thus amuse you. This, I hope, will help put you in the proper frame of mind to sing me into better humor. Speaking of which, be prepared to do your best—and your worst. After my time here, I feel in dire need of a rousing rendition of "Sune and the Satyr." Indeed, I could emulate the revels described therein, and not fully blunt the edge of my current despair. Tell me— do you think Khelben might be persuaded to participate? No, I didn't think so either.

With fondest regards, Laeral

Prelude: The Fall of Twilight

13th day of Mirtul, 1369 DR

rince Lamruil sauntered into the vast hall where his mother held court, well aware of the many pairs of disapproving eyes that followed him.

He had not been long in Evermeet—at Queen Amlaruil's insistence, he had taken to the mainland on an adventure for which he had little heart. The time away had been more eventful, the task given him more compelling, than he had anticipated. Yet his mother's hope—that Lamruil's absence might dim the passion that he shared with Maura—had been unrealized. At least the queen had the satisfaction of knowing that she had kept word of it from spreading. The gods would bear witness that Lamruil had done enough already to scandalize the court.

Since his arrival he had managed to further tarnish his reputation. Seemingly at whim, he'd decided to take up the study of magic. As a student at the Towers, he had managed to antagonize a number of powerful Gold elf families. What none of these nobles realized was that he did so deliberately. In his travels, Lamruil had observed that some Gold elves on the mainland held onto traditional, extremist views. He thought it wise to make some effort to ferret out any on Evermeet that might be allied with these extremists. Those who seemed most offended by the Moon elf prince's antics were likely suspects and worthy of closer, more subtle scrutiny.

Queen Amlaruil knew of Lamruil's tactics, and she did

not approve. For that matter, she approved of little that Lamruil had to do or say these days. He knew with grim certainly that she would not relish the news that he must give her, and that she would forbid him from doing what he had already decided must be done.

The prince strode to the dais and went down on one knee before his mother's throne.

"You are seldom in council, my son," she said in a voice that betrayed no hint of the curiosity that Lamruil knew she must feel. "Have you given up on the study of magic, then, to learn something of governance?"

"Not exactly," he said ruefully. "In truth, I must speak to you on a personal matter. A matter of considerable delicacy."

He saw the almost imperceptible flicker of her eyelids—for the wondrously controlled Amlaruil, that was tantamount to a shriek of panic. She clearly thought, as he meant her to, that this had to do with his forbidden relationship with Maura.

The queen politely but briskly cleared the council room. When they were alone, she turned a grim face to her errant son.

"Please do not tell me that another half-elven bastard is about to sully the Moonflower line," she said coldly.

"That would be a tragedy indeed," he returned with equal warmth. "May the gods bear witness to the fortitude with which we endure the disgrace brought upon us by half-breed bastards—such as my sister's daughter Arilyn."

Amlaruil sighed. She and Lamruil had sparred over this matter many times. Never had they come to a resolution. Never would they.

"Amnestria's daughter has served the People well," the queen admitted. "That does not give you license to increase the number of half-elves!"

"Content yourself, then, in knowing that I have not," Lamruil said grimly. "The news I bear you is of far more serious nature."

The queen's expression hinted that she doubted this.

In response, Lamruil handed her a letter. "This is from Arilyn's husband, whom I call not only nephew, but friend. He is human, but he writes the language well."

Amlaruil skimmed the elegant Elvish script. She looked up sharply. "Kymil Nimesin has slipped away from his Harper jailers! How is that possible?"

Lamruil grimaced. "Kymil Nimesin has powerful allies, unexpected ones. The sages say that Lloth and Malar once made an alliance against the People, though they hate each other nearly as much as they hate the children of Corellon. It appears that they might have done so again."

The queen's face paled to the color of new snow. "He should have been tried on Evermeet. This would never have happened!"

"On this, we agree."

"Where is he now?"

"The Harpers do not know."

"Has he elven allies still? You have been looking for them under every bed in Evermeet."

"A few, although none on Evermeet—at least, none that I could pinpoint with certainty," Lamruil said. "On the mainland, definitely. There are also other troubling alliances. In the past, Kymil has done business with the Zhentarim. He struck a bargain with the wizards of Thay. To what end, we can only imagine."

"Yes," the queen said softly. Her eyes filled with a sorrow and loss that the passing of decades had not diminished. "I know all too well the cost of Kymil Nimesin's ambitions."

The young prince felt suddenly awkward in the presence of such immense grief. But he placed his hands on her shoulders and met her eyes. "I will find the traitor, this I swear. One way or another, I will bring him back to Evermeet to stand trial."

A chill passed through Amlaruil at these words, like a portent of heartache yet to come. "How will you find him when the Harpers cannot?"

The prince smiled grimly. "I know Kymil Nimesin. I

185

know what he needs, and where he must go to find it. Ambitions like his need the support of vast wealth. He and I took a fortune that rivals a red dragon's hoard from the elven ruins. Kymil has hidden it, and will try to retrieve it. I will go there and confront him."

"He might expect you to do this."

"Of course he will," Lamruil agreed. "And he will set a trap for me. He will not expect that I will anticipate this trap, and walk into it of my own will."

Amlaruil stared at her son. "Why would you do this?"

"Kymil Nimesin has little regard for any Silver elf, and holds me in utter contempt," the prince said candidly. "He expects me to run bumbling into his traps in defense of queen and country. What he does *not* expect, however, is a bumbling prince who offers himself as an ally."

A small, startled cry escaped from the queen's mouth. "You cannot!"

Lamruil winced. "Have you so little regard for me? I would not truly ally myself with the traitor who killed my father and my sister."

"I never thought you would. Yet I cannot allow this ruse. If you do this thing, you will never rule Evermeet after me!"

"I never expected to," Lamruil retorted. "Ilyrana is the heir to the throne, and well loved by the people. Since I am not burdened by their regard, I am free to take such risks on their behalf. Let me learn of Kymil's plan, and undo it from within. I must," he said earnestly when the queen began to protest. "Do you think that a single elf, however powerful, would dare act alone? If he endeavors to complete the task he has started, be assured that it will be with the backing of powerful allies. And such alliances often set complex events in motion—events that might well continue with or without Kymil Nimesin. No, I think we must know more."

The queen's eyes searched his face as if she might find there an argument to refute his words. Finally she sighed, defeated.

"There is truth, even wisdom, in what you say. Yet I wish there was another who could take up this task!"

"You fear I am not suited?"

"No," she said softly, sadly. "You alone on all of Evermeet are suited for it. No one else has your knowledge of our foe. It is a terrible burden, I think."

"But a needed one," he said.

Amlaruil was silent for a long moment. "Yes," she said at last. "Yes, it is."

"I may go, then?" he said in surprise.

To his astonishment, a genuine if somewhat wry smile curved his mother's lips. "Would you have stayed, had I forbidden you?"

"No," he admitted.

The queen laughed briefly, then her face turned wistful. "You are much like your sister, Amnestria. I did not trust her to do what was best for herself and her People. Permit me to learn from my mistakes."

The implication of her words moved Lamruil deeply. "Are you saying that you trust me in this?"

Amlaruil looked surprised. "Of course I do. Did you not know that? I have always trusted you. Despite your mischief, there is much of your father in you."

The prince dropped to one knee and took both of her hands in his. "Then trust me until the end of this, I beg you. Trust me when your councilors tell you that you should not, when your own senses insist that you must not!"

"Bring Kymil Nimesin to me," the queen said softly.

Lamruil nodded softly. The seeming non sequitur told him that his mother understood what he intended to do. The risk was enormous, and Amlaruil was no doubt right in saying that even if he succeeded, he would never be accepted as Evermeet's king. In his mind, that was a small enough price to pay.

"By your leave, then, I will begin."

The queen nodded, then reached out and framed her youngest child's face with her hands. She leaned forward and kissed his forehead. "You are Zaor's son indeed," she said softly. "What a king you would have made!"

"With Maura as my queen?" he teased.

Amlaruil grimaced. "I suppose you could not resist that; even so, you should have made an effort. Go then, and make your farewells."

The young prince rose and bowed deeply. He turned and strode from the palace. He claimed his moon-horse from the groom who held its bridle, and then rode swiftly toward Ruith. In the forests just south of that fortress city he would find his love.

No other place on Evermeet suited Maura as well. Maura had been fostered by the forest elves of Eagle Hills, but now that she was a grown woman, she lived alone in the forested peninsula north of Leuthilspar, in a small chamber in the heart of a living tree. The rocky coast, the curtain of snow-crested mountains that framed the forest, echoed the wildness of her own nature. The proximity of Ruith, a fortress city that housed the heart of the elven military, provided her with sparring partners when she wished a match—which was often. Even in a society of champions, she was seldom defeated.

She looked up expectantly as Lamruil entered her home. "What have you learned? Can you stop this foolish charade among the city folk yet?"

During his time in Leuthilspar, Lamruil had insinuated himself into the confidences of certain Gold elves and given them to know that he was impatient to assume the throne. He had implied that he was eager to see his mother step down, hinted that he might be willing to facilitate the same end by other means. Maura knew these things, and had railed against them in terms that made Amlaruil's disapproval seem a pale thing.

"I learned a few things," he said vaguely. "At the moment, they are of minor importance. I must leave Evermeet at once."

He showed her the letter, and told her what he planned to do. He steeled himself for the girl's fury. Maura did not disappoint him.

"Why must you take the trouble and risk to bring this Kymil Nimesin back to Evermeet? Kill him outright, and have done with it. By all the gods—he killed your father! The right of vengeance is yours."

For a moment, Lamruil was honestly tempted to do as she urged. "But I am not the only one who has suffered loss. This matter is for the People to judge. I can best serve them by delivering the traitor to their judgment. I must also bide my time, and do what I can to uncover other threats to the throne."

The elf maid's glare faded, pushed aside by dawning apprehension. "You're starting to sound like a king," she said, her tone wavering between jest and worry.

A huge grin split Lamruil's face. "There are several thousand elves on this island who would be happy to dispute that with you," he said without rancor.

"Still, it is possible."

Lamruil shrugged, puzzled by her uncharacteristic gravity. "I am a prince. In theory, yes, it is possible. But Ilyrana is much loved, and will probably take the throne. Even if she declines, it is likely that an elf from another noble house would be chosen over an untried youth."

"Perhaps to act as regent in your stead," Maura persisted. "The result would be delayed, but it would be the same for all that!"

The prince took her hands in his. "What is this about, really?"

Her eyes were fierce when they met his; even so, twin tears glistened in their emerald depths. "A king will need a queen. A *proper* queen."

For a moment, Lamruil was at a loss for words. He knew the truth behind Maura's words; even if the nobles accepted him as their king, they would certainly insist that he take one of their own to reign with him. They would not countenance a wild thing like Maura on the throne of Evermeet, not even if she were fully elven. Nor, he realized, would she be long content in the moonstone palace of Leuthilspar.

The prince longed to wipe the silvery tracks from

Maura's cheeks, but he knew with the sure wisdom of love that she would not thank him for acknowledging her tears.

"Wait here," he said suddenly. Turning from her, he ducked out of the tree and sprinted off into the forest. In moments he found what he sought—wild laurel. A few flowers still clung to the plant, filling the air with a heady fragrance. He cut a few of the woody vines with his knife and hurriedly fashioned them into a circlet. The result fell far short of symmetry, but it would serve.

He returned to the girl and placed the crown of leaves and flowers on her head. "You are the queen of my heart," he said softly. "While you live, I will take no other."

"And why should you? You've already taken all the others," she retorted.

Lamruil lifted one brow. "Is it seemly to bring up my youthful exploits on this our wedding day? I think not—we are long past such discussions."

She crossed her arms and glared at him. "I will not wed you."

Lamruil grinned. Placing a finger under her chin, he raised her stubborn face to his. "Too late," he said lightly. "You just did."

"But—"

The elf stilled her protests with a kiss. Maura stiffened but did not pull away. After a moment her arms twined around his neck, and she returned his kiss with an urgency that bordered on desperation.

Finally the prince eased out of her embrace. "It is past time. I must go."

Maura nodded. She walked with him to the forest's edge. She watched as he descended the steep path to the harbor, and kept watching until Lamruil's ship was little more than a golden dot on the far horizon. She watched with eyes misted with grief born not only of loss, but understanding.

For the first time, she realized the truth of her love. Lamruil was meant to be a king—it was a role he was growing into, though in ways that few of Evermeet's elves might recognize. The day would come when he would be ready. And on that day, she would lose him to Evermeet.

"Long live Queen Amlaruil," she whispered with a fervor that had nothing to do with her genuine respect for Evermeet's monarch.

* * * * *

More than two years passed before Lamruil returned to the island. To the elves, this was no great time, but every day, every moment of it weighed heavily upon Maura. She had a task to do. She and Lamruil were one in their purpose, and she did her part with a determination that bemused her elven instructors. She threw herself into sword practice with a fervor that rivaled that of the most dedicated bladesinger. She did so, not only because she was a fighter at heart and because she loved the dance of battle, but because she, unlike the elves, fully expected a war to come.

And so she trained for it, watched for it, lived for it. Even so, when it came, she was unprepared.

They were all unprepared, the proud elves of Evermeet. The threat came from the place they least expected, from an enemy that all assumed was too far removed for concern. From Below they came—the unthinkable. The drow.

The attack came on the northernmost shore of the island. Throughout the long autumn night, the tunnels below the ancient ruins of Craulnober Keep echoed with the clash of weapons and the faint, instinctive cries that even the bravest of warriors could not hold back when a blade sank home. But the sounds had faded into grim silence, sure proof that the first battle was nearly over.

Was nearly lost.

Reinforcements came from Ruith's Lightspear Keep and from the lonely strongholds of the Eagle Hills. Maura came with them, to stand beside the elves who had raised and trained her.

The defenders struggled to regain the ancient castle from the dark-elven invaders that poured forth like seething, deadly lava from the depths of the stone. The approach of dawn brought a turn in the tide of battle, for as the drow began to fall back in anticipation of the coming light, the elves managed to breach the ancient curtain wall of the keep. With renewed ferocity, the elves took the battle to the dark elves who held the castle. Many dark bodies lay amid the fallen of Evermeet. With the coming of dawn, the surviving drow withdrew to the tunnels from whence they had come.

Too soon, the proud elves counted their victory. Following the command of Shonassir Durothil, they pursued. Nearly all the elves abandoned their positions on the cliffs and hills beyond the castle and came into the abandoned keep, determined to pursue and destroy the invaders.

No sooner had they entered the walls, however, than the doors swung shut behind them and sealed so completely that gates and walls seemed to have been melted into a single, unbroken expanse of stone.

A cloud of darkness settled over the castle, shrouding the elven fighters in an impenetrable mist and a chilling aura of pure evil.

Into this darkness the drow returned, silent and invisible, armed with terrible weapons and confusing magic. Here and there pinpricks of red light darted about like malevolent will o'wisps. Those elves who took these to be the drow's heat-sensitive eyes found, in giving chase, that they followed an illusion. Their reward was invariably an invisible dagger in the spine, and a faint burst of mocking laughter—music as beautiful and terrible as the faerie bells of the Unseelie courts.

The elves fought on amid the darkness and despair. They fought bravely and well, but they died all the same.

A few of the warriors managed to find their way into the tunnels. These pursued the drow back toward the island of Tilrith, through tunnels that hundreds of years of dark elven work and magic had reopened.

And in the darkness they died, for in the tunnels beyond the keep lurked the only two creatures that were perhaps even more feared than the drow. One of these, a beautiful dark elven female, shrieked with elation each time one of Corellon Larethian's children perished.

Lloth had come at last to Evermeet. Though magic barred her from setting foot upon the island itself, the tunnels below were hers to command.

No such strictures were placed upon the creature with her, a terrible thing that resembled nothing so much as a gigantic, three-legged cockroach. The monster surged toward the keep. Its probing snout swept along the tunnel walls, and the ironhard maw churned busily as the creature chiseled through the stone to make way for its bulk. Nearly as large as a dragon and covered with impenetrable armor, the monster was one that was all too familiar to many of Evermeet's elves.

Malar's creature, the Ityak-Ortheel, had followed Lloth from her home on the Abyss. Finally, the Beastlord and the Queen of Spiders had found a way to unite their strengths in a strike against Evermeet. The dreaded elf-eater needed a gate from the Abyss and Lloth had been able to provide one.

The elf-eater surged upward, exploding from the stone floor of the keep. Scores of tentacles probed the air, testing for the airborne taste of nearby prey. The creature was relentless, devouring both living and dead elves until the keep was silent and empty. With the speed of a galloping horse, the creature plunged into the ancient wall. The stone shattered, sending a cloud of dust and rubble hurtling out of the blackness that encircled the castle and threatened to engulf all of Evermeet.

One warrior survived—the only one whose blood was not sufficiently elven to call to the elf-eater. Alone, Maura watched in despair as the elf-eater turned away from the keep, heading south with a linear intensity that even a crow's flight could not match. Maura could guess all too well its destination, and its intent.

The monster was heading for Corellon's grave, the nearest elven settlement—not coincidentally, one of the seats of Evermeet's power. Many of the most powerful clerics came together to study and pray, to cast clerical magic to aid the People here and now, and to contemplate the wonders that awaited them in the realms of Arvandor. There, amid the temples of Corellon's Grove, the elf-eater would once again feed.

This was horror enough, but one more thought added the extra measure of urgency needed to tear Maura from her exhaustion and despair: The Princess Ilyrana, a priestess of the goddess Angharradh, made her home in the Grove.

A shrilling cry burst from Maura's lips, a shriek that to human ears would have been indistinguishable from an eagle's call. Maura, who had been raised among the Eagle Hills, knew of the giant birds and had heard the elves call them many times. Never had she summoned them, never had she ridden one. She wasn't certain she could succeed at either. It would not be the first time, however, that an untried warrior had ridden such a steed into battle.

She had not long to wait. An enormous bird dropped from the sky with unnerving silence, coming to rest on a pile of rubble that the elf-eater had left behind when it crashed through the keep. The eagle was as large as a war-horse, and beautiful. The slanting rays of the rising sun turned its feathers to gold. It was also fearsome, with a hooked beak larger than Maura's head, and talons the size of the dagger she carried.

The bird cocked its head in inquisition. "Who you? What want?" it demanded in a shrill voice.

Maura's chin came up proudly. "I am Maura of Evermeet, wife to Prince Lamruil and daughter by marriage to King Zaor. Take me into battle, as your ancestor once took the king. Evermeet's need is greater now than it was then—greater than ever it was."

"You not elf," the eagle observed.

"No. But then, neither are you. Do you fight less fiercely for your home, because of this?"

Her answer seemed to please the bird. The eagle spread its wings, until the golden feathers nearly spanned the bloodstained courtyard.

"Up, up," it urged her impatiently. "Get on back, hold tight. We show how fierce we the not-elves fight for Evermeet home!"

Book Three

Constancy and Change

"Some legends say that Evermeet is a piece of Arvandor descended to the mortal world. Some consider it a bridge between the worlds, a place where the line between the mortal and the divine blurs. To some, it is merely a prize to be won. But this much is clear to all: from the day of its creation, Evermeet became the ancient homeland of Faerûn's People. This is not a simple matter to understand or explain, but when has truth ever been utterly devoid of paradox?"

—Excerpt from a letter from Elasha Evanara, Priestess
of Labelas,
Keeper of the Queen's Library

11

Inviolate

alar the Beast Lord considered no wild lands beyond his claim. The deep forests of Evermeet should have been his to rove, and all living things upon the island should have been his rightful prey. If elves were numbered among this prey, so much the better.

But, the bestial god was barred from the elven retreat. A net of powerful magic covered the island and kept the gods of the anti-Seldarine from making a direct attack upon Corellon Larethian's children. And this time, there was no treacherous elven goddess to open the way for him from within.

No, Malar mused, he could not reach the island. But perhaps there were others who could. Once, long ago, a coalition had come near to defeating the elven pantheon in their own sacred forest. Why could he not gather a similar group of gods and direct the combined efforts of their mortal followers? Once and for all, he would crush the mortal elves whose very existence reminded him of his humiliating defeat at the hands of Corellon.

The sea, Malar reasoned, was his first barrier to success, and a formidable one. For the most part his own followers were orcs, humans who gloried in the hunt, and beings from a score or so of the other predatory races. These hunters lived upon the mainlands and did not have the ships or the skills needed to cross the vast watery divide. In time, perhaps, he could find godly and mortal allies who could remedy this lack. But it seemed clear to him that the first, logical step in building such an alliance would be to enlist the powers and the creatures of the depths.

And so the Beast Lord sought out a remote and rocky island, far to the north of Evermeet, and took on his bestial avatar form. He sent out a summons and then he settled down upon a high and ragged cliff to wait.

The sea winds that swept the island quickened to gale force as the sky darkened to indigo. Waves reared up and dashed themselves against the cliff below, growing higher and higher until the Beast Lord's black fur was drenched by the salty spray. Just as Malar thought the angry waters might engulf the island, and his avatar with it, a massive wave rose straight up from the sea and formed itself into a beautiful, wild-eyed woman.

The goddess Umberlee loomed over the island, quivering in the crest of that great, dangerously undulating wave. "What do you want of me, land dweller?" she demanded in a thrumming voice.

Malar eyed the sea goddess with a touch of apprehension. Her powers and her watery domain were far beyond his experience or understanding. Yet it might be that he could find a common ground, or at least some blandishment that would catch her fancy and mold her purposes to his. This would not be without risks. By all accounts, the goddess of the waves was dangerously capricious.

"I come in peace, Umberlee, and I bring warning. The elves travel your oceans to settle the island of Evermeet," he began.

Lightning sizzled forth from Umberlee's eyes, and the gnarled beach plum bushes on Malar's left exploded into flame. "You presume to summon me, and then speak as if I know not what happens within my own domain?" she raged. "What does it matter if the elves travel the seas, as long as they pay proper tribute to me?"

"But they do not merely travel your seas. They think to rule the ocean, with Evermeet as their base," Malar persisted. "This I know from a goddess of the elves."

The water goddess retreated a little as if in surprise, and a different sort of wrath kindled in her eyes. "No one rules the oceans but Umberlee!"

"The seagoing elves do you homage, that is true, but they revere only their own gods. Even the Sea elves do not worship you, but rather Deep Sashales."

"That is the way of things," the goddess said in a sullen voice. "Many are the creatures that inhabit my oceans, and all worship their own gods. But all they who live within or venture upon the waves pay tribute to me, and they say prayers to win my forbearance and stave off my wrath!"

"Do the elves who now live upon Evermeet so entreat you, or are they too content with the protection of their own gods?" Malar asked slyly. "Aerdrie Faenya has cast about the island wardings such that no ill wind or weather can ever destroy the island. The elves of the Seldarine believe that Evermeet is beyond the power wielded by other gods. And yet, surely there is something that Umberlee, one of the great Gods of Fury, can do to thwart these presumptuous elves!"

Malar watched as this shot sank home, as Lloth had predicted it would. He would have preferred to bring Umberlee into line with brute force and rending talons, but, as the dark goddess had pointed out, there comes a time in many a hunt when the prey must be herded to a place of the hunter's choice.

"There are many things I could do," the proud goddess boasted. "If there is chaos enough in the seas surrounding Evermeet, the elves will come to know and revere my power!"

The Beast Lord listened as Umberlee began to spin her plans for the Coral Kingdom, a vast and disparate group of enemies who would trouble the elves whenever they set sail. Some of these creatures could even venture onto the island itself, for the protection of the elven gods did not—could not—exclude all the followers of other gods. For such revenge as Malar had in mind, mortal beings would do what the gods could not.

And as he listened to the sea goddess boast and plot, Malar marveled at the cunning of Lloth, who had so deftly planned how to bring Umberlee's power against their elven foe. He tried not to dwell overlong on the end results of the dark goddess's last campaign, or on his dawning suspicion that he himself might have been as handily manipulated, both then and now, as was Umberlee.

Such dark thoughts served him best when they were turned into anger—a fine and killing rage that Malar could focus utterly against Corellon's children.

*   *   *   *   *

In the years that followed, large communities of strange and evil creatures began to gather in the warm waters surrounding Evermeet.

The scrags were the worst of them. These ten-foot, seagoing trolls were nearly impossible to defeat, for they healed themselves of battle wounds with astonishing speed. They could easily swarm over an elven ship, regenerating as fast as the elves could cut them down. Setting them aflame only ensured the destruction of the ship, and left the elven crew at the mercy of those scrags still in the sea. Few elves survived the swim through troll-infested waters. Travel between the mainland and Evermeet grew exceedingly perilous, and more ships were lost than made harbor.

In addition to the marine trolls were the sahuagin, dark and hideous fish-men who were driven by a soul-deep enmity toward Sea elves. Many were the battles that raged beneath the waves between these ancient enemies. In a few short decades, the peaceful Sea elves who lived near Evermeet, who guided elven ships and scouted ahead for dangers that hid beneath the waves, were nearly destroyed.

It was a dark time for the elves of Evermeet. Cut off from the powerful kingdom of Aryvandaar except for the Tower-sent messages, bereft of the formidable protective barrier once provided by the Sea elves, they found to their horror that their sacred homeland was not, as they had fondly hoped, impervious to attack.

* * * * *

Nearly four hundred years had passed since the first ships from Aryvandaar had sailed past the mountainous island outpost known as Sumbrar and into the deep, sheltering bay on Evermeet's southern shore. Here, at the mouth of the Ardulith river, they had founded Leuthilspar, "Forest Home."

From gem and crystal, from living stone and mighty ancient trees, the High Magi of Aryvandaar brought forth in the forests of Evermeet a city to rival any in the kingdoms of Faerûn. These buildings of Leuthilspar grew from the land itself, increasing in size as the years passed to accommodate the growing clans who dwelt within, as well as the settlers who came later. Even in its infancy, Leuthilspar was a city of incomparable beauty. Spiraling towers leaped toward the sky like graceful dancers, and even the common roadways were fashioned from gems coaxed from the hidden depths.

Although complete harmony among the elven nobility remained an elusive goal, Keishara Amarillis served well in bringing the contentious factions together. And when the time came for her to answer the call to Arvandor, Rolim Durothil accepted the duty of High Councilor with a humility and resolve that would have astonished those who had known him as a proud Gold elven warrior of Aryvandaar.

Rolim and his wife, the Silver elf mage Ava Moonflower, set an example for harmony among the clans and the races of elves. Theirs was an unusually large family, and their children increased both the Durothil and the Moonflower clans. Those children who took after their Gold elf patriarch were counted among the Durothils; those who favored their mother added to the numbers and power of the Moonflower clan.

Elaine Cunningham

It was a wise solution and a fine example—on this the elves of Leuthilspar were quick to agree. Few of them, however, followed in the High Councilor's footsteps. Unions between the various races of elves had become increasingly rare, and although relationships among the Gold, Silver and wild elves remained amicable, the various peoples began to draw off from each other.

As time passed, some of the more adventurous elves left Leuthilspar and spread across the island. A few of these travelers mingled with the wild elves that lived in the deep forest, and in doing so gave themselves over fully to a life lived in harmony with the sacred island. But most settled on the broad, fertile plains in the northwest to raise crops or train their fleet and nimble war-horses.

In the far north of the island were rugged, heavily forested hills and mountains. Wresting a living from this wild northern land was not an easy task, but it was a task well suited to the energies of the burgeoning Craulnober clan.

Theirs was a minor noble family, brought to Evermeet as honor guards in service to their liege clan, Moonflower. At the head of the family was Allannia Craulnober, a warrior who, despite her diminutive size, had survived the battles of the Crown Wars and had fought back the waves of monsters, orcs and dark elven raiders that threatened Aryvandaar. She knew all too well the horrors of battle, and the need for constant vigilance.

The growing complacency of Leuthilspar's elves, their utter certainty that Evermeet was an inviolate haven, were matters of deep concern to Allannia. She therefore chose a land that would test her strength, and would demand that she keep both her wits and her sword's edge sharp. Amid the struggles of life in their wild holdings, Allannia raised her children to be warriors.

Chief among these was Darthoridan, her eldest son. He was unusually tall for an elf, and more powerfully built than most of his kin. When he was yet a boy, still growing toward his full height, Allannia foresaw that no sword in the Craulnober armory would suit his strength. She sent word to the finest swordsmith in Leuthilspar, and had him create a broadsword of a size and weight seldom seen among the elves. *Sea-Riven* she called it, for reasons that were not entirely known to her.

As he grew toward adulthood, Darthoridan became increasingly restless. He spent his days in endless training, drilling with his warrior mother and his brothers and sisters for a battle that never came. Though he did not complain, he felt a keen sense of frustration over the singular focus of life in Craulnober Keep. Yes, he and his kin were becoming fine warriors, even by elven standards. Even so, the young elf longed to be so much more. He could not rid himself of the growing premonition that skill with the sword was not enough.

One day, when his hours of practice were over, Darthoridan sheathed Sea-Riven and wandered down to the shore. He spent many hours there, ignoring the dull aches in his battle-weary muscles as he challenged his strength and agility by climbing the sheer cliffs. More often, though, he merely sat and gazed out to sea, reliving the stories brought by travelers from the wondrous cities to the south.

This evening his mood was especially pensive, for his mother had decreed that the time was coming soon when he should travel to Leuthilspar and find a wife. This news was not at all unpleasing to the young elf, but he found that the prospect of transforming dream into reality was a bit daunting.

After all, the Craulnober clan holdings were isolated, and their keep was a simple tower of stone lifted from the rocky cliffs. Darthoridan knew little of the customs or culture of the great city. In her concern for a strong defense, Allannia Craulnober had focused on nothing else, and had taught her children nothing but the art of warfare. Darthoridan was hardly prepared for life in Leuthilspar; he did not feel confident in his ability to court and win a suitable bride.

If Allannia had her way, he mused with mingled

frustration and wry humor, then he would simply march into the elven city, challenge a likely looking battle-maid to a match, defeat her, and carry her off to the north.

Darthoridan sighed. Ridiculous though this image might be, in truth, this was all he was equipped to do.

When he was head of the clan it would be otherwise, vowed the young warrior. If he had only his own will to consult, his chosen wife would be a lady of high station and exquisite grace. She would teach their children what he could not. In addition, all Craulnober younglings would be sent into fosterage with noble families in the south, were they could learn the arts and the magical sciences which flourished in Leuthilspar. They would learn to master the magic that was their heritage—and the results would far outstrip the few experimental spells that Darthoridan managed to fashion in his scant spare time.

Despite the dreams that swirled pleasantly through his thoughts, Darthoridan remained alert to his surroundings. He noted a small blotch of darkness in an oncoming wave. He squinted against the light of the setting sun as he tried to discern its nature. As he watched, the surging waves tossed the unresisting object back and forth, as if toying with it before casting it upon the shore.

With a sigh, Darthoridan rose and began the descent down the cliff to the water's edge. He had little doubt as to what he would find. From time to time, the torn body of a Sea elf washed up on the northern shore, a grim testament to the wars that raged beneath the waves. It would not be the first time he had given the mortal body of a sea-brother to the cleansing flames, and sung the prayers that sped the soul to Arvandor. At moments like this, he found that he did not regret his hours of training with sword and spear.

As he suspected, yet another victim of the Coral Kingdom lay in shallow waters, rocked gently by the waves. Darthoridan waded out and lifted the dead elf in his arms, bearing her with honor to her place of final rest. As he stacked the stones and gathered driftwood for the bier, he tried not to dwell upon the Sea elf's garish wounds, long since bled white and washed clean by the seas, or on how young the little warrior had been when she died.

"If the battle is not over before the children must fight, then it is already lost," Darthoridan whispered, quoting his warrior mother. And as he worked, as he watched the flames leap up to greet the setting sun, he prayed that this young warrior's fate would not be shared by his youngest brothers and sisters, or by the children he himself hoped to sire. Yet if calm did not come to the seas, how long could they avoid a similar fate?

When at last the fire burned low, Darthoridan turned away and began to walk along the shore, hoping that the soothing rhythm of the waves would calm his troubled heart. The receding tide left the shore strewn with the sea's debris: broken shells, bits and pieces of ships lost at sea, long rubbery strands of kelp. Here and there small creatures scuttled for the sea, or busily tucked themselves in for the night in the tidal pools that dotted the shore.

As Darthoridan skirted one of these pools, he noted the odd shape of a piece of mossy driftwood that thrust up from the water. It was shaped rather like an enormous, hideous nose, right down to the flaring nostrils. He looked closer, squinting into the tangle of seaweed that floated on the surface of the pool.

A silent alarm sounded in his mind, and his hand went to the hilt of Sea-Riven. But before he could draw the sword, the tidal pool exploded with a salt-laden spray and a roar like that of an enraged sea lion bull.

From the waters leaped a scrag. Darthoridan stared in horrified awe as the creature rose to its full height. Nearly ten feet tall, the sea troll was armored by thick, gray-and-green mottled hide as well as an odd chain mail vest fashioned of shells. The strange armor clanked ominously as the scrag lifted its massive hands for the attack.

Darthoridan instinctively leaped back. Tall though he was, his arm and sword combined could never match the scag's reach. The creature's knuckles nearly dragged the ground, and though it held no weapons, its talons were

207

formidable. If the scrag got hold of him, it would shred him as it had no doubt slain the Sea elf girl.

The elf raised Sea-Riven into a defensive position and waited for the first attack. Darting forward, the scrag took a mighty, openhanded swipe at the elf. Darthoridan ducked under the blow, spinning away from the troll. He lifted the sword high overhead and brought it down hard on the troll's spindly, still-outstretched arm. The elven blade bit hard and deep, and the severed forearm fell to lie twitching on the sand.

Darthoridan dashed the spray of ichor from his face and lifted Sea-Riven again. Just in time—the scrag came on in a frenzy, its massive jaws clicking as it gibbered with pain and rage. Its one remaining hand lunged for the elf's throat. Darthoridan managed to slap the creature's hand out wide, then he dived between the scrag's legs and rolled up onto his feet.

Marshalling all his strength, the young elf gripped his sword as he might hold an axe, screaming out an incoherent battle cry as he swung at the back of the creature's leg.

Sea-Riven connected hard; the scrag toppled and went down. Now it was Darthoridan's turn at frenzy—his sword flashed in the dying light as it rose and fell again and again. As he chopped his foe into bits, he kicked or flung the gory pieces as far as his strength allowed. The troll could heal itself, but the task would be longer and more difficult if it had to gather its scattered parts.

A sudden pressure on his foot distracted the elf from his grisly work. He glanced down just as the scrag's severed hand clamped around his ankle. As the talons dug through his boot and deep into his flesh, Darthoridan shouted another battle cry, striving to focus his pain and fear into something he could use. He thrust the blade of Sea-Riven between himself and the disembodied hand. Driving the point deep into the wet sand, he pushed with all his strength. His sword cut into the scrag's palm, but the hand stubbornly refused to let go. Worse, one of the talons began to wriggle its way toward the tendon at the back of the elf's leg.

Desperate now, Darthoridan threw himself face forward onto the sand. With his free foot, he kicked out at the sword to keep it from falling with him. The sword remained upright, and finally pried the scrag's fingers from his boot.

Immediately the disembodied hand skittered away, running sideways on its fingers like some ghastly variety of crab. The hand groped blindly as it sought the limb from which it had been severed.

Breathing hard, the elf rolled to his feet and yanked his sword from the sand. He ignored the burning pain in his leg, and forced aside the impulse to avenge his wounds by chasing down the offending hand and crushing it underfoot. But it was painfully clear that this action would gain him nothing. Even now, several pieces of the scrag had managed to regroup, and gray-green flesh grew rapidly to fill in the missing parts. Worse, new creatures were starting to form from some of the more widely scattered parts. This was an eventuality that Darthoridan had not foreseen. Soon he would be facing an army of scrags.

He cast a quick glance at the distant towers of Craulnober Keep, plainly visible from the shore. Within the walls, preparing to enjoy the evening meal and a quiet hour or two before revery, were all his kin. His younger siblings were not helpless, certainly, but they were no more prepared for this sort of battle than he. And though Darthoridan was no expert on scrags, he suspected that trolls of any kind would not be sated by the death of a single elf.

Darthoridan turned and sprinted for the Sea elf's bier. He snatched up a still-glowing piece of driftwood and raced back to the burgeoning army of scrag. The elf skidded to a stop beyond the original creature's reach and snatched a small bag from his sword belt. It was time to test both his fledgling magic and his courage.

The elf dumped the contents of the bag into his hand. The discarded shells of several sea snails rolled out. Darthoridan had filled the cavity with volatile oil, and then sealed the opening with a thin layer of waxy ambergris. A thin linen wick poked out of the shell, awaiting the touch of fire. Darthoridan had played with these small, flaming missiles as a child, but never once had he tested the effect of the magic he'd placed upon the oil. For all he knew, he would set himself aflame long before he managed to toss one of the shells at the scrags.

So be it, he decided grimly. If that happened, he would charge the scrags and set them afire with his own hands. As long as he kept the creatures from ravaging the Craulnober lands, it would be a death well earned. He thrust the wick of the first shell into the driftwood flame.

The roar of light and heat and power sent Darthoridan hurtling back. He landed on his backside, hard enough to send a numbing surge of pain through his limbs that almost, but not quite, masked the searing pain in his hands.

Even so, he was content, for the explosive weapon had done its work well enough. The young elf watched with grim satisfaction as flaming trolls parts rolled in dying anguish on the sands. He rose to his feet, stalking the burning shore in grim determination that every vestige of his enemy be destroyed. Again and again the elf lit and tossed the flaming shells, until all that was left of the invading scrag were scattered spots of grease and soot upon the sands.

Later that night, Allannia Craulnober was oddly silent as she bandaged her son's blistered hands and poured healing potion into a glass of spiced wine for him to drink. Darthoridan, who was accustomed to maternal instructions delivered with a relentless vehemence that a harpy might envy, found his mother's mood disconcerting.

When he was certain that he would soon burst from the strain of waiting for his mother's verbal assault to begin, the elven matriarch finally spoke her mind.

"They will come again, these sea trolls. All our strength of arms will avail us nothing."

Her quiet, thoughtful tone surprised Darthoridan. "Fire will destroy them," he reminded her.

"But if they come in great numbers? Unless we are willing to risk burning down the keep and laying waste the forest and moorlands, we could not raise fire enough to hold back a large assault."

The elven warrior squared her shoulders and met her son's troubled gaze. "Go to Leuthilspar with the coming of dawn, and stay long enough to learn all those things that you long to know, the things that you try so hard to pretend mean little to you. And when you seek a wife, consider the wisdom of bringing north someone who can teach magic to the Craulnober young," she said. "It is time we learned new ways."

Allannia smiled faintly at the thunderstruck expression on her son's face. "Close your mouth, my son. A good warrior sees much—and knows when the time has come to share the field of battle."

* * * * *

In the years to come, attacks upon the elves by the scrags and their sahuagin allies grew more frequent and vicious. But leaders emerged among the people of Evermeet, including Darthoridan Craulnober and his wife Anarzee Moonflower, the daughter of High Counselor Rolim Durothil.

Although Anarzee was not a High Mage but a priestess of Deep Sashales, she possessed a considerable grasp of magic. She also had a keen knowledge of the ways of the sea, and the creatures who made their home beneath the waves. The priestess and warrior combined their skills to raise and train an army of elves to protect the shores with swords and magic.

But as time passed, Anarzee felt that this was not enough. If the elves were ever to prevail over the Coral Kingdom, they must take the battle to the seas. This burden fell to her, for there was no elf on all of Evermeet who could bear it as well.

All her life, Anarzee had felt a special affinity for the

sea. She felt its rhythms as surely as most elves responded to the cycles of moonlight. Even her appearance echoed the sea, for her hair was a rare shade of deep blue, and her eyes a changeful blue-green. As a child, her favorite playground had been the white sands of Siiluth, and her playmates had been the sea birds, selkie pups, and the Sea elf children who lived near its shores.

But now most of those children were dead. Even Anarzee's mentor, an ancient Sea-elven priest of Deep Sashales, had been slain in the endless battles with the sea trolls. The selkies, too, had disappeared, seeking the islands to the distant north where they might raise their young in safety. Thus it was that Anarzee, though she was born into a large and vibrant clan, and though the wonders of Leuthilspar surrounded her, was at a young age left very much alone.

The coming of the young warrior Darthoridan Craulnober to Leuthilspar had changed all that. He and Anarzee had fallen in love nearly at first sight. She went with him gladly to the northern coast, and together they fought the creatures who had destroyed her world, and who threatened his. With the birth of Seanchai, their firstborn son, the two worlds became one and the same for Anarzee. She would do whatever was needed to ensure her child's future.

Anarzee's eyes clung to the towers of Craulnober Keep as her ship left the safety of the docks. It was bitterly difficult to leave Seanchai, although he was weaned now and just starting to toddle. If the choice was entirely hers to make, she would spend every moment of his too-brief childhood delighting in her babe, singing him the songs he loved and telling the tales that kindled dreams in his eyes. After all, in just a few short decades, he would be a child no more!

The elf woman sighed, taking some comfort from the knowledge that Darthoridan remained behind in command of the shore's army. Anarzee had insisted that he remain. If this first strike should fail, the clan—and especially their son—must be protected from the certain retaliation meted out by the Coral Kingdom.

Even if her mission were to fail, it would not be the last. The ship upon which Anarzee stood was the first of many. Specially designed to resist scrag attack, armed with powerful elven magic and over a hundred fighters, it would strike a decisive blow against the sea trolls and begin the process of reclaiming the waves. Anarzee ran her hand along the thin, translucent tube that ran the length of the ship's rail. The scrags might notice that this ship was different, but they would never suspect what lay in store for them. And how could they know? Never before had an elven ship deliberately set itself aflame.

The ship was still within sight of the coast when the first of the scrags struck. The vessel jolted to a stop, then began to pitch and rock as powerful, unseen hands scrambled at its underside.

Anarzee knew all too well what the creatures were doing. Scrags would board when necessary, but they preferred to scuttle a ship by tearing holes in its hull, thereby forcing the elves into the water. But the outside of *this* ship was perfectly smooth and very hard—it had been grown from crystal and provided no handholds for the scrags to grasp. Nor could the creatures break through it with their teeth or talons. They would be forced to fight, and on elven terms.

A small, grim smile tightened Anarzees lips, and she nodded first to the small Circle of High Magi, then to the archers who stood waiting by blazing fireboxes. "It won't be long," she murmured. "Begin chanting the spell. Light the arrows . . . *now!*"

Even as she spoke, several pairs of scaly hands clutched at the rail. The archers dipped their arrows into the fire and took aim. Anarzee lifted one hand, her eyes intent upon the swarming scrags. Timing was crucial—if the archers fired too soon, the creatures would simply fall back into the water, where the flames would die and the creatures' arrow-torn flesh regenerate.

213

The sea trolls moved fast, and they often moved together like enormous, schooling fish. In the span of two heartbeats, all the scrags had swarmed aboard. It was a large hunting party—over a score of full-grown trolls.

Anarzee dropped her hand and shrieked, *"Now!"*

Flaming arrows streaked toward the scrags, sending them staggering back toward the side of the ship. Some of the creatures began to climb the rail, instinctively heading for the safety of the waves.

But at that moment the magi's spell was unleashed. With a sound that suggested a hundred goblets shattering against a wall, the crystal vials embedded in the rail exploded and released the fluid that bubbled within. A wall of flame leapt up all along the ship's rail, barring the scrags' escape and setting alight many of those that had escaped the archers flaming arrows.

Shrieking and flailing, the burning trolls instinctively darted away from the eldritch flame behind them. Elven warriors rushed forward to meet them, armed with protective spells against the heat and flame. They fought with grim fury, determined that no scrag would break through their line. Slowly, inexorably, they pressed the dying trolls back into the flames.

It seemed to Anarzee that the fire and the battle raged for hours, but she knew it could not truly be so. Trolls burned quickly. Behind the warrior elves, the Circle continued chanting the magic that sustained both the fighters and the flame—and that kept the fire from breaking past the wall of elven warriors. Sooner than Anarzee had dared to hope possible, the battle neared its end.

It was then that the sahuagin came. The first one to board the ship did so not of its own will or power. Shrieking and thrashing, a sahuagin tumbled through the wall of flame—no doubt having been picked up bodily by its comrades and thrown through the magic fire. Like a living bombard, the sahuagin hurtled toward the elven defenders.

A startled elf managed to bring his sword up in time,

impaling the creature as it fell. But the weight of the fish-man brought the elf down, too.

The sahuagin might have been unwilling at first, but it knew what to do now. Claws and teeth scrabbled and tore at the pinned elf's face and neck. By the time the elves pulled the creature off their brother, the sahuagin horde had claimed its first kill.

Other sahuagin followed in like manner, tossed up onto the ship by the unseen creatures beyond and falling like hideous hail upon the deck. Some of them survived the fall, and the battle began anew.

Anarzee spun toward the magi. "The flame wall slows them down, but it cannot keep them out! What else can you do?"

The white-haired male who served as Center pondered briefly. "We can heat the water right around the ship itself to scalding. What creatures this does not kill, it will drive off."

She frowned. "And the ship?"

"It will be at risk," the mage admitted. "The heat will make the crystal hull more brittle and fragile. But even if the sahuagin were to understand this weakness, they could not stand the heat long enough to take advantage."

"Do it," Anarzee said tersely, for there was little time to waste in speech. A sahuagin had broken through the fighting. Its black, webbed feet slapped the deck as it raced toward the magi's Circle.

The priestess snatched a harpoon from the weapon rack and braced it against her hip. At the last moment, the creature veered away, slashing out with its claws—not at the armed elf woman, but at one of the chanting magi.

Anarzee leaped at the sahuagin, thrusting out with all her strength. The harpoon sank home. She dropped the weapon at once, sickened by the dying creature's screams, which were echoed by a hellish chorus of the scalded sahuagin in the seething sea beyond.

For a moment, it all threatened to overwhelm her—the scent of burning troll flesh, the slick wash of elven blood and vile ichor upon the crystal deck, the pervasive cloud of evil that surrounded the sea creatures. The priestess closed her eyes and took a deep, shuddering breath.

In that brief moment, all was lost.

The dying sahuagin seized the nearest weapon—the still-smoldering, severed hand of a troll that lay on the deck nearby. With all its remaining strength, the sahuagin hurled the hand at the white-haired mage who acted as Center to the circle of spellcasters. The sahuagin's aim was true, and the scrag hand clamped around the elf's throat in a killing grip. Smoking black talons sought the vessels of life, and plunged in deep.

When the Center died, the magic of the Circle simply dissolved. The wall of fire that warded the ship flared high, then disappeared. The billowing steam from the magically heated sea wafted off to become just one more fleecy cloud in a summer sky. In the sudden silence, the elven magi looked about, dazed and disoriented, as they struggled to emerge from the disrupted spell.

At that moment a dull, clinking thud resounded through the ship, and then another. The sahuagin survivors had returned to renew the fight. The sea was too vast, too alive with movement, for the heated water to remain a barrier for long.

The captain of the elven fighters ran to Anarzee's side. "The sahuagin have metal weapons," she said urgently. "It is possible that they will break through the weakened hull. If we are thrown into the water, we can do nothing to fight them."

"Not as we are," the priestess agreed.

In a few terse words, she told the captain of the desperate plan that was forming in her mind. The warrior nodded her agreement without hesitation, and hastened off to prepare her fighters for what might befall them. This ship and the elves who sailed it were doomed, but if the gods were willing, they might yet serve the People of Evermeet.

Anarzee fell to her knees and began the most earnest

prayer of her life. She called upon Deep Sashales, not for deliverance, but for transformation.

As she prayed, the air around her seemed to change, to become unnaturally thin and dry. Her hearing took on new dimensions, as well. She could hear the terrible thuds and crackles that bespoke the shattering hull, and the whoops and cackling laughter of the triumphant sahuagin. But mingled with this airborne cacophony were other, subtler and more distant sounds—sounds from beneath the waves themselves.

As water lapped over the deck and soaked the kneeling priestess's robe, Anarzee found that she did not fear the depths, or the creatures in them. She leaped to her feet and ripped off the encumbering garments of a land-dwelling elf. Snatching up a harpoon with a newly webbed hand, the priestess—now a Sea elf—leaped from the dying ship and into the waves.

All around her, the new-made Sea elves fell upon the sahuagin with weapons and magic. This wonder cheered the priestess and sped her in battle, for naturally born Sea elves did not possess magic! This was what was needed to defeat the Coral Kingdom. Why had she not seen it sooner? As magic-wielded sea People, what a force they would be for Evermeet's defense!

Only much later, when the sahuagin were defeated and driven away, when the exhilaration of battle slipped away and the euphoria of victory faded, did the full realization of her sacrifice strike home.

Anarzee did not regret what she had done, nor did any of the other elves cast recriminations upon her. All were pledged to protect Evermeet, and they were resigned to do so as fate decreed.

But oh, what she had lost!

That evening, the Sea-elven priestess slipped from the waves to walk silently upon the rocky shores under Craulnober Keep. As she anticipated, her Darthoridan was there, gazing out to sea with eyes glazed with grief. She stopped several paces from him, and softly called his name.

He started and whirled to face her, his hand on the hilt of his mighty sword. For a long moment, he merely stared. Puzzlement, then startled realization, then dawning horror came over his face.

Anarzee understood all these emotions. She was not surprised that her love did not recognize her at first, for she was much changed. Her body, always slender, had become streamlined and reed-thin, and her once-white skin was now mottled with swirls of blue and green. The sides of her neck were slashed by several lines of gills, and her fingers and toes were longer and connected by delicate webbing. Even her magnificent sapphire-colored hair was not what it once had been, and she wore the blue-and-green strands plaited tightly into a single braid. Only her sea green eyes had remained constant.

"The raising of Iumathiashae has begun," she said softly, for it was their custom to speak of matters of warfare and governance before turning to their personal concerns. "A great Sea-elven city will stand between the Coral Kingdom and Evermeet, for High Magic has returned to the elves of Evermeet's seas. We will re-people the seas, and provide a balance for these forces of evil. The shores of Evermeet will be secure; the seas will again be safe. Tell the People these things," she concluded in a whisper.

Darthoridan nodded. He could not speak for the scalding pain in his chest. But he opened his arms, and Anarzee embraced him.

"I accept my duty and my fate," the Sea elf said in a voice rich with tears. "But by all the gods, how I shall miss you!"

"But surely you can spend much time ashore," he managed.

Anarzee drew back from him and shook her head. "I cannot bear the sun, and the nights are when the evil creatures are most active, and my duty most urgent. I will do what I can, and what I must. This twilight hour will be our time, brief though it is."

Darthoridan gently lifted her webbed hand and kissed

the mottled fingers. "Thus it is ever with time. The only difference between us and any other lovers who draw breath is that we know what others seek to ignore. Joy is always measured in moments. For us, that must be enough."

* * * * *

And so it was. Each night when the sunset colors gilded the waves, Anarzee would come to speak with her love and to play with her babe. When at last she had to relinquish Seanchai to his nurse, she would linger in the water below the keep and sing lullabies to her child.

In the years that followed, the lovers found that their times together came less and less often. Darthoridan was called often to the councils in the south, and Anarzee roved the seas in defense of her homeland. But she returned to the wild northland coast as often as she could, and to her son she gave the one gift she had to give: the songs taught to her by the merfolk and the sea sirens and the great whales, stories of honor and mystery from a hundred shores.

So it was that this boychild grew to become one of the greatest elven minstrels ever known, and not merely for his store of tales and songs of heartbreaking beauty. Even his name, Seanchai, came to denote a storyteller of rare skill. But there was never another who equaled his particular magic, for the noble spirit of Anarzee flowed through all his tales like air and like water.

12

The Starwing Alliance

he harbor of Leuthilspar was silvered with the promise of dawn when Rolim Durothil and Ava Moonflower slipped away from the home they had shared for many years. They left behind them a large gathering of their kin—Gold and Silver elves alike—as well as a multitude of elves from all clans and races who had come to do honor to Evermeet's High Councilor and his consort, the Lady High Mage.

It was difficult for Rolim not to reflect upon what he was leaving behind. He and Ava had been blessed with an unusually large family. They had raised seventeen healthy children, who had in turn given them grandchildren to the third and fourth generation. These offspring had increased both the Durothil and the Moonflower clans. Some of their kin had gone on to form alliances with other ancient houses, as well as with newcomers—elves who had come to Evermeet by sea, or through the magical gates that linked the island to places hidden within the elven realms. He and Ava had been fortunate in their family, and in each other. They had lost kinfolk, that was true. Their daughter Anarzee was all but lost to the sea, though she served Evermeet still as a Sea elf, and a few of their grandchildren had perished in the sea battles that, though less common, were still a grim reality of life on the elven island. But the losses had been somewhat easier to bear for Rolim, in that he had such strength ever at his side.

Rolim looked fondly upon his wife of over seven centuries. Her gray eyes were serene, and the oddly dull, kitten-soft gray of her hair was streaked at last with elven silver.

But for that, there was little in her face or form to mark the passage of years. Ava appeared to be nearly as youthful as the day they married, and in his eyes she was far more beautiful.

Together the aged couple climbed the easy slope of the mountain that overlooked the river and the city beyond. For a long time they stood there, looking out over the place that had been their home.

On this, her last day upon Evermeet, Ava's heart was filled with a poignant mix of joy and sadness. She had loved this land and the People in it, but she was prepared to go. Her farewells had all been said in a celebration that had lasted three days. No one had come to the mountain to see them off. This time was theirs alone. She smiled at Rolim, and was surprised to see that furrows lined his brow. He looked deeply troubled—an odd thing, considering the peace that awaited them.

Ava tucked her arm into his. "You have served Evermeet with honor, my lord," she reminded him. "And Tammson Amarillis will be a fine High Councilor. You have trained him well."

The Gold elf sighed. "I have no fear of Tammson. It is our own brood, and their hot-blooded young friends, who give me pause."

It was not the first time Rolim had spoken of this concern to her. There were among their Gold elven descendants some who were not immune to the growing pride of the self proclaimed Ar-Tel'Quessir—the "high elves." It had been a matter of no little concern to Rolim. Gold elven sentiments concerning the innate superiority of their kind was growing to the point where the young elves threatened to mirror the dangerous attitudes of Aryvandaar's ruling elite. Among the youngest two or three generations there were many elves who were bitterly unhappy with the

221

decision to return the Council of Elders to the control of a Moon elf. Tammson Amarillis, for all his talents, would not have an easy road ahead.

"The burden is no longer yours," Ava reminded him. "You have ceded your place to Tammson."

"I know. But even with Arvandor ahead, it is not an easy thing to leave Evermeet," he said ruefully.

"Even so, it is time."

It *was* time, and Rolim knew it well. He and Ava, bonded together by the soul-deep rapport that was rare even among the elves, had both felt the call of Arvandor for many years. So pressing were their duties, so firm was their sense of responsibility to the People, that they had delayed their departure for far too long. But the voice of Arvandor, sweet and compelling, had beckoned to them in every waking hour, and sung them into revery at night. The need for this final homecoming had become too strong for either to resist.

The elves closed their eyes and sank deep into meditation. As he did, Rolim's awareness began to sharpen. With ever-increasing acuity, he began to see and hear and feel in ways that far surpassed his mortal senses. As barriers slipped away, he noted with wonderment that the rapport he had shared with Ava was spreading, reaching out until it encompassed all of Evermeet. On he went, traveling out to touch the communities of People upon distant shores.

It was a communion beyond anything Rolim had ever known or imagined, and he was awed and humbled. In his heightened awareness, he was exquisitely aware of Ava's thoughts and emotions. She was more accustomed to such wonders than he, for she had spent a lifetime as a High Mage in the communion of her magical Circles. Yet she also took her place in the larger elven community with mingled joy and humility.

Rolim understood at last what the call to Arvandor was: a summons into the very heart of magic, into the Weave of Life itself. As the centuries of their mortal lives began to press upon them, elves could no more disregard this call

than an elven toddler could push aside the driving desire
to walk and form speech. One way or another, the call to
deeper community had to be answered. It was no marvel to
Rolim, now that he saw the way of it, that more and more
often the High Magi were found only among the aged—
elders who deferred the call of Arvandor for centuries to
serve the People upon the mortal world, finding the needed
communion in the Circles. In these days, young practition-
ers of High Magic—such as his great grandson Vhoori—
were becoming exceedingly rare.

Vhoori. For a moment, Rolim's thoughts slipped back
into the mortal world, tugged there by his concern for the
brilliant and ambitious young mage.

*Be at peace. The son of your son's son will bring great
wonders to the People, and power such as few who walk as
mortals on this world have imagined.*

Oddly enough, Rolim was not particularly startled by the
voice that sounded in his mind, soothing as the cadences of
the sea. For he was reaching out now beyond the bounds of
his mortal world, and entering communion with the
Elders—those elves who had gone before him. Rolim sensed
more of them now, but not as a cacophony of conflicting
voices. It was rather like walking into a vast room, and
being greeted with smiles of welcome by well-known
friends. In this homecoming was a peace—a unity—that
filled some unnamed corner of his soul, that place which
gave birth to every yearning he had ever known.

Dimly, Rolim felt Ava take his hand in hers. There was
little sensation of warmth or pressure, though, for their
bodies were fading away into translucent, glowing shadows. Yet he knew that Ava's tiny hand was secure in his,
for they were both truly one with their People.

The morning sun broke through the canopy of leaves
overhead, sending glowing shafts slanting down through
the trees. The last few motes of silver and gold swirled
together in a brief, giddy flurry, as if they danced to greet
the light.

Elaine Cunningham

* * * * *

The Durothil mansion was one of the finest and most whimsical in all of Leuthilspar. At a distance, it resembled nothing so much as a flock of swans startled into sudden, graceful flight. One only had to look at the leaping towers to know that many powerful mages dwelt herein, for it took great power to raise a building of any kind from the soil.

The newest addition to the mansion was also one of the tallest and most imaginative. Two spiraling crystal towers wound around each other in a way that suggested, but did not precisely portray, a pair of entwined elven dancers. From the tower flowed gracefully curving buttresses, some of which rooted the structure to the sacred island, and others that reached seeking hands toward the starlight. The interior of the tower was less whimsical. It was divided into a number of small rooms, each devoted by its creator to a specific purpose.

In one of these rooms, the young Gold elf warrior Brindarry Nierde paced the floor restlessly as he dredged his mind for some way to talk sense into the young wizard who sat calmly before him—floating in midair, his legs crossed and his hands resting on his knees. It was difficult for Brindarry to become too angry with his friend however, for Vhoori Durothil was the epitome of all that Brindarry held dear.

For one thing, the wizard was the quintessence of Gold elven beauty, with his pale tawny skin, night-black hair, and large, almond-shaped eyes the color of a summer meadow. His hands were long-fingered and graceful, and his sharp, finely molded features and triangular face called to mind the ancient, enchanted sculptures of the gods that their ancestors had brought from Aryvandaar. Vhoori Durothil was tall, like his illustrious grandfather Rolim, and as lithe as that famous warrior. But his was a different talent. He had come to magic at an early age, and had already proven to have exceptional potential. Already he was acting as the Center of a small circle, and he received from his peers a deference that was out of proportion to his age and accomplishments. Most elves assumed that Vhoori Durothil would in time become the most powerful High Mage on all of Evermeet, and treated him as such. Yet in Brindarry's opinion, the young mage was content to settle for far too little.

"It is an outrage," Brindarry burst out when his patience reached an end. "By Corellon's sacred blood! The Gray elves rule in Evermeet, and you simply drift along with events, as unconcerned as the clouds on a summer breeze."

The mage lifted one brow, and Brindarry flushed as he remembered that his friend's great-grandmother, the High Mage Ava Moonflower, had been a member of that maligned race.

"Gray elf" was more than a mildly derisive term for the People who were usually called Moon or Silver elves. A slight inflection of Elvish transformed the insult to the word for "dross," that which was common and low, the waste product left over when objects of precious metal—by implication, the "Gold" elves—were created. From the lips of another elf, "Gray" was a deadly insult.

But Vhoori seemed inclined to let it pass. He gracefully unfolded his limbs and stepped down to stand on the floor. "And what would you have me do, my impatient friend? Strike down the new High Councilor with a fireball, or perhaps lay him low with a single blow from a phantom sword?"

"It would be better than doing nothing at all," muttered Brindarry. "You certainly have the power to take action!"

"No, I do not. At least, not yet."

Those cryptic words were as close as Vhoori had ever come to giving voice to the ambitions they shared. Brindarry's eyes glinted with excitement as he regarded his friend.

"It is about time you thought of taking your due!" he exulted. "You have been playing the role of messenger boy for far too long!"

A wry smile lifted the corners of Vhoori's lips. "A

messenger boy. Never have I heard it put quite that way," he said mildly. "I suppose I should point out that the sending of messages from one tower of High Magi to another is an important part of the Circles' work. It is true that this is my primary task, but considering my youth, the Elders think it best that I learn one thing very well before moving on."

Brindarry threw up his hands in exasperation. "How do you expect to rule in Evermeet if all you ever do is chat with the magi of Aryvandaar?"

"Ah, but there is power in information."

"Power that is shared by every other elf in your Circle," the warrior retorted.

"Even so," Vhoori said with a small, secretive smile. "But there will come a time when that is no longer true. Come—there is something I want you to see."

The mage led the way up a tightly spiraling stair to the very top of the tower. In the center of the small, dome-shaped room was an alabaster column, from which rose a scepterlike object. It was about the length of an elf's arm and made of some satiny metal that was neither gold nor silver in color, but some subtle shade for which even the precise esthetics of Elvish had no name. Intricate carvings seemed to lie beneath the surface, which appeared to be utterly smooth. It was a marvelous work of art and magic, justly crowned by a large, golden gem.

"The Accumulator," Vhoori said, stroking the smooth metal with a lover's hand. "With this, I can store power from each spell that I cast. In time, I will have stored so much power that I can act alone, and cast High Magic as a Circle of one."

Brindarry let out a victory whoop. "And then you need no longer answer to the dotards who rule and restrict the use of magic! Your power will be tremendous. It will be an easy matter to oust the Amarillis pretender," he concluded happily.

"Not so easy as you seem to think," Vhoori cautioned him. "Tradition, my friend, is a powerful thing. Tammson Amarillis is armed not only with his own merits, which are considerable, but also all those of his illustrious forebears. Even if every disgruntled Gold elf upon this island were to rally under my standard, we would have little hope of staging a successful coup—at least, not by traditional methods of warfare. No, it is time to find not only new powers, but new ways. And perhaps," he mused, "new allies."

The Nierde snorted. "And where will you find these allies?"

"By doing what I do best," Vhoori said dryly, "by being the very best 'messenger boy' that Evermeet has ever known."

* * * * *

The elven ship was dying. Captain Mariona Leafbower knew that even as she gave the order for a reciprocal attack.

She felt its death as a physical pain. Not in all her decades of travel among the stars had she known a ship that was its equal. In appearance it was rather like a titanic butterfly, with its two sets of sails that glimmered every shade of green known to her verdant homeworld. So vast were these winglike sails that the body of the ship— a sturdy structure with a keel length of over one hundred feet—was almost lost from sight among them. Mariona had inherited the graceful man-o-war from her uncle, who had grown and nurtured it himself, and she had carried on the Leafbower tradition of exploration, trade, and travel for the sheer joy of the journey. She knew this ship as well as any mounted warrior knew her pegasus, and she felt its dying agonies as keenly as if it were in fact a beloved steed.

The captain watched stoically as her crew cranked the ballistae into firing position and loaded the catapult with grape shot. Hers was a well-armed ship, with two mounted ballistae that shot enormous metal bolts with the accuracy of an elven archer's longbow, and a catapult capable of delivering a large load of scattershot missiles with devastating force. Even so, it would not be enough, and she knew it. The ship would die, that was certain, and the elven crew, as well. But at least they would take a few of the Q'nidar with them.

Mariona cursed under her breath as she watched the next approach of the Q'nidar. A flock of them flapped toward the ship in precise, single-line formation. The Q'nidar—hideous, batlike creatures with a fifteen-foot wingspan and long, barbed tails like those of a wyvern—were as black as the wildspace in which they hunted, but on their crystalline wings glittered every color within both the light and heat spectrums. Q'nidar were heat-eaters who traveled the vast spaces between the stars. They spoke by breathing intricate patterns of heat and energy that were detected and understood by others of their kind. Disaster usually occurred whenever they attempted to "speak" with star-traveling ships. Indeed, they were often drawn to such ships, attracted by the heat and light and activity.

These Q'nidar, however, were not merely curious. This was a hunting party, and they desperately needed to feed. Mariona could tell this from the unusually close-knit formation of the flying monsters. They flew nearly nose-to-tail, so that each Q'nidar could feed upon the heat emitted by the creature in front of it.

Their first attack on the ship had been unexpected—from a distance they unleashed a blast of breath so hot that it had ignited the protective bubble that surrounded the ship and kept the life-giving envelope of air and warmth in place. The off-duty helmsman, a wizard of considerable power, had drained his magic to put out the flames. He had succeeded—but not before their air supply had been dangerously heated and thinned.

It was still hot on the ship. Mariona's hair clung to her scalp in lank silver strands, and the pain in her blistered hands and face was intensified by her keen awareness of the ship's ills. The ship's crystal hull had been cracked by the sudden burst of heat, and the wings were seared and brittle. Her ship yet lived, but barely. It could not survive another hit. And the Q'nidar were closing in, eager to ignite the ship and feed upon the energy of the flames.

Mariona waited until the lead Q'nidar was within range, and then screamed out the order to fire. The first ballista thudded, sending a giant bolt streaking toward the creature. The weapon caught the Q'nidar squarely in the upper chest, sending it hurtling back into the ranks of its followers. A few of the Q'nidar at the far end of the formation managed to peel off in time, but for several moments most of the creatures struggled and thrashed in a tangle of bat wings and barbed tails.

At that moment, the elven fighters fired the catapult. A spray of small spiked metal balls, lengths of chain, and odds and ends of nails and scrap metal burst toward the tangle of Q'nidar. The shrieks of wounded and dying monsters reverberated through the ship's atmosphere like a chorus from the Abyss. Some of the less-wounded Q'nidar took off in rapid, desperate flight toward the nearest star. A few of the creatures, torn and silent, began to drift off into the blackness of wildspace. One of these floated directly toward the man-o-war.

"Hard astern!" Mariona shouted into the speaking tube that led from the deck down to the navigation room. The helmsman—the wizard whose magic combined with the power of the magical, thronelike helm to give power to the ship—acknowledged her order. Mariona noted with deep concern that his voice sounded thin and weary. Passilorris had been at the helm for much too long. His strength and his magic were nearly depleted.

The ship began to trace a leisurely arc toward the right as the helmsman urged the ailing vessel in an evasive maneuver. Not fast enough. The Q'nidar flopped down onto the ship's envelope, its black wings spread wide like a pall over the ship, its body bouncing slightly from the impact with the protective shield. So diminished was the air envelope that the creature hung low, bobbing gently between the ship's paired wings.

To Mariona's horror, the creature's eyes opened, focused, and then narrowed with malevolence as they glared directly into hers. The Q'nidar's chest slowly expanded as it prepared to expend its last breath in a killing blast.

"Fire!" she shrieked, pointing up toward the Q'nidar.

The ballista crew threw their weight against the massive weapon, swiveling it around and tilting it up to aim at the new threat. The bolt tore upward and plunged through the creature's heart.

A shimmering glow spread outward from the dead Q'nidar to engulf the protective bubble. The bubble's surface began to seethe and bulge like water just coming to a boil. A blast of hot air burst down through the opening, scalding the ballista crew before the magical shield could close in to repair the gap.

Mariona noted with grim relief that the ballista bolt had gone clear through the creature, thus allowing much of the hot air from its lungs to escape into wildspace. Had it not, the full force of the blast might have killed many more elves. Either way, however, they were better off than if the creature had "*screamed.*" At such close range the force from such a heat weapon would have reduced the ship to ash.

But the threat did not die with that single Q'nidar. The creatures who had scattered and fled were regrouping. Mariona could see the distant flash of reflected starlight on their wings as they hurtled in for the final assault.

The final assault. Of that, there could be no doubt.

"Captain, we're receiving a communication!"

The navigator's voice echoed up through the speaking tube, shrill with excitement and hope reborn.

Mariona's heart quickened. To the best of their knowledge, there were no spelljamming ships in this section of wildspace, and no civilization on the nearest world capable of star travel. It would be wonderful to be proved wrong!

"On my way," she said, taking off at a run for the narrow steps that led down into the hold.

Her eye fell first upon the helmsman, a Silver elf of middle years. He was nearly gray with exhaustion, and his white-knuckled hands gripped the armrests of the helm as if to squeeze from it just a few more drops of power. Mariona rested a hand on his shoulder, briefly, and turned to the navigator.

Shi'larra was bent over a scrying crystal, her black eyes intense in her tattooed face. She glanced up at the captain. "The crystal has been pulsing, as if receiving a message. It is powerful magic—definitely elven—but subtly different from anything we know. According to the latest report from the Imperial Fleet, there are no elven ships in this area."

Mariona understood at once the implications of the navigator's words. From time to time, an elven civilization upon some outpost world found its own way to star-flight. The first contacts between these fledgling ships and the well-established elven navy that ruled wildspace was usually jarring in the extreme to the newcomers. There were strict protocols concerning how these encounters should be handled. Protocol, however, was a luxury that the desperate crew could not afford.

The elf woman lay her palm on the crystal, letting the powerful material absorb her personal magic. And powerful it undoubtedly was—the globe had been fashioned from the crystallized remains of a Q'nidar that had flung itself into a star. Such artifacts were rare and powerful, and she'd considered herself fortunate to have happened upon it in the debris that floated along a common trade route. Now the crystal offered a chance to stave off the utter destruction of ship and crew. Later, perhaps, she would ponder the irony of this.

"Captain Mariona Leafbower, of *Green Monarch,* a man-o-war of Elven Imperial Navy," she said crisply. "We are under attack and have sustained heavy damage. We are near the moon of Aber-toril. The navigator will give you our precise star coordinates. Can you help?"

There was a moment of silence. "You are flying? You are near Selûne?" demanded a melodious, disembodied male voice.

"We are still star-borne, yes," Mariona said, puzzled by the incredulous note in the elf's voice. "Identify yourself and your ship."

"I am Vhoori Durothil, a High Mage of Evermeet," the unseen elf said. "And I am not on a ship at all, but on land. Sumbrar, to be precise, an outpost island just beyond Evermeet's bay of Leuthilspar."

Mariona and Shi'larra exchanged incredulous glances. Land-to-ship communication was incredibly difficult, and required magical technology of an extremely high level. They had not known that the elves of Aber-toril possessed such magic.

"Do you have spelljamming ships in this area?" she repeated.

"We have no such ships," Vhoori said. "But I can guide yours to a sheltered bay near the island."

Another blast of Q'nidar breath hit the dwindling shield, and another thrumming crack shuddered through the hull. Mariona winced. "Our ship is breaking apart. We don't have time to make landfall. Even if we did, we would be pursued by creatures that want the ship."

"I fear I cannot help you in such a battle. Can you leave the ship to your enemies? Have you lifeboats?"

Shi'larra nodded, her face grim. "It's that or nothing, captain."

Mariona glanced with concern at the failing mage in the helm. His head jerked upright, suddenly, as if he were trying to keep himself awake by force of will. "Passilorris can't bring us down. Ghilanna is dead, Llewellenar isn't feeling much better. We don't have another helmsman."

"What is a helmsman, please?" the unseen elf inquired.

The captain hissed in exasperation. Her ship was soaring toward oblivion, and this land-bound mage wanted a primer in spelljamming technology? "A wizard," she gritted out. "His spells power the helm—a magical chair of sorts—that powers the ship."

"Ah. Then perhaps I *can* help you. Get your crew to the

lifeboat, and place your communication device upon this . . . helm."

"You cannot power a helm from a distance—not even the minor helm on the lifeboat! It has never been done," Mariona said.

"That does not mean it is not worth trying. And I can sense the thread of magic between my communication device and yours. I will bring you down in safety," the elf said confidently.

Since she had no better ideas, Mariona turned to the watchful navigator. "Give the order, get everyone aboard. I'll follow with Passilorris."

Shi'larra seized the scrying globe and darted up the steps. The captain gave her a few minutes to gather the survivors and get them aboard the lifeboat, a small, open craft that looked rather like an oversized canoe. But it was light and it was fast; provided, that was, that a mage of sufficient power sat at the helm.

In moments Shi'larra's trademark signal—the high, shrieking cry of a hunting hawk—informed the captain that all was in readiness. Taking a deep breath, she dragged the nearly comatose mage from the helm and flung him over her shoulder.

Instantly the air in the helm room heated to nearly a furnace blast as the magical connection, however feeble, between mage and helm was broken. In a few moments, the air envelope would dissipate, as well. Mariona staggered up the stairs with her burden and made her way over to the rail where the boat was waiting.

It took all her power of will to keep her eyes upon the lifeboat rather than on her ship's flaming sails or the flock of Q'nidar that circled the burning ship, emitting triumphant shrieks and cackles as they drew sustenance from its funeral pyre.

At least the wretched creatures were distracted, Mariona thought grimly as she eased Passilorris off her shoulder and into the waiting hands of the survivors.

There were only ten elves aboard the lifeboat—all that

remained after the last attack. But as Mariona took her place, she noted the awe on each face as they stared at the helm and the crystal scrying globe that sat in the center of the magical chair. The crystal glowed with intense inner power. It appeared that the land-bound mage could do what he claimed: The air that encircled the lifeboat was cool and fresh, which meant that power was indeed flowing to the helm.

"Looks as if we might make it, after all," Mariona muttered.

"Of that, Lady Captain, you may have no doubt." Their rescuer's voice sounded different, more vibrant—magnified, perhaps, by the power that flowed through the crystal. "By your leave, I will not speak again until we meet in person, except in necessity. The concentration needed to maintain the thread of magic is considerable."

"Of course," Mariona replied. "Let me know if there is anything we can do that might help."

There was a brief pause. "Actually, there is one thing," the unseen elf said wistfully. "Speak to me of the stars, and tell me what your eyes see on your journey to Evermeet."

Mariona cut the ropes that bound the lifeboat to the ship, then nodded to Cameron Starsong, a bard who had purchased passage aboard ship. As the small craft floated out into the darkness of wildspace, she settled back and listened as the elf strummed his lyre—which he had adamantly refused to leave behind—and declaimed in rhythmic, musical cadences a spontaneous ode to the wonders of starflight.

As the captain listened, it struck her that the life she took for granted would be the fabric of legend to an elf such as Vhoori Durothil. And the fact that she herself was headed for such a primitive world was disheartening in the extreme.

Mariona grimly took stock of the situation. Her ship was lost. At best, it would be many, many years before she could grow another. It was entirely possible that the surviving crew would spend the rest of their natural lives upon Aber-toril.

The elf woman sighed and turned her head to look back at her burning ship. Her eyes widened with surprise; Green Monarch was no more than a flicker of red light. She turned to Shi'larra, who was watching the rapidly diminishing light with narrowed eyes.

"How fast do you figure we're moving?" she demanded.

Shi'larra shrugged. "It's hard to say, without my instruments and charts. But I can tell you this much, we're traveling at least twice as fast as Monarch could at full power. Look down," she said suddenly, seizing the captain's arm and pointing to the rapidly approaching world. "There's Aber-toril, and already I can see the island. By the stars, never have I seen a place so green! And from this height!"

"You will be landing soon," Vhoori Durothil declared, in a voice made thin by exhaustion. "We will have boats ready to bring you in. Healers are preparing spells and herbs and will tend your wounded."

"Herbs and healers," Mariona muttered, rolling her eyes in Shi'larra's direction. "If we had to become land-bound, we've drawn a hell of a world for it!"

A fey smile lit Shi'larra's tattooed face. "Do not sneer until you have seen this world," she said softly. "It might be such that you will have no desire to leave."

"Oh yes. *That* will happen," the captain said caustically. "And as for you—your homeworld is almost unique in that it has no oceans. You're accustomed to endless forests, watered by a network of vast rivers. You're telling me you could be happy on that tiny island?"

The forest elf shrugged, and her eyes were fixed upon the rapidly approaching blur of green forest and sapphire seas. "All I can tell you is this: I have the oddest feeling that I'm going home," she murmured.

Before Mariona could respond to this odd pronouncement, the boat jerked suddenly as the untried mage who controlled it tried to slow the craft's descent. A second jolt quickly followed, sending the boat into a slow roll. The captain seized the crystal globe and held it firmly against the helm, shouting for the others to help her keep the magical device in place.

Again and again the little craft shuddered and jolted as Vhoori Durothil inexpertly slowed its descent into the sea. Even so, the boat hit the water with a force that shattered the wooden hull and hurled the elven crew into the water.

Mariona plunged down deep, her hands flailing about as she instinctively sought to find and save the helm. The water that swirled around her was dark with blood, and she knew from the fierce throbbing in her temples that she had taken a head wound, perhaps a serious one. All she could think of, however, was the need to find the helm. If she could not, she would never again travel the stars.

Suddenly she felt small, strong hands close on her wrists, and her frantic eyes looked up into the face of the strangest elf she had ever seen. A blue-haired, green-skinned female gave her a reassuring smile, and began to draw her up toward the surface. Mariona glanced at her rescuer's hands. They were striped in rippling patterns of blue and green, and there was delicate webbing between the unnaturally long fingers. Jaded as she was by her years of travel and her encounters with fantastic creatures from a dozen worlds, Mariona had never seen a creature that struck her as quite so bizarre as this Sea-elven creature.

Her last thought, before the darkness engulfed her, was that she'd picked a hell of a world to be stranded on.

* * * * *

The next thing Captain Mariona Leafbower knew was the soft, lilting sound of elven voices lifted in song. There was a healing power to the music that seemed to draw the pain from her head and the aching lethargy from her limbs.

Cautiously, Mariona opened her eyes. She was warm and dry, clad in a silken robe and tucked into a bed that, if the one right next to her was any indication, floated above the floor in a subtle, undulating motion.

236

"Captain Leafbower."

Mariona knew that voice. Painfully she turned her head and looked up into the smiling face of a young Gold elf. She was not in such a bad way that she didn't take note of the fact that he was probably the handsomest elf she had ever seen. Even so, there were more important matters on her mind.

"The helm . . ." she began.

"Do not concern yourself," Vhoori Durothil said. "The Sea elves have already found most of the pieces. In time, we will reconstruct it."

"It can't be done. You don't have the technology," she said in a voice dulled with despair.

"It seems to me that you said something very much like that before," the elf replied with a touch of wry humor. "And yet, here you are."

Mariona shifted her shoulders in an approximation of a shrug. "I'll grant that your magic is impressive. Maybe we can learn a thing or two from each other."

"That is my hope." Vhoori paused, and glanced at the elves who ringed her bedside. They discretely melted away. When he and Mariona were alone, he said, "You want to leave this world. You have said as much, repeatedly, in the days you lay in healing revery."

"Days?" she interjected in disbelief.

"Even so. Most of your crew are up and about. I regret to tell you that one elf perished in the landing."

"Passilorris," she said immediately, without a hint of doubt. "I was not certain that he would survive, regardless of the ease of landfall." She cast a fierce look at the mage, as if daring him to accuse the helmsman of some weakness. "He was a hero. Without his effort, all would have died!"

"He has been accorded a hero's passage," Vhoori assured her, "and a place of honor in the history of Evermeet. I regret the loss deeply. There is much that I would like to have learned from him about the magic of star travel."

Mariona sniffed. She and Passilorris had been lovers not too very long ago, so she supposed that she was excused from the need to sympathize with Vhoori Durothil over his loss of a potential teacher.

She swallowed the unexpected lump in her throat and swept the room with an inquiring glare. It was a large, perfectly circular room with walls that seemed to be made of a single stone. Large, arched windows looked out over a sparkling sea.

"Where the hell am I?" she demanded.

"This is the island known as Sumbrar. This house is mine, and the elves who tended you with spell-song are part of my Circle. The magic that contacted your ship, however, was entirely my own." He paused. "Perhaps it is best that this fact does not leave Sumbrar, at least for the time."

"Why?"

Vhoori drew a scepter from the folds of his robe and showed it to her. "For years now, I have been storing magical power in this device. I drained much of its power to bring you to Evermeet."

"So?"

The elf hesitated, his green eyes searching her face as if taking her measure. "My colleagues in magic do not know of this device. They have no idea that I can work such powerful magic alone. I would not have them learn of this before I am able to restore the Accumulator to its previous level."

Mariona's chuckle was utterly devoid of humor. "The gods forbid that the Elders should take away your toy. How old are you, by the way? Ninety? One hundred?"

"I have seen over two hundred springs," the elf said with dignity. "And I assure you, your silence is as much to your benefit as mine."

The captain nodded cautiously. She was not a fool, and knew that any elf who could command the sort of magic this one had wielded was a force with which to reckon. If Vhoori Durothil had a proposition for her, she would at least hear him out.

"Every elf on this island saw your craft fall from the sky.

They will have questions. Tell them what you will, but do not mention my part in the matter. Not yet, at least."

The star-traveler's eyes narrowed suspiciously. "What are you planning to do? You're not planning some sort of attack on the main island, are you? Because if you are, you can count me out now. I've never fought elves, nor will I."

"And you shall not."

A faint rustle at the open door captured Vhoori's attention. He hurriedly tucked the Accumulator out of sight and looked with ill-concealed impatience at the young female who clung to the door's lintel. "What is it, Ester?"

"There is a communication from Aryvandaar, Lord Durothil," she said. "You are needed in the Circle."

Vhoori frowned. "Ygrainne can act as Center in my stead. Bring word to me if the message is urgent."

The elven woman bowed and hurried from the room.

"Aryvandaar," Mariona said, a question in her voice.

"A great and ancient kingdom, many days' travel by sea from this island," he explained. "Many of our ancestors came from this land."

"Tell me," she requested. Her eyelids were beginning to feel heavy, and at the moment she welcomed the soothing, melodious sound of the young elf's voice. She relaxed back against her pillows as Vhoori spun tales of wonder and warfare, and a land as beautiful and dangerous as any she had seen or imagined. As he spoke, she slid comfortably back toward revery, lulled into a state of contentment that was rare indeed for her restless spirit, and certain that the dreams that awaited her would be pleasant.

A sudden, terrible blast tore Mariona from her comfortable state. She sat bolt upright, stunned by a force that utterly dwarfed the shattering of Green Monarch's hull. Oddly enough, there was no sign of destruction. The room's luxurious furnishings were undisturbed, the birdsong outside the windows continued unbroken. There was no sound of battle, no scent of smoke or death. Only upon the face of Vhoori Durothil was the devastation written; the young mage's face was pale as parchment and twisted in nameless anguish.

"What the nine bloody hells was that?" Mariona demanded.

Before Vhoori could respond, an elven warrior bolted into the room, his flaxen hair flying about him in disarray and his black eyes wild. "Vhoori, the Circle is destroyed! Every elf who cast the High Magi is gone—gone! Utterly vanished. I would not have believed it had I not been in the spell chamber and seen it with my own eyes!"

"Did you hear the message from Aryvandaar?" Vhoori asked in a dry whisper.

"I did," the warrior said grimly. "It was a call for help from the tower at Sharlarion—they wanted us to send warriors and magi through the gates at once. Then came a blast that nearly drove me mad, and then—nothing. Quite literally nothing. I was the only elf left in the chamber. What does it mean?"

Vhoori abruptly turned away from the dazed and babbling elf and walked to the window. He was silent for a long moment, staring out over the water toward Evermeet with eyes that for once did not see the beauty of his homeland. A beauty that was all the more poignant now, for the added importance that this day's events had given the elven island.

"Brindarry, the day you have longed for may well be at hand. Evermeet will determine her own path in a way that she has never done before, and who is to say that this path will not lie along the road you yourself have envisioned? And your task, Captain Leafbower, is made all the easier. All those who saw your ship fall from the sky are dead, but for your crew, we three in this room and the sea people, who know only that your ship was destroyed by a powerful blast. It will be easy enough to fashion an explanation that will content them. Thus we can work here on Sumbrar in privacy, without fear that our task will be detected or our effects deterred. All things have changed this day," he concluded softly.

"These are words I have longed to hear," Brindarry said, his brow furrowed in puzzlement. "Why then, can I not fathom their meaning?"

Vhoori spun to face his old friend and his new ally.

"Then I will speak plainly. Brindarry, our time is near at hand. Your destiny, Captain Leafbower, is intrinsically bound with my own. There is no other to whom you can turn. You see, the Crown Wars have taken their toll, after these many centuries of warfare. The ancient kingdom of Aryvandaar has fallen. Evermeet, for good or ill, now stands alone."

13

Tides of Fury

n icy wind whipped the island, coating the Beast Lord's black fur with salt-scented icicles. Malar hunched his massive shoulders in a futile attempt to ward off the chill, listening with uncharacteristic patience as the goddess Umberlee wailed and shrieked out her frustration. The sea goddess smashed at the waves with her fists again and again, sending sprays of water leaping up over the rocky coast with each blow.

Umberlee's minions, the fearful creatures of the Coral Kingdom who were supposed to bring the sea-faring elves to heel, had been, if not bested, at least contained. Magic had returned to the Sea elves of Evermeet. And this, through the intervention of an elven god! Long and bitter had been Umberlee's jealousy of Deep Sashales, and terrible was her fury against this perceived insult.

"There are other creatures in the sea that you can command, are there not?" inquired Malar when at last his rumbling voice could be heard over the roar and crash of the waves.

Umberlee stopped in mid-wail. She subsided, sinking down into the crest of the wave she rode as she pondered this suggestion. Her countenance softened a little as she considered the possibilities. "There are many," she agreed. "There are terrible creatures in the depths which will surely come to my bidding. I will send them at once!"

"And storms," Malar added as he broke off a daggerlike

icicle that hung from his furred chin, and that gave proof of the icy potency of the goddess's fury. "You cannot over-whelm the island itself, but surely you can disrupt sea traffic. Many elves will flee the troubles on the mainland to sail for Evermeet." His red eyes glowed with intense, evil light. "I see no reason why they should reach the island."

"Nor do I," agreed the sea goddess delightedly. She surged forward suddenly and flung her arms around the bestial god, drenching him with frigid sea water. Then she was gone, leaving behind a sea that was as calm as a wood nymph's pool.

Malar let out a grating, whuffling chuckle. The sea god-dess's chilly embrace was a minor discomfort, a minor indignity. In his estimation, things were going well.

The centuries-long devastation of the Crown Wars had been deeply satisfying to the Great Hunter. He was not entirely disappointed by the defeat of the dark elves—or drow, as they were now called. Despite his ties with the goddess Lloth, Malar was not fond of any elves, fair or dark. He was willing enough to enjoy the drow's warfare against Corellon's faithful children, but the deaths of dark raiders pleased him equally as well as the slaughter of peaceful forest elves. In fact, he thought it a delightful turn of events that brought the elves to be pitted against each other in this manner. Not only did such inner strife serve his purpose, but it was also most entertaining to observe.

The elves on Faerûn had been dealt a series of devas-tating blows. His followers—orcs and goblins, for the most part—would continue to harry the settlements that were scattered through the forests. The time was right to turn his enmity once again upon the elven island. He would let Umberlee do what she could, and what she could for *him*. Also, there were humans who called themselves the Wolves of the Waves, and who showed considerable prom-ise as raiders. They would be a fine foil to the sea goddess's wrath. And though these humans were not strictly follow-ers of Malar, the god felt certain he could find ways to entice them into joining the hunt for elves. These actions would suffice for now.

Yet Malar, the Great Hunter, knew full well that he would not be forever content to concede to others the challenge of the hunt, or the pleasure of the kill.

* * * * *

Anarzee Sea-elven, once a daughter and a matron of the noble Moon elf families of Evermeet, swam south with all possible speed toward the city of Leuthilspar.

Years had passed since the peculiar shipwreck off the eastern coast of Sumbrar. There had not been a single day since that Anarzee had not pondered the strange events of that day. Not that shipwrecks were rare occurrences—far from it. The storms that raged beyond Evermeet's protective bounds sent many an elven vessel into the depths. The Sea elves of the great city Iumathiashae were kept busy rescuing those elves they could, and bearing grim tidings concerning the fate of those they could not aid. But there had been something very odd about that long-ago wreck. The incredible force with which the small craft had been sundered suggested that some new and powerful force was at work.

It had taken Anarzee a long time to piece together an answer to her lingering questions. But when at last she had found her way to this answer, she'd been at a loss to know what to do.

As she swam southward, Anarzee batted aside a bit of floating seaweed with a hand that was long-fingered and delicately webbed. The sight of her own Sea-elven hands no longer seemed strange to her. She was now a Sea elf in thought and impulse as well as in physical appearance. Even so, her sense of allegiance to her land-dwelling clans was still strong. Right or wrong, Vhoori Durothil was kin to her, the son's son of her own brother. It ran against everything that she had once held dear to speak against him.

And yet, how could she not?

The Sea elf's decision was made all the more difficult in that she had no idea what use Vhoori planned to make of his new-found power. Elven magic was nearly endless in variety, and it was no uncommon thing for elves to use magic to give flight to common objects. But the sort of magic that could empower an entire ship to fly, that could surround it with air so that it could travel beneath the waves or among the stars, this was more power than any one elf should possess.

And what concerned Anarzee most was the secrecy with which the Gold elven wizard had gone about his work. It was unnatural for any elf—especially a High Mage—to hold himself apart from his brothers and sisters as did Vhoori. And it was dangerous for the mages of a powerful Tower to keep so much of their work secret from the larger community. For all Anarzee knew, Vhoori Durothil might be plotting to overtake Evermeet itself. But there was only so much she could learn, and very little that she could do, from her home in the sea.

After much private deliberation, she decided to lay the matter at Darthoridan's feet. He would know what must be done. Though he was no longer her husband, Anarzee still sought him out when she could and found that his wisdom had more than kept pace with the passing of years.

In the decades since Anarzee's self-imposed exile, Darthoridan had become as skilled a diplomat as he was a warrior. Under his leadership, the Craulnober family had gained in power and honor. They now merited seats on the Council of Elders; in fact, Darthoridan's was among the names spoken when the elves of Leuthilspar speculated upon who might succeed Tammson Amarillis as High Councilor. Accordingly, Darthoridan spent more and more of his time in Leuthilspar, tending to matters of governance.

He was there now, or so Anarzee's daughter—the second and last child she had borne to Darthoridan—had curtly informed her. The Sea elf had not lingered at Craulnober

Keep. She had turned toward the south at once, and not just for the urgency of the message she carried.

The memory of that meeting stabbed Anarzee's heart anew with pain sharper than a manta's sting. She had given birth to a daughter two years after her transformation into a Sea elf. But children born of parents from two different elven races did not inherit from both: there was no blending of the moon and the sea in Darthoridan and Anarzee's daughter. The Sea elf had given birth to a perfect Moon elf maiden—and had given the babe into the hands of a land-dwelling nurse to love and to raise.

Abandoning yet another child had nearly broken Anarzee's heart. Upon her insistence, her marriage to Darthoridan had been dissolved, for she could not bear another such loss.

As for Darthoridan, though Anarzee saw him with ever diminishing frequency, her love for him had not been altered by her change of form. It had not been dimmed by the passage of time, or by the grief she carried over the loss of her children. He was her lover only occasionally—and that, not for quite some time—but he would always be her love. She would trust Darthoridan to make good use of her knowledge of Vhoori Durothil, as she trusted him in all things.

The sun rose and set more than once during Anarzee's journey from Craulnober Keep to the southern city. But she pressed on, scarcely pausing for rest or food. When at last the weary Sea elf passed the outpost island Sumbrar and broke the surface, she beheld a harbor ablaze with lights. Though it was near to midnight, the docks and streets of Leuthilspar were bright with festive lanterns, globes of magical fire, and the flickering, darting pinpricks of light that bespoke the presence of tiny fey creatures—sprites, most likely, and perhaps even a faerie dragon or two.

None of these lights were fairer than those that festooned a ship moored just off the docks. An ever-shifting pattern of colored lights played against the rippling sails, and the crystal hull glittered like a dragon's hoard in the reflected light.

A wistful smile curved the Sea elf's lips as she gazed at the wondrous sight. It occurred to her that it must be near to midsummer, the time when elves made merry and celebrated alliances of all kinds. Weddings were usually made at midsummer. It was likely that this ship was bedecked to carry a newly wedded couple to the home they would share. It had been so when Darthoridan had first taken her from Leuthilspar to his keep upon the wild northern shores they both had loved.

Anarzee's smile faded as another, less joyous memory edged into her mind. There was something disturbingly familiar about the ship. The Sea elf swam into the harbor and circled around the ship to read the name engraved onto the crystal prow. Her heart thudded painfully as her eyes fell upon the bold runes.

The ship's name was *Sea-Riven*.

Anarzee dove beneath the water and swam quickly toward the city's docks, her thoughts whirling. Surely it was a coincidence that this ship should bear the same name as Darthoridan's sword! Yet she could not deny that the ship was much like the first vessel they had fashioned together for their fight against the sea trolls, the ship that Anarzee had sailed on her last day as a Moon elf. The ship that had nearly been her tomb was reborn and bedecked for a wedding.

Perhaps Seanchai had taken a bride. He was nearly of age, Anarzee pondered as she climbed a ladder that led from the sea up onto the docks. Even as her mind formed the thought, her ears caught the sound of faint and distant music. It was not so faint that she could not immediately discern the rare beauty of the singing. This made perfect sense. Her son was already a noted bard—his wedding would draw the finest musicians in all of Evermeet to pay tribute.

But if this were so, why had she not been told? Her landdwelling daughter shunned her, but Seanchai was truly the child of her heart! He would not marry without somehow sending word to his mother.

From her perch on the ladder, Anarzee scanned the

bustling dock for an unfamiliar face. She did not want to hear of her son's wedding from someone who had known her as the Moon elf she once had been. Anarzee's shoulders had carried many burdens, but pity was a load too heavy for the proud elf woman to bear.

Her searching gaze fell upon a Gold elf youth. He seemed a likely choice. His simple garb proclaimed him a commoner. He was barefoot and stripped to the waist, displaying the lean strength of one who made a living through hard labor. His clean-shaven head and the large gold hoops in one pointed ear gave him a raffish, almost piratical air, but neither that affectation nor the large goblet in his hand could disguise the fact that he was very young—barely into adulthood. This elf had not yet been born when she was Anarzee Moonflower, daughter of the High Councilor Rolim Durothil and wife to Darthoridan Craulnober. Nor would he have frequented her circle, in any case. The lad might had heard the story of her transformation, but he would have no reason to make any connection between the heroic priestess extolled in song and story, and the weary, aging Sea elf before him.

Anarzee climbed onto the deck and softly hailed the youth. His eyes lit up when they fell upon her, and he made his way toward her with an unsteady gait. To Anarzee's surprise, the dock worker promptly enfolded her in an exuberant hug.

"Welcome, pretty maid," he said with great enthusiasm—and exceedingly fuzzy diction. "Come from the sea to celebrate midsummer with me, are you? Sea and celebrate . . . sea shellebration," he improvised, grinning with pride over a jest that apparently struck him as quite clever—and proclaimed him to be very tipsy indeed.

Anarzee wrinkled her nose against the heavy scent of feywine on the lad's breath. "If you take me for a maid, you have drunk far more than that single goblet could hold," she said dryly as she tried to wriggle away.

The young elf leaned back a bit and endeavored to

focus his bleary eyes on her face. "Not young," he conceded. "But so very pretty. And blue hair," he marveled, easing his hold long enough to finger one of Anarzee's damp, curling locks.

The Sea elf twisted away and then nimbly sidestepped the lad's attempt to reclaim her. With one hand, she caught his wrist, and with the other she snatched a strand of rosy pearls from her bag and dangled it before his eyes.

"Enough of this foolishness! These are yours, in exchange for some information. A fine midsummer gift for a pretty maid," she suggested, hoping to banish the crestfallen look from the young elf's face. "And surely you will have need of such a trinket! The night is yet young."

He brightened considerably at this thought. "Ask anything, and I will answer as best I can."

"Whose wedding procession is that?" she demanded, raising her voice to be heard over the approaching musicians.

"A northern lord. Clan Craulnober. I drink to his health!" So saying, the young elf raised his goblet for a sip. He looked puzzled for a moment, then made a face when he realized anew that the cup was empty.

"So it is Seanchai," she murmured sadly.

"No, not the bard," the lad corrected her. "The councilor. Darthoridan. Have you not heard of him? He's a famed warrior. Ran the scrags back into the sea, he did, and gave the sahuagin reason to fear the People of Evermeet! Some say he'll be the next High Councilor," he continued importantly, clearly pleased to be imparting such information.

But Anarzee no longer heard him. It seemed to her that a vise had clamped around her heart. Her fingers clenched in sympathetic agony around the necklace she held. The delicate thread broke, spilling pearls like falling petals.

"Hey, now!" protested the lad, seeing his reward slipping away. He dived for the dock and began to gather up the rolling pearls.

Anarzee whirled and ran for the far side of the dock. The joyous throng was almost to the dock. She did not want to look upon the face of the elf woman who had taken her place in Darthoridan's heart.

The Sea elf dived into the water of the harbor and plunged deep. She swam frantically, as if she could outrace the full realization of all she had lost.

When she was certain that her heart would burst from mingled pain and exhaustion, she stopped and clung to a thick stand of sea grass until she could again draw breath. As soon as she could, she sent out the clicking, whistling call that would summon any dolphin who might be nearby.

Before long a sleek gray form sped toward her. Dolphins were friends to the Sea elves, and this one was known to her. He circled the Sea elf playfully, bumping gently against her in a manner that recalled the behavior of the cats she used to keep for companionship and comfort. For once, however, the creature's permanent, impish grin failed to elicit an answering smile from Anarzee.

The dolphin seemed to sense her mood, for he bobbed his head rapidly then cocked it to one side in an oddly inquisitive gesture.

Take me far from this place, she pleaded in his language.

In response, the dolphin rolled a bit to present her with his top fin. Anarzee grasped the offered hold and clung as the dolphin sped off for the open sea.

The stunned and grieving Sea elf gave little thought to the passing of time or to the distance they traveled. But it seemed to her that not much of either had elapsed before the dolphin drew up short. The creature looked up toward the distant sky, chattering in surprise and alarm.

Anarzee followed the line of his gaze. Through the deep curtain of water, the full moon was clearly visible. But as she looked, a huge, circular form passed overhead, eclipsing the light so rapidly that it appeared as if some massive creature had simply swallowed the moon. Then, just as suddenly, the light was back, shimmering through the troubled water in a way that brought to Anarzee's fear-struck mind the image of a trembling child.

The apparition had passed over with startling speed,

but not so fast that Anarzee didn't get to catch a glimpse of the four massive, churning legs and the lashing tail that had propelled the creature with such speed.

Dragon turtle? she asked the dolphin. The creature nodded rapidly, nervously. After a moment's hesitation, he indicated in clicks and squeals that he needed to rise to the surface to breathe.

Though Anarzee had no such need herself, she went with the dolphin. The creature did not ask this of her, but she sensed that he had no desire to go anywhere near the place where the dragon turtle had passed. Dolphins feared them, and with good reason. Such creatures were seldom seen, but all who lived in the sea knew of their power. Dragon turtles possessed a keen, if somewhat unfathomable, intelligence. It was not pleasant to ponder what this one might have in mind, what might bring it so close to Evermeet's shores. Indeed, the dragon turtle had been swimming straight for the elven island.

As they neared the surface, Anarzee noticed an unusual turbulence sweeping the surface of the water—far too much to be explained by the dragon turtle's passage. She came up into the air to be greeted by a chill blast of wind from the north, and buffeted by the surging, restless waves. Yet the sky was clear and cloudless, and the stars shone almost as brightly as Leuthilspar's festival lights. Whatever troubled the sea was no natural storm.

A large wave caught Anarzee and tossed her high. Just before she was slapped back into the sea, she caught sight of a distant, brightly lit ship, gliding northward on calm waters.

Anarzee's breath caught in her throat as she recognized Darthoridan's ship. But her pain was immediately overtaken by a surge of relief. The waters surrounding Evermeet were protected from storms by Aerdrie Faenya herself. Her beloved was safe in the hands of a powerful elven goddess. His wedding ship could not be swept away by this storm unless it deliberately ventured out into the troubled sea.

Or unless it was forced.

Suddenly the Sea elf suspected what mischief the dragon turtle had in mind. She dived deep and frantically called the dolphin back to her side.

I need to see that ship. We must leap above the waves! she urged him.

The dolphin was not easily convinced. For many moments they argued in vehement clicks and chattering that transformed the waters around them into a dizzying whorl of vibrating sound. At last the dolphin conceded and allowed Anarzee to take hold of his dorsal fin. Both of the sea folk swam upward with all their strength, and then hurtled themselves up into the final spring.

As Anarzee clung to the leaping dolphin, she saw her beloved's ship lurch suddenly toward the east. It was as she feared: The dragon turtle was forcibly herding Darthoridan out to sea.

Without pausing for thought, Anarzee left the dolphin behind and sped toward the doomed ship.

* * * * *

The night was nearly spent when Vhoori Durothil's skiff touched the docks of Sumbrar. On the main island, the mid-summer festival was still in full celebration. All the people of Evermeet, not only the elves of every race but all the other fey creatures who made the island their home, marked the longest day of summer with music and dance, feasting and revelry. Though Vhoori was not adverse to gaiety, he was eager to return to his island, and his tower, and his all-consuming work.

Vhoori's accomplishments had outstripped most early predictions of his potential. His skill at magical communications, in particular, was uncanny. Many times he had foreseen approaching danger and given warning, and so effective was he at this task that the entire outpost island of Sumbrar had been placed under his rule. A large contingent of warriors were garrisoned there, and a score of fighting ships were kept on alert. But perhaps Sumbrar's most potent defense was the magic wielded by its Circle. Vhoori Durothil's tower had become one of the largest in the elven realm. Many young mages vied for the honor of training with Sumbrar's High Mage.

Yet there were back on Evermeet many elves who feared Vhoori Durothil's growing power, and who spoke out against the dangers of isolating a tower of High Magi, and the dubious wisdom of placing a considerable fighting force in the hands of a single elf. Chief among these dissenting voices was that of Darthoridan Craulnober.

Vhoori gritted his teeth at the thought of his rival. At the last council meeting, not more than a fortnight past, Darthoridan had spoken long and eloquently about the dangerous divisions growing between the various races of elves. He had even had the nerve to point out that only Gold elves were accepted into Sumbrar Tower, and that only Gold elves fought in the outpost guard.

This was true enough. In Vhoori's eyes, this practice was merely a matter of preference and convenience, but Darthoridan's words had made it appear a sinister plot. The seeds of suspicion had been planted in many a fertile Moon-elven mind. This, Vhoori could not allow. The mage could ill afford to have attention focused upon his work, and he had no intention in any event of becoming accountable to a Gray elf.

Nor was this the worst that Darthoridan had done. The Craulnober upstart was gaining ground in the Council, and was even spoken of as a possible High Councilor. Vhoori Durothil fully intended that this honor would be his. He had chosen his wedding gift for Darthoridan accordingly.

Somewhat cheered by this thought, the mage alighted from his skiff and hastened to the uppermost room of his tower. There he kept the Accumulator, as well as many, many other magical objects he had collected or created. Even now, in the darkest hour of the night, the room would be bright with the combined light of a hundred softly glowing spheres.

As Vhoori entered the chamber, he noted that he was

not alone. Before one such globe sat Mariona Leafbower, her eyes fixed upon the globe and her pale face twisted in an expression of intense longing.

Vhoori pulled up short, startled by the captain's presence in this, his inner sanctum. His next thought was concern for what the elf woman might have seen. Each magical globe was a window, and some of the sights they revealed were for his eyes alone.

But predictably enough, the captain gazed into the globe that probed the stars beyond Selûne.

The mage cleared his throat. "If you wished to see the stars, Captain Leafbower, you had only to walk outside the tower. This is my private room. There is no reason for you to be here."

Mariona glanced up. A wry smiled lifted one corner of her mouth as she took note of her host's consternation. "No reason?" she echoed dryly. "It's midsummer night, Vhoori. Maybe I came here hoping to celebrate with you."

A startled moment passed before the mage understood this comment for what it was. He could not imagine intimacy of any kind with this tart-tongued elf woman, but he had become well acquainted with her tendency to say things meant to throw him off stride. That had worked, once. These days he merely responded in kind.

"I am surprised you noted the changing of seasons, much less the coming of the solstice," Vhoori said mildly. "Perhaps you have become more attuned to this world than you like to admit."

Mariona's lip curled into a sneer. "Not likely! The sooner I shake the sand of this wretched place off my boots, the happier I'll be!" She rose abruptly and stalked over to the mage, her fists planted on her hips. "And speaking of which, when can I leave?"

"Leave?"

"Don't play the fool!" she snapped. "The first ship is nearly full-grown. The original helm has been rebuilt and tested beneath the waves. The air envelope held; the ship is fully maneuverable. I can leave this place, and I want to do so at once."

Vhoori sighed. "We have had this conversation many times, Captain Leafbower. Yes, there is one ship ready for starflight. But tell me, who would crew this ship? Who but you is eager to make this long trip? Shi'larra?"

Mariona glared at the mage, but she could not refute his words. She had not seen her former navigator for years. Shi'larra had declared herself utterly content with her new home, and had long ago disappeared into the deep forests of Evermeet.

Nor was the forest elf the only member of Green Monarch's crew to have gone native. One by one, the elves had slipped ashore, armed with papers of introduction from Lord Durothil himself.

The captain hissed in frustration. The fools had probably spent the night dancing beneath the stars, never giving a thought to the days when they had traveled among them!

Well, to the Abyss with them. Surely there was another way off this rock.

"What about your wizards?" she asked grudgingly.

In the years since she'd made landfall, Vhoori had learned some of the secrets of star travel, mostly by experimentation, and had taught them to several young magi of his Circle. Any one of the Gold elven wizards could get her where she wanted to go. Mariona had seen better helmsmen in her time, but she'd certainly also seen worse. And Sumbrar's warriors were an elite group, well trained and highly skilled in the ways of ships and seas. Surely some of them would be eager to travel the stars. There was glory and adventure, and even treasure aplenty to be had in the service of the Elven Imperial Navy.

"My people know their roles, and they are content with them," Vhoori said. "And truly, why would any elf want to leave Evermeet, but for Arvandor itself?"

The mage spoke simply, calmly, as if stating a widely accepted truth. As indeed it was, Mariona reluctantly acknowledged. At that moment, the captain understood at last the futility of her long-cherished dream.

She let out an oath and backhanded the nearest globe. The priceless, magical crystal flew across the small room and shattered against the wall.

Anger flared in the High Mage's eyes. Mariona lifted her chin and stared him down, almost daring him to strike. At this moment of anger and loss and utter frustration, she would have welcomed the killing blow.

But Vhoori's face softened, and he came to her and placed a gentle hand on her shoulder. "You have not lost the stars. If only you would open your heart, you would experience their wonder again."

The elf woman spun away from him and threw herself into a chair. Never had she felt so utterly defeated. "All these years on this gods-forsaken rock, and for what? I will never leave—I'll be trapped on Sumbrar until I die!"

"This world is a wide place, Captain Leafbower. I have come to know you and your nature, and have heard from your former crew the reputation of your adventurous clan. You are not content to remain long in any one place. But the seas of Aber-toril, the scattered lands and ancient cultures, are not these things worth exploring? If you so desire, I will see that you have a ship and crew."

A tendril of interest worked its way into Mariona's benumbed mind. It was not wildspace, but even so . . .

"I don't suppose you have decent maps and star charts," she muttered.

Vhoori suppressed a smile. "As to that, you may judge for yourself. My library is at your disposal. Star charts we have, but it may well be that you can greatly improve them. Certainly, you have an insight that no one on Evermeet can equal. Your work will guide elven ships for many centuries to come." He paused, as if beset by sudden doubt. "That is, if you can captain a ship upon the water. It is easier, I would think, to sail through the endless void than to deal with matters of tides and winds."

The captain's eyes kindled. "I was walking the deck of

sea-going ships when you were still in nappies, and furthermore—"

She broke off suddenly, for the mage had dissolved into ringing laughter. Realizing that she was being teased—and more importantly, that he had deliberately reminded her of a time and a work that she had loved—Mariona gave him a grudging smile.

"Now that you mention it, I wouldn't mind sailing these waters myself!"

With these words, she caught up one of the many globes that showed a sea-scape and tossed it playfully to the mage. Vhoori caught it, glanced down. His eyes widened, and he returned his gaze to the image within.

"Well, indeed. It would seem that my gift to Darthoridan Craulnober was fortunately timed," he murmured.

Curious, Mariona rose and came to look over Vhoori's shoulder into the globe. Within the magical sphere she saw the image of a ship, crystal-grown like an elven man-o-war. The sails, which glowed with multicolored light, hung slack, flapping helplessly in the gathering wind despite the efforts of the elven sailors who labored at the ropes. Another cluster of elves gathered at the stern, firing upon the enormous creature that nudged and prodded the boat out into an odd, unnatural band of turbulence. The creature, by all appearances a titanic turtle, was odd enough. But stranger still—at least to Mariona's eyes—was the invisible boundary that abruptly separated the calm sea from the storm.

"The dragon turtle wishes to destroy the ship," Vhoori reasoned. He did not sound particularly displeased.

"Not so," the captain said. "Just look at the size of that thing! It could shatter a crystal hull with a few swats of its tail. And I'd be willing to bet my favorite dagger that this dragon has other weapons worth using."

"Its breath," Vhoori admitted. "If the dragon turtle wished to do so, it could send a scalding cloud of steam over the ship that would certainly kill most of the crew."

"And likely damage the ship, as well," Mariona retorted. "That's not its intent."

"What, then?" the mage demanded, not liking the direction that her reasoning was taking.

The captain tapped the globe with one finger. "Three ships," she said, indicating three specks of heat and color in the distant seas. "My guess is, these people want your ship. The dragon turtle is in alliance with them—or more likely, they're both answering to whoever sent this wizard weather."

"This is no wizard's work," Vhoori mused as he studied intently the storm raging within the globe. Already the ships that Mariona's sharp eyes had discerned were coming fully into sight. They were long and low, each bearing a single large, square sail. Vhoori had seen such ships before. They belonged to pirates from the north, primitive humans who lacked the sort of magic needed to create such a storm.

There was only one explanation for such a gale: It was the work of Umberlee herself. For whatever reason, the capricious goddess had made the raiders' purpose her own.

By her power, every bit of speed had been coaxed from the sturdy little ships. The sails were tightly curved and as full of wind as they could be without rending under the force. Even the masts seemed to be bent almost to the breaking point.

"Raiders, I'll warrant. They want to capture the elven ship unharmed," Mariona said, answering Vhoori's question before he could put words to it. "It will be easier for them to slip past Evermeet's defenses in an elven ship, to strike at other ships or even to raid coastal towns."

"This we cannot allow," Vhoori said. He raised his gaze to Mariona Leafbower's eyes, and saw grim determination reflected back as if from a mirror.

"You promised me a ship. I can sail those waters," she said, nodding toward the globe and its image of wild seas.

"No doubt," Vhoori responded. "But we could never reach the elven ship in time to bring aid. At least, not by sea. Come." He turned and strode quickly from the tower room.

The elf woman's brow furrowed with puzzlement. Then Vhoori's meaning came to her, and a fierce smile set flame to her eyes. She fell into step beside the mage. "You said 'we.' You're coming in to battle?"

"This night Evermeet's first starwing ship will take its maiden flight," the mage said. "Who better to take the helm?"

The captain nodded. "Good. You've got more power than any helmsman I've sailed with. But remember, I'm the captain and this battle is mine. Do you think you remember how to take orders?"

"That is not my strongest skill," he said dryly. "But yes, this battle is yours to fight—and mine to win."

Mariona cast a sharp, sidelong glance at the mage. She did not care who got the credit for this victory. The prospect of walking again upon the deck of an airborne ship was enough for her. But there was an odd note in Vhoori's voice that she disliked and mistrusted. More was brewing than an eminent battle against a dragon turtle, a trio of human pirate ships, and an angry sea goddess—as if *that* wasn't enough!

To steady her nerves, Mariona brought to mind one of her favorite maxims: "If it were easy, it wouldn't be worth doing," she muttered. By that token, or so the elven captain strongly suspected, her night's work would be worthwhile indeed.

* * * * *

As Anarzee swam desperately toward her beloved's ship, a large, moon-cast shadow fell over her. Another followed swiftly. The Sea elf paused in her headlong race just long enough to glance up as the third ship swept past her.

Human ships. The Sea elf had seen such ships before, and knew well what manner of human sailed them.

"Pirates," she murmured, sending a rift of bubbles floating up into the troubled sea.

259

The dragon turtle's part in this was now apparent. Since no human ship could pass unbidden through the magical barriers surrounding Evermeet, the pirates had made a bargain with the sea monster. Anarzee wondered what the humans had offered the dragon turtle in exchange for delivery of the elven ship. Treasure, most likely, for the promise of elves to devour was a hollow one—if that had been the dragon turtle's only purpose, the creature could surely have carried it out without the aid of human pirates.

Anarzee twisted in the water and swam upward with quick, powerful strokes. Her head broke the surface and she bobbed there in the turbulent waters as she took stock of the situation.

The elven warriors aboard Sea-Riven fought desperately against their gigantic foe. Magic was not a viable solution, not at such close range. Any spells powerful enough to hurt the creature would almost certainly destroy the ship, as well. Their arrows, even the huge ballista bolts, merely bounced off the dragon turtle's armor. Any vulnerable areas the creature possessed were hidden beneath the waves.

As if his thoughts echoed Anarzee's, Darthoridan vaulted over the rail of the ship and plunged down toward the monstrous turtle. In his hand was a long metal tube, from which protruded the barbed tip of a spear. A second spear was strapped to his back.

Anarzee caught her breath; Darthoridan's attack was a brave and desperate move. The turtle's shell was a mass of ridges and spikes, and Darthoridan might as well have been leaping headlong into a mass of braced and ready weapons.

But Darthoridan came up onto his feet and at once began to pick his way along the spiny center ridge of the shell, heading for the creature's head.

A small cry of relief escaped the Sea elf. Darthoridan's shoulder was bleeding badly, but at least he had survived the leap. She began to swim for the dragon turtle, never once taking her eyes from the brave warrior she loved.

Just then the dragon turtle butted the ship again. The impact cost Darthoridan his footing; the elf stumbled and rolled painfully down the bumpy curve of the creature's back. He slammed into one of the ridges that lined the edge of the shell. Not bothering to rise, he began to work his away around the macabre island, using the ridges as handholds, toward the opening from which protruded the massive front leg.

Anarzee nodded grimly. The harpoon Darthoridan carried could fire with considerable force. If he could get a clear shot through the folds of tough, leathery skin of the dragon turtle's leg, he could pierce the creature's heart.

Even wounded, Darthoridan moved quickly. In moments he'd reached his target. Hooking his feet around one bony ridge, he lowered himself and his harpoon into the water. The Sea elf's keen ears caught the sharp *click* of the harpoon's release, carried to her by the water.

A terrible roar split the night. The dragon turtle reared like an angry stallion and then wheeled about, swinging its massive head this way and that as it searched for the source of the attack. Its yellow eyes fell upon the elf clinging to the edge of its shell. The reptilian orbs narrowed with malevolence, and the turtle's head craned back, jaws snapping. But Darthoridan had rolled back onto the shell, and was scrambling to the center where he was well out of reach.

The dragon turtle changed tactics and went into a roll. Once, twice, the pale armor of its belly glinted in the moonlight as it tried to rid itself of the troublesome elf. The creature's spin created twin surges of water that caught the elven vessel and carried it ever closer to the turbulent sea—and the rapidly approaching pirates.

Anarzee wailed and swam all the faster, though she knew there was little she could do. Once Darthoridan was cast into the water, the sea creature could finish him off with a single snap.

But when the turtle righted itself, the elven warrior clung

to the center ridge of the shell, stubborn as a barnacle. He could not do so for long, however; a wash of bright blood mingled with the water that flowed down the slope of the creature's shell. No warrior could ignore such wounds forever.

Suddenly the sea around Anarzee went still. The unnatural winds eased off, and the surging, white-capped waves sank into the sea, sending small restless ripples skittering off. Anarzee heard the guttural shouts of surprise as pirates trimmed their sails to adjust for the diminishing wind. They no longer needed such wind, Anarzee noted, for they would soon be upon Darthoridan's ship.

For a moment the Sea elf knew despair. As she gazed out over the quieting sea, inspiration struck her, as clearly as if the voice of Deep Sashales whispered in her ear.

Without the marker provided by the restless waves, the humans had no way of telling where the dangerous shields lay!

The Sea-elven priestess began to chant a clerical spell, praying for an illusion that would turn the serene waters surrounding Evermeet into a mirror—a mirror that would reflect the still-choppy waves of Umberlee's storm.

Anarzee completed her spell and then dived deep—a heartbeat before one of the pirate ships blundered into the magical barrier.

A flare of light transformed the dying night into midday, and turned the ship into a torch. The Sea elf plunged downward to escape the sudden heat, and to avoid the flailing limbs of the pirates who had survived the first blast and who had leaped—or been thrown—into the water.

The boom and crackle of the fire, the bellowing of the angry dragon turtle, the thrashing of the wounded humans—these things filled Anarzee's senses like a chorus of triumphant music. Too late she caught the vibrations that bespoke a new presence in the waters nearby. Instinctively she twisted to one side—just as a sleek gray form brushed past her.

For a moment Anarzee thought the dolphin had

returned to join the battle. But the rough hide that rasped painfully against her arm could belong to only one creature. The sharks, drawn by the commotion of battle and the scent of spilled blood, had come to feed.

Anarzee drew a knife from her belt and dived deeper still. She slashed off a length of kelp and quickly bound the arm that had been abraded by the brush with the shark. There was not much blood, nor would there be, but even a few drops in the water around her could mean her death. At the moment, the sharks were driven to a frenzy by the abundance before them. They would be busy with the pirates for quite some time. But few sharks ever became so sated that they would forbear to hunt their favorite food: a wounded Sea elf.

She placed the knife between her teeth and swam up to the enormous shapes silhouetted against the burning sky. The dragon turtle had turned its attention back to the elven ship, and was nudging it relentlessly toward the open sea—and the two ships that awaited the prize. A thin line of blood streamed into the water from behind the creature's leg, diminishing even as Anarzee drew near. Darthoridan's shot had done little more than nick the turtle's hide. It fell to her to do better.

The Sea elf lunged for the enormous tail. She caught hold of the tip, then pulled herself against the tail and wrapped her legs around it as tightly as she could. With one hand, she took her knife from between her teeth and drove it deep into the tail. She pulled it down with all her strength, tearing a gash in the hide.

Again the dragon turtle roared, a terrible sound that reverberated through the water and even created a lull in the sharks' grim feasting. Anarzee held on as the tail lashed fiercely back and forth through the water. When this method did not avail, the turtle raised the tail above the water and flicked it upward with one quick, hard motion. The Sea elf released her hold, letting the momentum throw her up onto the turtle's spiked shell.

She was not so fortunate as Darthoridan. Waves of

Elaine Cunningham

agony swept through her as she slammed facedown onto the bony ridge. But she tore herself upright, off the short spike that grated against her hip bone, and came up onto her hands and knees. Ignoring as best she could the searing, numbing pain, she forced herself to look at the wound. There was blood, far too much of it. In a shark-infested sea, such a wound would prove mortal—of that she had no doubt. But perhaps she could survive long enough to complete the task before her.

Still on her knees, the Sea elf made her way over to where Darthoridan lay. He was hurt worse than she had first thought, and near to losing consciousness. She slapped and shouted and pleaded until at last his eyes focused on her.

"Anarzee," he whispered. "Oh, my poor, lost love. There are so many things I must say . . ."

"No time," she told him grimly. With one torn hand, she gestured toward the elven ship. It had passed the barrier, and pirates swarmed up onto its crystal decks. "The humans must not have this ship! You know what use will be made of it."

A female's scream, shrill with pain and terror, rang out over the sounds of battle. Darthoridan swore bitterly as two of the humans dragged a struggling elf woman up from the hold. The elf woman's bright gown, the circlet of summer flowers hanging askew in her tangled hair, left little doubt in Anarzee's mind as to her identity.

Darthoridan struggled to his feet, but he did not immediately go to his new wife's aid. He seized the harpoon and thrust a second spear into the metal tube. As clearly as if he spoke his thoughts aloud, Anarzee knew what was in his mind. His first task was to keep the ship in elven hands. As long as the dragon turtle lived, the ship was lost.

The Sea elf looked down into the churning sea, where the sharks were still avidly feeding. No land-dwelling elf was nimble enough in water to avoid them. If Darthoridan tried again to stop the dragon turtle, he would surely be dead, and his efforts would be for nothing.

Anarzee seized the harpoon with her one good hand. "Go," she demanded, nodding toward the rope ladder that the pirates had draped down the ship's crystal hull.

"You are hurt," he protested, noting at last the blood that stained her mottled skin.

"I am dying," she said simply. "Go, and let me die well. You must save the ship, and the People upon it."

Before Darthoridan could respond, the Sea elf scrambled down the turtle's shell and dived into the water. The Moon elf took a long, shuddering breath and made his way up to the shell just behind the turtle's head. Although the creature's task was done—the elven ship had been herded beyond the magical shields—it remained nearby, circling the ship like a waiting shark.

Darthoridan waited until the creature circled back around to the place where the pirates' boarding ladder hung. He leaped, catching the lower rungs as he fell. The pain as he slammed into the crystal hull was nearly overwhelming, as was the dull throb in his torn shoulder. But he pulled himself up and rolled over the rail onto the ship.

Battle, bloody and fierce, raged all around him. As the elves fought for their lives. But Darthoridan's comrades were no army—just a few friends and kindred who had accompanied the newly wed couple on the northward trip.

The ship lurched suddenly as a rolling wave caught it. Darthoridan seized the rail to steady himself, and suddenly found he was eye-to-eye with the dragon turtle. The creature's eyes were frantic, and its gigantic mouth was flung wide, held open by the harpoon imbedded in the roof of its mouth. It could not shut its jaws without driving the weapon up and into its brain.

Even as he took note of this, Darthoridan saw the slender, webbed hands clutching at the base of the spear. Anarzee had not gotten off a killing shot, but the determined Sea elf would bring down her quarry even if that meant swimming into its mouth! For a moment he knew hope—Anarzee had wedged the spear in securely, and perhaps she would consider her task done and escape into the water. Even as the thought formed, a cloud of steam puffed from the dragon's mouth, turning crimson as it caught the light of the rising sun. The dragon turtle let out a garbled roar and tossed its head high. Anarzee's limp hands slid from the spear, disappeared down into the crimson mist.

Darthoridan dashed a hand across his tear-blinded eyes and turned to face the battle before him. One of the pirate ships had emptied its human cargo onto the deck of Sea-Riven, and another was closing in. The elves would soon be overwhelmed.

A silver streak shot down from the clouds toward the approaching ship. Darthoridan gaped as a ballista bolt struck and splintered the ship's single mast. The beam fell, smashing one side of the wooden ship and covering the pirates in a shroud of canvas.

The elf looked up in the direction of the attack. Incredibly, their rescuer was an airborne ship, a glittering elven vessel that swooped down upon the pirates like a vengeful butterfly.

* * * * *

Mariona Leafbower let out a whoop as the ballista bolt struck home. The frustrating years on Sumbrar fell away as the captain's blood sang anew with the wonder of flight, and the joy of battle.

"Well shot," commented a too-familiar voice behind her.

The captain whirled to see Vhoori Durothil, watching the battle with calm detachment and cradling in his arms a staff that was crowned with a glowing, golden gem.

"Who's on the helm?" she snapped.

"Chandrelle is quite capable," the mage replied. "No one could have brought this ship to battle more swiftly than I, but at this moment, my skills are best employed elsewhere."

"I can handle the fighting!"

"Can you also handle *that*?" he said, pointing with the staff toward the enraged dragon turtle. "When facing two foes, is it not best to pit one against the other?"

"But—"

"Enough!" Vhoori thundered. "I will do as I must. See to the battle as you will, but do not hinder me."

Mariona fell back a step, startled by the vehemence, the sheer power in the Gold elf's voice. For once, she had no inclination to argue.

The mage pointed the staff at the sea creature and began to chant. As he spoke, the light in the gem began to intensify. To Mariona's surprise, the Gold elf chanted a powerful spell of summoning and binding, using the magic as a frame for soothing words of friendship and promise— words spoken to the dragon turtle!

The sky-borne ship was closer now, and Mariona could see the spear lodged in the gigantic turtle's mouth. The creature was not an immediate threat to the elves, but neither was he of much good as an ally. What did Vhoori have in mind?

She did not have time to ponder the matter. Although the pirate ship she'd hit was badly damaged and taking on water fast, a number of pirates had managed to cut their way through the canvas. The last, undamaged ship was swinging around to come to their aid. Soon the elven fighters would be overwhelmed.

Mariona leaned down to the speaking tube. "Helmsman, set us down on the water, as close to the elven ship as you dare!"

She spun, ready to shout orders to the crew. They were already about their business—hauling up the lower wings of the sails, readying boarding pikes and ropes, gathering weapons. A fleeting moment of regret touched Mariona— what adventures she might share with elves such as these in wildspace! But the thought was hard to hold, chased as it was by the prospect of the battle ahead.

By now the water was spinning up to meet them. The

captain braced her feet wide, accepted the surprisingly small jolt of impact when the ship touched down. She went to the rail. Seizing a coiled rope, she twirled it briefly and then let fly. The three-pronged hook at the end caught the side of the embattled ship. Other lines flew, and most of her Gold elf crew threw themselves against the ropes, leaning back hard and pulling in hand over hand as they brought the elven ships together.

Mariona did not wait for the two crystal hulls to touch. As soon as she dared, she leaped over the watery divide and threw herself into the melee.

* * * * *

Crimson and gold spilled into the sea as the sun broke over the horizon. The night was gone, and with it, the last of his strength. Darthoridan could fight no more. He was utterly spent, drained not only by wounds and exhaustion, but by the crushing sense of guilt and grief. Anarzee had remained constant, while he had given thought only to increasing his clan and his personal power. For these reasons he'd taken a new wife—a lady of high family and many accomplishments. Her beauty and her skill at harp and verse made her an ornament to his castle, and to the court. She would help increase the Craulnober lines, for she was young—younger even than his own son—and would bear many children to the clan. Already her belly was slightly rounded under her bedraggled finery.

Darthoridan's eyes sought her now. The elf woman stood with her back against the mast, her eyes frantic as she watched the battle rage around her, and her hands pressed to her mouth as if to hold back cries of horror. No warrior, she.

As if from a distance, Darthoridan heard the clatter of a falling sword, then a dull, echoing thud. Dimly he realized that his sword had fallen from his hand, and that he had dropped to his knees.

The elf heard his wife's voice screaming out his name. He managed to look up as a curved sword slashed toward his neck. It was not in him to do more.

The shriek of metal against metal sang out over the clatter of battle. A rangy, silver-haired elf woman had darted in just in time to catch the pirate's blade with her own. She flung the enjoined swords high. Before the pirate could recover from the parry, she barreled in, driving her forehead into his face and then bringing her knee up hard. She danced back. The man folded, bleating out a strangled oath.

The elven warrior lifted her sword high, swept it down viciously at the back of the pirate's neck. Even as she brought the bloody sword back up, she kicked the rolling, bearded approaching pirate. The man stumbled, his arms windmilling as he sought his balance. Before he could get his feet firmly beneath him and his weapon into guard position, the elf woman whirled in a tight, precise circle. Darthoridan did not actually see her sword's stroke, but he saw the man fall, his throat sliced cleanly across.

The fierce elf woman took off at a run in search of another fight. But there was none to be found. By now the rescuers—all Gold elves, wearing the uniform of the Sumbrar guard—were tossing the last of the humans into the sea.

The fight was over, and at last Darthoridan allowed himself to yield to the seductive darkness. As it swept over him, he felt small, cool hands stroking his face.

"Anarzee," he murmured.

The hands stilled abruptly. "Anarzee is dead, my lord," his new wife said. "Slain by the dragon turtle. It was horrible to see!"

Darthoridan remembered all. Grief would come later. Even the darkness would have to wait, for there was one more battle to fight. "Help me up," he rasped. "We must rally the fighters and finish off the creature!"

"Take ease, Lord Craulnober," said a familiar voice. "The creature, as you call it, is alive and well, and now an ally of the People." As if to give evidence, Vhoori Durothil held out the two broken pieces of the harpoon that Anarzee had planted at such cost.

Darthoridan stared with disbelief at the calm, golden face of Sumbrar's ruling mage. "The monster killed Anarzee Moonflower, your own kinswoman!"

"That is a great loss, and I will join the many who will mourn her passing. But we have need of such allies as this dragon turtle, and cannot allow grief to overtake reason. If you will excuse me, I have yet to solidify our alliance."

The mage walked over to the rail. "One question yet remains, great Zhorntar," he called out. "What did the sea goddess offer, in return for your help? It might be that the People can do as well for you and better."

"Umberlee promised a rich domain to rule as I wish," the dragon turtle said in a deep, sonorous voice. Steam rose from the water with each word. "All passing ships would give tribute, and great would be the sport when I chose to hunt!"

"That you will have, and more," the mage promised. "The seas surrounding Evermeet will be yours to patrol, and every vessel that does not bear elven runes carved onto the bottom of its hull will be your rightful prey. All treasure that you take from would-be invaders is yours. This domain will be yours, and you will pass it down to your heirs. You shall have fame if you wish, or secrecy if that is your preference. Agreed?"

"You are mad," Darthoridan said hotly. "Will you invite the fox to bed down among the hens? The creature will follow its nature, and elven ships will fall prey!"

"Zhorntar will not touch an elven ship," the mage said confidently.

"How can you know this?"

In response, Vhoori reached out and plucked an ancient, jeweled dagger from Darthoridan's belt. He murmured a few arcane words, and then hurled the blade into the sea.

Darthoridan squinted out over the water. There

paddled the dragon turtle. The knife was embedded deep in the turtle's shell—only the glowing hilt, its gems pulsing with magic, was still visible.

"I will now be able to observe the creature," Vhoori said. "And rest assured, even if my eyes are averted, the blade will sink down and find its way to Zhorntar's heart if ever he gives in to the temptation to hunt elves."

"A fine ornament," the turtle admitted, craning his head around to admire the gems. "But what of my heirs?"

"They can pluck it from your shell upon your death. It is ensorcelled, and will release itself to your chosen successor."

"Well done. It is agreed," the turtle said, and sank down into the ocean.

Darthoridan's eyes flamed as he rounded on the High Mage. "You gave me that dagger as a wedding gift so that you might watch me!"

"And you should be glad of it," the Gold elf retorted. "Had I not, you would be dead and this ship would be in human hands."

That was true enough, but the warrior eyed Vhoori suspiciously. "I cannot believe you gave such a gift because you wished me well."

"I came to your rescue, did I not?" the mage said impatiently.

Darthoridan nodded. "What do you want of me, then?"

"First, your silence. None need know of the Starwing fleet, or of Evermeet's newest protector," Vhoori said, nodding to the now-quiet sea. "Second, your support. I wish to become the next High Councilor."

Darthoridan laughed, briefly and without humor. "You command ships that fly, magic enough to bind one of the sea's most powerful creatures—"

"Two, actually," the mage interjected. "There is already a kraken patrolling the waters north of Sumbrar."

The Moon elf threw up his hands. "Why do you need my support? You could simply take what you desire!"

Vhoori Durothil shook his head. "You still do not

understand. I have no wish to conquer, but to serve. The powers I have, I will wield for the good of Evermeet."

"According to your lights," Darthoridan said sarcastically.

"According to my *right*." The mage's usually calm voice rose with sudden passion. "The Durothil clan is the most ancient and honored of all those on this island. Our ancestors ruled Aryvandaar, and before that, Faerie itself. The Council's time is nearly past. Evermeet must have one ruler, a worthy ruler from a worthy and proven dynasty. And who better than me and mine?"

"You wish to be a king," Darthoridan said, thunderstruck.

Vhoori did not disagree. "I have ruled Sumbrar well. Evermeet is my due. There is more," he said, breaking off the Moon elf's attempted protest. "With my magic, I can look among the stars, below the sea, and to the Circles that gather in every corner of this world. Sometimes, dimly, I catch a glimpse of what will be. And this I tell you in all assurance: Evermeet will have a king."

"And have you also foreseen that you are to be this king?"

The mage shrugged. "Perhaps I presume too much in seeking Evermeet's throne. But more likely, in doing so I only hasten my own destiny. I tell you this because you are a strong voice in the council. Your word will go far. Swear fealty to me now, and in return you will hold your northern lands in the name of the crown. You will have power and honor beyond what most Silver elf clans could hope to achieve."

Before Darthoridan could respond, he felt a gentle pressure on his shoulder. He looked down into his wife's face. She nodded, her lovely features set in determination. "If swearing to Durothil will bring honor and position to our house, my lord, do so at once."

The Moon elf was too weary to argue. He could not dispute Vhoori's vision or his wife's desire for a place of power in the court. Did he not wish the same thing? Was this not what he had desired all his life?

"Agreed," he said curtly. "But beware of me, if you do not rule well."

Vhoori's smile was complacent. "There is little chance of that. Evermeet is becoming what she was meant to be. The dawn you see before you is that of a new and—you should pardon the expression—*golden* era."

14

The Flight of the Dragons

he forest trees shook as Malar the Beast Lord screamed his rage into the night sky. Snarling and cursing, he paced the forest and set the mountains of Faerûn quivering with the reverberating echoes of his wrath.

This deep inland woodland was his haunt now. Not for him the remote islands and the angry waves of the sea. He was done with Umberlee, and she with him.

Twice now had the goddess of the sea fallen short of Malar's expectations. It was not that Umberlee lacked power, but she was simply too capricious. The goddess had none of Malar's single-minded focus. She was just as happy tormenting sailors off the sunny coasts of Chult as she was speeding human pirates on a raid to Evermeet. If one endeavor should fail, the goddess merely shrugged a white-capped shoulder and turned her attention elsewhere. The seas of Aber-toril were broad, and a single elven island could not hold Umberlee's attention for long.

But Malar wondered if he would ever be able to think of anything else. The passing of centuries had done little to cool his hatred for elves or to blunt his desire to see Corellon Larethian bested. It was becoming increasingly clear, however, that an invasion of Evermeet was no easy matter.

Finally wearied by his ranting, the Beast Lord flung himself to the ground. Leaning his black-furred head against the trunk of an ancient oak, he sat and stared with malevolent red eyes up into the blackness of a moonless night. The night was as dark as any he had seen. A fine layer of clouds obscured the stars. This pleased Malar, for starlight was a source of joy and magic to the accursed elves. In his current mood he needed no such reminder of his elusive foes.

A faint, rosy pinprick of light in the eastern sky caught the brooding god's attention. He squinted up, trying to remember what about it seemed so familiar. Suddenly the years fell away, and Malar remembered a distant time, a time of terrible destruction at the hands of the mightiest hunters known to this world.

The god sprang to his feet and sprinted through the forest. To the nearest mountain he ran, and he did not pause until he had left the tree line below him. Finally he stood near the mountaintop. The night sky lay open before him, a naked void of darkness bereft of any light but one.

By now the new star had risen high in the sky, huge and bright enough to shine through the mist. It hung over the mountains, glimmering like a single crimson eye. Malar threw up his arms and crowed with triumph. It was as he thought. The King-Killer had returned.

Perhaps some gods understood the rhythm of the stars, and marked the occasional coming of the brilliant red star. Malar was not such a god. But he remembered one thing— one very important thing. For reasons unknown, when the King-Killer shone bright above Faerûn, the dragons gathered and took flight.

At last, Malar knew how best to serve vengeance to Evermeet.

The god began to dance in the dim red light of the King-Killer. Tendrils of godly magic wafted off to search for the Beast Lord's followers, and to slip into the dreams of those who listened. To all his priests and shamans Malar sent the same message:

Gather the faithful. The time has come for a Great Hunt.

* * * * *

The orc horde crashed through the forest, making no effort to conceal their presence or to mute the sound of their approach. There didn't seem to be much point. The path of the dragonflight had passed over this land, leaving a broad swath of charred and lifeless forest.

"Don' know why we's acomin' thisaway," muttered a young, gray-hided orc who trailed along near the end of the procession. This was his first raid, and so far it had fallen far short of his expectations. A Great Hunt, indeed! They had yet to kill a single elf. Even four-legged game was scarce.

His companion shrugged and shifted his own unbloodied spear to the other shoulder. "Vapgard sez come, we come."

"Not find nothing here," the gray grumbled. "Why dragons gotta burn forest, anyhow?"

"Hmmph! You not remember the hungry winter? Hard snow. Too many wolves come south. Hard for orcs to find game."

The gray orc grunted. Of course he remembered. He had not yet been old enough to be accounted a fighter, but he'd been old enough to hunt. His ears still rang with the memories of his mother's blows when he came back to the cave day after day with an empty bag.

"What we do back then?" his companion persisted.

"Ah!" The orc bared his fangs in a grin as he grasped the meaning. "Some orcs burn forest. Other orcs, many many, wait by river."

"I hear Vapgard's brother float boats down river. Boats carry many orcs—more than many. They wait. We come behind." The orc stopped his march and planted his spear into the thick layer of ash. He held up his taloned hands. "Them, us," he said gesturing first with one hand, then the other. With a fierce grin, he smacked his palms together.

"Smash 'em," agreed the gray happily.

So encouraged, the young orc marched without complaint through the remainder of the day. By late afternoon, the horde had left the ruined forest behind. Ancient charred trees gave way to scrub, and then to meadow.

A howl of excitement started at the front of the mob and rippled back through the horde. The orcs began to surge forward. The gray waited for the wave of movement to reach him, and grant him space to run—and to kill.

"Long past time," he grunted when at last he could level his spear. He ran out onto the meadow, noting that the grass was not only dried and brittle from dragonfire, but slick with blood. He pulled up short to keep from stumbling over what appeared to have been the haunch of a wood buffalo. Probably a morsel that fell from some dragon's mouth.

The horde had spread out by now, and the orc had a better view of the battlefield. It was not what he had hoped for.

The field was littered with bodies—some of them forest creatures that the dragons had not eaten, but most of them elves. Some had been torn by massive claws and fangs, some blasted by dragonfire, others melted to the bone by a black dragon's acid breath. The carnage was entertaining to observe, but it offered neither sport nor satiation. The young orc wanted to kill. He needed to kill.

Baring his fangs, he began to zigzag back and forth across the field, imitating the older orcs who kicked and prodded at the elven bodies. Every now and then, one of them found an elf who yet breathed. Each discovery was heralded by triumphant howls, and the sounds of thudding clubs and spears.

But the young orc's status had placed him too near the back of the horde, and he was too late to claim any of the trophies taken that day. It occurred to him, when at last the secondhand battlefield fell silent, that this was not hunting at all, not really. They were more like ravens and wolves, cleaning up after the dragons.

The gray shrugged. Ravens and wolves—these were not so bad to be. And if he could not kill elves today, then tomorrow was nearly as good. The river was but a half day's march to the south. Along the edge of the river was a large elven settlement. Though it had been fortified with walls and magic, it would fall readily enough. How could it not? The forest elves, archers and fighters who were the city's advance defenders, were all dead. Moreover, the dragonflight usually followed the course of the river, and surely dragonfire had tumbled parts of the walls, perhaps even toppled those wicked Towers. And there were many, many orcs on the move, orcs who were in near-frenzy from their first taste of slaughter.

Tomorrow, the elven city. Tomorrow, the joy of the hunt and the pride of many trophies would be his.

* * * * *

Chandrelle Durothil, the powerful daughter of Evermeet's high councilor, led her Circle in yet another spell of summoning. Even through the deep concentration of the spell, she could hear the unmistakable sounds of dragonflight beyond the tower windows—the thumping of giant wings, the screams and roars the massive creatures emitted as they wheeled and swooped.

She could also feel the powerful crackle of the magic that thrummed through the air. On all of Aber-toril, no creatures, not even the elves, were as inherently magical as the dragons. Only the rebirth of the dragonriders, the union of dragons and elves in an incredible joining of magic, offered the elves hope of survival against the approachng orc hordes.

The elves of Faerûn were not the only people to suffer from the flight of rampaging dragons. Wars between the races of dragons had been long and costly. Now the evil dragons of the south—red dragons, mostly, with a few smaller but no less deadly blacks—gathered together in nearly unprecedented numbers for the northward migration. Along the way, they deliberately destroyed the holdings of the peace-loving wyrms. Bronze dragons found their lakes reduced to drifting steam and cracked, lifeless beds. Gouts of flame melted rock, sealing entrances to the caves of silver and gold dragons and trapping many of the creatures within.

Chandrelle had been among the first elves to travel through the new gates that in recent years had linked Evermeet to the mainland. Her husband, a newcomer and a distant relative who also bore the name Durothil, had helped establish the gate between Evermeet and the city of his birth.

Now the city lay in near ruin. Once, it had been a fair place, protected by walls and powerful magic, and situated on the banks of a broad, trout-filled river. Dragonfire had destroyed the farmlands and forests beyond, and had blasted huge gaps in the walls. An entire quarter lay in smoking ruins. Only the mithal, a powerful shield of magic, had kept the city from utter destruction.

But the Tower still stood, High magi joined with the scores of other magi sent from Evermeet to help buttress the tower. They chanted powerful spells that summoned and bound the goodly dragons. In ancient times, drag-onriders trained their mounts from birth, bonding to them with deep and mystical connections. There was no time for this now.

Shouts of excitement from the city below alerted the magi to their success. Chandrelle skillfully tapered off the flow of power and released the magi from their collective spellcasting.

"Seven more have come," she said in a voice that still thrummed with power. "There are now enough dragons for us all."

Along with the other mages, Chandrelle hurried from the tower to greet the newcomers. One of the dragons, a gold female, stepped forward and dipped her massive head in a gesture of respect to the High Mage.

"We have heard what you plan to do," the dragon announced in a voice that shook the Tower. "It is madness."

"It is needed," Chandrelle insisted. "Your people cannot fight the evil dragons alone, nor can we. We need your powers of flight to overtake and surround those who fly north. You need our High Magic to stop them."

"And when they are slain? What then?"

"Then your kind can once again live in peace, and we elves can rebuild our cities."

The dragon shook her golden head. "So much power, so little wisdom," she murmured.

"You will not help us?" Chandrelle pressed.

"We have little choice. Your magic compelled us to come— it compels most of us to serve."

It was not the endorsement that Chandrelle would have liked, but it would have to do. The mage quickly explained to the newly arrived dragons their part in the plan. Hastily fashioned saddles were brought and strapped onto the creatures. Today was the practice flight. There could be only one.

Excitement mingled with trepidation as Chandrelle climbed onto her dragon mount. Dragonriders had used magic for centuries, but never before had a Circle attempted to join together while riding dragons!

The creature's wings unfolded with a loud, booming crash. Before Chandrelle could catch her breath, the dragon was airborne.

As a High Mage of Evermeet, during her years in the Towers of Aryvandaar Chandrelle had seen many wonders. None of them equalled dragonflight for sheer exhilaration. They soared upward like a shooting star in reverse. In moments the city was as vague as a forgotten dream, the river a mere ribbon. The elf threw back her head and laughed into the racing wind.

When the clouds lay below them like mounds of snow and mist, the dragon leveled off and began to circle. Other dragons broke through the clouds, and one by one they fell into formation. It was time for the casting to begin.

Chandrelle sank deep into herself, seeking the magic that flowed through her and with it reaching out to the minds of the other magi. One by one, she pulled them into the Weave. The elf gathered the threads and wove them into a single spell of destruction—the most powerful spell attempted since that which had sundered the One Land in a time of legend.

At first light the following day, the High Magi and their dragon mounts gathered for final preparations. Their mood was somber, even though the testing of the spell had gone well. Perhaps, *because* it had gone so well. The magnitude of the destruction they would soon unleash was not an easy thing to contemplate.

Nevertheless, more than a hundred pairs of dragons and riders took to the air that morning. They climbed high into the sky until they were well above the sunrise clouds, and then flew with magically enhanced swiftness toward the north.

The path of the dragonflight was not difficult to follow. Sometimes in search of prey to fuel their flight, sometimes just for the love of destruction, the evil dragons burned the land and slaughtered all the creatures they found. Black and red these dragons were, and in the charred and blood-soaked land they left a grim reflection of themselves.

Before highsun, the dragonriders overtook their quarry. The horde of evil dragons swept low to the ground, intent upon their orgy of destruction. At that height the winds were capricious, the air thick with a blend of morning mist and smoke from the burning woodlands. The evil dragons could not fly as swiftly as those that pursued them.

At a signal from Chandrelle, the dragonriders dispersed and began to form a wide circle over the horde of dragons below. They flew in careful formation, like an enormous flock of glittering gold and silver geese.

The elven magi began the chant, summoning the magic and spinning it in a dizzy circle. Together they formed a whirling cone of air and magic, a storm larger than any the world had known, and sent it plunging down toward the dragons below.

There was no warning, no time for the migrating dragons to pull away from the attack. One moment, the sounds filling the air were those of their own making: the boom and crackle of the burning woodlands, the distant cries of fear and pain from the forest creatures below, their own triumphant roars. All these were muted, suddenly and completely, by the descending cone of magic.

The whirling winds caught the dragons and spun them helplessly about. Many were killed in the first sudden rush of explosive sound and power. Their enormous bodies acted as bludgeons as the wind whipped them against their still-living comrades.

Nor did the destruction stop there. Burning trees were torn from their roots and sucked up into the vortex. Within moments, the whirling cloud was a ghastly shade of reddish gray, a mixture of smoke and carnage.

The gold and silver dragons above instinctively shied away from the force in their midst, fearing, despite the success of the day before, that they themselves might be drawn into the surging, killing magic.

But as suddenly as it came, the whirlwind died. A terrible black and crimson storm rained down upon the blasted countryside as the slain dragons—perhaps as many as two hundred—were released from the terrible vortex.

And just as suddenly, Chandrelle was falling. The magic she had fashioned was gone. For the first time in her life a spell had disappeared too fast for her to withdraw carefully. Dimly, she noted that her grasping hands still held the dragon's reins, that the forest below was still passing by in the giddy blur of dragonflight. Her mortal body was safe, but nonetheless, *she* was falling.

Instinctively, the mage realized what had occurred. The death of so many dragons, so many magical creatures, had severely torn the fabric of the Weave. Her own magical essence, which had been bound inextricably into the casting of this spell, has been ripped free of the mortal world along with the dragons her magic had slain. She was dead. Her body simply had not yet had the chance to grasp this reality.

As if from a distance, Chandrelle saw her form grow translucent and fade away into motes of golden light. Her dragon mount seemed dazed and confused by the sudden break in the magical bond they had shared. The creature veered wildly aside—directly into the path of a venerable silver dragon.

The crash of impact reverberated over the ruined land. The silver's elven rider was thrown off; the mage's limbs floated limply as he spun helplessly, unknowingly, down toward the uprushing ground. The pair of dragons grappled helplessly as they strove to release themselves from the tangle of wings and elven livery.

Too late they broke apart. Just as Chandrelle's dragon managed to spread her wings, the massive, jagged trunk of a pine thrust up through her body like a spear. The impaled dragon struggled briefly, then sagged down, a glint of tarnished gold against the charred landscape. The silver dragon pulled into a glide, but there was nowhere for him to go. Nearby the flames had flared up high and hot, stoked into a frenzy by the swirling winds. The dragon's brief and desperate flight ended in a thick bank of black smoke, and the sucking winds that swept him toward the crackling inferno beyond.

* * * * *

Vhoori Durothil, the High Councilor of Evermeet, listened in silence to the grim tidings brought from Sumbrar's tower.

A flight of dragons was wending its way northward across Faerûn, laying waste to the land. Many elven settlements had fallen, either as prey to the dragons or to the ravening orcs and goblins that followed in their wake.

"What of the dragonriders?" he asked. "My daughter Chandrell sent word of her plan. We have sent many High Magi to support her."

A long silence met his words.

The mage's old friend, Brindarry Nierde had risen nearly as high in his chosen work as had Vhoori. The Gold elf warrior now commanded not only Sumbrar, but all of Evermeet's fighters.

The mage sighed and leaned back in his chair. He knew

all too well that light in his friend Brindarry's eyes—a near manic eagerness for battle. Clearly, the elven warrior had a plan in mind. "What do you recommend?"

"We cannot ignore the suffering of the People. There are a few magical gates between the island and the mainland. I say we create more. Many more."

"Those are not easily created, and should never be used lightly. The cost of magical travel is high."

"And the cost paid by the mainland elves is not?" retorted Brindarry. "We must send warriors to help counter the orcs and Circles of High Magi to fight the dragons."

"And what of Evermeet? If we do as you suggest, her defenses will be dangerously reduced."

Brindarry sniffed. "I think not. Under your leadership, the island has been secured against all possible attack. When was the last time anyone saw a scrag or a sahuagin? When was the last time a hostile ship came anywhere near the island? Between the Guardians and the Starwing fleet, no foe can get near."

"Say that I agree with you," Vhoori suggested. "Even so, the council almost certainly will not."

"Then dissolve the council. Their time has passed."

The mage considered this. Elven tradition had long considered the best governance to be a council of elders, a body that would give advice through collective wisdom rather than enforce compliance through power. Though the People nearly always followed the council's advice, they put high value on individual thought and freedom of personal choice. The elves of Evermeet would resist bitterly any perceived attempt to curtail these long-held rights.

On the other hand, news of the mainland troubles would send many elves scurrying to arms. Some of them had not been long in Evermeet, and many of these newcomers had near kin living in the areas scourged by the dragonflight. Other elves held firmly to the principle of unity among the People, and would fight just as fiercely for a stranger as they would their own kin. And regardless of personal circumstances, all the elves of Evermeet shared a sense of destiny, and their place in it. Evermeet represented hope and haven for all elves. In times of such darkness, hope must be brought to the elves who were too beleaguered to seek it. Even if the council voted otherwise, the elves, with a little encouragement, would almost certainly rally in great numbers to the rescue of their distant kin.

And when Evermeet was nearly emptied of warriors and magic, when the noble clans who held council seats were busy elsewhere, Vhoori Durothil would declare himself king. Who would gainsay him, when the battles were over? Not even the most querulous Gray elf on the council could argue with success.

"Start gathering your forces," Vhoori said. "We will summon the Circles, and begin creation of the gates at once."

Back in the shattered elven city, Brindarry Nierde stood ready with his warriors. In the first moments of dragonflight, Chandrelle Durothil had spotted the advancing orcs and had sent word to him through one of her father's speaking gems. Brindarry was ready, even eager, for the battle to begin.

He had lived all his life on Evermeet, and so he had never had the opportunity to fight the People's traditional enemy. In his mind, this day he and his would relive the legendary battle of Corellon Larethian and Gruumsh One-Eye. His elves would prevail just as surely as did Corellon, and they would join in the legends and the glory of the elven god of battle.

Suddenly the Gold elf's senses tingled weirdly. Something had changed, something important. It felt rather like the rain and mist of a summer shower had disappeared in the blink of an eye, leaving the skies utterly dry and clear. To the elf's fey sensibilities, the air suddenly felt—thin. Empty.

"The mithal," breathed the elf, understanding what had happened. The magical shield that had staved off the city's utter destruction was no more.

A moment's panic swept through the warrior. He was

confident of his skills and those of his elven fighters, but he acknowledged the cost of a failure would be enormous. If the defenders should fall, the gate to Evermeet would be left open. Never had Brindarry imagined that it might be possible for orcs to set foot upon the island.

The warrior snatched up the speaking gem that linked him to Chandrelle Durothil. The stone was cold and silent, the magic gone. Chandrelle was dead. The dragonriders would not be returning to lend their combination of dragon and elven magic to the battle.

Brindarry possessed one more magical gem, one that was even more powerful. He tugged a golden pendant from beneath his tunic and focused all his will upon the large, smooth stone set into it. In moments, the angular face of Vhoori Durothil appeared within.

There was little time for words, no time at all for explanations. Already the city resounded with the clash of weapons along the breached walls, and the dull thuds of bombards as the orcs sought to batter down the riverside gates.

"What is it, my friend?" Vhoori demanded. "I hear battle. Do you need aid? More warriors, magic? What can I do?"

Just then the vast wooden gate splintered, and orcs spilled through the city wall like water through a broken dam. Brindarry pulled his sword and spoke his final words to his dearest friend.

"There is but one thing you can do. *Close the gates to Evermeet.*"

* * * * *

Two days passed before seven dragons and their elven partners limped back to the city. The survivors found a river polluted with the bodies of thousands slain, streets that were red with dried blood, beautiful buildings reduced to rubble. Even the Tower, one of the proudest survivors of the High Magic tradition of ancient Aryvandaar, had been tumbled and despoiled.

The elves camped that night in the ruined city. Even the dragons bedded down in empty courtyards and ruined marketplaces, and attempted to tend their wounds and gather their wits. The fey creatures that had survived the dragonriders' battle were left dazed and stunned by the aftermath of the spell.

None of the remaining magi could agree on what to do next. The magical gates had been closed—they could not return to Evermeet by such means. It was unlikely that new gates would be created soon. The island kingdom had been drained of both wizards and warriors. The few remaining High Magi on Evermeet would have other, more pressing work, and the warriors were too few to protect new gates against possible invasion. One thing was clear: The personal power of any single surviving mage was not what it had been. The destruction of the evil dragons might have saved many elven lives, but the damage to the fabric of the Weave was beyond measure.

In the years that followed, the stranded magi of Evermeet scattered like autumn leaves. Some stayed near the river to rebuild the city, or took off into the forest in search of other elven settlements. Others had been entranced and entrapped by their taste of dragonflight, and stayed to form bonds with their dragon mounts.

Not long after the crimson star known as King-Killer faded unmourned from the sky, a new wonder appeared in the heavens. A scattering of small, glowing lights began to follow the moon in her path through the night sky, like goslings pattering faithfully after their mother.

The poets named this phenomena the Tears of Selûne. No one knew for certain what they were, or what they meant. Some of the elves took heart at the sight, remembering the legends that claimed the People were born through the mingled blood of Corellon and the tears of the moon. The dwindling number of People, the destruction of so many of their ancient cultures—this, they claimed, was about to end.

Others argued that the Tears of Selûne were a sign of

the gods' favor, a mark of approval for the tremendous heights the elves had reached in their mastery of magic.

In truth, the appearance of these heavenly bodies represented, if anything, the end of an era.

Slowly, inexorably, High Magic was disappearing from the land. A few isolated enclaves of such magic still stood: Darthiir Wood, Winterwood, Tangletrees, Evermeet. Among the elven seers were those who predicted that soon such magic could be cast only on Evermeet. As this grim prediction came closer and closer to fruition, the island haven took on a whole new level of meaning to the elves.

Vhoori Durothil had been wrong about a good many things. He never ascended the throne of Evermeet, though he and his descendants controlled the council for many years to come. Evermeet's resources were not without limit, as the attempted rescue showed.

But about one thing Durothil was entirely correct: A new era was beginning for the elves. It was not to be the golden era he envisioned, but a time of great trouble and confusion. Evermeet's importance grew as the troubles of the mainland elves steadily increased.

It seemed to many elves that the tears of the moon—the very thing that legend credited with the birth of the elven people—might well signal their end upon Faerûn.

To Danilo Thann does Athol of Candlekeep send greetings. Reluctantly.

Very well, I read your last letter, and the one before it, and the several that preceded them. In truth, I shudder to contemplate what your bills for parchment and ink must be.

But this, I suppose, is the way it should be. If you are to do this task and do it well, you must be relentless and prolific in your pursuit of information. That does not mean, however, that you cannot be brief.

Start by sparing me your fine flourishes and your flattery. Though I doubt not your sincerity, such niceties only serve to raise my hackles. Perhaps this is because I remember all too well the times you insisted that she who named me must have been speaking with a lisp.

Be that as it may.

I regret that I cannot send you the volume you last requested. It is an ancient book, perhaps one of the five oldest in this library, and its fragile pages and bindings would not survive the trip. The best I could do was to hire a scribe to copy it for you. Enclosed herewith are some sample pages. If you are satisfied with the effort, I will engage her to complete the work. A reasonable fee for such a task would be 5,000 gold pieces—it would be considerably more, but the scribe is a first-year student.

And yes, I am still cheaper than an ugly courtesan, to coin one of your youthful gibes. Though I must admit the reason for bothering with frugality eludes me; after all, I am spending your money, not mine.

I am returning with this letter the ink powder that you sent me. Perhaps it truly does glow in the dark, but I have no

Elaine Cunningham

desire to stand in the spot where lightning once struck me.

The excerpt from the lorebook Of Blades and Blooded Honor *you requested follows.*

Regards,
Athol the Beardless

* * * * *

It was the time of man.

To many elves, it seemed that the humans flourished in all things even as they, the children of Corellon, faded.

As the number of People dwindled like sands slipping through an hourglass, the humans swelled their ranks at an indecent rate. The elven communities retreated into the forests as humans spread out into every land and every clime. As High Magic became a rare and secret thing, human mages discovered ancient scrolls that enabled them to reach in their few short years of life incredible levels of power. Mighty human kingdoms had risen—and fallen. Fabled Netheril was a memory, but from its ashes magelords were rising to command the settlements and cities of the north-lands. The humans pressed even into the deep forest, seeking to settle amid the ancient trees and pleasant dales that were the elves' last stronghold on Faerûn.

Everywhere, contact between elves and humans was increasing. Half-elves, once rare and pitiable beings who were almost invariably the result of war crimes, were becoming almost common. As a people, the elves were not at all certain what to make of these developments, nor were they of a single mind concerning how best to deal with the ubiquitous humans. On one thing all agreed, however: Evermeet must remain sacred to the People.

Few humans knew of Evermeet. Most who heard the tales thought of the island as an elven fancy, a legendary place of wonder and beauty and harmony. But there were a few, mostly sea-going folk, who had reason to know that something existed in the distant western seas. Those who ventured too far into the sunset were met by terrible storms, bands of warlike Sea elves, and magical barriers of all kinds. These hearty men—those few who survived these encounters—began to speak more often of the rich island kingdom in the sea.

The image of Evermeet that emerged was colored by the humans' experience with the elves of Faerûn. The humans thought that the island, if it existed at all, was a place of serene beauty and utter harmony, where elves joined as one in their pursuit of the arts of magic and warfare, and to contemplate the wonders of sky and forest.

The truth was something rather different.

For millennia, the noble Gold elf families of Evermeet had vied for control of the ruling Council of Elders. Most often, the Durothil clan held sway, but this right was strongly contested by the Nierde, the Nimesin, and the Starym families. Nor were the Moon elven clans content to leave the positions of power and influence uncontested.

The disputes between the races and the clans never actually devolved into warfare, but the island became a warren of intrigue. Elven culture, which had once been focused upon the creation of beauty and the assurance of a strong defense, focused instead upon the art of political maneuverings. Clans vied with each other in their wealth, their forces at arms, and in the stockpiling of magical weaponry.

Predictably enough, at this time the most powerful seat of elven culture was not Evermeet at all, but the forest of Cormanthyr. As ambitious Gold elves came to realize this, many of them began to leave the island and settle in the burgeoning cities of Cormanthyr.

But even there, differences arose among these clans. The Nierde elves were generally willing to compromise with the Moon elves and the forest elves who had proceeded them. They even tolerated the insurgence of humans, halflings, and dwarves into the forest community. But the more xenophobic of the Gold clans—among others the Starym, Nimesin and Ni'Tessine—loudly proclaimed the need for isolation.

After much debate, the Elven Council of Cormanthyr

*opened the forest lands to human settlement. The Standing
Stone was raised as a monument to peace and cooperation
among the many races. That much of the story is well-
known. But long before this year, a year of events so great
that it became a measure by which time was reckoned, other,
more secret events had occurred that were to shape the very
course of the elven race.*

*When the long destruction of the Crown Wars had final-
ly come to an end (about -9000 by Dale Reckoning) some
elves became concerned that such a period of strife might
come yet again in the long history of the elves. They were
determined to do everything in their power to prevent such
a disaster.*

*There was in Cormanthyr at this time an ancient elven seer
known as Ethlando, a survivor from the ancient kingdom of
Aryvandaar. He believed that this increasing division among
the elves could lead to the destruction of all. Ethlando had
lived long past the normal years for an elf, and was well into
his second millennia of life. He was widely believed to have a
special connection with the Seldarine, for the visions that were
granted him proved infallible. Even in small matters, his word
was greatly respected in the land. Oftentimes his opinion was
sought—and followed—when arbitration between the more
contentious clans was necessary.*

*During the years when Cormanthyr's fate was still hotly
debated, Ethlando declared that Evermeet must be ruled by
a single royal family—this, he claimed, was the will of the
gods. The plan that he gave for the selection of this clan was
so complex, so dependent upon a magic beyond the reach of
mortal mages, that the Council decided that the Seldarine
did indeed speak through the seer.*

*On one matter, though, they held firm: Ethlando insisted
that only Moon elf clans could apply for this honor. But the
Gold elves held sway in Cormanthyr, and the ruling class
decreed that all noble clans—excepting of course the drow
elves—who wished to make a claim for Evermeet's throne
could do so.*

Three hundred master weaponsmiths were chosen, and

each was charged with creating a single sword. Though each artisan was given license in the crafting, certain things were to be constant. All were to be double-edged broadswords, and the hilt of each was to be set with a large moonstone. Of all the gems known to elves, the moonstone was the purest, most fluid conductor of magic. Yet the swordcrafters were not to imbue the weapons with any magical powers whatsoever. That, Ethlando insisted, would come when the time was right.

By the year of the Standing Stone, the swords were completed. In due time, the question of elven royalty would be settled beyond question or dispute.

Prelude: Shadows Deeper

(1371 DR)

he silver dragon swooped down on Sumbrar, flying with dangerous speed directly toward the high, rounded Tower. She was a Guardian, and her task was to warn the elves of the approaching danger. She had reason to fear that her warning might already be too late.

Her glittering wings beat against the air to halt her desperate flight, and her taloned feet caught and clung to the whimsical carvings that ringed the rounded dome roof of Sumbrar's tower. The dragon draped her wings down over the smooth stone walls to steady her perch, then craned her neck down to look into the high, arched window of the upper tower. There the magi gathered to cast their Circle magic. She only hoped that they did not die of fright at the sudden appearance of her enormous, scaly silver visage in their window!

But to her surprise, the chamber was empty. Silent. No magi gathered to meet the coming threat. The dragon's first thought was that they did not know. Then her keen ears caught the sound of a rumbling deep within the caves of Sumbrar, and her senses quickened with the surge of magic that emanated from the depths of the outpost island.

As the Guardian watched, six ancient dragons burst from their age-long slumber and took to the sky. She watched in awe as the legendary heroes of her people leaped into flight as if from the pages of the lorebooks. Even so, her wonder was overwhelmed by a deep and profound feeling of dread. It was written that only in times of deepest peril would the Sleeping Ones be called forth.

The Guardian spread her silver wings and rose into the sky, setting a course for the Eagle Hills. There she would seek out the dragonriders, and learn what fate had befallen her elven partner. Shonassir Durothil had not responded to her silent call. Though she feared the answer, she must know what she—indeed, what all of Evermeet—faced.

* * * * *

Far from the shores of Evermeet, in a very different tower that stood in the shadow of Waterdeep's single mountain, another of Evermeet's guardians threw back her silvery head and let out a wail of mixed anguish and frustration.

Khelben Arunsun, the human mage who ruled this tower, came forward and gently pried the guardian's white-knuckled fingers from the gilded frame of her enchanted mirror.

"It is no good, Laeral," he said firmly, taking the woman by her shoulders and turning her to face him. "Everywhere, it is the same thing. All the gates to Evermeet have been barred. There is nothing you or I or anyone else can do to change this."

"But this elfgate is different! No one should be able to close it. Do you not remember how we struggled simply to conceal and move it?"

"If ever anything in this world went as it *should,* rather than as it *does,* it is possible that we would all perish from the shock," Khelben said without thought of humor. "Laeral, I would give anything if this were otherwise. You must accept that the battle for Evermeet is in the hands of her People."

The woman moaned and sank forward into the archmage's embrace. "We could make a difference, Khelben. You and I, my sisters. There must be a way we can help!"

The mage stroked Laeral's silvery hair, a strange shade that proclaimed her elven heritage and served as a reminder of the ties that bound the woman to Evermeet. Improbably, the human mage and the elven queen had long ago become fast friends, and Laeral wore on her finger one of the elfrunes that named her a trusted agent of Evermeet's queen. But even the magic of the ring had been silenced, its fey light blotted out by the strange pall that had fallen over the distant island.

Evermeet was truly alone.

"Trust in the elves," the archmage urged her. "They have weathered many storms, and may yet find their way to a port in this one."

Laeral slipped away from the shelter of Khelben's arms. "There is more," she whispered as tears began to spill down her cheeks. "Oh, there is more. I never told you about Maura. . . ."

* * * * *

Flying high above the trees of Evermeet, Maura clung to fistfuls of golden feathers and leaned down low over the giant eagle's neck. Her black hair whipped wildly about her in the rush of wind, and her face was grim as she scanned the ground below for sign of the elf-eater's passage.

Finally she caught sight of the monster as it crashed through a stream, sending water spraying wildly upward in sheets and flying droplets that glistened briefly in the bright morning light.

"Down here!" she shouted to her eagle mount, daring to let go with one hand in order to point. "Follow that thing!"

"Ooh. Big bug," the eagle commented as he eyed the domed carapace of the monstrous elf-eater. "Crack shell, get meat for many eagles. We two not-elves fight that?"

"Eventually. First we must fly past it to Corellon's Grove and warn the elves there of its approach. Do you know where it is?"

"Hmph! Know where every rabbit den is. You tell, I find. Fight soon, yes?"

"Soon," Maura agreed.

The eagle banked sharply as the elf-eater veered toward the east. Maura clutched at the bird's feathers as the eagle redoubled his efforts. The speed stole her breath; the buffeting force of his beating wings alone nearly tore her from her perch.

Fast though the eagle was, several moments passed before the giant bird was able to pull ahead of the monster. An eternity seemed to slip by before Maura caught sight of the elven temples.

"Set me down over there," she shouted, pointing to a domed, green-crystal shrine.

"Not sit there," the eagle countered. "See elf enemy by river, many many. Fish-people, very bad. We fight now, yes?"

"Fight now, not!" Maura screamed, letting go of one handhold to pound on the eagles' back. "Warn elves first!"

The bird darted a puzzled look over his shoulder. "You talk funny."

Maura shrieked in pure frustration. She leaned forward and talked loud and fast into the eagle's ear. "Your people know of the elf king? Well, his daughter is there in one of those buildings. If we don't get her away, the big bug will eat her!"

The eagle let out a piercing cry that matched Maura's for rage and surpassed it in sheer power. "Bug eat Zaor's elf-chick, not," he promised grimly. Without further warning, he swung around in a tight circle and then dipped into a screaming dive.

Racing wind tore at Maura's streaming clothes and stung her eyes into near-blindness. She buried her face in the eagle's neck feathers and clung to the creature with all her might. The sudden, frenetic battering of wings against wind warned her of their eminent landing. She lifted her head and squinted. Her eyes flew open wide, heedless of the painful wind.

They were flying directly toward the elf-eater's churning maw.

There was little that Maura could do, but she instinctively seized a knife from her belt to throw into that gaping, ravenous cavern—although she doubted it would inconvenience the monster in the slightest. Nor did she have any confidence that the eagle's attack would avail. The creature apparently thought that his giant hooked talons and rending beak were sufficient to the challenge. Unlike Maura, he had not seen the elf-eater at work.

"Up! Up!" she shrieked.

The eagle responded to the urgency in her voice. He tilted his wings to get the flow of wind beneath them and began to pull up into a soaring rise.

Too late. A long tentacle shot forward and seized the eagle by the leg. The bird came to a painfully abrupt halt. Maura did not. She sailed over the eagle's head and landed with bone-jarring force amid the flowers of one of the temple gardens.

Ignoring the surging pain that coursed through her every limb, the woman leaped to her feet, her dagger ready.

Sprays of golden feathers filled the air, mingling with the furious screams of the captured eagle. The giant bird put up a brave fight, but despite its struggles the monster drew it slowly, inexorably, toward its rapacious maw. Maura lifted her dagger high and started forward.

"Don't!" warned the eagle as its fierce eyes fell upon his fellow "not-elf." "Go find Zaor's elf-chick!"

For a moment the woman hesitated. It was not in her to leave an ally, or turn away from battle.

"Go!" screamed the eagle. He was jerked sharply toward the monster. There was a horrid crunching sound, and then his massive wings dropped limp.

Maura turned and ran for the tower that was Anghar-radh's temple. Even as she did, she realized that she was probably too late. If Ilyrana was anything like her younger brother, she would not use her clerical magic to flee from this place. The princess would try to stop the elf-eater, even at the cost of her life.

Maura found herself in sudden and complete accord with this, even though Ilyrana's death would mean Maura would almost certainly lose Lamruil to the duties of his clan and its crown.

The thought made her chest ache with a dull, hollow pain, but somehow her sorrow seemed a small thing compared with the evil facing her adopted home. She understood with her whole heart the choice that Lamruil had made, the choice that Ilyrana would almost certainly make. Nor could Maura do otherwise. If she could help Ilyrana, she would do it.

     * * * * *

Wave after wave of sahuagin invaders swarmed the coasts of Evermeet, overwhelming the elven vessels and slipping through to fight the elves hand to hand on the red-stained shores.

For two days the battle raged. When at last some of the creatures broke past the elven defenders, they roiled inland, taking to the Ardulith river and swimming up into the very heart of Evermeet. Behind them came the scrags, terrible creatures that devoured with grim delight any being that had fallen to the talons and tridents of the fishmen.

Along the way, villagers and fisherfolk gathered to do battle. Bonfires dotted the shores of the Ardulith, and clouds of oily smoke roiled into the skies as the elven fighters consigned the slain sea trolls to the flames.

In the waters beyond Evermeet's shore, the Sea elves struggled to hold back the tidal wave of invaders. But they, too, had been taken unawares by the massive, multisided attack. Those Sea elves on patrol fought as best they could, but all others were trapped inside their coral city by a siege force of enormous size. The kraken and the dragon turtle that patrolled the waters fed well, but even they could not hold back the swarms of sea creatures that swept over the elven shores.

The elven navy, the wonder of the seas, fared somewhat better. In the waters beyond Evermeet's magical shields, elven man-o-wars and swanships battled against a vast fleet of pirate ships. They sent ship after ship into Umberlee's arms. And better still, they cleared a safe way for several vessels that fled for Evermeet, closely—and deceptively—pursued by the pirates.

"Fools," Kymil Nimesin observed as he watched the fiery battle raging behind his ship.

Captain Blethis, the human who commanded the flag ship *Rightful Place,* licked his lips nervously. "That's nearly the last of our fleet, Lord Nimesin. There will soon be but six ships left."

"That will suffice," the Gold elf said calmly. "The elven ships will go one to various ports, as we agreed. One will go aground on the beaches of Siiluth, and from there our forces will march inland to take and hold Drelagara. The next will sail around to Nimlith, and hold that city. Continuing northward, we will take the Farmeadows. This victory is key, both for food supplies and the horses we will need to ride south and inland. From the east we attack three points: The Thayvians will sail to the northern city of Elion to engage and destroy the drow scum that hold the keep there—certainly, the dark elves' usefulness is ended."

"From what I've heard of drow, that task might be harder than the telling suggests," Blethis muttered.

Kymil Nimesin cast an arch look in his direction. "And have you also heard of the red wizard's magic? The two are well matched—in power as well as loathsomeness. Those few vermin who survive the encounter will be easy enough to dispatch. The problem with this invasion," he concluded dryly, "is not so much in the conquering, but in knowing how best to rid ourselves of our allies."

The captain kept silent, though the elf's words set him

to wondering how well he and the other humans would fare once the island was taken.

"We will accept the surrender of Lightspear Keep at Ruith," the elf continued. "And this ship, as planned, will enter the Leuthilspar bay to take over the court."

"You make it sound easy," Blethis commented.

"It has been anything but!" snapped the elf. "All my life, for more than six hundred years, I have been working toward this final attack. I have won and spent a dozen fortunes in funding it, formed alliances that will leave a stench on my soul throughout eternity! You have been told what you need to know. Believe me when I say that our ships will make port in a land that has been ravaged almost beyond repair."

"Almost, but not quite," Kymil added. "In times past, the People have rebuilt from less than we will leave them. The elves will merely be purified by this crucible, and the gold will rise above the dross at last. Evermeet will be restored in the image of ancient Aryvandaar. And from this place, the elves will once again reach out to expand and conquer."

It occurred to Blethis that the elf was no longer talking to him. Kymil Nimesin was reciting a litany, reliving the image that had ruled and shaped his centuries of life. Whether or not there was any truth in this vision, or even any sanity, the human could no longer say.

* * * * *

If Kymil Nimesin could have seen the battle playing out amid the temples of Corellon's Grove, it is possible that he himself would have doubted the sanity of his quest. Not even his blind zeal could excuse the unleashing of Malar's vengeance upon the elven homeland.

The elf-eater battered through a circle of standing stone, and a score of writhing tentacles reached out to ensnare the cluster of forest elf shaman who chanted spells of warding. As carelessly as a courtesan might pluck at a bunch of grapes, the monster thrust one elf after another into its churning maw. A few of the elves fled into the forest. Most stayed, fighting back with whatever weapons of steel or faith or magic they had at hand.

From her window in a high tower of Angharradh's temple, the princess Ilyrana gazed in horror at the carnage below. Her memory cast up an image of the last time she had seen this creature—during the terrible destruction of the Synnorian elves of the Moonshae Islands. It had been a day beyond horror, and the worst of it was witnessing the disappearance of a blue-haired elven lad into that ravenous maw. Which of her younger brothers had met this fate, she never knew, nor had she ever been able to learn if the other twin had somehow survived. The failure she had felt then, the utter impotence of a young and untried priestess, washed over her anew.

A young human female, scarlet-clad and decidedly disheveled, skidded into the room. It took Ilyrana a moment to recognize her as Laeral Elf-friend's daughter.

The woman propped her fists on her hips and glared at the princess. "The way I see it, you can either fight or flee—but you've got to pick one of those *now!*"

"Maura, isn't it?" Ilyrana murmured in her gentle voice.

"Not for long it isn't, unless you take action." The woman drew her sword and stepped to the door.

For a moment the elven priestess thought Maura intended to force her to flee. She realized, suddenly, that she did not wish to do so. She would stay and she would fight

Maura, who was keenly observing the princess's face, nodded with satisfaction. "Do what you must—I will stand guard as long as I am able."

The elven priestess reached out for the magical threads that bound her to Arvandor. A familiar presence flooded her mind in silent rebuke even as a tendril of warmth and strength stole into her benumbed thoughts. She sank deep into the mystic prayer, opening herself fully to Angharradh, her goddess.

303

The mystery that Ilyrana had contemplated her whole life suddenly seemed to have been laid out plainly before her. Angharradh, the goddess that was three and yet one, was not so very different from the other gods of the Seldarine. Nor was she so different from the unique magic that sustained Evermeet. Many, and yet one. Perhaps the magi were not the only elves who could summon a Circle's combined magical strength.

Ilyrana closed her eyes and sank deeper still into the meditative prayer, until the power of the goddess seemed to flow through her like air, binding her in silver threads to the web. She reached out, seeking the power of the other priest and priestesses. One by one, she reached out to touch the startled minds of desperately praying clerics of Hanali Celanil, Aerdrie, Sehanine Moonbow—all of the goddesses whose essence was mirrored in Angharradh. They were many, yet they became one, even as the goddess herself had been given birth.

As an awareness of Ilyrana's spell spread through the embattled grove, the priests and priestess of all the gods of the Seldarine followed the princess, lending the force of their prayers and their magic to this not-quite-mortal child of Angharradh.

Ilyrana gathered their combined power, instinctively forming it into a new and terrible goddess form. In response to the collective prayer, a warrior maiden clad in gleaming plate armor rose from the soil of Evermeet. Tall as an ancient oak, she held a spear the size of a ship's mast.

The warrior stood her ground as the elf-eater thundered toward her, and thrust her spear's point deep into the monster's mouth. With all her strength she pushed the blunt end of the spear down, levering it toward the ground. Then she dug in her heels, and held on.

The impaling spear thrust deep, abruptly stopping the monster's headlong rush. Although the mighty shaft bent like an arched bow, although the wood shrieked and groaned and crackled from the strain, the warrior did not release her hold. Then, suddenly, she threw herself backward, preleasing the spear.

As the lowered end of the spear sprang straight and high, the creature was thrust violently in the opposite direction. It flipped, landing on its rounded carapace and rocking like an up-ended turtle. Its three massive legs churned the air and its tentacles flailed wildly, but it could not right itself.

One of the tentacles found and seized the warrior, wrapping around her arm and pulling her close. The magical elf drew a knife and severed the limb, then ripped the clinging length from her arm. Circles of blood welled up on her arm where the tentacle's suction cups had found purchase, but the warrior paid no attention to these wounds.

The warrior maiden took a gossamer net from her belt and whirled it briefly. It flew over the creature, entangling it in a silvery web of magic. She turned to the tower, nodding toward the watchful elven princess who had given her form and substance. And then she was gone, and the elf-eater with her.

Gone, too, were many of the clerics, for their spirits had been bound up in the casting. Of all the elves who had raised the warrior goddess from their combined power, only Ilyrana lingered.

But her spirit, too, had flown. As Maura knelt beside the too-still princess, she noted a pattern of bloody circles upon the flesh of one white arm.

The woman ran to the window and called for help. The surviving clerics hurried to her aid, but nothing any of the survivors could do had any effect on Ilyrana's deathless slumber.

At last they somberly prepared to take the princess to Leuthilspar. If anyone would understand this unfathomable blending of the mortal elf with the divine, it would be Queen Amlaruil herself.

Maura went with them. As she tended the princess, she noted with dread and fascination that other wounds

Elaine Cunningham

appeared on the elfwoman's silent form. It seemed that somewhere, in some battle that only the gods could witness, Ilyrana was fighting still.

Book Four

The Royal Family

"Duty to clan and family, to people and homeland—this is the truth that guides the life path and heats the fighting blood of the Moonshae Ffolk. But I've come to learn in these many years of my life that the honor held so dear by my highland kin is but a pale thing compared to that of the elves. 'Tis a truth that makes me humble indeed before these wondrous folk—and, I admit in all candor, more than a wee bit frightened."

—Excerpt from a letter from Carreigh Macumail: Captain
of *Mist-Walker*,
Friend of the People—

15

The Moonblades (-9000 DR)

he claiming of the king-making swords was set for twilight on the eve of the summer solstice—a time of powerful magic. From all over Aber-toril, elven nobles gathered in the forests of Cormanthyr for the ceremony. With them came High Magi, three hundred of them, one for each of the swords.

When the sun began to sink below its zenith, they all gathered in a broad valley. Ethlando awaited them, standing in a vast circle of swords lying with the hilts turned outward. The magi took their places, as well, standing within the parameters of the swords, near to but not touching the points of the gleaming blades.

Anticipation hung heavy in the air—even the birds seemed hushed as they listened to Ethlando's magically enhanced voice describe at last the full role of the magic swords.

"Many years ago, I was given a spell by Corellon Larethian himself," Ethlando began, his voice resonant and sure despite his great age, and flavored with the quaint accent of lost Aryvandaar. "This spell have I taught to these magi. Its magic will give to the swords two things that no other magic weapon possesses: the ability to determine what powers it will possess, and the judgment to chose who is worthy to wield these powers."

The ancient mage cast a slow, searching glance over the gathered elves. On each face, he saw written confidence, expectation. No one among the assemblage appeared to think himself less than worthy of this honor. Ethlando hoped that not too many would die before they learned otherwise.

"Each clan has chosen and sent representatives. Many who will claim the swords today come from ancient lines, and they can point with pride to many illustrious ancestors. This is a fine thing, but it is not the measure that the swords will use."

A few brows furrowed in puzzlement or consternation as the elves contemplated these words. How else would a royal house be chosen, but for the honor of lineage?

Ethlando took this as a good sign. At least they were thinking.

"Today, the swords will select their first wielders. In time, they will chose a worthy clan with a proven succession. You see, these are hereditary blades, meant to be passed down to worthy descendants for as long as the line lasts. Claiming a sword will become more difficult as time goes on, for the sword will choose only those who have the potential strength and the character to wield *all* of the powers of the sword. With each passing generation, the task will grow more difficult."

"How will we know if the sword has chosen us?"

Ethlando turned to face the young elf who asked the question. "If you are still alive, you have been deemed worthy."

The seer let this statement hang for several moments in the silence. "Yes, the swords—the moonblades—will take the life of any who are not worthy. This may seem harsh, but consider how great the power of these weapons will be when ten generations have past! Safeguards must be taken, lest their magic fall into evil hands and evil use. Once a sword is claimed, only the sword's rightful wielder can unsheathe it and live."

The elves nodded cautiously as they considered the practicalities involved in safeguarding weapons so potentially powerful. None spoke, though, for all were intent upon hearing the seer's words.

"Any elf can decline the honor of inheritance. There is no compulsion today, nor will there ever be. But know this: those who lay hold of a moonblade also pledge themselves to the service of the People. They do so at great cost.

"The magic each wielder adds to the sword is that part of the Weave that the elf calls his own. You will serve the sword and the People after your death, and forgo the joys of Arvandor. Yet this is not an eternal sentence," Ethlando added quickly. "When the sword's work is done, it becomes dormant. Its magic flees—and the essence of all its wielders is released to Arvandor."

The seer paused to let each elf absorb the magnitude of the commitment, then turned to the matter for which they all had gathered.

"The moonblades will select a royal family through two means. First, the swords will narrow down the field. In a few millenia, only a few worthy clans will still hold blades. These will demonstrate a proven succession of worthy elves. It is possible that a few thousand years hence, some clans might yet have more than one blade in service to the People.

"Second, the powers with which a particular sword is imbued will determine the clan's worthiness to rule. Some swords will become formidable weapons for highly skilled fighters, others will become like the mage's staffs that hold spellpower. One, or perhaps two or three, will become such a sword as a king might wield."

Ethlando let the words echo long. "There is one thing I would ask of you. This is not the directive of the gods, but my own request. Do not let more than two elves from any one clan fail this day. If you so desire, an unclaimed sword may be kept by the clan in trust for some future wielder to use in the service of the People. But understand that those clans who do not succeed today, bear little hope of aspiring to Evermeet's throne.

"Now is the time to speak, if you have any questions. This is not a choice to be made lightly. No elf will be thought the less of for choosing not to claim a moonblade, now or ever. There are many ways to serve the People. This is but one."

Predictably enough, there was no sound but the restless shifting of elven feet, no emotion written on the waiting faces but confidence of the outcome—and impatience to begin.

Ethlando smiled ruefully. "Very well, then. These are the last words you will have of me. When the casting is done, the magi will see to the ceremony of choosing."

The ancient elf's eyes drifted shut, and he began to sway as he hummed an eerie melody. One by one, the circle of magi took up the weird casting. Before the wondering eyes of the elven throng, Ethlando began to glow with faint blue light. His form grew translucent, shimmering with gathering power. The chanting magi, themselves enchanted, began to add words to their spell, albeit words that no mortal elf had heard or spoken before. Ethlando's form took on height and power as the spell drew magic from the Weave, and wisdom from the gods.

Finally the spell ended on a single high, ringing note. Ethlando's glowing form burst apart as if he were a crystal shattered by sound. The light that was Ethlando shot out like rays from a cerulean sun. Blue bolts of magic and power flashed to each of the moonblades. The swords were suddenly alive with magic, and glowing with intense blue light.

The watching elves flung up hands to ward off the sudden brilliant flare. When their eyes adjusted to the magical light, they saw that though the moonblades were still alight, Ethlando was gone.

The meaning of this was clear to all. It had been as Ethlando said: The power of the moonblades would be fashioned from the essence of the noble elves who would wield them. The first power, that which formed the basis for all that would follow, was the ability to see and to judge. Who better for this task, than the revered seer himself?

A moment of reverent silence passed before one of the High Magi spoke. "Three hundred swords, three hundred elves. Let the clans who aspire to Evermeet, step forward."

Without hesitation the first representatives of the clans came. The elves formed a circle around the glowing blades, knelt briefly in prayer to the gods and dedication to the People. At a signal from the magi, they reached as one for the hilts of their moonblades.

Blue light ripped through the valley, and an explosion sent shudders through the ancient trees. In the heavy silence that followed, fewer than two hundred elves rose to their feet, glowing swords in their hands. The others lay dead, blasted by the magical fire.

Disbelief and horror was etched upon the countenance of every witness. The slain elves were some of the finest fighters, the greatest mages! If they were not worthy, who could be?

And yet, the answer stood before them. One hundred and seventy-two elves slipped moonblades into the empty scabbards on their belts and stepped away from the circles. Their faces were alight, not with pride, but with awe.

The High Mage spoke again. "Those clans who wish to attempt a second claim, may do so now. First, remove your dead, and remember them with pride. There is no dishonor in their death. It is given to some creatures to fly, others to swim, and still others to hunt. Not every elf is gifted with the potential to reign, and not every clan carries the seed of kings and queens."

It was apparent, however, that most of the elves present felt that their clan was destined for this honor. Every one of the failed clans sent members forward to try again. This time, only two elves were left standing.

"Moon elves," murmured Claire Durothil, a young mage who stood fourth in line for the honor of establishing her clan's succession. "All those who carry the blades are of the Moon elf people! What does this mean?"

Her question rippled through the crowd, murmurs that swiftly grew to the fury of a tempest. Finally the Coronal, the elf who sat at the head of Cormanthyr's council, came forward to quell the angry elves.

"It is true that Ethlando suggested that only Moon elves be given the trial," he admitted. "He argued that as a race, the Moon people are best equipped by temperament and inclination to deal with the folk of other races. We elves have become the few among the many. Ethlando feared that rulers who sought to blind themselves to the realities of a changing world, would lack the insight and knowledge needed to keep Evermeet secure."

"And you let us try, knowing all this?" Claire Durothil demanded.

The Coronal sighed. "Would the knowing have changed your choice? Even now, is there any among you who wish to try a third time?"

The silence was long and heavy. Then, ten Gold elves stepped forward to claim their clan's honor.

Heartsick, the elves watched as all ten were reduced to ash and charred bone.

When the clans carried the remnants of their slain kin away, Claire Durothil stepped forward.

"I claim a moonblade in the name of the Durothil clan. This is my right, by the word of Ethlando. Though I do not profess to understand all that has happened this day, it may well be that the Gold elves are not destined to rule Evermeet. But I am certain that there have been many great and worthy elves in my family, and that there will be many more. Give me this blade, and an elf of my clan will claim it when the time is right."

The High Mage slipped a sheath over the blade, then handed the muted weapon to the Gold elf. Clair took the sheathed weapon without hesitation or fear, and then returned to her somber clan.

Several more Gold elves followed her example. The Nimesin, the Ni'Tessine, and the Starym all carried away unclaimed blades that day.

Silently, all the elves acknowledged that there was honor in this, for surely a time would come when the sword would chose the proper wielder. And Ethlando did not say that it was *impossible* that a Gold elf might gain the throne, only that it was *unlikely*.

Long into the night the rite of claiming went on. Some Moon elf clans claimed several blades—even a few commoners gained that night a magic sword, and with it the right to found a noble house. There was no protest, no contention over the results, for there was no denying the power at work among them. Most of the Gold elves were willing to bide their time, to wait out the succession process. Few of them believed that they were entirely excluded.

When dawn crept over the valley, it found no sign of magic, or death, or the elves whose kindred had earned one or the other. The People had returned to their homes to ponder what had happened. Many years would pass before the rulers of Evermeet were chosen. Yet every elf who now carried a moonblade knew that regardless of how the test of succession played out, a great destiny would be his.

16

The King Sword
(715 DR)

light snow fell upon the forests of Evermeet.
Big, downy flakes whirled and spun as they
drifted through the winter-bare trees. A few
of the flakes clung to Zaor Moonflower's
hair, looking like icy stars amid the twilight
sheen of the elf's luxuriant, dark-blue locks.

But Zaor was oblivious to the beauty of the forest and
the striking image he himself presented. He was an elf in
the prime of life, and had seen and done much in his two
centuries. Though the passing years had left little mark
on him, no one who set eyes upon him would mistake him
for a callow youth.

For one thing, Zaor was exceedingly tall, and nearly as
muscular as a human warrior. At more than a hand-
breadth over six feet, he was a giant among elves. His
coloring was striking as well, for his hair was the most
unusual color known to the Moon elf people—a deep,
glowing blue that brought to mind sapphires or stormy
seas.

And there was nothing of youth in Zaor's eyes. They
were also blue, and flecked with gold, yet their natural
luster was dimmed by a deep and profound sadness.
Those eyes had seen more battle, more death, more
horror, than most elves who could claim his years and
more.

Zaor had not been long in Evermeet. He was one of the
few survivors of Myth Drannor's fall who had sought
refuge in the island kingdom.

But for Zaor, Evermeet brought no peace. Even a year after that final siege, his ears still echoed with the cries of dying Myth Drannor, and he still felt the emptiness, like a physical pain, left behind when the mithal that had upheld the wondrous city had been destroyed.

Indeed, Zaor had found nothing but bitterness in the company of the island's elves. The people of fabled Leuthilspar, with their endless petty intrigues and their deeply entrenched sense of privilege, simply galled him. Perhaps if they had spent a quarter of their hoarded wealth and wasted energies on the defense of Myth Drannor, the city might not have fallen!

But even as the thought formed, Zaor knew there was little truth in it. All his life he had battled the foes who pressed the wondrous city. That was his task, and his calling. He was a ranger, and the forests surrounding Myth Drannor were his to keep. And because he was a ranger, he had not been within the walls during the final siege, and thus he had survived the last, terrible battle.

Zaor Moonflower had survived, but the guilt of his continued existence pressed heavily upon him.

It did not seem right, that he should be alive when so many thousands—indeed, a whole civilization—had died. He felt he could not bear to see such a thing happen again. Yet the elves of Evermeet—who were so like the people of Myth Drannor in their pride and complacency—were as much at risk as that lost city had been.

Zaor sighed and lowered his gaze to the fresh blanket of snow, willing his mind to imitate the smooth, untroubled surface.

His eyes narrowed as they fell upon a strange mark. The elf dropped to one knee to examine it more closely. The mark was like that of a horse's hoof, but slightly cloven and far more delicate. And it was not so much a print, but a glittering shadow upon the snow.

Only one creature would leave such a trail. Wonder—a feeling that Zaor had thought was forever banished from his heart—flowed over him in rippling waves. Silently, carefully, the ranger followed the silvery prints deep into the forest and into a snow-shrouded glade.

The sight before him stole his breath. Two unicorns—wondrous creatures whose coats were so white as to render them nearly invisible against the unblemished snow—broke away from the pristine background. They minced toward the center of the glade, tossing their silvery horns and nickering softly.

This was wonder enough, but Zaor found his eyes lingering less on the rare and magical creatures than on the pair of elven maidens who awaited the unicorns with outstretched hands.

Both of the maidens were Moon elves, and by the looks of them initiates of some religious order. They were clad in simple white robes and swathed in white cloaks, and there was a stillness about them that came only with strenuous training and great personal discipline. With their snow-colored garments, milky skin and bright red tresses, they looked like statues fashioned from ice and flame.

Zaor watched, barely breathing, as the unicorns came up and nuzzled the maidens' outstretched hands. One of them, a tall girl whose hair fell in a riot of tangled curls about her shoulders, sprang onto her unicorn's back.

"Come, Amlaruil," she chided when the other girl held back. "Why do you wait? The unicorns have accepted us—we can leave behind the stuffy towers for good and all, and seek adventure at last!"

The other girl's face was wistful, but she shook her head even as she caressed the second unicorn's silky mane. "You know I cannot, Ialantha. This is your dream, and I wish you well of it, but my place is elsewhere." She smiled up at her friend. "Think of me, from time to time, when you are captain of the unicorn riders."

The girl called Ialantha snorted, as if amused by such visions of grandeur. "All I want is a bit of excitement and an open sky! A year and a day—that is all the service a unicorn will give! And after that, I will be on to the next adventure."

"We can set our feet upon a path, but we cannot always choose where that path might take us," Amlaruil said seriously. She reached out and patted her friend's fey mount. "I think you have found not only a year's partner, but a destiny."

Ialantha's eyes widened. "You have seen this for me, then?"

The girl hesitated. "There is need for unicorn riders," she said carefully. "I think this unicorn has chosen well. You could ride before you could walk, and you were reaching for a sword before you could do either! No one in the Towers rides or fights as well as you. Who better than you to revive the old ways, and to train and command the swordmaidens?"

"Who indeed?" Ialantha echoed teasingly. Her face turned serious, and she extended her hand to her friend. The girls clasped wrists with the gravity of warriors.

Ialantha lifted her white hood to conceal her bright hair, and then tapped her heels against the unicorn's sides. The creature reared, pawing the air with hoofs as delicate as the falling snow. With the speed of thought, the unicorn and her rider melted away into the forest. The second, riderless unicorn followed like a white shadow.

After a moment, Amlaruil turned toward the thicket where Zaor crouched. "You might as well come out now," she said in a clear, bell-like voice. "I will do you no harm."

Zaor's first response was mingled surprise and chagrin that the elf maid perceived his presence so easily. Then the irony of her remark struck Zaor as rather amusing. The girl seemed to be little more than a child, and slim as a birch tree and by all appearances fragile as a dream. She might make half his weight, had she been soaking wet.

But he rose and entered the clearing, stopping several paces from her as propriety demanded.

He managed a bow that he thought would not disgrace him too badly. "Zaor Moonflower, at the etrielle's service," he said, using the polite term for an elven female of honorable birth and character.

The girls' large, blue eyes lit up like stars. "Oh! Then we are kin! I am of the Moonflower clan, also. How is it we have never met?"

Zaor managed, just barely, to hold her gaze. "I am recently come from Cormanthyr."

He steeled himself for the usual barrage of questions, or the formal expressions of regret, or the words of acclaim lavished upon the "heroes" of Myth Drannor. To his relief, the girl merely nodded. "That explains it, then. My name is Amlaruil."

"I heard."

"I know." Her sudden smile lent her face such beauty that Zaor had to drop his eyes to keep from staring. A moment before, she had seemed nothing but a skinny child with long red-gold plaits of hair and huge, serious eyes. The fleeting smile transformed her into the reflection of a goddess.

Zaor took a moment to compose his thoughts. "You spoke of a Tower."

"Yes. I am a student of High Magic at the Towers of the Sun and Moon. They are not far from here."

The ranger frowned. "I have never seen these towers."

"Nor will you, unless you know where to look." The girl laughed at the aggrieved expression that crossed Zaor's face. "Do not take offense—the magic that shields the towers hides them even from the birds and wood nymphs. But rest assured, you will see them one day."

Zaor's brows lifted at this odd pronouncement. There was a strange note in her voice as she spoke these last few words, an abstracted tone that had been missing a moment before.

"You sound very certain of this. Can you read portents, then?" he asked, thinking to humor the child.

"Sometimes," she said in all seriousness. "It is easier to do if the person carries an object of power. I do not know why that is, but it is so."

Her eyes fell to the sword on Zaor's hip. Although sheathed, the ornate hilt with its crowning moonstone gem was clearly visible. Before Zaor could divine her intent, she reached out and ran her fingertips over the smooth, milky surface of the stone.

With an oath, Zaor jerked away. No one could safely touch such a sword but the wielder—surely the foolish child knew that!

But apparently she did not. Amlaruil regarded him in surprise, her eyes wide. After a moment Zaor realized that she had gone unscathed. The slender fingers that by all rights should have been blackened by a blast of killing magic were as smooth and white as the winter snow.

For some reason, this shook Zaor almost as deeply as the thought that the girl had come to harm through his carelessness. "You should never touch such a sword," he told her sternly. "This is a moonblade, and can mean death to any but he who wields it."

Amlaruil's eyes grew still wider. "A moonblade. Oh, then that explains . . ." Her voice trailed off uncertainly and her gaze slid to one side.

"You really did see something, didn't you?" he asked, intrigued.

The girl nodded, her face grave. "This is the king sword. Who rules this sword, will also rule Evermeet."

Zaor stared at her, not wanting to believe the words she spoke with such uncanny certainty. Yet there was something about the girl that lent weight to her words. He believed her, even if he did not wish to do so.

"There is nothing of the king about me," he said dully. How could there be? It was the final duty of any elven king to die for his people. Myth Drannor lay dead, and he stood hale and unblemished, half a world away in the glades of Evermeet. "My children, perhaps, might someday serve—that is, if their mother can make up for my lacks."

"Perhaps," she echoed in a tone that gave away nothing of her thoughts.

Zaor shook aside the girl's troubling pronouncement and turned to something that lay closer to his ken. "You touched the sword without harm. How can that be?"

Suddenly, Amlaruil did not look so much a child as she had a moment before. A faint flush stained the snow of her cheeks. "As to that, I cannot say," she murmured.

"Cannot, or will not?" Zaor pressed.

Again, that incandescent smile. "Yes," was all she said.

The elves joined in a burst of laughter. It seemed to Zaor that suddenly the burden that had weighed down his heart for so long was easier to bear.

After the shared laughter faded, they stood gazing at each other for a long moment. Amlaruil was first to break the silence. "I must return to the Towers. I have been away too long."

"We will meet again, though?"

The girl hesitated, as if not sure how to answer. Then slowly, deliberately, she reached out and curled her fingers around the hilt of Zaor's sword.

And then she was gone, disappearing into the forest as quickly and silently as the elusive unicorns.

In the white silence of the woodland glade, Zaor bowed his head and struggled to absorb what had just happened. In the passing of a few moments, his life had been utterly changed. One burden—the terrible load of guilt and grief—had been lifted; another, still greater burden had taken its place.

Amlaruil's vision for him was beyond anything Zaor had ever imagined. Even so, he found he had no desire to shy away from it.

The ranger turned and headed southward with a swift and determined stride. All that he had seen and suffered, all the lessons he had learned to his sorrow, he would share. He would find a way to make the complacent elves of Leuthilspar hear what he had to say. Evermeet would not suffer the same fate as Myth Drannor, not while Zaor Moonflower lived.

Even as he made this silent vow, Zaor drew the moonblade—the king sword—from its sheath. He was not surprised to note that a new rune was etched upon the blade. Amlaruil's vision was now his own, and the magical sword he carried had responded with the needed power. No longer did he fear or doubt the destiny before him.

Who ruled the sword, would also rule Evermeet.

* * * * *

Keryth Blackhelm shook his head. "It won't work, Zaor," he said ruefully. "I'm too young—I've yet to reach my first centennial! Nor am I nobly born. By the gods, I can't even name my father, much less trace my ancestors back into Faerie and beyond! The Leuthilspar guard will have nothing to do with the likes of me, and you know it well."

"I know that you possess the finest mind of any battlemaster I've met," the ranger insisted.

With a wry grin, Keryth lifted his cup as if to toast himself. "And the strongest sword arm, too."

"We'll contest that matter another day," Zaor retorted good-naturedly. "But if you haven't the sense to pick a battle you've a hope of winning, perhaps I will have to revise my opinion of your skills as battlemaster!"

The friends joined in a brief chuckle. The third member of their trio, a slight, silver-haired Moon elf about Keryth's age, fixed a thoughtful gaze upon Zaor. "You have a plan," he observed.

"A plan? I wouldn't put it quite that high," Zaor said in a dry tone. "A notion, perhaps. If it works, then we'll call it a plan."

"Agreed. What's your notion, then?"

"It seems to me that an elf's worth must be proven, and that there is no time like the moment at hand."

Myronthilar Silverspear nodded, as if this made perfect sense. He put down his cup and swept the tavern with his calm silver gaze. "By Corellon, it looks as if half the city guard drinks in this place!"

"The half that's on duty, no doubt," Keryth put in.

"All the better." Zaor turned to Myronthilar. "You first?"

The small elf lifted a silver brow. "But of course."

Myron hopped lightly from his stool and strolled over to where a cluster of guards, Gold elves all, lolled indolently over a table littered with bottles and goblets. One of them eyed the Moon elf with a supercilious smile, then elbowed his neighbor. He said something that sent a ripple of laughter through the group.

Watching this, Zaor lifted a hand to his lips to hide a smirk. The haughty elves were due for a lesson in the importance of open minds and keen observation. Had they the wit to look beyond their first impression, they would never have discounted the small Moon elf.

There was a remarkable economy about Myronthilar's every movement, a precision and purpose to each step and gesture. He was like a dagger: slender, finely honed, perfectly balanced—and deadly. The results of this encounter, Zaor mused, would be a good start to the necessary reeducation of Evermeet's elves.

Myronthilar stopped and regarded the assembly soberly. "Well met, Saida Evanara," he said politely, regarding a suddenly wary Gold elf female. "I'm afraid I must be the bearer of ill news. Myth Drannor has fallen."

The female's eyes narrowed. "And well I know it. I was there until the final battle ended!"

"Yes, I have heard minstrels sing that tale," Myron said. "*Paid* minstrels. There are others, though, whose stories claim that you ran like a rat." He looked around the elegant taproom. "Of course, such as they would never perform in so fine an establishment as this."

Saida's face flushed with outrage. "How dare you! Never in my life have I been so insulted!"

"Actually, that is not entirely true. You really ought to

listen to a wider range of bardic tales," Myron said helpfully.

One of the guards leaped to his feet and stood menacingly over the diminutive Moon elf. "Have a care how you speak. Saida Evanara is my kinswoman," he said in a low, ominous tone.

"You have my sympathy," the Moon elf returned. "Of course, since none of us can chose our kin, I shall not hold that against you."

The elf scowled and reached for his sword with a slow, dramatic flourish. A look of utter befuddlement crossed his face when his fingers closed around an empty scabbard. His puzzled frown was chased away by an expression of sheer panic as he regarded the length of steel at this throat. It was very familiar steel. Myron had beat him to the draw—and with his own sword!

The Moon elf lifted the "borrowed" blade to his forehead in a mocking salute.

Saida hissed with rage and leaped to her feet. Before she could draw her weapon, Myron tossed her the stolen blade. Instinctively, she caught it, and then lunged. The Moon elf dodged, spun, and parried Saida's second attack—with her sword.

With her free hand, Saida groped at the scabbard at her hip, unwilling to believe the evidence of her eyes. It was indeed empty. Her eyes narrowed with malevolence.

"You're quick, Gray," the Evanara warrior admitted as she shifted into battle stance. "But when I'm finished with you, you'll think you've been stomped by a warhorse!"

"I've heard that," Myron said conversationally. "You really ought to chose lovers less inclined to bemoan their experiences."

"Enough!" snarled the guard whose sword Saida wielded. "By Corellon, I will have your hide tanned for shoe leather!"

The enraged elf leaped at Myronthilar. He never came

close. In fact, he never touched the floor. Instead, he found himself gasping for air, his feet dangling, as he looked into the eyes of the biggest elf he had ever seen— a blue-haired giant who held him aloft with one hand by the collar of his uniform, as a boy might hoist a puppy by the scruff of the neck.

"As you can see, the quessir is already engaged," Zaor said, referring to Myron in the term reserved for noble elven males. "If it is the custom of the guard to fight two and three against one, by all means—choose an assortment of your comrades and I will be happy to oblige you."

The elf's face, already red from his struggle for air, turned purple with rage. Three of the guards leaped to their feet and rushed to his defense. The Moon elf casually tossed his captive at them, bringing all four down in a heap.

Myron and Saida were fully engaged now, and the ring and clash of their weapons filled the tavern with grim music. The remaining two guards rose from the table to take the blue-haired elf's challenge. They reached for their swords, only to find that their scabbards were empty, as well.

They whirled. Behind them stood Keryth, a sword in each hand. "Excuse me," he said politely, walking past the bemused elves to hand one of the blades to Zaor. He turned the other sword and offered it hilt-first to its owner.

"My apologies for the inconvenience, but you see, my friend cannot fight you with his own sword. Bad form, you know, using a moonblade in a tavern brawl—especially against honorable People such as yourselves."

In almost comic unison, the guards turned to stare at the sword on Zaor's hip. A mixture of chagrin and grudging respect dawned on their faces. One of the elves, a raven-haired male who wore the insignia of a captain, rose to his feet. He wiped a line of blood from his chin with his sleeve and eyed Zaor with genuine curiosity.

"What's this about, then?"

"I wish to apply for a position in the guard," Zaor said.

A dry chuckle escaped the captain. "You chose an unusual way to do so! Why didn't you just come right out and say you were a moonfighter? No order or regiment would refuse you."

"Had I done so, would you have considered my friends, as well?"

"No," the captain admitted. "Though they are as quick and skilled as any elf under my command."

Zaor tactfully declined to point out the obvious flaw in the captain's claim. "The three of us, then," he pressed.

The Gold elf shrugged. "Done."

At that moment a sharp thud resounded through the tavern. They turned, observing as Saida gritted her teeth and tugged at the blade embedded in the living wood of the tavern wall. Myronthilar, who had just sidestepped her lunge, was examining his fingernails in an exaggerated gesture of patience.

"One more thing. Call off your lieutenant before she takes the edge off her kinsman's blade," Zaor requested dryly.

The captain sniffed, as if in derisive agreement. He slanted a look up at the blue-haired elf. "What your friend said of Saida Evanara's courage in battle—was there any truth to it, or was he merely taunting her to start this fight?"

Zaor shrugged. "As to that, you must judge for yourself. Myronthilar Silverspear's words had a purpose, and they served their purpose well. Saida Evanara is under your command. Her measure is not mine to take."

"Fair enough." The captain cupped his hands to his mouth and shouted, "Hold!"

Myron responded instantly, dancing back out of his opponent's reach and dropping his sword to a low guard. He inclined his head to Saida, the respectful gesture of one fighter to another to mark the end of an honorable practice match.

But the female stood still, her sword poised for a

strike and her entire body quivering with rage and indecision.

"I said *hold!*" snapped the captain. He strode over to the elf woman and seized her wrist. Saida's gaze snapped onto his face. Her eyes grew wary, then guarded.

"On your command," she agreed, then added, "I would not have struck, captain."

The Gold elf searched her face. "I wonder," he murmured.

He dropped her wrist and turned away. "Follow me to the guards barracks. You have much to learn."

The three Moon elves exchanged triumphant smiles and fell into step behind the captain. But the Gold elf whirled, and fixed a stare upon the company of guards behind them.

"I was talking," he said grimly, "to *you.*"

* * * * *

Lady Mylaerla Durothil, the formidable matriarch who headed the city's most powerful Gold elf clan, regarded her visitor with interest.

She was not a young elf, and had left the midpoint of her mortal life behind many summers past. But she was not too old to appreciate so handsome an elf as the one who sat before her. If the young captain of the guard had charm enough to waste on an old elf woman, why not give him the chance to use it? More, his plan intrigued her.

"You are certain that Ahskahala Durothil is of my kindred?" Mylaerla asked.

"Beyond a doubt," Zaor said stoutly. "I have made a study of the Durothil linage, and can assure you that she, like you, is a direct descendant of the Rolim Durothil who first settled Evermeet. Her ancestors fought against the dragonflight in the year of Malar's Great Hunt. She is a worthy descendant of all these illustrious elves; moreover, she is the finest, fiercest dragonrider I have ever seen."

"Is it so? Then how is it that she survived Myth

Drannor's fall, when so many fine, fierce warriors did not?"

It was a hard question, but an important one. Nearly as important was the manner in which Zaor posed the answer.

"Ahskahala has little patience with the habits and concerns of city dwellers," he said carefully. "She preferred to live in the wild places, and she served the People of Cormanthyr by guarding the outposts. But for her efforts, the city would have fallen much sooner than it did. More than one marauding band of orcs or goblins met their end due to her diligence. But her dragon was wounded during the early days of the siege, stranding both of them in their mountain lair. When at last they could take flight, the time for battle had passed."

"Hmm. How would we contact this dragonrider?"

Zaor inclined his head in a gesture of respect. "The abilities of House Durothil in matters of communication are legendary. I do not think this task would pose much challenge to your magi."

"Well said. But what makes you think she would come to Evermeet now?" the elf woman asked shrewdly. "What gain would she hope to find here? Power? Honor? Wealth?"

"Ahskahala has seen one elven culture fall. She would not wish the same on another."

Mylaerla blinked, startled by the young warrior's bluntness. "You think it possible that Evermeet could share Myth Drannor's fate?"

"Don't you?"

For a long moment, the elves regarded each other keenly. Then Mylaerla leaned back in her chair, and a mask seemed to drop from her face.

"You are more right than you know about many things, Zaor Moonflower," she said bitterly. "I cannot tell you how weary I am of the Durothil clan's endless concern with magic-aided chitchat. It was not always so. The first dragonrider was a Durothil—*the* Durothil. Did you know that?"

Not waiting for an answer, she hissed out an earthy curse and shook her head in frustration. "My clan are descendants of Durothil, and what have we become? Effete, tower-bound layabouts, content to waste our brief centuries of life using magic to exchange gossip and to peek into distant bedchambers! Bah!"

Zaor leaned forward. "There are yet dragons on Evermeet, are there not?"

Mylaerla considered this. "I believe so, yes. I've heard talk of fairly recent sightings of a gold and a mated pair of silvers flying above the Eagle Hills." She lifted an inquiring eyebrow. "If Ahskahala is all you say, I doubt she would have much difficulty in training the dragons to this task. My concern is this: How would she deal with the Durothils of Evermeet and their ilk?"

"Your kindred will not have an easy time of it," Zaor admitted.

The elf woman nodded. "Good," she said with grim satisfaction. "In that case, we will send for her at once."

Hearing the dismissal in her words, Zaor rose to leave.

Mylaerla sighed heavily. Something in the sound froze Zaor in the midst of his polite bow of leave-taking. He straightened and met her eyes, nodding encouragement for her to continue.

"This visit has reminded me of many things I should not have forgotten. For one, I have been too long in this city. It has been many years since I climbed the slopes of Eagle Hills. I do not even know for certain whether there still are dragons upon Evermeet!" She looked up at Zaor, and her smile was strangely tentative. "Tell me something, youngling, do you think that even such as I could ride a dragon?"

As she spoke, a wistful expression crept into her eyes and softened her aging face. But her poignant longing did not in the least blunt the steel in her voice or the forceful impact of her presence.

Zaor could not keep the smile from his face. "My lady, I don't think there's a dragon alive who could keep you from it."

The elf woman burst into surprised and delighted laughter. Still smiling warmly, she rose and extended her hand to the young warrior as one adventurer to another. "Then it is settled. The dragonriders will become Evermeet's guardians. Her shores will be kept inviolate."

"As the gods will," Zaor responded fervently.

Mylaerla cocked her head. "I meant what I said, you know, about learning the craft myself. But what of you? Will you be joining those who ride the winds?"

"Regretfully, no. My responsibility lies elsewhere."

Lady Durothil regarded him for a long moment. Then she nodded thoughtfully. "Yes. Yes, it may indeed be so."

17

Heirs of Destiny

o many of Evermeet's elves, the Towers of the Sun and Moon represented the epitome of elven culture.

Fashioned of white stone that had been raised by magic from the heart of the elven land, the Towers were surrounded by wondrous gardens and hidden in the heart of a deep forest. Here were housed some of the most powerful magical artifacts known to elvenkind. Here gathered wizards and High Magi for study and contemplation, for the casting of the Circles, and for the instruction of promising students.

Of all the Tower's students, none showed more promise than Amlaruil Moonflower. Magic seemed to flow through the girl as naturally as rain from a summer cloud. Secretly, the magi believed that she could become the most powerful mage since the legendary Vhoori Durothil. Already she was being groomed to take the place of Jannalor Nierde, Evermeet's Grand Mage.

Yet there were some in the Towers who doubted that the elf maid's destiny was all that certain. Among these was Nakiasha, a Green elf sorceress of considerable ability who had taken upon herself the role of Amlaruil's mentor and confidante.

As was their custom, the two elf women, their day's work completed, walked the paths that curved through the Tower grounds. They walked in silence, to better enjoy the beauty of the evening. Birdsong filled the cooling air, and the chirp of crickets and other forest creatures heralded the coming night.

It was the time of day that they both preferred to all others, when the last, long rays of sunlight bathed everything in a golden haze. But it seemed to Nakiasha that her young friend seemed distracted, and quite removed from their small, self-contained world of magic and scholarship.

"Where are you today, child?" the sorceress asked.

Amlaruil dropped her eyes to the gravel path, and not because she wished to contemplate the exquisite walkway. It was a wondrous thing, to be sure, for the gravel was actually bits of marble in shades that represented all the goodly races of elves: gold, silver, green for the wild elves, and blue for the sea folk. Some whimsical bit of magic kept the colors shifting in an ever-changing mosaic. At the moment, however, Amlaruil wanted merely to escape her teacher's searching gaze.

"I am sorry, Nakiasha," she murmured. "Please forgive my inattention."

"The day's lessons are over. I only wondered if all is well with you," the sorceress said. As she spoke, she peered up into the girl's face—no easy task, for Amlaruil was exceedingly tall. Nakiasha's shrewd eyes took note of the flush on the girl's face.

"By Hanali! You aren't in love, are you?"

Amlaruil slanted a look at her teacher from beneath lowered lashes. "Would that be so bad?"

"Perhaps not." Nakiasha shrugged. "Though to be sure, some of the magi here might worry that your spring fancies might interfere with your studies. It's a wonder," she added with asperity, "that with such thinking, the Gold elf people have not died out long ere this! Who is the lad? Laeroth? A good choice. Very talented."

The girl answered only with a shrug. Laeroth was a fellow student and a good friend. Even so, she could not help but picture the young mage standing alongside Zaor Moonflower. Though Laeroth was nearly six feet tall—nearly as tall as Amlaruil herself—he seemed dwarfed in comparison with the warrior. Amlaruil suspected that in her eyes, it would always be so.

Even so, maidenly yearnings had little to do with Amlaruil's distraction. She had been strangely restless all day. Her spirit felt for all the world like a hawk buffeted by too-strong winds.

With a sigh, she came to a stop at the foot of the Totem, a monument honoring the spirit magic peculiar to the Green elves. Amlaruil's eyes swept up the massive statue, lingering on each of the stark, powerfully portrayed totem animals it depicted. The totem protected the Tower grounds in ways that few of the elves fully understood. Until today, Amlaruil had often found comfort and reassurance in its massive shade. Now, for reasons that she could not define, she found herself wondering if the totem—or anything else—would be enough.

"Primitive art, by Gold elf standards," Nakiasha observed with a touch of sarcasm, "but no one can deny its power! The Totem has protected the Towers from rival spells for many centuries."

Amlaruil nodded, though she knew that in these days of diminished magic, spellbattle between towers occurred only in minstrels' tales. Though such challenges might have been common before the Sundering, no magical battle had ever taken place on Evermeet.

Nakiasha patted her arm. "It is nearly time for evenfeast. Go, and meet your young gallant."

"You are not coming?" Amlaruil eyed the older elf. Nakiasha seldom took time to eat or even to seek revery, and her bones were nearly as bare as winter wood. The elf maid often wondered what source fueled the sorceress's unending energy. Once, she had asked. Nakiasha had merely smiled and replied that she would learn the secret herself in due time.

Predictably enough, the sorceress shook her head. "I have work awaiting me. You know of the Accumulator, of course, and you know that it absorbs the magical energies of Evermeet itself. For some reason, the artifact's power is rapidly increasing—it nearly hums with magical energy! We do not yet know why, and this we must know."

"I have felt something beyond the ordinary," Amlaruil admitted.

"Have you, now?" the sorceress said, eying the girl thoughtfully. "If anything more comes to you, be sure to seek me out at once. But go now, and refresh yourself. It might be that we will have need of your youth and strength."

Nakiasha ended her words with a smile, but to Amlaruil's ears they still sounded more like a warning than a compliment.

The elf maid turned down the path that led to the Tower of the Moon. While the Tower of the Sun was devoted to the storing and casting of magic, the Moon tower tended humbler, more personal needs. Here were kept the living quarters, small rooms dedicated to contemplation or study, and finally the kitchen and dining hall. All meals were taken at the narrow, spiraling table that filled the lower hall.

Laeroth was waiting for her at the door. As she often did, Amlaruil noted that there was something otherworldly about the young mage. It was not merely his appearance, though that was odd enough. Laeroth looked disturbingly akin to the ancient statues that depicted the Faerie People. Tall and exceedingly thin, he was all sharp angles and eerily precise grace. His eyes were black, and they slanted upward at the corners beneath similarly winged, black brows. Only his mop of wheat-colored hair, which was in its usual state of disarray, seemed to place him rightfully in the mortal world.

The young mage sprang at Amlaruil, seizing her by both shoulders. "Where have you been? I have awaited you this hour and more!"

The intensity in his burning black eyes unnerved the girl, especially considering her recent conversation with Nakiasha.

"As ambushes go, that was rather poorly done," she said with a smile, trying to lighten the tone between them. "It is not common practice to show yourself until the moment of attack."

Laeroth released her and ran a long-fingered hand through his unruly hair. "The moon has risen. It will soon be dark enough to see."

"See?"

The young mage took her arm and led her away from the Tower. "The lights here are too bright—they dampen the stars," he explained. "I think we must go into the forest."

Amlaruil followed without comment, caught up in his urgency. The two elves slipped deep into the trees, into the hidden dale where Amlaruil had met the unicorn—and glimpsed her disturbing, improbable destiny.

Laeroth stopped and pointed up into the night sky. "It should be there between the fourth and fifth of Selûne's Tears, and slightly to the north."

The elf maid studied the sky, seeing nothing beyond the lights that were familiar friends. But as her eyes sought deeper, she did indeed notice something new. Faint and distant, more like the ghost of a star than a true light, it crouched amid the glowing tears like a crimson shadow.

"By the gods!" she breathed. "The King-Killer star!"

Laeroth nodded, his narrow face set in grim lines. "You see it, then. I thought so, but I had to be sure. Usually its path arcs over Faerûn and as far east as Kara-Tur. Never has it been seen on Evermeet."

"What does this mean?"

"I wish I knew," Laeroth said. "This mystery will tax even the magi."

Amlaruil stared at him. "*Will* tax? You haven't told anyone?"

"I only just found out this evening. In fact, you saw its light before I did." He hesitated. "It's hard to explain, but I think I *felt* the star's presence. At the very least, I felt *something*. All this day I have spent in the library, studying the lore for some clue. It was about time for another appearance of the King-Killer star, so . . ." his voice trailed off, and he shrugged.

Amlaruil's eyes widened. "The Accumulator! Perhaps

the appearance of the King-Killer might help explain the magic surge. Nakiasha will wish to know this at once!"

The pair hurried to the Tower of the Sun and told the sorceress what they had seen. Nakiasha led them to the Chamber of a Thousand Eyes.

Here they found Jannalor Nierde, gazing into a long looking tube. The lens was aimed at the far wall, but Amlaruil doubted he was engaged in a study of the tapestry that hung there. The magical device could see nearly any spot on Faerûn.

Jannalor disengaged himself from the looking tube and listened gravely to their tale. "I hope that you are wrong," he said when they were finished speaking. "Nonetheless, let us have a look."

The Grand Mage cast an incantation and then trained the looking tube at a high, arched window. He studied the image for a long moment, then swept the lens back and forth as if scanning distant skies.

Suddenly the mage stopped, stiffened, and swore a low, fervent oath. He straightened and gestured for Amlaruil to look within the tube.

The girl peered into the looking glass, and was greeted by Selûne's bright, silvery light. As she gazed, a shape like that of an enormous bat winged across the moon. More followed, so many that they nearly blotted out the light.

Horror clenched her throat like a monstrous hand as Amlaruil realized she was gazing upon the deadliest, most dreaded phenomena known to Aber-toril.

"A flight of dragons," she murmured hoarsely.

This, then, was what she had felt. The magical creatures had a powerful aura, and certain mages could sense their near presence. So, apparently, could the Accumulator, for the artifact was no doubt absorbing some of the dragons' power.

"Where are they?" she asked, moving aside to give Laeroth a turn at the glass.

"Far out to sea, praise the gods," Jannalor replied in a worried tone. "But they are flying straight toward

Evermeet. We must get word of the coming attack to every corner of the island!"

"But Evermeet is protected by magical shields, woven by Corellon himself," protested Laeroth.

"Think, boy!" growled the mage. "What creature is more magical than a dragon? Any shield that would keep out the magic of a hundred dragons would also block the flow of the Weave of Magic. If Evermeet were so protected, we could not work magic; indeed, under such a shield, we elves would die as surely as the summer lighting bugs that careless children gather and leave too long under a glass! Mark me: there *will* be an attack."

Nakiasha took the girl's arm. "Come, child. Let the Gold elf attend to sending messages. We must form the Circle, and lend the warriors what help we can."

* * * * *

The door to Horith Evanara's office flew open, striking a ringing blow against the living rock of the chamber wall.

Captain Horith was not at all surprised when Zaor Moonflower burst into the room. The tall, blue-haired Moon elf had swiftly climbed the ranks of the Leuthilspar guard, and had sought reassignment to the fortress city of Ruith. Already Zaor had made his command into perhaps the finest fighting unit among the many that trained and garrisoned within the walls of Lightspear Keep. Zaor was well liked by the fighters, but he did not always show proper respect for either the rank or the wisdom of the keep's commanders.

"I heard of the approaching flight of dragons. Why have you not called forth the dragonriders?" the young warrior demanded.

The captain fixed a cool stare upon his most promising— and most troublesome—officer. "You mean the squadron commanded by those Durothil crones? I think not. This battle—if indeed there *is* a battle—belongs to me."

"You cannot be serious! You've never seen the destruction a rampaging dragon can leave behind. I have. This matter goes far beyond clan rivalry, or personal pride!"

"Have a care how you speak," the Gold elf said coldly. "I assure you, the situation is under control. The Durothil dragonriders need not hear of it."

"You have not even sent word?" said Zaor in disbelief.

Angry now, Captain Horith rose—and immediately regretted the act. It was difficult to assert authority over an elf who stood head and shoulders above him. Though, in truth, he suspected that Zaor Moonflower would be formidable even at half his size.

"The situation is under control," the Gold elf repeated in a tight voice. "The dragonriders are not needed, and neither, Captain Zaor, is your presence in my office. You are dismissed."

But the Moon elf stood his ground. "Warriors afoot have little chance against a single dragon, much less a hundred. You know that as well as I. What, then, do you intend to do?"

When Horith hesitated, Zaor slammed the desk with one fist in sudden wrath. "This is as much my affair as yours! I've a hundred elves under my command, and I'll be damned as a drow before I'll march them blindly to their deaths! If you have a plan, speak!"

"The Starwing fleet," Horith said grudgingly. "Star ships, man-o-wars that sail through the clouds as nimbly as common ships do the seas. They are kept in secret in the sea caves of Sumbrar. Beyond the Council members and the ships' crew, few elves know of them."

Zaor fell back a step as he absorbed this wonder. "How many ships?"

"Ten. All well-crewed and heavily armed," the Gold elf said with pride. "Finer warships do not exist, on this world or any other. If the need arises, I will command the battle myself from the flagship."

"Even so, what chance have ten ships against a hundred dragons?" Zaor shook his head. "No, Lady Mylaerla must be alerted at once." He spun and stalked from the office.

341

"If you do," hissed the captain, "I will see you stripped of rank."

Zaor did not pause. "And If I don't," he returned with grim certainty and in a voice that rang though the corridors, "we will all be dead."

Leaving the Gold elf sputtering with rage, the Moon elf captain hurried through the halls of Lightspear Keep to the stables beyond. In the adjoining pasture awaited his horse. No common beast, this, but a moon-horse, a magical beast capable of great speed. He would have need of it, for the Eagle Hills were nearly fifty miles to the west, and too much time had been wasted on Horith Evanara's pride.

Zaor leaped upon the stallion's back and urged it forward with a thought. As he rode through the streets to the western gates, the Moon elf's gaze fell upon a round, white-marble tower, one of the finest buildings in all of Ruith. This was the Pegasi Aerie. Even now, winged horses and their riders were circling the city, landing on the flat roof of the Aerie, practicing the endless, complex maneuvers that had shaped them into a legendary defensive force.

For a moment, Zaor was tempted to stop and try to persuade the Gold elf commander into joining his mutiny. But he knew that such an effort would fail; furthermore, he doubted that a score of winged horses would have much effect upon a hundred rampaging dragons.

Zaor turned away, riding through one of the randomly shifting gates in Ruith's transparent walls. He could feel his moon-horse's relief as they left the city behind. The stallion sped toward the hills, then climbed the first rugged slope as nimbly as a mountain goat.

The Moon elf called a halt at the mouth of a cave. He dismounted, then urged the moon-horse to take refuge in the meadows to the west of the mountains. If all went as he hoped, he would not have need of such a mount in the battle to come.

When the magical creature was safely out of sight, Zaor took up a curving bronze horn that hung from a hook at the cave's entrance. He placed it to his lips and blew three quick blasts.

Before the final echoes died away, Zaor found himself gazing into two pairs of golden eyes. One belonged to Ahskahala Durothil, the other to Haklashara, the venerable gold wyrm who was her partner. At that moment, Zaor could not say with certainty which of the two was the more formidable.

The elf woman's odd, almost reptilian eyes were the only hint of color about her. White of hair and skin, draped in pale chain mail and a silver-gray tunic, Ahskahala closely resembled the spear she carried: tall, slender, lethal. There was more warmth in the dragon's amber gaze than in hers, and less menace.

The warrior listened, tight-lipped, to Zaor's warnings.

"I can meet the flight with thirty dragonriders," she said at last. "But I tell you now, it will not be enough. Monst of the dragons are younglings. Even if they were not, the numbers are against us."

"Perhaps the starwing ships will turn the balance," Zaor said. Even as he spoke, he realized how hollow the words sounded.

The dragon Haklashara cleared his throat, a horrible grating sound that reminded Zaor of the first stage of a rock slide.

"What of the giant eagles that nest on the high crags?" suggested the wyrm. "Many times I have told you, elf woman, that they also might be persuaded to take on the training of you elves. At the very least, they might remove some of the burden of Evermeet's defense from the shoulders of the dragon folk!"

The elf glared at her mount. "This is not the time to sing that old song! Even if you were right—and mind you, I'm not saying you are—there is no time for it. Such birds must begin training the moment they emerge from their eggs. No untrained eagle would be able to work with an elven rider."

"Or vice versa," the dragon put in snootily.

Despite the bantering nature of this exchange, the

dragon's words gave Zaor a sudden, desperate idea. He knew that all the creatures who made Evermeet their home were closely bound to the magic isle. A common eagle in defense of its nest was a fearsome adversary. Perhaps as many as fifty giant eagles lived in the mountains to which they lent their name. If he could convince these creatures to join the coming battle, they might have a real chance.

"Who leads the giant eagles?" he demanded of Haklashara.

"Hmm." The dragon raised a paw and tapped reflectively at his scaly chin with one massive claw. "That would be WindShriek, I believe."

"Do you know where to find him? Can you take me there?"

"Her," the dragon corrected. "WindShriek is a female, and as nasty-tempered as this other two-legged one before you. As to your questions, yes and yes. I know where her nest is, and I will take you there." The enormous creature slipped from the cave, sinuous as a snake, then crouched down to allow Zaor to mount his back.

"You would permit another elf to ride you?" demanded Ahskahala in astonishment.

The dragon shot a look of pure, gloating delight at his elven partner. "Only an elf who possesses the good sense to recognize wisdom when he hears it," he said slyly. A cryptic expression crossed his scaled visage, and he added in more serious tones, "And only the elf who bears such a sword."

Before Ahskahala could voice further protest, the dragon flexed his wings and leaped into the air.

The sudden rush of wind and speed nearly tore Zaor from his seat. He grasped the horn of the saddle with both hands, hanging on for his life and swearing with a soldier's fluency.

A low, grating chuckle thrummed through the shrieking wind. "Get used to it, elf king," advised the dragon. "As much as it pains me to admit, WindShriek in a dive flies even swifter than I!"

Haklashara climbed steadily until all that lay beneath them was a bank of clouds. Suddenly he curved his wings in a tight arch and spun down in a sweeping circle.

As they burst from the clouds, Zaor's eyes widened in pure panic. The dragon was hurtling with incredible speed toward the sheer rock wall of a mountain.

The wyrm's deep, booming chuckle bounced off the mountain, to be echoed again and again by the hills beyond. Just as Zaor was certain he could glimpse before him the shadows of Arvandor's trees, Haklashara wheeled abruptly to one side, then glided down to land with astonishing lightness and ease upon a large stone ledge.

The winds still roared in Zaor's ears as he leaped down from the saddle. Even so, he was nearly deafened by a shrieking cry, a scream so powerful that it shook loose rocks and sent them tumbling down the rocky face of the mountain. With a flurry of wings, WindShriek rushed at the invaders.

Zaor's moonblade hissed free of its scabbard. The elf brought the sword up in guard position and held his ground.

An aura of power, like a shining blue haze, surrounded the elf. Magic gleamed like captured lightning along the rune-carved length of the sword. Yet Zaor did not attack the wondrous bird.

Taller than a war-horse and garbed with golden feathers, the giant eagle was magnificent in her fury. Zaor only hoped that WindShriek, like Haklashara, recognized the significance of the magic sword and the destiny of the elf who wielded it.

WindShriek halted beyond the glowing aura, her wings batting wildly and her furious golden eyes fixed upon the dragon. The buffeting winds from her flailing wings threatened to sweep Zaor from his feet despite the sword's protective shield of magic.

"Why you come by my nest, dragon?" demanded the eagle in a high, ringing voice. "Bring lotsa blue magic, elf with sword. How come? You wanna steal egg, you plenty late! Eggs hatch, hatchlings now fledglings. Children not here—fly far and strong!"

"Do you take me for a starling or a squirrel? I'm no nest robber, and well you know it!" the dragon huffed.

Zaor took a single step forward. "Do not blame Haklashara for this intrusion, Queen WindShriek. Evermeet has need of you and your strong children."

The eagle cocked her head and examined the elf. "Who you?"

"For a creature with your legendarily keen eyesight, you're remarkably slow to see what's before you," the dragon said dryly. "You don't recognize the power of the sword, do you? It pulses as if it were the heart of Evermeet! 'Lotsa blue magic,' indeed! This is the elven king, you feather-brained dolt! He has come at last."

It was not a claim that Zaor felt he could make, nor one he wished to reaffirm. To his relief, WindShriek accepted the dragon's pronouncement without question. "Why you come by my nest, elf king?"

"I come to bring word of great danger to your people and mine," the elf said. "You are not a night bird, so it might be that word might not have reached you. A bright red star shines in the eastern sky. When this happens, oftentimes a flock of evil dragons gathers to join in a flight of destruction. This time, they are heading directly for Evermeet. We must stop them before they reach the island."

The giant eagle pondered this. "What you want Wind-Shriek to do, elf king?"

"You are queen of your kind. Lead them into battle. The risks will be great," he told her gravely, "and many of your own will not return. The same is true of all who will fight, be they eagles or dragon folk or elves. Yet there is no other choice before us, but death for all."

"Hmm. Eagle people never fight dragons," WindShriek mused, but there was no fear in her voice.

"I have," Zaor asserted, "and I trust that your battle prowess is equal to the task. If you will work with me, I believe together we can turn them back."

"Trust, elf king?"

WindShriek stared at the elf for a moment, her wild

eyes unreadable. Then she lunged at him, her hooked beak diving toward his throat.

Trusting his instinct, Zaor did not flinch or attempt to parry the attack. The enormous beak snapped shut a finger's breadth from his face. Nearly eye to eye, the eagle and the elf regarded each other.

The giant eagle stepped back. "You plenty brave, elf king," she said approvingly. "You trust WindShriek, Wind-Shriek trust you. Eagle people fight with elves and dragons this day."

"Now that that's settled," the dragon said, "I'll take my leave. Ahskahala is not the most patient of elves, and her disposition does not improve with pending battle. Your majesties." Without irony, the great creature inclined his horned head to the eagle and the elf, and then leaped from the ledge into the air.

WindShriek spread her wings, as well. "You not gonna walk, are you?"

This effectively settled Zaor's next problem—how to persuade the giant eagle to allow him to ride upon her back. The elf climbed onto her wide shoulders sitting just behind her enormous golden head. With a shrilling cry, the eagle climbed into the sky.

* * * * *

In the Tower of the Sun, Amlaruil joined with the other High Magi in a spell of seeking. In the combined vision of the Circle, the elves reached out across the miles, out over the open sea, to the dragons that winged steadily toward Evermeet.

There were perhaps seventy of them. Many of the dragons bore the scars of their long flight: scales dulled or molting, wings frayed by storms and sea winds, the leathery hide of the neck hanging in loose folds over depleted flesh. In response to the strange compulsion of dragonflight, the great creatures had flown far without rest or food.

But the elves did not take too much heart from this evidence of the dragons' weariness. By now, the creatures were desperate, and in their imperative need to reach Evermeet, they would certainly throw all their remaining strength against the defenders.

Even as the elves struggled to absorb the horrendous mental image of the dragonflight, a new wonder edged its way into their vast magical canvas. Amlaruil caught her breath in awe at her first glimpse of the Starwing fleet.

There were ten of them, all man-o-wars, and they swept toward the invading dragons like a flock of titanic butterflies. Their slender crystal hulls cut through the air as swiftly as did the dragons' sleek forms, and their glistening, brightly colored pairs of double sails seized every breath of wind.

As Amlaruil watched, the blood-red ship in the lead position fired her ballista. An enormous, iron-tipped bolt streaked toward the nearest black dragon.

To the elf's astonishment, the black wyrm deftly snatched the weapon from the air with one forepaw. Immediately it bought the spear up against its body, so that the force of the stopped bolt was not borne by that one limb. Then the dragon twirled the ballista bolt around, nimbly as an elven fighter might spin his staff. Its massive black tongue lolled out and licked at the wicked tip.

A corrosive hiss and the stench of burning metal filled the air as the black dragon's acid began to melt through the iron tip. Holding the weapon like a javelin, the creature reared back in the air and hurled the ballista bolt back toward the lead ship.

The man-o-war pulled hard to one side, but the tainted weapon tore through the starboard wing. The tattered hole it left behind began to grow as the acid spread, eating its way through the crimson wing and sending melting drops falling like blood to the deck below. The cries of wounded elves echoed horribly. The ship began to falter, sinking down toward the waiting sea.

Swiftly the remaining ships fanned out to form a

defensive line between the island and the approaching dragons. Thump after thump filled the air as their catapults loosed a steady barrage of scattershot at the approaching dragons.

The deadly fire had effect. Four of the creatures spiraled down to the waters, their wings torn and useless. But the others, even those who had been wounded, came steadily on. In their lead was a young red dragon, a large male. The bands of armor encircling the dragon's mighty chest swelled as the creature fueled itself for the killing blast.

Fire shields, now!

Jannalor Nierde's voice, imperative and desperate, sounded in the minds of each elf in the Circle. As one, the High Magi chanted the words that would fashion the protective spell.

Fire burst from the creature's mouth, pouring out in a stream of flame that went on and on in a seemingly endless gout of heat and destruction. The immense, curved shield of magic that warded the ships turned back the flame, but within moments the once-invisible barrier was red-hot, the surface blistered and bubbling like melting glass.

Most of the onrushing dragons ducked under the reflected waves of fire. They glided under the ships, letting the searing heat and flame waft upward harmlessly. Only two of the dragons were caught in the updraft and tossed high into the sky.

Well enough, thought Amlaruil in relief. The ships had survived the dragons' worst weapon, and they were above most of the wyrms, and thus in a far more defensible position.

Immediately the man-o-wars began to maneuver into a new formation. The ships on the outer edges of the line swept around to the west, the others following until all nine had formed a circle. The dragons, however, knew no such organization. They swarmed toward the ships from all sides in sudden, terrible, relentless attack.

Gone, too, was all hope of an organized defense. Wizards aboard all the ships loosed countering weapons. Massive fireballs tore toward the red dragons, meeting answering fire in bursts of multicolored light and shattering explosions of sound. Enchanted arrows flew from bows passed down by ancient heroes as the fighters sought the vulnerable eyes and wide-flung mouths of the attacking wyrms.

The Circle did what they could, following Jannalor's lead and lending their combined strength to one elven attack after another. But the dragons were simply too many. They battered the elven vessels with magic, swooped down and caught up elven fighters in their talons, slashed at the sails with their rending teeth and talons, and slammed the crystal hulls with their own enormous bodies. They fought in near-frenzy, driven by their own desperate hunger and the compelling, mysterious urging of the dragonflight.

Nor did the Starwings' defensive stance aid the magi, for there was no one attack to which to lend their strength. One after another, the ships were shattered by dragonfire, or melted by the terrible clouds of acid breath, or left so damaged or bereft of crew that they were forced to limp down toward the sea.

A sudden surge of magic, like sunlight breaking through winter clouds, flooded the joined minds of the Circle's elves. As one, they soared upward in thought to seek its source.

Winging toward the battle in precise formation were thirty gold and silver dragons, each bearing an elven warrior.

Amlaruil's lips curved in a triumphant smile. She recognized the formidable Lady Mylaerla Durothil. The matron sat astride a venerable silver and looked as if she'd been born to battle. The grim, Gray elf woman who rode at her right wing tip could only be the legendary Ahskahala. With such heroes as these fighting for Evermeet, surely victory would not be long in coming!

Yet even as she watched, lending her magic to the Circle as Jannalor wove a net of power that supported the dragonriders like a favorable wind, Amlaruil realized that the battle would not be easily won.

The dragonriders came in from above, attacking the invaders with great, swooping dives and pulses of magical power. But the evil dragons countered with their own fearful weapons. Amid the terrible confusion of blood and steel and flame and smoke and magic, pairs of the gigantic creatures grappled in the sky. Here and there the entwined dragons plummeted from the fiery clouds, only to be swallowed by the waiting sea.

Above the roar of the embattled dragons and the answering shouts of elven fighters, a shrill, distant voice took up the elven battle cries. Giant eagles, nearly as large as some of the dragons, hurtled down from the sky. Leading them was a wondrous golden female, and on her back rode Zaor Moonflower. His wild dark blue hair streaked behind him like a storm cloud, and the moonblade he brandished blazed with arcane fire.

Amlaruil instinctively reached out to him. Her magic strengthened his arm as he slashed out to meet the snapping jaws of a red dragon. The sword slapped the dragon's head to one side, and the hooked beak of Zaor's eagle partner sank deep into the vulnerable neck.

The young mage felt the swell of gathering magic nearby, and she flashed her attention to the small black dragon who drew breath for an attack upon the deadly eagle-rider. Amlaruil sensed the moonblade's protective shield, and she lent her magic to calling it forth. The dragon spat acid in a fetid stream. It hit the moonblade-created shield and dissolved into a foul smelling cloud, as easily as a cup of water might be dispersed if tossed upon a dwarven forge.

Deep into the magic of Zaor's sword Amlaruil went, finding its secrets and lending her magic to his strength. Unknowing, she slipped free of her place in the Circle and bound herself instead to ties still deeper and more mystical. Yet in a distant corner of her mind, she could still hear Jannalor's voice, still feel the wondering thoughts of the magi as they focused their efforts upon bolstering the new and powerful Center who had unexpectedly taken over the course of the battle.

Zaor seemed to be everywhere, his sword flashing and diving as he battled the invading dragons. He and his magnificent eagle worked together as if one creature. Dimly, Amlaruil could hear the elf's voice as he shouted encouragement and instruction to the aptly named Wind-Shriek. But more than that, she felt the distinctive magic of the elven isle itself pulsing through Zaor's moonblade, and binding the defenders together. It was a magic she knew, for it coursed through her body and sang in her veins.

Nor was she the only one to sense the power of Zaor and his sword. The other eagles, even the dragonriders, rallied to the Moon elf warrior as the magic of the king sword subtly reached out to touch and inspire each child of Evermeet.

The eagles attacked relentlessly, gouging the invading dragons with their hooked beaks and shredding at their leathery wings with talons as long and sharp as any sword. The eagles swooped down in groups of two and three, slamming into the dragons as the dragons had in turn attacked the elven ships.

Not all of the giant birds survived. A burst of dragonfire caught one of the eagles in mid-dive, filling the air with a spray of golden feathers, and the stench of charred flesh. Another spun down to the sea, a broken wing hanging over the long bloody gash that scored its side so deeply that it exposed a neat row of bones.

But at last the battle was over. A single elven ship, a dozen pairs of dragonriders and wyrms, and less than a score of giant eagles winged wearily back toward the island. They left behind skies still dark with smoke, and a sea that still steamed and seethed from the burning destruction of the ships and the gigantic warriors.

Slowly, gently, Jannalor Nierde reclaimed control of the Circle from the young mage.

We have yet another task to do, one that will challenge our remaining strength. You were all bound up with the magic of the goodly dragons—you know that those few who survive are without exception gravely wounded. We must put them into healing slumber, else all will die, the Grand Mage said somberly.

I will take half the Circle—all the males, let us say—to the tower at Sumbrar. Some of the more gravely wounded dragons will surely stop there, at the nearest land. There are hidden caves where they can sleep. Nakiasha, take the others to the Eagle Hills, and do the same.

In response, the elves eased away from their shared Circle and reformed the magical ties into two groups. Along with the other female magi, Amlaruil focused her will into the casting of the spell that would carry them along magic's silver path to the Eagle Hills.

It was the first time she had experienced magical travel. White light enveloped her in a sudden, dizzying whirl. Swept into the vortex, Amlaruil held tight to the threads of magic that bound her to her Circle—and the deeper, more personal tie that guided her to the place she needed to go.

As the magic faded away, Amlaruil felt the chill sweep of wind against her face. She opened her eyes cautiously, and found that she and her Circle were standing perhaps halfway up the western slope of a mountain. Above them wheeled and soared five silver dragons, and one great gold. Following them like bright shadows were the eagles.

The gold dragon was clearly in trouble. One wing was badly tattered. Torn flesh showed through the gap where melted scales dripped like liquid gold down his wounded flank. Ahskahala was not in much better shape. Her face was blackened with soot and dried blood, and much of her hair and tunic had been singed away. Zaor and his eagle partner kept close to the wounded dragon's side. Through senses still attuned to the warrior, Amlaruil heard his voice, felt his sword's magic, joined in bracing harmony as they urged the faltering wyrm on.

The dragon that Zaor called Haklashara lumbered to the ground, hitting far too hard and skidding painfully over the rock-strewn hillside. His head—now bereft of one of its proud, curling horns, twisted back to regard his elven partner. An oddly contented smile curved his reptilian maw as he noted that Ahskahala still held her seat.

Amlaruil rushed forward and caught the wounded elf woman as she fell. "You must speak to the dragon, help him find his way into the cave," she urged as she lowered Ahskahala to the ground. "We will put him into deep, magical slumber. He will heal, and live to serve Evermeet again."

The warrior's red-rimmed eyes fastened on Amlaruil's face. "I will join him," she croaked.

"But—"

"I will join him," Ahskahala said in a stronger voice, one that neither invited nor permitted argument. "Haklashara and I will heal together, and awaken together. You must do this, mage!"

A gentle hand rested on Amlaruil's shoulder. She knew before looking up that Zaor had come to her side. "She will not live, else," he said softly.

The young mage nodded. Zaor swept the dragonrider up into his arms, and the three elves made their way into the cave, followed by the gravely wounded dragon.

When they were deep within the mountain, Ahskahala called a halt. She gritted her teeth as Zaor lowered her carefully to the ground, then looked with contentment at the stone chamber, and the dragon who curled around her like a gigantic cat preparing to nap.

"It is well. Here we will stay until Evermeet's need is as grave as it was this day. When and if that day comes, call us forth."

The warrior took a ring from her hand and gave it to Zaor. "Speak my name, my lord, and the dragonriders will answer your call. If the gods are kind and the day long in coming, you must give this ring to whosoever rules after you."

"You know," Zaor said in wonderment.

A faint smile crossed the elf woman's blackened face. "If one so dense as Haklashara can see what you are, do you think that I cannot?"

"I heard that, elf," the dragon rumbled.

With a soft chuckle, Ahskahala leaned back against her partner's scaly side. "Go about your work, mage. We are very tired."

A moment of pure panic threatened to claim Amlaruil. The spell that she must cast was High Magic, an enchantment so powerful that it could not be safely cast outside of the strength and support of a Circle. And that was considering just the spell for the dragon alone; to send an elf into endless revery was more difficult still.

And yet, what else could she do? The dragon and elven heroes would die before Amlaruil could gather the other elves, who, for that matter, would be busy with their other dragon charges.

The mage took a long breath to steady her resolve, then sank deep into the magic. She called forth the spell, her body swaying and her hands gesturing gracefully as she chanted, summoning the threads of magic and weaving them into the needed pattern. As she worked, she could feel the silvery web take shape, and then sink down over the pair of warriors like a comforting blanket.

Swept up in the power of the magic, Amlaruil had no sense of the passing of time. Nor did she feel the hunger or exhaustion that so often plagued the magi after the workings of the Circle. If anything, she felt invigorated by the flow of magic.

Almost regretfully, she released herself from the spell and left Ahskahala and her dragon friend to their long slumber. Without speaking, she and Zaor made their way from the cave.

The mountainside was deserted when they emerged,

and the sunset colors stained the distance hills. "The others must have returned to the Towers," Amlaruil murmured. "Working together, they could have completed the task faster than one alone."

After a moment's silence, Zaor reached out and took her hands in his. "I felt you with me during the battle, you know. Your magic, your strength."

The elf woman nodded. The bond that had formed between them still sang in her blood and filled her soul. A shy smile curved her lips as she looked into the warrior's searching eyes and saw a similar knowledge there.

Amlaruil did not return to the Towers that night, nor did Zaor turn his steps southward toward the fortress at Ruith. In a stone chamber in the heart of Evermeet, bathed in the soft light of the king sword, they acknowledged what both had known from their first meeting. That night, with words and with loving actions, they pledged themselves gladly to the future. They belonged to each other, and together, to Evermeet.

With the coming of dawn's first light, the lovers said their farewells, each content in the knowledge that their joined destiny would surely bring them back into each other's arms.

Amlaruil stood long at the mouth of the cave and watched the warrior descend the mountain, hurrying toward a handful of surviving dragonriders who had gathered in the valley below.

Despite all Zaor had told her of his leave-taking from Lightspear Keep, Amlaruil had little fear that censure awaited him. For one thing, Captain Horith Evanara's ship was gone, crushed into shards of crystal by the weight of a falling dragon. Even had the Captain survived, he could not have denied that Zaor Moonflower was one of the battle's true heroes. Without the dragonriders, without the giant eagles, the flight of evil dragons would have slipped through Evermeet's shields and laid waste the island.

And more than that, Amlaruil had faith in the destiny

whispered to her by the moonblade Zaor carried. He was destined to rule, and she with him.

Bright dreams filled her thoughts as she summoned the silver path that would carry her back to the Towers. But as the whirl and rush of the magic travel faded, she was greeted by the sound of anguished elven mourning.

High, wordless keening filled the air as the elves of the Towers gave themselves over to grief. Amlaruil gathered up her skirts and ran for the Tower of the Sun. She burst into the lower chamber, in which stood a single elf, draped and cowled in the robes of the Grand Mage of the Towers.

"Jannalor! What happened? What is wrong?" she cried.

"Hush, child." To Amlaruil's surprise, the voice belonged not to Jannalor, but to Nakiasha. The forest elf turned to face the young mage, and lowered the cowl that obscured her tear-streaked face. "Do not speak his name while his spirit is yet so near to Evermeet, lest he turn away from Arvandor for love of you."

To the young mage, this seemed impossible. For as long as she had lived—nearly three and a half centuries—Jannalor Nierde had ruled the Towers of the Sun and Moon. His calm presence seemed as constant and predictable as the dawn.

"Surely he is not dead!" she protested.

"Along with the other magi who ensorcelled the dragons," Nakiasha said sadly. "The task was too great, the magic that bound us all together too strained by the battle and by our far distance from each other. You were not part of the Circle, so you could not know. But each of the five magi who went with us to the Eagle Hills attended the silver dragons in separate, distant chambers among the caves. I felt them die when the enchantment was done, yet I could do nothing to save them."

Amlaruil stared at her mentor, her thoughts spinning in confusion and stunned grief. Among the magi were many of her closest friends, and nearest kin. "How then do you and I still live? It does not seem possible. It does not seem—"

"Right?" the older elf finished. "Do not think that I have not asked that same question, many times. But to do so is to doubt the will of the gods. You and I, Amlaruil, carry the special blessing of the Seldarine. How old do you think me?"

The girl blinked, startled by the seeming non sequitur. "You are past midlife, perhaps in your fifth century."

Nakiasha snorted. "Double that, you'd be closer. It will be much the same for you. Do not look so doubtful! You have lived three centuries and more, yet most who behold you take you for a maiden fresh from childhood. And what of your power? You should not have been able to cast the spell upon the dragon alone, and yet you did. You survived, even while those joined in a Circle could not bear the flow of magic. It is a hard fact, but you must accustom yourself to it, for it is your destiny. As is this."

The forest elf shrugged off the Grand Mage mantle and came forward to drape it over Amlaruil's shoulders. "It was the will of he who ruled these Towers that you succeed him. I but kept it in trust for your arrival."

Amlaruil stared at her mentor, unable to take in all that she had said. "But I am pledged elsewhere," she whispered.

"Are you, now?" Nakiasha looked at her shrewdly. "Ah. I see the way of it. The young warrior whom you supported through the battle, is it not?

"Even so," the sorceress said briskly, not awaiting an answer. "Was the nature of your pledge merely that of a young lover, or she who wishes to serve all her People?"

"Must I choose between them?"

"Perhaps."

Amlaruil's fingers tangled in the folds of the Grand Mage's mantle, as if uncertain whether to draw it close or cast it aside. Yet there was no denying Nakiasha's words. The promises that she and Zaor had exchanged during the long, sweet hours of the night sang in her heart, and she would hold true to them. They were pledged to each other—and to the service of Evermeet.

In her heart, Amlaruil knew herself to be Zaor's true

queen. But surely a long and difficult road lay before Zaor before he was acclaimed Evermeet's king. Perhaps she could best serve his destiny by accepting that which had been laid upon her by the former Grand Mage.

The elf maid lifted her head in an unconscious gesture of command. "We must gather the magi. With so many of us gone, there is much that must be done to rebuild the strength of the Towers, and to lift the spirits of those who remain."

A faint smile, one that was both proud and sad, crossed Nakiasha's face. Jannalor Nierde had chosen well—Amlaruil filled the mantle of power as if she had been fashioned for the task. The sorceress bowed her head in a gesture of respect, and followed the new Grand Mage out into the Tower courtyard.

18

For the Good of
the People

he elves who sat at the table of the Council of Elders watched in stunned amazement as Lady Mylaerla Durothil put aside her cloak of office.

"Do not look so dismayed," the elf woman said dryly. "In recent years, the title of High Councilor has been largely honorary. It is, quite frankly, an honor I can live without."

"It has never been the way of Durothil to turn aside from duty," Belstram Durothil said in a tight, angry voice.

"Nor do I," retorted the matron. "The recent battle has shown me how I can best serve the People and myself. I am less suited to court life than a general's command, and I say without intention of giving offense that I prefer a dragon's company to that of any elf in this room," she added, gazing pointedly at her great-great-nephew. Belstram flushed angrily and looked away.

"In resigning as High Councilor," Lady Durothil continued, "I do not suggest that the Council itself be dissolved. But mark me, its role, like my own, must change."

"Lady Durothil," interrupted Saida Evanara in a supercilious voice. "With or without you, the Council has ruled Evermeet for centuries untold. It is tradition. What you suggest is absurd."

"Is it?" the matron said tartly. "Perhaps my time in the Eagle Hills has given me the distance needed for clear sight. Do you wish to discuss absurdity? Very well. While this council in my absence debated a course of action, while the commanders of the various forces scrambled for personal glory, a flight of dragons came within a day's ship-travel from our shores! Your own kinsman, Horith Evanara, was slain in this battle. Had he not acted as he did, going into battle without either consulting the council or summoning the dragonriders, we would not have before us the task of choosing his replacement!"

"As to that, I do not see why the council should debate this matter. The command should fall to me," Saida stated, seizing upon the one item in Lady Durothil's speech of personal interest. "Perhaps I am have not been long in Evermeet, but in my clan I stand next to Horith in military rank and experience."

"The Nierde clan is not unique in producing able warriors," Francessca Silverspear pointed out. "Nor are you, Saida, the only elf seated here who fought for the life of Myth Drannor!"

"That is true enough, but would you have us toss aside all tradition in one afternoon?" returned Saida heatedly. "For centuries, the Nierde clan has held Ruith and commanded Sumbrar!"

"And what of Ruith now?" inquired Montagor Amarillis, a young noble with the bright red hair characteristic of his clan. "What of Sumbrar? The Starwing fleet is all but demolished. Many of the Sumbrar Tower's magi perished in an attempt to save the surviving dragons. Our reserves of arms and magic have been dangerously depleted by the actions of the last Evanara to hold Lightspear Keep. I, for one, am not eager to see Horith Evanara's legacy continued!"

Saida turned a coldly furious gaze upon the Moon elf. "The Amarillis have always been ambitious, Montagor. You would be delighted to see control of Evermeet's military seized from the Gold elves. Next, you're going to argue that it's time for Evermeet to succumb to a Moon elven royalty!"

"That is precisely what *I* think, and it is the reason why I called the council together this day," Lady Durothil announced firmly, turning Saida's mockery into a statement of truth.

She let the silence linger so that it might give weight to her next words. "I know that many of the noble families, particularly the Gold elven clans such as my own, will be resistant to this. But all of us knew that the time would come! I say that it is here, now."

"It is true that with a single voice commanding all the forces of Evermeet, we would be better able to respond to a sudden threat," admitted Yalathanil Symbaern. "According to Lady Durothil's reports, the tide of battle was turned when young Zaor Moonflower took command. I can only speak according to what I have seen, but I believe that if Myth Drannor had been led by a single, capable ruler rather than a contentious council of its own, its fate might have been quite different. Evermeet must learn, and move forward."

Several members of the council nodded thoughtfully. Had this opinion come from a Moon elf, it would not have fallen into such receptive soil. But the Symbaern house was ancient and honorable, even if the Gold elf wizard himself was a new voice in the council. Yalathanil and several other survivors from his clan had fled the destruction of Myth Drannor to settle Evermeet. He was already widely respected for both his magical skills and his wisdom.

"I agree with Lady Durothil's opinion of Zaor Moonflower," added Keerla Hawksong, the aged minstrel who led her Silver elf clan. "His recruitment of the giant eagles was brilliant. Already members of my house have followed up this victory, and are discussing with Queen WindShriek the possibility of forming a permanent troop of Eagle Riders."

"We are wandering from the point at hand," Montagor Amarillis pointed out. "According to our High Councilor, it is time for the People of Evermeet to choose a royal family. I say that the council put the matter to vote this very day!"

"The young have so little regard for history," Lady Durothil said dryly. "Are you forgetting that the choice will be made, not by the council, but by the will of the gods, as interpreted by enchanted swords?"

"Forget? That is hardly likely," sneered Saida, "considering that the Amarillis clan still holds a living moonblade! It is said that Montagor Amarillis has a bit of the seer about him. Perhaps in his dreams of the future he fancies himself a king."

"As to that, it is for the gods to say," Montagor said piously. "Yet it is true that the Amarillis moonblade is unclaimed. My grandmother, Chin'nesstre, was among the commanders of Lightspear Keep who took the Starwing fleet against the invaders. She was slain by dragonfire; her sword was recovered from the charred remains of the ship."

"Your grandmother's sword is not the only Amarillis moonblade still in service to the People," Francessca Silverspear asserted. As she spoke, the warrior touched the moonstone in the hilt of her own blade. "This I know, for I fought beside many of your kin. In the fall of Myth Drannor, many heroes died, including many moonfighters. Some of these swords are unclaimed, others have been lost."

"How are we to know that one of these lost swords might not have been meant to determine kingship?" Saida Evanara demanded. "How can such a decision be made now, when not all of the moonblades can be accounted for?"

"In that, we will have to trust the gods," Mi'tilarro Aelorothi said firmly. Such was the weight of the Gold elf's words that all protest fell silent, for the patriarch of the ancient Gold elf clan was also a high priest of Corellon Larethian.

"It is decided, then," Lady Durothil said firmly. "Send word to all clans of Evermeet, and to all elves bearing moonblades upon the mainland. When the summer solstice arrives, all will gather in the meadowlands surrounding Drelagara."

Montagor's attention was suddenly fixed intently upon the goblet before him. "As you have pointed out, Lady Durothil, my knowledge of history is perhaps not what it should be. Tell me, what will happen if more than one clan demonstrates through possession of a moonblade a viable claim to the throne?"

Mylaerla Durothil's face turned grim. "It will be as it has always been: a matter for the gods to decide. Each sword has developed certain powers, and the elf who wields the sword must be equal to the challenge of his or her blade. Who holds the most powerful sword, and who wields it best, the same shall win the throne."

"You mean that elves of noble blood must fight each other?" Montagor asked, clearly appalled.

The elf woman's smile was ironic in the extreme. "Since when, young Lord Amarillis, have we ever done anything else?"

* * * * *

There were few places on all of Evermeet as lovely as Drelagara. A small city, it made up in symmetry and quiet beauty what it lacked in grandeur. The buildings were all of white marble, magically raised from the depths of Evermeet, and the whole was located in the center of an expanse of gently rolling meadows that measured more than sixty miles wide. This meadowland was surrounded on all sides by forests, and within a day's ride of the wondrous white-sand beaches of Siiluth.

The moon-horses, those magical white beasts who were the willing allies and friends of the elves, made their home in the meadows of Drelagara. As the day of the summer solstice dawned the moon-horses were as much in evidence as the elves. Their glossy coats gleamed in the pale light that proceeded sunrise as they pranced among the gathered people and the bright silk pavilions, accepting the caresses of elven children, tossing their flower-braided manes as if they were gracious hosts giving welcome to their elven visitors.

From all over Evermeet the elves gathered in the Drelagara meadow, along with representatives from many distant elven communities. This, the selection of Evermeet's ruling house, was a matter that concerned all the People.

Many of the wild elves ventured from the forest depths for the occasion, though no one there could get a true sense of their number. The fey folk kept to the shadows of the forest's edge, or gathered beneath the meadow's scattered trees. Like elusive deer, they were nearly invisible until they showed their presence with movement.

There were also a number of Sea elven representatives who wore amulets to aid them in breathing air so that they might observe the ceremony.

Moon elves were much in evidence, of course. Each clan gathered under the bright banners of its house standard. Those who possessed moonblades would contend for the honor of rulership, and these clans were given the prime locations nearest the center of the gathering place.

And all the Gold elf clans were present, though it was widely noted and softly commented that many of these elves did not look pleased with the prospect of eminent Moon elven rule.

Members of all the other fey races gathered in Drelagara as well, for Evermeet's king would be the ruler of them all. Massive centaur warriors stood at the perimeter of the forest, eyeing the large, silvery forms of the nearby lythari—the elusive, shapeshifting elven wolf-people—with wary respect. Unicorns and pegasi exchanged silent gossip. Faerie dragons flitted about the meadow, some of them amusing themselves by playing tricks on the elves, some giggling wildly as they chased the delegation of sprites about as if they were herding a flock of tiny, airborne sheep. Pixies sat comfortably upon the leafy arms of a giant treant, an ancient, sentient tree-person who watched over the proceedings with solemn patience.

A place of honor near the very center of the gathering had been granted to the delegation from the Towers of the Sun and Moon. In her own private pavilion, Amlaruil prepared herself for the festivities with more than her usual care. As Lady of the Tower, she held a position nearly the equal of the soon-to-be chosen ruler. This was her first state appearance, and she would be the focus of many eyes this day.

Amlaruil wished to do honor to the Towers, but in her preparations she answered another, more personal motive. Several months had passed since she and Zaor had made their pledges in the heady aftermath of battle. She had not seen him since. Everything must be right for this, their first meeting.

The elf woman carefully arranged her red-gold hair in elaborate curls, and donned the jewels passed down to her from distant generations. Her gown, though lovely and fashioned of silk the color of summer skies, was of less importance, for it would be covered by the flowing mantle that proclaimed her office.

"And a good thing, too," Amlaruil murmured. A small, secret smile curved her lips as she smoothed her hands over the clinging silk of her gown. Though she took nothing but joy in the tiny life that slept within the growing curve of her belly, she wanted Zaor to see *her*, first and foremost, and not the child who would be his heir.

His *royal* heir.

Of this, Amlaruil was as certain as sunrise. In her few months as Grand Mage, and under the careful tutelage of the sorceress Nakiasha, she had come to accept the unusual link between her spirit and the gods of the Seldarine. Attuned to Evermeet in ways that she could not yet begin to understand, Amlaruil knew and recognized the power of the sword Zaor carried. She also felt the innate nobility of the elf who wielded it. In Amlaruil's mind, Zaor *was* Evermeet's king. This day would only affirm what she knew to be true.

"My lady?"

The sound of Nakiasha's voice, coming from outside the pavilion, startled Amlaruil from her thoughts. She snatched up her mantle and quickly draped it about her shoulders.

"Come," she said, schooling her face to serenity before turning to meet her mentor.

Nakiasha brushed aside the tent's closing and surveyed the young elf woman with a mother's pride. "You are beautiful, child," she said, forgetting for the moment the formality due to Amlaruil's position. "It's nearly time for the ceremony—you must take your place among the members of the Council."

Amlaruil nodded, and followed the sorceress from the pavilion. In her heightened state of excitement, she was keenly aware of the eyes that followed her as she ascended the platform to her assigned place. This was the first time that she had appeared at any ceremony as Lady of the Towers, and the elves were understandably curious about the new Grand Mage.

But even without the mantle of office, Amlaruil would have drawn wondering stares. She was exceedingly tall—a full head taller than most elves, and she moved with an ethereal grace that lent her even more presence. Her red-gold hair was an unusual and striking shade, and she knew without vanity that she was accounted beautiful. Even Laeroth, her fellow mage and the most unromantic and practical elf of her acquaintance, once commented that her face tended to linger in memory like a haunting melody. Amlaruil found herself hoping that Zaor's memory had been thus afflicted.

She took her place next to the matron of the Nimesin clan, a Gold elf woman hugely rounded with child. A sympathetic smile curved Amlaruil's lips, but her words of congratulations died unborn as the elf woman met her friendly smile with a gaze icy enough to freeze the tides.

"Well. Now that I see you, I understand why a Gray elf wench rules in the Towers," the elf said coldly. "Jannalor Nierde always was a fool for a pretty face and a summer night's frolic! You, I take it, were his favorite plaything."

A slow, hot flush spread over Amlaruil's face. "You do not know me, Lady, yet Jannalor Nierde was widely revered for his wisdom and honor. Your words do him grave injustice."

The bitter lines around the elf woman's mouth

367

deepened, and she continued to regard the Grand Mage with the disdain usually reserved for the half-eaten offerings of a hunting house cat. "Is it not enough to demand that the People endure a Moon elf royalty? Why must the honor of the Towers be sullied, as well?"

"I have done the Towers no dishonor, nor will I," Amlaruil said. Her voice was calm and soft, yet full of power.

The animosity in the Gold elf's eyes faltered, as if she suddenly felt uncertain of an easy quarry. "The ceremony is soon to begin," the elf woman said grudgingly, but she sounded oddly grateful for the excuse to turn away from the conversation—and the young Moon elf's unshakable dignity.

As the heirs to the unclaimed moonblades stepped forward, Amlaruil forgot the Nimesin matron's bitter comments. Though her own brother possessed such a sword, Amlaruil had never seen the ceremony in which the swords were claimed.

It was beautiful, and it was terrible. The recent battles had left several swords unclaimed. Ten elves, all nobles of ancient house and good reputation, pledged themselves to the power of the swords and the service of the People. Of them, only six survived the ceremony.

For two of these survivors, there was no triumph. The magic in the blades they held went silent and dormant in their hands. They had been proved unequal to the task of wielding the powers within their family blades; as the last living descendant of the original wielders, they were spared a sudden death. The expression of stunned disbelief on the two elves' faces suggested that they would perhaps have preferred death to this living realization of their loss.

In the heavy silence that followed the first claiming, the four Moon elf houses who had lost their first and best hope of the future tried again, and yet again, to claim the honor of Evermeet's throne.

Amlaruil's eyes burned with tears of mingled pride and grief as she watched one young elf after another step forward to die, like so many moths flinging themselves against the seductive promise of a lantern's heat and light.

Yet not one of the elven houses yielded, not until the last surviving member of the clan stood alive, but defeated. Their moonblades, their task of selection completed, went dormant at last.

In the grim and reverent silence that followed the claiming, Lady Mylaerla Durothil rose to speak, the last time in her office of High Councilor of Evermeet.

"The Council of Elders honors all those who came this day to stand before the People and the gods of the Seldarine, and to dare the crucible of the moonblade's magic. No dishonor tarnishes the houses who were not selected, and a place in Arvandor awaits all those who had the courage to take up a moonblade. To those new moonfighters among us, we extend congratulations."

The Gold elf's gaze swept the small group of Moon elves before her. "The task ahead is more difficult still. There are yet five-and-twenty living moonblades. Legend says that when four-and-twenty remain, the king sword will announce itself and its wielder. We are one too many, and thus the royal family must be determined by its collective strength. Moonfighters, please gather by clans."

The keepers of the magic swords shifted, each coming to stand beside his or her family standard. In all houses but two, there was but a single wielder. Of these, the Moonflower clan clearly possessed the stronger claim.

Three Moonflower fighters gathered under the banner of the blue rose. Giullio, Amlaruil's much-older brother, appeared greatly ill at ease in the center of so many eyes. Slight of stature and diffident in manner, the solitary, scholarly elf devoted himself to the veneration of Labelas Enoreth, the god of years. Giullio was a worthy claimant to his moonblade, which possessed magics of healing and inspiration, but he was no king. Only with great difficulty had he been persuaded to come to Drelagara at all. Thasitalia, a distant relative, was an adventuress who had never before stepped foot upon the elven isle. By her own words, she was eager to leave. Hers was a restless spirit, and her sword was fashioned for the fighting of solitary battles. Then there was Zaor, standing head and shoulders above every other elf in the field. The young warrior held himself with quiet confidence as he awaited the decision that had been set in motion centuries earlier.

The Amarillis clan possessed two living moonblades. One was a sword recently recovered from the ruins of ancient Aryvandaar, newly claimed by a flame-haired girl-child known as Echo. The other was wielded by a mage from the mainland settlement of Tangletrees.

"By the strength of numbers, Moonflower has proven a strong succession and thus has passed the first test given for the royal clan," Lady Durothil began.

"With your permission, Lady, I must object," interrupted a voice from the crowd.

A low murmur rippled through the crowd as Montagor Amarillis stepped forward to join his two kin. The Moon elf was strangely pale, and his face was the color of snow beneath the thick shock of bright red hair characteristic of his family. He unbuckled his weapons belt and held high a sheathed blade, turning slowly so that all might see the glowing moonstone in the hilt.

"This sword belonged to my grandmother. It was her will that it pass to me. There are therefore three living moonblades in House Amarillis, making us the equal of Moonflower."

Lady Durothil stared, dumbfounded, at the young noble. "Why did you not come forward for the claiming ceremony?"

"It is the right of every elf to decline his hereditary blade," Montagor said in a steady tone. "I claim the right to keep this sword in trust for my oldest child, as yet unborn."

Montagor turned to his two kin. "These worthy elves are not of Evermeet, and have told me they have no desire to stay or to rule. If there is to be an Amarillis king, he will be of my blood." He looked over to the three elves who stood beneath the blue rose standard. "Have the Moon-flowers likewise come to an understanding?"

"I make no claim to royalty, and I would decline the throne if it were offered," Thasitalia Moonflower announced in a clear, low voice.

"And you, Giullio?" Lady Durothil prompted.

In response, the cleric drew his moonblade and saluted Zaor.

"That is clear enough," Montagor said, a smile of satisfaction playing about his lips. "I, too, will pledge my support to Zaor Moonflower, provided that he agrees to honor and acknowledge the rights of clan Amarillis."

Zaor stepped forward to face the red-haired noble. "The honor of Amarillis is beyond question," he said in a puzzled voice. "But of what rights do you speak?"

"The rights of royalty," Montagor said firmly. "The swords of Myth Drannor declare that this right is ours as much as yours. If you deny this, know that the Moonflower family will not hold the throne uncontested."

"You would have me divide the kingdom?" Zaor demanded.

"I would have you unite the two clans," Montagor countered. "Take my sister, Lydi'aleera, as your queen, and we will consider the matter settled."

The noble turned and extended a peremptory hand. A small, golden-haired elf woman came forward from beneath the green dolphin crest that marked the pavilion of House Amarillis. Montagor took her hand, which he in turn presented, in obvious symbolism, to Zaor.

Stunned into immobility, the warrior stared down at the girl. She was very beautiful, though her pale coloring set her apart from the ruddy elves of Amarillis. Her gown was spring green—which in ancient legend was considered the color of elven royalty—and a wreath of flowers clung to her hair as if she were already prepared for a wedding.

As he gazed at the elf maid, Zaor silently cursed Montagor for putting him in this untenable position. His eyes darted to the place where the Grand Mage of the Towers sat.

Amlaruil's blue eyes were unreadable, her face utterly still. Not even her posture yielded any clues as to her thoughts, for the flowing mantle of her office obscured her form.

Since he could hardly refuse to acknowledge the girl, Zaor took the elf maid's offered hand and bowed over it. Yet as soon as he decently could, he released the slim white fingers and turned his attention back to Montagor.

"I am honored by the offer of union with Amarillis, and by the consent of this noble lady," he said carefully. "But the decision of what house will rule Evermeet was never mine to make. The moonblades alone must decide."

"You would chose battle between our clans rather than union?" Montagor asked incredulously. "What would be the cost of such a blood war to Evermeet? The Moonflowers and the Amarillis are ancient families with ties to many houses. Craulnober would surely come to your defense, and behind them the northland commoners who have given allegiance to them! The Silverspear newcomers are aligned with you, as is the commoner captain of the Leuthilspar guard! But the Hawksongs, the Eroths, the Alenuath—they have blood ties and close loyalties to Amarillis. Think carefully on what you would begin."

"Battle, if such there must be, would not involve all these elves!" Zaor protested. "Only those who hold the moonblades must contend for the throne."

"I have declined mine in favor of my heir. Would you let the question of kingship wait until I have a son or daughter to challenge you for it? Would a delay of a hundred years or more serve Evermeet?"

With great difficulty, Zaor held onto his temper. He recognized the layers of sophistry in the elf's argument, and he did not feel equal to meeting them. And there was enough truth in Montagor's words to be disturbing. Perhaps his rejection of the Amarillis alliance would not trigger a full-scale civil war, but it would cause a deep resentment, a division among the Moon elf families. And there were many Gold elves who would be quick to seize

Montagor's suggestion, in hope of holding onto the Council rule for a few decades more.

"It seems to me that this matter cannot be resolved between you and me. I should consult with both the Council of Elders and with my advisers," Zaor said. "Let us all meet again this night, when the Tears of Selûne are in midsky. Perhaps the reminder that we are all of the blood of Corellon and the tears of the Lady Moon might help us unite as we must."

Montagor's jaw tightened with anger, but he could not refute such a reasonable and pious request. He inclined his head to Zaor—a bow between equals, no more. "I agree. It will be as you suggest."

He turned and stalked away, leaving Lydi'aleera standing alone with the Moon elf. Zaor bowed to the young elf woman and strode from the field, not entirely sure where he should go.

Lady Mylaerla caught him by the arm and led him into her pavilion. "I have sent messengers to gather some of the People you'll wish to consult: some of the Elders, leaders among the warriors, a few of the clerics and magi, your circle of trusted friends," she said as she settled down in a chair. "They will be along shortly. I thought it best that we speak alone first."

Zaor paced restlessly about the tent. "What do you think of Montagor's claim?"

"He shows more subtlety than I had thought him capable of mustering," she admitted. "And he's in a good position to carry out his threat of delaying the selection of a royal house."

"And the possibility of clan warfare between Amarillis and Moonflower?"

"Unlikely. But you know that many of the Gold elves resent their exclusion from the process of selection. Of all the Moon elf families, Amarillis has the most demand upon their loyalties. High Councilors, when not of the Durothil lines, were usually from Amarillis. The family is one long, nearly unbroken line of warriors, mages, legendary heroes. If you turn away from an alliance with Amarillis, you stand to alienate most of Evermeet. Believe me, Montagor knows what you will refuse if you refuse Lydi'aleera. And doing that, in and of itself, would give Amarillis—and most of Evermeet—ample cause to take offense."

"I have no wish to insult the girl," Zaor said in deep frustration, "but even less desire to wed her!"

"It was unconscionable for Montagor to put either you or his sister in such a position," the elf woman agreed. "Yet Lydi'aleera is a reasonable choice for queen, even apart from her high family. The girl is beautiful and well mannered. She is an accomplished singer, and well versed in the arts. Many would consider her an ornament to the court. Ah, here are the others," she said, turning to beckon to the small, somber group that gathered at the open door of her pavilion.

As the elves entered, Zaor took note of how they aligned themselves. The Council members stayed together, forming a small group at the far side of the tent. His friends Keryth Blackhelm, who now commanded the Leuthilspar guard, and Myronthilar Silverspear, a captain of the guard, came to flank him in unspoken support.

Only Amlaruil stood apart and alone, as isolated and solitary as the Towers she ruled. Zaor could not bring himself to meet her eyes, for fear of what he might reveal before the gathered elves. He could only imagine what use Montagor Amarillis might make of the knowledge that Zaor had already pledged his heart—and to an elf woman of his own clan!

He turned to the Council. "Will you as a group support the Moonflower claim?"

"How can we, when the task of the moonblades is incomplete?" responded Yalathanil Symbaern.

Francessca Silverspear snorted and crossed her arms over her chest. "Then let it be completed! Let the Amarillis pup draw his moonblade, if he dares, and then further dare to fight Zaor for the throne!"

"We cannot compel him to do so," said Mi'tilarro Aelorothi firmly, his golden fingers curving around the holy symbol of Corellon Larethian that hung over his heart. "The rules for the selection of the royal family were given by the gods. Montagor Amarillis is within his rights."

"You see how it is," Lady Durothil said dryly, tossing an exasperated glance at Zaor. "The Council is not of one mind about this matter, or any other. Montagor Amarillis plays upon these divisions like a master minstrel his harp!"

Zaor nodded, and turned to Keryth Blackhelm. "You know the minds of Leuthilspar's warriors. What do you think? Can I hold Evermeet without the support of Amarillis?"

The captain thought this over. "The warriors respect you. There's no doubt that they would follow you in battle. It's *peace* that worries me. You and I are warriors, Zaor, but neither of us understands the sort of bloodless battle waged among the noble houses. The truth, then? No. I don't believe that you can rule without Amarillis. Not as it should be done, at least."

Zaor stood silent, his head bowed, as he struggled to find his way through the tangle. Finally he looked up, his eyes at last falling upon Amlaruil.

"My friends, I would like to consult with the Lady of the Towers," he said softly. "I thank you all for your advice. I will not leave you waiting long for my decision."

Lady Durothil cast a glance at Amlaruil Moonflower's inscrutable face, then turned a searching gaze upon the Moon elf warrior. She seemed deeply disturbed by what she saw. She rose hastily.

"Come, all of you," she said briskly. "The sooner we're away, the sooner Zaor can make his choice."

Amlaruil sat silently as the Gold elf matron herded the others from the pavilion, as relentlessly and efficiently as a Craulnober hound might drive a flock of northland sheep from a pasture.

"She knows," the mage said simply when at last she and Zaor were alone. "She knows, and does not approve."

375

"Lady Durothil has been High Councilor for many years," Zaor said hastily. "She knows how the noble clans will respond to news of our love. She has spent a lifetime dealing with the nobles and their small intrigues."

"Which only give more weight to her opinion."

"It doesn't matter. None of it matters." Zaor covered the distance between them in a few steps and took both of her cold hands in his. "Amlaruil, we made a pledge to each other. Whatever happens, I intend to honor that! There can be no one for me but you."

Amlaruil's gaze was sad, but steady. "If you refuse this alliance with Amarillis, war among the clans—the very threat that the moonblades were intended to forestall—seems possible. Even if you rule in peace, offending Amarillis will almost certainly ensure the failure of the very task for which you were chosen: bringing unity to the elves. You must understand that clan Amarillis forms both a link and a buffer between Moon elves and Gold. Without Amarillis, you might as well take scepter and crown and place them directly into Durothil hands."

Gently, she slipped her fingers from Zaor's grasp. "The gods have chosen you as Evermeet's king. They have chosen me to help you, and so I must."

The Grand Mage of the Towers went down on her knees before the appalled elf. "I pledge my personal allegiance, as well as all the power of the Towers of the Sun and the Moon, to Zaor, King of Evermeet, and to Lydi'aleera his queen. May you both live long, and reign well." Tears sparkled in her eyes, but her voice was firm.

Before Zaor could speak, Amlaruil disappeared. Only a faint silver sparkle of magic in the air, and the tiny mark of two fallen tears upon the earthen floor of the pavilion, betrayed that she had ever been there at all.

The Moon elf warrior dashed from the tent, looking frantically about for a glimpse of Amlaruil's beautiful red-gold hair among the crowds of elves. She was nowhere to be seen.

Lady Durothil came forward and grasped him by his forearms, her eyes searching his stricken face. Relief and sympathy mingled on her countenance. "You have chosen well," she said gently.

"I did not choose at all!" he blurted out. For a moment, the Moon elf's loss and heartache was naked in his eyes.

"The Lady of the Towers has acted with honor," Lady Durothil said softly. "And she has taken the worst burden— the burden of choice—from your shoulders. She did what she must, and now so must you."

Zaor was silent for a long moment. "I have always heard that the sacrifices demanded of those who would lead can be great. Had I any idea of what would be required of me, I would have wanted no part of this!" he said passionately.

The matron sighed. "If the gods are kind, it might be that you've already endured the worst! But come, my lord—the others are waiting."

* * * * *

For the remainder of that summer, the High Magi of the Towers of the Sun and the Moon lavished their magic upon the creation of Evermeet's court. The Moonstone Palace, a wondrous structure fashioned from marble and moonstone and roofed with gold, rose from the heart of Evermeet.

The labor was bittersweet for Amlaruil. Though she rejoiced to see Zaor as king, her part in his kingmaking was hardly what she had dreamed it might be.

As the summer passed and the brilliant colors of autumn faded from the land, Amlaruil went into seclusion to prepare for the birth of her daughter. Only Nakiasha attended her on the night that Zaor's heir drew breath, and stood witness to the elf woman's tears of mingled joy and loss.

In the months that followed, Amlaruil found immense comfort in her daughter. But she could not escape the feeling that this child was merely loaned to her. Amlaruil's ties to the Seldarine were deep and mystical, but it seemed to her that this babe was more a child of the gods than of mortal elves.

From birth Ilyrana was oddly silent, and her large, sea-blue eyes were grave and ancient. Nor did the babe resemble either of her parents. Tiny and ethereally pale, her white skin seemed tinged with blue, and her snow-colored baby curls held a touch of palest green. Amlaruil named her Ilyrana, from the Elvish word for opal.

Never once did Amlaruil speak the name of her baby's father. As an elf woman of noble birth, a High Mage, and Grand Mage of the Towers, she was beyond reproach in such matters. The child was *hers,* and if any of the elves of the Tower cared to speculate further, they did so with unusual discretion. Amlaruil had already won the respect and love of most of the young magi. Most of them grasped that it was her wish to keep the child from common sight and knowledge, and they protected their lady and her child as they did any of the Towers' other legacies.

What none of the magi understood, however, was that Amlaruil's reticence was based on something far darker than discretion and a desire for privacy.

The machinations displayed during the kingmaking at the previous summer solstice had opened her eyes to the nobles of Evermeet. The Lady of the Towers kept a careful watch on the multilayered affairs of the court. The more she learned, the deeper became her concern, not only for Zaor, but for all of Evermeet.

* * * * *

"Really, Montagor, I find your offer singularly ignorant, even considering that it came from a Gray elf," sneered Vashti Nimesin. "You are of less use to me than Lydi'aleera is to clan Amarillis! Surely you know that any offspring of Zaor will be accounted part of clan Moonflower. You can evoke every long-dead Amarillis hero whose name you can recall, and it will not change that fact!"

The Amarillis heir sipped at his goblet of feywine,

buying time to collect his thoughts. He had spent many days currying the favor of the wealthy and increasingly powerful Nimesin clan. Finally, he had finagled an invitation to one of Vashti's elite parties. Judging from her disdainful tone, it would clearly be a mistake to count his successes too soon.

"Perhaps my sister's child will be a Moonflower," he allowed, "but Lydi'aleera is still of House Amarillis! There is much that a queen can do to influence royal policy."

Lady Nimesin snickered. "And you're claiming she has the wit to do so, I suppose? That little twit?"

"Lydi'aleera has always been guided by me," Montagor said stoutly. "I tell you, there is much that can be gained from an alliance with Amarillis."

The matron's appraising gaze slid over the young Moon elf. Vashti Nimesin was well aware of Montagor's ambitions, and in fact she approved of most of the steps he had taken to consolidate his clan's influence and power in the newly established court. Foisting that insipid little wench upon Zaor Moonflower had been a masterful stroke. It was to Montagor's credit that he also sought out ties with the members of powerful Gold elf clans.

But it was patently clear to Lady Nimesin that Montagor was not quite up to the standard of his illustrious ancestors. In his naked desire for power, he was vulnerable—and more of a willing tool even than his insipid little sister.

Vashti Nimesin smiled. "There is in fact a service you can do for me. My son, Kymil, shows great promise in both magic and arms. I would have him trained at the Towers of the Sun and Moon. Perhaps you could escort him there, and present him to the ruling mage?"

Montagor bowed deeply. "It would be my great pleasure," he said sincerely, though he had little illusion about the reason for Lady Nimesin's request. She clearly disliked the fact that a Moon elf ruled in the Towers and was unwilling to submit herself in the position of supplicant to Amlaruil Moonflower. In sending the

Amarillis heir as an errand boy, Vashti would make a statement of her high position and her contempt for Moon elves.

So be it. It was a price worth paying for Nimesin's favor.

Montagor turned his gaze upon Kymil Nimesin, who stood talking with a small group of young Gold elves. He was a singularly handsome youth, with the golden skin of his race contrasting with the ebony luster of his black hair and eyes. Yet he was still a child, far too young for admittance to the tower.

At that moment, Kymil turned and met Montagor's curious gaze. The Moon elf recoiled, stunned by the sheer malevolence of those eyes. But the moment passed, so swiftly that Montagor was left wondering if he'd imagined that hate-filled stare. Young Kymil came willingly enough to his mother's beckoning, and his handsome face was a model of civility as he greeted the Amarillis heir.

"Montagor Amarillis will escort you to the Towers, my son," Lady Nimesin said in a satisfied voice. "You will leave at first light. See that you are a credit to your people and your house."

"Yes, mother," the boy said automatically. There was nothing in his face or voice to suggest he was other than a dutiful son, and there was no mockery in the bow he gave the Moon elf noble. Yet Montagor felt deeply uneasy as he contemplated the young elf.

From time to time, Montagor caught a glimpse of what might yet be. He had not claimed the moonblade because he suspected that he would not survive the attempt. Now, looking at young Kymil Nimesin, he had the same feeling of impending death. There was something stirring in the mists of this boy's future, something that Montagor could neither see nor grasp. It reached out to him, all the same, taunting him with dire possibilities.

The Moon elf quickly brushed aside his unease. A moonblade, with its powerful and killing magic, was something to be feared and respected. This boy, however, was a mere stripling. Surely Montagor Amarillis was more than Kymil's match.

And so the two left for the Towers the next day, as Lady Nimesin had decreed. Kymil rode well, but he was strangely silent during the northward trip, with none of the questions or chatter that Montagor would have expected from a boy his age.

Finally the silence began to wear on Montagor. "I trained in the Towers myself, briefly," he said. "If there is anything you'd like to discuss, I'd be happy to oblige."

The boy slanted a look at him. "Thank you, no," he said politely. "I shall do fine."

"Have you friends at the Tower?" Montagor persisted. "I don't imagine there are many elves your age."

"There is at least one," Kymil said in a dark tone. He grimaced, as if even that terse remark was more than he had intended to say.

Montagor was intrigued. "I had not known that the Tower magi accepted children."

"From time to time, children are born to the Tower magi," the boy said matter-of-factly. "And sometimes a prodigy is accepted at an early age. Tanyl Evanara, a distant cousin of mine, is much my age and nearly my equal at arms and magic. We will learn together."

"Ah. And what use will you make of the magic you acquire?" the Moon elf asked in the patronizing tone often used toward the very young.

A hard smile played at the corner of the Gold elf's lips. "What would you say, Lord Amarillis, if I told you that I would use what I learn to do away with the travesty of a Moon elf royalty and restore the Elven Council?" he said softly. "Just for argument's sake, of course. Naturally, I would never attempt such a thing. No one but a fool would harbor such treasonous thoughts, or express them to the brother of the queen—not even considering that you yourself would profit from such a course of action. Amarillis will never hold the throne, but certainly you could become High Councilor were the Council restored. Again, just for argument's sake."

Montagor blinked, astonished by the levels of intrigue in the boy's words. He was being warned, courted, and threatened—all at once.

But even as he regarded the young elf, the sly hard look disappeared beneath the smooth golden mask of Kymil's handsome face.

A chill passed through Montagor, swiftly followed by a wave of bitter remorse for his part in delivering this child to the Towers. Whatever came of it, he would have a part. Kymil had implied as much.

Suddenly the Moon elf was less certain of his ability to control, or even to fathom, the ambitions of this Gold elf clan. But the spires of the Towers were now clearly visible to all in the escort party.

Come what may, it was too late to turn back now.

* * * * *

Several years passed before Montagor Amarillis was again summoned to the mansion of Lady Vashti Nimesin. He found the matron in a state of high excitement.

"It has begun," she said bluntly. "The first of the Gray elf pretenders to the throne has been slain. And you, my friend, have made it possible!"

Montagor stared at the Gold elf. "Zaor is dead?"

Vashti laughed scornfully. "Not even your sister could get close enough to the king to accomplish that wonder! No, I speak of Zaor's daughter."

"My sister the queen has no children," the Moon elf said, his brow furrowed in puzzlement.

"As all Evermeet well knows!" sneered Lady Vashti. "Amarillis blood is running thin—the best you can offer these days is a barren queen. No, Zaor has a bastard, and by the Lady of the Towers, no less!"

"Amlaruil Moonflower has a child?" Montagor demanded. "And you are certain that it is Zaor's?"

"Oh, yes. I suspected that she was breeding when I saw

her at the kingmaking. At the time, I assumed that it was some festival-got brat, or the result of climbing to her high office by currying Jannalor Nierde's favor—on her back," Lady Vashti said crudely. "But I made it my business to trace the wench's footsteps back. She and Zaor were together at the right time. There are magics that can determine a child's sire . . ."

She cast a sly look at the appalled Moon elf. "Why do you suppose I was so eager to place my son in the Towers? It was not from a desire to have him learn magic at the foot of a Gray elf, I assure you!"

"Kymil has slain Amlaruil's daughter," Montagor repeated in a dazed voice.

"Well, it appears that this elf can be taught," the Nimesin matron said with heavy sarcasm. "Ilyrana Moonflower is dead, or soon to be. It seems she fancies herself a priestess rather than a mage. She left the Towers to travel to Corellon's Grove as if it were some sacred pilgrimage. Kymil sent me word of this. Which brings us to your part in the matter."

"I will have no part of this!" Montagor said.

"An admirable sentiment, but a bit late in coming," Lady Vashti said dryly. "When you escorted Kymil to the Towers, he told you quite plainly of his intent. He said that you made no move to dissuade him or to disagree. We took your silence as assent, as will any who might hear of this matter now. Speak of it, and you will only condemn yourself."

The Moon elf slumped in his chair, defeated. "What must I do?"

Vashti Nimesin smiled coldly. "Many days will pass before Ilyrana is missed. By then, the poison which sent her into confused slumber will have run its course. It will be assumed that she, who has never been out of the Towers, simply lost her way in the forest and perished. Although it is unlikely that dark intent will be suspected, you will provide Kymil with a safeguard story. He left the Towers the day before Ilyrana departed. If any question is raised, you will say that he was hunting at your villa in the Eagle Hills, as your invited guest."

Montagor's thoughts whirled as he worked his way through this puzzle. All his life he had lived with the small intrigues, the endless positioning for power and influence, but never had he suspected that one elf would willingly slay another for gain. He wanted no part in any of it, yet he feared he was as firmly enmeshed as Lady Vashti claimed.

And yet, what would he lose if the Nimesin elves succeeded? Surely the Gold elf would not be content with killing Zaor's daughter. Lydi'aleera would be the next to go—perhaps Lady Nimesin would even require Montagor's hand in the matter! And for all that, what would keep her from eliminating the claimants of clan Amarillis, once the Moonflower elves were removed? No, this was not a path that Montagor could safely tread. He must set Lady Nimesin's foot upon another.

"I fear that this matter has gone beyond the simple remedy you suggest," Montagor said gravely. "As you know, my sister the queen has yet to bear an heir to the throne. You were not the only one to notice the looks that passed between Zaor and Amlaruil Moonflower during his kingmaking, or to search for possible by-blows of the king."

"What are you saying?" the elf woman demanded.

"Lydi'aleera knows that Amlaruil's daughter is Zaor's heir, and she has already taken steps to have the child brought to the palace for fosterage. Therein lies the problem. The death of a novice priestess might be mistaken as an accident; the death of a secret heir to the throne would certainly attract more scrutiny than either you or I could bear."

"How is this possible? You were surprised to hear of Amlaruil's child!"

Montagor spread his hands. "Forgive me for my prevarication, my lady. I had to feign ignorance, the better to learn the full extent of your knowledge. This is a delicate matter, and I'm sure you can understand."

"Has Lydi'aleera approached the king yet? Has he knowledge of this child?"

"Yes," Montagor said stoutly, praying that he might get word to his sister in time to bolster his plans.

The Gold elf wrung her hands in dismay. "Then all is lost! Had we known of this, Kymil would have chosen another way."

"There is yet a way to turn this around," Montagor said earnestly. "Kymil must find the princess before the poison takes effect, and bring her to the palace. I will swear that he acted all the while in behalf of Lydi'aleera."

"A Nimesin, errand runner for a Gray elf?" Vashti sneered.

"Better than being seen as a murderer and a traitor," Montagor pointed out coldly. "And do not think that you can implicate me in this. I have aided my sister in seeking out Zaor's heir—she will vouch for this! In this task, I have demonstrated my loyalty to the royal family, even placing it over the concerns and claims of Amarillis! In light of this, no one will believe I conspired with you against the crown princess. No, Nimesin will fall alone for this deed, on this you may believe me!"

He gave the elf woman time to absorb this new threat. "There is a way, however, that Nimesin can escape any taint of scandal," he said softly. "More than one Gold elf clan has left Evermeet for Cormanthyr— just last fortnight, every member of Ni'Tessine sailed for the mainland. Join them, and seek there the power that you have forfeited upon this island. If you go, I pledge upon my life and my honor that your secret will never be disclosed."

Lady Vashti glared at him with undisguised hatred. "Very well," she said at last. "Kymil will deliver the bastard princess and grit his teeth as he plays the role of heroic rescuer. Then I and all my house will leave this island. But do not think for a moment that we will cease to work for the good of the People!"

A familiar chill shivered through Montagor at these

words, for in them he glimpsed the shadow of deeds yet undone.

Yet he quickly comforted himself with this day's success. Once the Nimesins were safely off the island, he could surely stave off any future attacks. After all, was not Evermeet inviolate?

Lydi'aleera would not be pleased by these developments, but she was a pragmatic elf. Ensuring a strong succession to the throne was vital—that was the first lesson of the moonblades. Moreover, as a barren wife, she could not remain queen forever. Evermeet must have an heir, on that even the Gold elves agreed.

Montagor rose to his feet. "With your permission, Lady Nimesin, I am away to the palace. The queen needs to know that the princess is on her way, sooner than expected."

As he hurried through the streets of Leuthilspar toward the Moonstone Palace, Montagor wryly noted that his last words to Vashti Nimesin held much more truth than the elf woman could know.

19

Towers of the Sun and Moon

mlaruil sat alone in her chamber in the Tower of the Moon, staring at the framed picture in her hands. It was a small painting of Ilyrana as a child, done by one of the student mages not many years ago as a gift to the Lady of the Towers.

The mage studied the face of her only daughter, looking, as she often did, for some visible link between herself and Zaor. But Ilyrana was ever and always nothing but her own person.

Never had Amlaruil seen such oddly beautiful coloring as Ilyrana's. The elf maid closely resembled the opal for which she had been named; pure white, but for hints of pale colors that almost seemed to be reflected from some other source. Palest blue clung to her angular features, a flush of pink lingered about her lips and in the hollows of her cheeks, and a hint of green glinted among her white curls. Ilyrana was as beautiful—and nearly as remote—as the gods themselves.

With a sigh, Amlaruil put aside the portrait, silently berating herself for the terrible, numbing loss she felt over her daughter's absence. Surely that was nothing but selfishness!

And yet, even as the thought formed, Amlaruil knew it was untrue. She would have missed Ilyrana had the girl gone to the groves of Corellon to study as a priestess, but she would be content knowing that her daughter was following her chosen path. There was no peace in the knowledge that Ilyrana had been taken away from her own desires to be raised as a princess in the court of Leuthilspar.

It seemed to Amlaruil that there was reason for concern. One thing had Ilyrana inherited from her mother; her connection with the Seldarine was deep and profound, so much so that the girl often seemed detached from the mortal elves around her. How would she fare among the shallow, petty concerns of the Leuthilspar court? In the palace of Queen Lydi'aleera, fey and uncanny Ilyrana would be like a penned unicorn, or a pixie captured beneath a glass!

A soft knock at her door interrupted the mage's bitter thoughts. "Lady? I am bidden to summon you for evenfeast," came a tentative male voice from without.

Amlaruil started guiltily. Evenfeast, already? The day had slipped past unnoticed. It had not been the first.

She rose, smoothing the folds of her mantle about her, and bid the lad enter. Tanyl Evanara, a Gold elf boy whose slender limbs already held the promise of unusual grace and height, slipped into the room.

"Forgive the intrusion, Lady," he said, as his eyes darted to the portrait of Ilyrana.

"Not at all," Amlaruil said briskly, softening the words with a smile. "You merely did as you were bid, and well, as usual. Your studies are progressing, I trust?"

The boy's face lit up in a grin. "Shanyrria Alenuath says I will make a bladesinger, if that is my wish! I have both the sword and the voice for it, she says!"

"I am sure she is right," Amlaruil said, but she wondered if the fiery young bladesinger spoke more from impulse than wisdom. Shanyrria had that tendency. Yet truly, Tanyl showed promise in the use of both weapons and song magic, and perhaps the bladesinger's path was indeed his to follow. A bladesinger melded magic, music, and fighting into a uniquely elven technique, and was in many ways the epitome of an elven warrior. But bladesinging was not merely a fighting style, but a philosophy. Amlaruil could not picture the gregarious Tanyl as one of these self-contained warriors.

"I am sure that Shanyrria is right about your potential," Amlaruil repeated, "but remember that your path is your own to chose. Just because you *can* do a thing, it does not follow that you *must.*"

The boy's forehead furrowed as he contemplated this advice. "I will remember," he said somberly. He bowed then, and offered his arm to Amlaruil with the grace of a courtier.

"I am to escort you to evenfeast. You must eat—Naki-asha said so," he added with a grin, suddenly appearing to be the boy he was. He clearly took delight in their implied fellowship; after all, even the beautiful Grand Mage of the Towers had to listen to *someone!*

Smothering her own smile, Amlaruil took the arm Tanyl offered and walked with him down the spiraling stairs that led to the dining hall.

As she did, she could not help but wonder if her well-meaning words to this talented boy were based in reality. Had she herself chosen the path she now trod? Had Ilyrana, or even Zaor? In truth, did anyone?

The soft murmur of conversation that filled the dining hall dwindled to near silence as the Grand Mage entered the room. Amlaruil smiled and nodded to the gathered elves, indicating that they should continue. At proud Tanyl's side, she made her way into the very center of the spiraling table. As she took her place in the midst of them, a terrible desolation swept over her in sudden, devastating waves. None of this felt real—not the gathered elves, or the food on her plate, not even her presence in this chamber.

Amlaruil speared a bit of venison and pretended to eat. As she did, she noted the disapproving eyes of Belstram Durothil upon her.

A troubling thought edged into her mind. The young nobleman was highly ranked in his clan, and had even held a seat on the Council until his recent decision to

leave the court of Leuthilspar to study magic at the
Towers. Belstram was also a near relative of Mylaerla
Durothil, that too-perceptive matron who had seen what
had passed between Zaor and Amlaruil on the day of
Zaor's crowning. Lady Durothil was now one of Zaor's
most trusted generals, but it was possible that she had
spoken to her kin of the "nearly-averted disaster" that
had threatened the kingmaking alliance between Moonflower and Amarillis. Perhaps it had been Belstram who
had ferreted out the truth of Ilyrana's parentage, and had
taken word of the royal heir to Moonstone Palace. His
arrival at the Towers was certainly well timed.

Amlaruil dropped her gaze to her plate. It would not
help matters if her bitterness were to creep into her eyes,
and give further offense to any member of clan Durothil.
There were many among the Durothils who believed that
one of their members—or at the very least, another Gold
elf—should rule the Towers in Amlaruil's stead.

"Is my lady well?" Belstram inquired politely.

"No, and well you know it."

A long, silent moment passed before Amlaruil realized
that she had spoken the bitter words aloud. Amlaruil took
a long, steadying breath and forced herself to meet the
Gold elf's eyes.

"Forgive me, Lord Durothil, and all of you," she said
in a clear voice that reached to the edges of the chamber. "That was spoken without thought or purpose. I
have been too absorbed with my own affairs. It will not
continue."

"I am glad to hear these words, Lady Amlaruil. Do you
mean to say, then, that you will no longer remain in seclusion in these Towers?" Belstram pressed. "It is a matter
that must be addressed," he continued heatedly, silencing
the murmur of protest that rose from the assembled magi.
"Lady Amlaruil has not left these Tower grounds for nearly
fifteen years, not since the birth of her daughter. Indeed,
until recently it was not known beyond these walls that
she *had* a child."

Amlaruil rose in one swift movement. "And now that all the world knows?" she said in a choked voice. "What good has come of it?"

The Gold elf rose from his place and came to face the angry mage. "The royal house has an heir," Belstram said softly. "This was a needed thing. What Evermeet needs now, my lady, is a Grand Mage."

Several of the elves gasped at his effrontery, others rose in protest. The bladesinger Shanyrria, predictably enough, drew her sword in hot-tempered willingness to fight for the Lady of the Tower's honor.

Amlaruil gazed down at the Gold elf, astounded by his open challenge to her position before all the gathered magi. But to her astonishment, she read in Belstram's face not animosity, not even ambition, but deep and genuine concern. She saw, too, the truth in his accusation.

A sad smile curved her lips. "Thank you, Lord Durothil," she said softly. "Thank you for your honesty. Your words are hard, but fair. I have not been the Grand Mage that Evermeet deserves."

"You misunderstand," Belstram said, seeming genuinely appalled by Amlaruil's words. He further astounded her by going down on one knee before her.

"You are dying, Lady Amlaruil," he said bluntly. "With each day that passes, you slip closer to Arvandor. Evermeet needs a Grand Mage, yet you are willfully depriving her of perhaps the greatest to rule these towers. Once, I thought that Jannalor Nierde had chosen his successor unwisely. Do not continue on this path, and prove me right."

For many moments, the silence that filled the chamber was profound and absolute. Then Nakiasha huffed loudly. "It's about time someone other than me spoke sense in these halls," declared the opinionated sorceress. "Which leads me to an interesting question. Are you absolutely certain, Belstram, that you aren't a Green elf in disguise?"

The look of consternation that crossed the Durothil's face sent the forest elf sorceress into hoots of laughter.

Nakiasha's mirth was contagious, spreading throughout the dining hall and echoing long as the elves found in laughter a much-needed release. Even Belstram managed a self-conscious smile as he rose and made his way back to his place.

Both bolstered and shamed by the truth in Belstram's words, Amlaruil resumed her seat and made a real effort at downing some of the food. As the evening progressed, the lightened mood of the evenfeast spilled over into celebration, for the young High Mage was much loved, and great was the elves' relief to have their concerns for her given voice.

Much later, as the elves danced in the Tower gardens beneath a star-filled sky, Amlaruil slipped away into the forest to ponder the events and insights of the day. Following a sure instinct, she made her way to the clearing in which she had first met Zaor.

She stood in long silence, remembering her first meeting with Zaor and the vision which had come to her that day. She remembered also the night when the King-Killer star had appeared to her and Lamruil, and had ironically set in motion the events that led to the crowning of an elven monarch.

Much later that evening, Zaor found her there, as Nakiasha said he might. As the elven king gazed upon his lost love, he understood why the sorceress had sent for him.

The change in Amlaruil was appalling, and unmistakable. Once, Zaor had witnessed the passage of an elf to Arvandor. His own father, a ranger who spent his life in the defense of Myth Drannor's forests, had simply faded away, leaving behind like a final benediction a fleeting glimmer of silvery motes. Amlaruil was doing much the same thing. In the faint, fey light of the stars, her slender form looked almost translucent. Zaor could see the faint shadows of these glittering motes—not just silver, as he would expect, but also gold, blue, green and even a few tiny pinpricks of gleaming obsidian. Zaor did not wonder at this, for in his mind Amlaruil was the uncrowned queen of all the elven People. He felt a deep sadness, though, for the years of loss—not only the empty years he had spent in the Moonstone Palace, but the centuries that stretched before him, void of his one love, his true queen.

"Come back to us, Amlaruil," he said softly.

The elf woman whirled at the sound of his voice, her blue eyes wide and startled and one hand at her throat. She stared at Zaor for a moment as if not entirely certain that she had not conjured him with a thought. Then her too-angular face relaxed into a smile. "You still walk with the silence of a ranger, my lord."

She made move to kneel, but Zaor was at her side in a few quick steps. He grasped her arms and pulled her fiercely to him.

"What are doing?" he demanded in a raw, angry voice.

Amlaruil blinked. "I had thought to do proper reverence to Evermeet's king," she said dryly.

"Not that! You are slipping away—you are leaving Evermeet behind. I will not permit it!"

The elf woman sighed, undone by the anguish in Zaor's voice and the truth in his words. Her head sank down to rest on Zaor's shoulder. His arms enfolded her.

"Promise me that you will stay," he said in softer tones. "Swear that you will remain on Evermeet for as long as you are needed."

Amlaruil lifted her head to look into his eyes. "That is a difficult pledge, my lord, and beyond the scope even of Evermeet's king to demand."

"Even so, I think it is within your power to keep."

Even as he spoke the words, Zaor recognized the truth in them. All elves were slow to age, but time refused to touch Amlaruil with any but the kindest of hands. But for the fashion of her hair and the sadness in her eyes, she was still the lithesome elf maid he had glimpsed many years ago. And since the day that he had met Ilyrana, he had been beset by the suspicion that the girl was not entirely mortal. The gods had touched his daughter. Zaor could sense, if not fully understand, Ilyrana's deep communion and connection with the Seldarine. And through Ilyrana, he had come to better understand the nature of Ilyrana's mother. Whatever Amlaruil set her mind to, she could do.

Amlaruil was silent for a long moment, as if she, too, knew the truth of his words. "I swear it," she said at last.

With a faint smile, she eased out of Zaor's embrace. "How is Ilyrana?"

It was strangely comforting, to be discussing their child as if they were lovers wed, recently reunited after a small time apart. Zaor only wished he had more to tell Amlaruil.

"Ilyrana is hard to know," he admitted. "She is not a cold or rude girl, yet she remains aloof, distant."

"Has she taken well to court life?"

Zaor sighed. "On the face of it, well enough. Her manners are without flaw, and her beauty remarkable. Though she is not yet of age, already the young nobles are lining up to vie for her favors. But when not at her lessons or at court, she has little to do with anyone in the palace."

"The queen is kind to her?" Amlaruil said tentatively, hating to ask but needing to know.

"Lydi'aleera is not *unkind*. She does not know what to do with Ilyrana, though. She has no understanding of the girl. Not that I am much better," he added.

Amlaruil heard the guilt in his voice. "You cannot blame yourself. Ilyrana is a stranger to you. That choice was mine, for good or ill."

"You should have told me," Zaor said softly.

The elf woman shook her head, understanding what he meant. "If I had told you on the day of your kingmaking that I carried your child, you would never have agreed to the alliance with Amarillis. As things stand, the kingdom is secure, Evermeet's defenses have never been stronger, and even the most contentious Gold elves speak with grudging pride of their king. Would any of this have come to pass, had you passed over Lydi'aleera to wed your cousin?"

"But does it truly matter, compared to what we have lost?"

"It matters!" Amlaruil said with sudden passion. "Do not dismiss what we have accomplished, or demean the sacrifices that we have made! If I did not believe that what I did was for the good of Evermeet, I could not bear this life!"

Zaor again took the angry elf woman in his arms, soothing her with soft words and gentle hands. The years fell away from them both, and with joy he felt the familiar kindling of their shared flame. When he thought he could bear no more, Amlaruil broke away. Her eyes searched his.

"How is it that you have no heir within marriage?" she asked softly.

The elf grimaced but did not flinch away from the question. "Perhaps I have not your dedication to Evermeet, Amlaruil. But there are some duties that I cannot countenance. If that makes me less the king, so be it. Lydi'aleera agreed to this alliance for what it was—a political convenience and no more. Before we were wed, I told her in all honesty what would be between her and me, and what would not. I cannot be other than I am."

"And what is that?" murmured Amlaruil, reading the answer in his eyes but needing to hear the words.

"Yours," he replied. "Only yours."

"For this night," she agreed, taking his hands and drawing him down with her to the forest bed of deep, green-velvet moss.

"No," Zaor said softly. "For all time."

* * * * *

In the months that followed, Amlaruil fulfilled her promises of that night in ways that astounded even her most avid supporters.

She left the Towers at last, traveling Evermeet with a small Circle of magi and testing the sons and daughters of both noble and common houses. Those who showed talent were accepted for training, regardless of birth.

This did not please all the elves, particularly those scions of the powerful Gold elf families who felt that they had already lost enough. Amlaruil had a ready answer for these restless and disgruntled young elves. In a planned confrontation, during the midsummer gathering at the Drelagara meadows, she brought a Circle of magi in mock spell battle against the powerful war wizard Yalathanil Symbaern.

Though all understood that the magical jousting was meant as entertainment, the power of Yalathanil's magic staff, demonstrated before a large gathering of wizards, magi, and nobles, had the effect that Amlaruil desired.

Magic items, she insisted, were not merely family treasures to be hoarded. They were an important part of elven culture, a legacy of all elves. She pledged the support of the Towers to any adventurers who wished to recover elven artifacts from the ruins of lost elven civilizations, and to artisans who would create new ones. The result was a flurry of activity, and the harbors of Leuthilspar bloomed with ships sailing eastward to reclaim the glories of times past.

Inspired by the High Mage's example, the elves began to pursue the magical arts with renewed fervor. But as Amlaruil was soon to learn, nurturing the strengths of the elves was an easy matter. Dealing with their failures was quite another.

As the clans vied with each other for power in magical matters, the children of noble houses were increasingly urged to excel. There were some children sent to the Tower who, in less enthusiastic times, would not have been there. Chief among these was Rennyn Aelorothi.

The young Gold elf was rapidly becoming a problem. Like many of his kin, Rennyn was proud and even arrogant about his high birth. But unlike most elves, he had a barrier about his heart that kept him apart from any sort of deep communion. The Aelorothi clan was determined that their son become a High Mage, yet the intense sharing of the Circle magic was utterly beyond him.

For a while, Amlaruil tried to occupy Rennyn's talents elsewhere. But he disdained to learn the bladesinger's art from Shanyrria Alenuath, claiming he would not apprentice himself to a Moon elf. He showed some promise with battle spells and simple illusions, but as his training progressed it became clear that he simply possessed an unusually small amount of talent for any sort of magic.

Demand for places in the Tower was high, and elves of great promise waited for their turns. The other High Magi began to clamor for Rennyn's dismissal. But Amlaruil was unwilling to do this, and not just for fear of alienating the powerful Aelorothi family. She saw much to value in Rennyn. Although his skills were not those highly prized by the elven culture, she began to envision a role in which he could excel.

The day she called him to her private rooms, Rennyn came before her with the stiff pride of one who saw his fate approaching and was prepared to accept it standing tall.

"You know that I am dedicated to the service of these Towers, but I will be the first to admit that they are not all of Evermeet," Amlaruil began, putting the young elf immediately off guard. "There are other important tasks to be done. I think that an elf of your talents might do better for himself by looking beyond these Towers."

"And what talents might those be?" Rennyn said with bitterness. "I am a failed mage, however you wish to gild me with your golden words!"

"Not so," Amlaruil countered. "You have gained facility with many types of magic. You have not the makings of a High Mage, I agree with that, but with a little assistance from the right devices, you could accomplish any magical task you might need to undertake."

She took a ring from her hand and gave it to him. "There is a looking glass on the wall behind you. Put on the ring, and imagine that you need to speak with a forest elf, a stranger to you."

The elf gave her an incredulous look, but did as he was bid. He turned to face the mirror, only to pull back, startled by the strange face that gazed back at him. His own face, albeit copper in hue and swirled with green and brown tatoos, stared out from the glass with inscrutable black eyes. The familiar golden hair had darkened to brown, and was ornamented with weavings of feathers and beads. Rennyn lifted a wondering hand to touch his face, looking surprised anew as his reflection followed suit.

Amlaruil smiled. "The ring's magic suits you well. You have a natural talent, Rennyn, for being other than what you appear. I have seen you charm an elf maid with a smile, convince a soldier with a few bluff words that you are his comrade and friend. And yet—forgive me—you are never touched in turn. You hold yourself apart from those you easily befriend, and give only and precisely what you chose to give. And in truth, the elf maid and the soldier would not know you from each other's description."

Amlaruil leaned forward, her face earnest. "I have in mind for you a role in which you can truly excel. While it might not sound as grand as a councilor or a war wizard, it is every bit as important to Evermeet. I want you to be the eyes and ears of the Towers. You will travel, both on Evermeet and to distant lands, and send me word of such things as we here should know."

"You would have me be a spy?" he said, more in astonishment than disapproval.

"A hidden diplomat," she agreed. "You have fine judgment and excellent discretion, and if ever these talents should fall short of the task at hand, your fighting skills are impressive and should more than fill that gap. Your first task is an important one, something I would not entrust to an elf of lesser talents."

Amlaruil stood and shrugged off her mantle. The silken

folds of her gown clung to her rounded belly. "As you can see, I am again with child," she said serenely, her hands framing her belly as if cradling the life within. "Before the winter is past, I will bear twin sons to King Zaor. They will be raised in secret fosterage with my distant kin, and trained among the warriors of Craulnober Keep. You will accompany them as their guardian and bodyguard, and see that they are delivered safely. None must know of their identity, or yours." Amlaruil smiled at the astonished elf. "Would I give you a task so near my heart, if there was another better suited?"

With effort, Rennyn stopped gaping. "And the king?"

"Zaor knows of my choice, and approves it," Amlaruil told him. "When you have done this, you may sail for the mainland. The ring you wear is also an elfrune, a device of my creation. I have enspelled it so that you might speak to me at will. It will also transport you magically, instantly, back to Evermeet in times of grave danger. I will show you how to use these powers. But first," she suggested, "show me the guise you will use when you go to Craulnober Keep."

Rennyn turned back to the mirror. A faint, sardonic smile lifted his lips as he confronted his changed image. He was now a Moon elf warrior, white-skinned and silver-haired. His frame was heavier, almost human in appearance, and his arms and shoulders gave promise of daunting strength.

"Forgive me, lady," he murmured, "but I doubt my parents would approve this transformation."

Amlaruil came to stand beside him, her hand on his shoulder. "Trust me with your family, as I entrust you with mine," she told him firmly. "I will tell the Aelorothi whatever they need to know to help them understand how important their son is to Evermeet. Your kindred are honorable; they will keep their council and only say with pride that Rennyn travels on missions for the king."

The elf turned and bowed low to Amlaruil. "Thank you for allowing my family to save face."

"Do you still think that is my intent?" she demanded. "You are a remarkable elf, Rennyn, with unusual talents. And though you serve King Zaor, you will also be my personal representative and the guardian of my sons. I do not assign this task lightly."

"The queen's knight," Rennyn murmured thoughtfully, pride kindling in his eyes.

Amlaruil lifted one brow. "I do not think that Queen Lydi'aleera would thank you for that description," she said dryly.

"Lydi'aleera is a vapid fool," Rennyn responded without rancor. He shrugged. "Forgive me, but it seems to me that you, not Lydi'aleera Amarillis, are Evermeet's rightful queen. And I say this not just for the heirs you have given Zaor."

Before Amlaruil could respond to this pronouncement, Rennyn drew his sword and lay it at her feet. "I will serve you and your children, in secrecy and in honor, the hidden knight of a hidden queen," he said, and knelt before her.

Perhaps because the young elf looked up at her with such shining expectancy, perhaps because he needed so desperately to believe in his worth and hers, Amlaruil took up the sword and with reverent solemnity declared Rennyn Aelorothi a knight of Evermeet. And when he left, she found that she did not regret the action.

Amlaruil slipped back on the concealing mantle of High Mage. But before returning to her duties, she paused to gaze thoughtfully at the reflection in her mirror.

It seemed to her that the faint shadow of a crown lingered upon her forehead. And she wondered if, perhaps, the magic of Rennyn's ring allowed him to see through illusions as well as create them. The young elf had seen a truth that she herself was just coming to accept: Though she ruled only in the Towers of the Sun and Moon, in heart and spirit she was Evermeet's true queen. The gods knew it: for had not she as a girl touched Zaor's moonblade, the king sword, as if it were her own?

What did it matter that the elves did not recognize or

acknowledge her? She would still serve—a hidden queen, Rennyn had called her, but a queen nonetheless.

Well content, Amlaruil left her chambers to take up once again the rule of the Towers.

20

Windows on the World

mlaruil tried to look sternly upon the identical scamps standing before her, their tousled blue heads hanging sheepishly low and bare toes scuffing at the polished marble floor.

It was difficult, though, to summon anything resembling maternal wrath over the boys' latest misdeed. Indeed, it was all she could do to keep from sweeping both of them up into her arms and forgiving them outright for this, any past and all future offenses.

Xharlion and Zhoron, her twin sons, were small replicas of their warrior father. Sturdy and stubborn, they had inherited Zaor's sharp features—right down to the dent in the center of their chins—and their father's distinctive sapphire-colored curls. Amlaruil could not help but smile wistfully whenever she looked upon them, a blessing which came to her all too seldom.

"You boys are under the fosterage of Lord and Lady Craulnober," she reminded them with mock severity. "You are to obey them as you would me, and study with diligence all the things they would have you learn."

"But dancing?" Xharlion exclaimed, spitting out the word with exquisite disdain. "What need have warriors of Evermeet for that?"

"It is the custom of the Craulnobers to teach all the young elves in their care the ways of court life as well as the skills of the battlefield," Amlaruil reminded him. "It is, I might add, a custom with which I wholeheartedly agree. Life does not present us with a single task, and an elven noble must be able to comport himself well in many circumstances. And what have you against dancing, anyway? It is as important to an elf, and as natural, as magic!"

"Well, the two things aren't so bad, when you put 'em together," Zhoron observed, his blue eyes sparkling with mischief. The twins exchanged a sly look. Their shoulders shook as they snickered at their shared memory of the morning's events.

Amlaruil struggled to keep from joining in. The image of the primly sedate Chichlandra Craulnober shrieking and clutching at her fly-away skirts was almost Amlaruil's undoing.

"You should not have enspelled Lady Chichlandra to dance upon the ceiling rather than the floor," she admonished them.

"Lady Chicken-legs," Zhoron improvised, setting the twins off in another bout of giggles. "That one ought to wear longer bloomers, I'd say!"

"Dances like a chicken, too, she does," Xharlion said. He tucked his hands high up on his sides, flapping his elbows like wings as he minced through the first steps of a roundelay. His small face was set in an eerily precise imitation of Lady Chichlandra's tight, prissy smile.

At last Amlaruil succumbed to a chuckle, which earned her a pair of identical, conspiratorial grins.

"Do not think for a moment that I approve," she cautioned the boys. "Whatever your opinion of Lady Chichlandra's dancing—or her legs, for that matter— you need to show her proper respect. Terrifying and embarrassing your hostess is not the sort of behavior I expect from you."

The genuine disappointment in her voice finally pierced the twins' high spirits. They mumbled apologies, and when Amlaruil dismissed them, they actually *walked* from the room and down the hall that led to the garden, rather than bolting headlong through the open window as was their

usual custom. In moments, however, they had found
wooden swords and were bashing at each other with great
gusto, emitting battle whoops lusty enough to give pause
to a well-armed ogre.

Amlaruil sighed as she watched the boys at play.
"My work in the Towers keeps me from them far too
much."

"They are being well taught here, lady," Rennyn
Aelorothi assured her, coming from the shadows to stand
beside the mage. The Gold elf was a frequent visitor to
Craulnober Keep, and he had come to look upon the twins
as his personal charges. "There is no finer swordmaster
than Elanjar Craulnober on all of Evermeet."

The mage turned to smile at Rennyn. "Why, I never
thought to hear such sentiments from you concerning any
Silver elf!" she teased him.

Rennyn responded with a shrug. "I have seen much in
the last ten years. Things are not so simple as I once
thought them, nor are the Gold elves quite the paragons
we like to think ourselves. There are elven cultures that,
although very different from that of Evermeet, are worthy
of respect."

"So you said, earlier. Tell me more about the elves of the
Moonshaes," she prompted, knowing that her young advi-
sor was eager to speak more on the matter, having recently returned from a trip to these islands.

"They are fierce fighters and fine riders—on horseback,
they are as nimble as centaurs," Rennyn began, speaking
with great enthusiasm. "Their magic is different from ours,
too, and very much a part of the land. Even an elf would
have a difficult time finding their valley, for it is hidden
from common view by magic." He paused. "In fact, this
sheltered valley might be the very place for restless young
princes to begin exploring the world."

Amlaruil nodded thoughtfully as she watched the
warring twins. Their play had progressed from sheer
exuberance to fierce competition. As she watched, they
threw aside their swords and leaped at each other. They

fell together, rolling and pummeling as they went at it with fists and feet. Fortunately for Amlaruil's peace of mind, it appeared that the twins were dealing far more damage to Lady Craulnober's flower beds than to each other.

"They are too like their father in that they will need to find or form kingdoms of their own," she mused. "I fear there is little future for them here on Evermeet, since Ilyrana seems destined to rule."

"The Sonorian Valley may have need of such warriors as Xharlion and Zhoron will become," Rennyn said. "The elves are secure enough now, but I fear for them as humans become more numerous on the island. Perhaps the presence of the young princes will help persuade the elves to set up a gate between Evermeet and their valley."

"A fine idea," she commended him. "You have done well, Rennyn, in forming ties with other elven settlements, and in training the Ahmaquissar elves to follow your example."

The elf bowed. "I thank you for your words, my lady. They remind me, however, of my fear that we will soon lose the services of one of our agents. Nevarth Ahmaquissar."

"Oh?"

"He wishes to remain in the High Forest, in the company of a young elf woman."

"Ah." Amlaruil nodded in sympathy, even if she found the image hard to conjure. Nevarth was a roguish, carefree elf who changed ladyloves with a frequency that rivaled that of the new moons. "You have met this girl?"

A troubled look crossed Rennyn's face. "I have. She is very beautiful, and very bewitching. I suppose I can see why Nevarth is taken with her."

The mage heard and understood her agent's hesitation. Though she knew full well the power of young love, she also knew that Nevarth had trained long and hard to win his place among the High Mage's advisors. He would not lightly cast it aside.

"Perhaps I should summon him home, and try to learn more about his intentions."

"That would be wise. If you please, lady, I would as soon not be present when you speak to him." Rennyn paused, and again he looked disturbed. "He would not thank me for speaking against his ladylove. He is very jealous of her, and has already accused me of trying to come between them, thus to win her favors for myself."

Amlaruil frowned. That was very unlike Nevarth. He was sounding less and less like an elf enamored, and more like one ensorcelled. "I will speak to him now through the elfrune he carries. Go then, Rennyn, and I promise you I shall be discrete about my source of information."

The Gold elf bowed and left the room. As soon as she was alone, Amlaruil touched the ring on her small finger and spoke her agent's name, followed by an arcane phrase.

A few moments passed before Nevarth answered. His voice sounded unusually distracted, even impatient. Amlaruil, her concern increasing by the moment, insisted that he meet her at once, at the small lodge near the Lake of Dreams that the Grand Mage and her agents often used for such meetings.

When the light from her ring faded, along with Nevarth's reluctant assurances, Amlaruil gathered up her skirts and ran out into the garden that had become the boys' impromptu battlefield. There was but time for a quick embrace and a brief admonition concerning future behavior before her duties took her, once again, from those she loved.

* * * * *

"Why must you go?"

Nevarth Ahmaquissar stopped tugging on his boots long enough to cast a wistful glance at the elf woman curled up among the silken pillows of their shared bed. Even newly awakened, she was stunning—the most beautiful Moon elf he had ever seen. Her masses of night-black hair were still tousled from his touch, and the skin of her lithe, naked body was the rich, pale color of new cream. As if sensing a momentary weakness, Araushnee pouted prettily, then patted the cushions in renewed invitation.

"What is this Amlaruil to you? You do not rush so when I call you," she said in a voice that reminded Nevarth simultaneously of feywine and dark velvet.

"Rush?" The elf grinned. "Never that! You are meant to be savored, my love."

"Yet you are leaving me."

"Only for a while," he said in soothing tones. "I have business on Evermeet, and then I will return. And when I do, I need never leave again."

"Pretty words!" scoffed Araushnee. "How many elf maidens have heard the famed minstrel Nevarth sing *that* song?"

The elf caught one of her hands and raised it to his lips. "My heart is yours alone," he said, speaking with a simple dignity that was very unlike his accustomed banter. "You know this to be true."

Araushnee lifted her other hand and smoothed a finger over the ring Nevarth wore on the small finger of his hand. "Then give me a token to keep until you return. This ring."

"I cannot." He hesitated, as if wondering how much to reveal. The words came out in a rush. "I would give you this or anything else, but I cannot. The ring is enspelled. No one can wear it but me—it cannot even be removed from my finger while I live, and when I die its magic perishes with me."

The elf maid lifted one ebony brow. "Powerful magic for a simple minstrel to carry."

"Yes," he said, and though she waited, he did not offer further explanation.

After a moment, Araushnee sighed and took a ring from her own hand. "If you will not give me a token, at least wear one of mine! Take this to Evermeet with you, and think of me when you look upon it."

Nevarth willingly held out his hand to her. He glanced down at the ring she slipped onto his middle finger, noting that the band shifted to fit his larger hand. The stone, a ruby, seemed to stare up at him like a malevolent crimson eye. Nevarth blinked and shook his head as if to dispel the odd image. When he looked again, the ring was merely a lovely red stone, as bright and vital and wonderfully fierce as the elf woman who shared his bed and held his heart in her white hands.

Araushnee rose up on her knees, entwining her arms around his neck and lifting her face for one last kiss. Willingly, eagerly, the elf made his farewells. When at last he stepped away, his smile said without words that he would not need her token in order to remember her long and well.

The elf woman watched Nevarth slip away into the silver path of magic, waited until the heat shadow he left behind had faded utterly away. Then she herself began to change. The rich ebony color of her hair leached away, washing down over her skin like spilled ink. She took on height and power in a sudden rush. Her body became more lush, and it gleamed in the lamplight like polished obsidian as she rose from the bed and glided over to a locked chest. From it she took a blood-red scrying bowl. As she knelt and gazed into it, her large blue eyes changed to mirror the malevolent crimson of the ring that Nevarth wore in her honor.

The being known in ages long past as Araushnee studied the bowl intently as the last vestiges of her mortal disguise slipped away. Even with the sharp eyes of a drow, the avatar form of the goddess Lloth, she did not see anything. Nor did she truly expect to. The magic guarding Evermeet was powerful and subtle, and she could not penetrate it even with such magic as she possessed. Nothing that she or her agents had attempted could pierce the shield that Corellon had woven about his children.

Well, Araushnee—or Lloth, as she was now known—had children of her own, and none wove webs more skillfully than she. Beneath the lands that Corellon's children trod, beneath the seas they sailed, her people live in a maze of tunnels so convoluted and intricate that even they themselves could not number all their secrets.

For many hundreds of years, the drow had sought a passage under the seas to Evermeet. Always they had fallen short, for the spells of misdirection protecting the island were powerful. More than once, the work of many years had been ruined in a sudden, terrible flood as the seas rushed in to destroy a too-hasty tunnel. Evermeet had so far remained beyond Lloth's grasping hand.

But Nevarth, dear besotted little elfling that he was, would finally change that. Like so many of Evermeet's elves, he had devoted himself to following the will of this upstart, this Amlaruil.

Lloth hated Evermeet's Grand Mage with a passion that rivalled her loathing for Corellon himself. And yet, she was almost grateful to the Moon elf female. It was Amlaruil, after all, who was opening windows between Evermeet and the rest of Aber-toril.

Windows, that if properly used, could look both ways.

It had been no small thing for Lloth to take on an avatar form so different from her nature, no small thing to play the part of a Moon elf seductress. But if her gambit succeeded, the prize would be worth all the aggravation.

And when Nevarth returned to claim his "beloved," Lloth would take the small, added pleasure of killing the elf, slowly and with exquisite attention to every possible nuance of pain.

A smile of near-contentment crossed the goddess's dark face. Even when compared to her ruling passions—a consuming hatred of elves, a love of power, and an implacable thirst for vengeance—Nevarth's devotion to his precious Amlaruil was a powerful thing. It would give Lloth great pleasure to let him know that not only had he been betrayed, but that he had in turn betrayed Evermeet.

* * * * *

The white whirl and rush of magical travel faded away to be replaced by a deep green haze. As the verdant mist sharpened, Nevarth Ahmaquissar felt the familiar magic of Evermeet's forest reach out to enfold him as if in welcome.

And yet, something did not seem quite right. The elf heard a faint sound, squeals and cries that suggested a wounded animal. He followed the sounds until he stood at the lip of a deep, broad pit. Within the pit, bleeding from a dozen wounds and nearly frantic with pain and terror, was an enormous wild boar.

Nevarth frowned. It was not elven custom to dig pits for hunting, for there was a possibility that an animal might be left wounded and helpless. As he studied the wounded boar, he realized that this was even worse. It appeared that the creature's wounds had been inflicted by elven spears and arrows. The boar had been deliberately hurt, and left here. But why?

The faint sound of elven boots alerted him, and suggested that an answer might be soon in coming. Nevarth darted into the deep foliage, well beyond sight, and crouched down to listen.

"Is the trap in readiness?" inquired a melodious elven voice, a cultured voice belonging to a young male.

Nevarth shifted, trying to catch sight of the speaker, but the thick curtain of leaves blocked his view.

"All is as we discussed," another male responded. "King Zaor will come, and alone. Of that I am certain. When he passes between the twin oaks—as he must, to reach the lodge—the ropes will raise the net beneath the boar. The creature will be free of the pit, and in its pain and madness will attack anything within reach. No single elf, not even Zaor Moonflower, is a match for a wounded boar!"

"It is a fearsome animal, and in fine mettle for a fight," the first elf said. "You have done well, Fenian."

410

"I hope the creature is too far gone in pain and rage to come under the king's spell," the one called Fenian said in a worried tone. "My father knew Zaor in Cormanthyr. He said that as a ranger, Zaor was without equal. Do you think he can tame that boar?"

The elf laughed. "I doubt it. And even if Zaor should manage to tame or kill the beast, he will not find a smooth path back to Leuthilspar. Other traps await him. And if need arises, well, I'd be more than happy to do the deed myself. My mother bid me not to kill the Moon elf myself—since there is always the possibility of discovery—but I would relish the opportunity for battle. Have I not pledged to see every one of the Gray elf pretenders slain?"

Nevarth could bear no more. He exploded from his hiding place, drawing his sword as he rushed toward the traitorous elves.

The pair of them looked up, startled, as the Moon elf came at them. With a stab of surprise, Nevarth realized that he knew one of them. Fenian Ni'Tessine had left Evermeet with his Gold elf family years ago for the forests of Cormanthyr. The other, younger Gold elf was also familiar, but Nevarth could not place him.

Both elves drew their swords. In unspoken agreement, they whirled away from the onrushing elf, forcing Nevarth to chose a single target. The Moon elf settled on Fenian and came at him, sword held high for a slashing downward stroke.

As Nevarth hoped, Fenian countered, raising his blade to parry. The Moon elf swung down hard, meeting Fenian's sword with enough force to send sparks darting off into the forest shadows. Before the Gold elven traitor could recover from the blow and disengage his blade, Nevarth snatched a long knife from his belt and stepped in under the joined swords.

The second elf's sword thrust in hard, slashing a deep gash across the back of Nevarth's knife hand and spoiling his killing stroke. The Moon elf threw his arm wide and somehow managed to land a wild backhand punch to the attacker's face. He spun away, then faced the pair of Gold elves head on. They stalked in like hunting cats, swords before them.

Nevarth did what he could, but his two blades could not match the swords of the Gold elven traitors. Again and again they broke through his guard, their swords leaving long and bloody trails across his arms, his chest, his face.

Still Nevarth fought on, not only for his life, but for that of the king. He had to survive, or Zaor would walk into a traitor's snare.

A female voice called his name, and suddenly Nevarth knew the fight was won. "That is Amlaruil—the Grand Mage," he informed the elves, speaking the words between the rapid exchange of blows. "You are as good as dead."

A look of deep hatred swept the face of the younger elf, but he danced back beyond the reach of Nevarth's sword. "Fenian, to the trees! Let the king's whore find her slain champion. You can bring her down with an arrow while she mourns him!"

Nevarth thought this a bit presumptuous, considering that he was far from dead. Yet even as the thought formed, the Gold elf whirled forward, his sword flashing up and around so rapidly that its path seemed to linger as a solid, silvery circle. Nevarth did not feel the cut, but dimly he felt the blood-soaked ground rush up to meet him. In some distant, fading part of his mind he saw the Gold elf sheath his blade and melt into the forest.

He tried to warn Amlaruil, tried to wave her away, tried to bid her no when she knelt beside him. But his limbs were so terribly cold, and they would no longer answer his will. No words could rise through his torn throat.

He thought, briefly, of his Araushnee, but oddly enough he could not bring to mind an image of her face. The light faded from before his eyes, until all that was left to him was an image of the glowing ruby on his hand, and a deep, terrible sense of failure. Amlaruil would die because of him.

Yes, she will die, and all of Corellon's children with her, exulted a familiar dark-velvet voice in his mind.

Nevarth heard Amlaruil's startled intake of breath, and realized that she, too, heard the silent voice. And then he was gone, spinning away from his torn body.

Amlaruil stared in disbelief at the dead elf, her mind whirling as she tried to sort through what had happened. He had been in fierce battle—she had heard the clash of swords from the lodge nearby. His enemies could not have gone far. And what of that terrible, malevolent voice, the sense of dark and evil magic that hung about him like a miasma?

Answers she must have, no matter how they were gotten. Amlaruil took a deep breath and prepared to do what was anathema to any elf: interfere with the afterlife of another. To delay the passage to Arvandor, for any reason, was a terrible thing. But Amlaruil was certain that this she must do.

She was no priestess, yet her connection to the Seldarine was deep and direct. Amlaruil sent her thoughts along the path to Arvandor, the same path that Nevarth was surely taking.

In the gray mist between the mortal world and the immortal, she felt the uncertain spirit of the Moon elf agent. Urgently she demanded to know what had happened. Nevarth told her without words, transferring his thoughts, his fears and failures. He gave her the name he knew—Fenien—and warned her there were other traitors. He yielded his regrets, his hopes, his dearest dreams. As the information surged into her mind, one thing stood out—a name from the ancient mythos of her people. A sense of dread and terror filled Amlaruil as she realized what Nevarth had brought with him to Evermeet. Yet as his spirit drifted away, his final and most urgent message was not of the goddess Araushnee, but of an immediate and mortal danger.

Acting on instinct, Amlaruil thrust Nevarth's body aside and rolled away. Two arrows, in rapid succession, plunged into the dead Moon elf.

The High Mage sprang to her feet, her blue eyes blazing with battle light and her hands outstretched. A small pulse of power burst from her fingertips and sizzled upward along the path that the arrow had taken. A cry of pain rang out through the forest, and the trees overhead rustled as the hidden foes drew away.

For a moment, Amlaruil was tempted to pursue. Yet another, more pressing matter weighed upon her. Zaor was in grave danger. Nevarth did not know the location or the nature of all the traps these traitors had laid for the king, so Amlaruil could do little to forestall them. She did not know where Zaor himself might be, nor did she have any means of reaching him through magic.

But there was one who did. Amlaruil steeled herself for the confrontation ahead. Never, not once, had she faced Zaor's consort. Yet Lydi'aleera wore an elfrune attuned to the king, a gift from the Towers fashioned by Amlaruil herself.

The High Mage stooped and gathered Nevarth's torn body in her arms. Eyes closed, she murmured the phrase that would summon the silver threads of magic, and carry them both to the very heart of the elven court.

A jangle of harpstrings and a shriek of mixed terror and disgust was Amlaruil's welcome to the Moonstone Palace. She opened her eyes and looked up into the white, startled face of Zaor's queen.

The spell Amlaruil cast was designed to bring her to the presence of the elfrune's wearer. She had come upon Queen Lydi'aleera at a time when the queen was alone and at leisure, amusing herself in a chamber filled with artworks and with wondrous musical instruments. The queen had sprung to her feet, upending both the padded bench on which she had been sitting and the golden harp before her. Her wide, staring eyes were fixed upon the slain elf.

With all the dignity she could muster, Amlaruil rose to

face Zaor's consort. She was keenly aware of the flare of resentment in Lydi'aleera's eyes as she recognized her visitor, and the disdain on the elf woman's face as she took in Amlaruil's disheveled appearance and blood-stained robes.

"Forgive me for this intrusion, my lady," Amlaruil began, "but this is a matter of great urgency. You must contact the king at once."

Lydi'aleera's chin came up. "Who are you, to tell me what I must do?" she said with a mixture of hatred and hauteur that might have been chilling, had Amlaruil not had far greater concerns.

The mage snatched up the queen's small, white hand and turned it so the elfrune was apparent. "With this ring you can speak to Zaor. Do so now, or he will die! There are traitors and traps awaiting him—I know not exactly how many or where they might be! But he must turn back at once. At once!"

The urgency in Amlaruil's voice finally began to pierce the cloud of resentment that seemed to enshroud the queen. A small, sly smile lifted the corners of her lips.

"Very well, I will do as you suggest," the queen agreed, "but at a price."

Amlaruil reeled back, staring in disbelief. "You would put a price upon Zaor's life?" she demanded.

"Is not *my* life of value?" Lydi'aleera returned in a shrill, tight voice. "What of me? Am I utterly without worth, that I must sit by and see another woman's child made my husband's heir?"

"If you do not act now then Ilyrana will inherit sooner than any of us would like," the mage pointed out, taking another tact.

"Do not place that little witch upon my conscience," the queen hissed. "She is none of my doing, and I swear that she will not have the throne! She will not!"

"That is in the hands of the gods. Zaor's life, however, is in your hands. Name your price, and quickly," Amlaruil said, willing to do anything to calm the queen.

Lydi'aleera seemed to sense this. A faint, feral smile lit her thin face. "Very well. I want you to give me a potion that will make Zaor hold no image in his heart but mine, and another that will enable me—*me!*—to conceive an heir to Evermeet's throne!"

21

The Sword of Zaor

ow can you ask this now?" Amlaruil said in disbelief. "How can you think of anything at all but the fact that the king is in danger?"

"I would give Zaor a lawful heir!" Lydi'aleera said implacably. "Surely you, the King's most devoted subject, could desire no less for him."

"Zaor already has an heir, as well you know! You have taken my daughter from me. How much more will you demand?"

"Just a bit of magic," Lydi'aleera said, shrugging negligently. "A potion. Any wood-witch or commoner crone could put together a few herbs and create the same effect."

"If you believe that to be so, then why do you trouble me for this magic, but for spite?"

Lydi'aleera's pale faced flamed. "Remember your place, mage, and have a care how you speak to me!"

"My place is in the Towers," Amlaruil said in a tight voice. "Permit me to return there at once."

The queen stepped forward, her hand outstretched so that Amlaruil could see the enchanted ring. Her pale eyes were set with resolve. "Go then. But do so knowing that you have been the death of your beloved king! Give me what I desire, and I will alert him of danger. If you do not pledge to do as I say, he will die, and be lost to us both. I would rather have it so, than remain as things are."

The two elf women locked eyes in a silent, bitter battle. Finally Amlaruil bowed her head, defeated. "You have my pledge. Alert the king, and I will make you your potions."

Smiling in triumph, the queen lifted the ring to her lips and spoke a single arcane word. The ring began to glow with faint, fey light. In a moment, Zaor's voice drifted into the room.

"How may I serve you, Queen Lydi'aleera?" inquired the voice in formal, distant tones.

"My lord king, I have grave news," the queen said, a faint smirk on her lips as she held Amlaruil's gaze. "Are you alone to hear it?"

"There are none with me."

At these words, Amlaruil's concern increased fourfold. What possessed the king to go into the forest alone? Where were his soldiers? Where was Myronthilar Silverspear, his pledged guard?

"You must retrace your path at once," Lydi'aleera said. "Gold elf traitors have planned that an accident befall you."

"That is most unlikely," the king said impatiently.

The queen's expression tightened. "Even so, it is true. I have before me a messenger from the Towers of the Sun and the Moon. The magi have foreseen this plot, and sent word."

There was a moment's silence. "I cannot return to the palace, but thank the magi for their diligence."

Amlaruil sprang forward and seized the queen's hand. "Zaor, you must!" she said urgently. "They have laid traps for you! I saw one myself, near the lodge at the Lake of Dreams, and one of my agents heard the conspirators speak of others! There are armed elves awaiting you, as well—two that I know of, perhaps more. How is it that you are alone, leaving no word where you go?"

"Amlaruil?" his voice said, brightening with hope. "Did you hear any word of our sons? Xharlion and Zhoron? Are they yet alive?"

Suddenly the mage understood what had lured the king into the forest. "I have come this day from Craulnober Keep," she assured him. "The boys are well, and safe. This is but a cruel ruse to draw you off alone!"

"Thank the gods," Zaor said fervently. "I will return to Leuthilspar at once."

The light in Lydi'aleera's ring winked out. "He would not consider the warning on the merit of my words alone," the queen said bitterly. "Oh no. He listens only to the mother of his children! Well, you will lose your sole claim to that place soon enough."

Amlaruil did not offer comment. "With your permission, I must return to the Towers. I will have the potions sent to you."

"Oh, no," the queen said softly. "You will bring them yourself, and place them into my hand. If there were a way to do so without offending proprieties, I would have you stay and witness the results, from the first sip of wine to the birth of Evermeet's true heir!"

The High Mage turned away, unable to face the cruelty in the elf woman's face. She fled from the chamber with no thought to dignity, and ran headlong into a flame-haired elf just entering the room.

Montagor Amarillis caught at her elbows to steady her. "Lady Moonflower," he said, his tone slightly mocking. "It is a surprise to see you here, considering that the king is not at court. Nothing is amiss with the princess, I trust?"

Amlaruil tore herself away from him and flung both arms high in a sudden, desperate gesture. She disappeared in a flash of silver fire.

The noble blinked. "Well. Unusually flashy, for our lady mage. She must have been most eager to divest herself of our presence. What mischief have you been up to, my sister?"

Smiling like a cream-sated cat, Lydi'aleera tucked her arm into his and drew him out onto the balcony. As they walked, she told him what had transpired. Montagor listened, openmouthed, to the queen's words. When she was finished, he chuckled softly, shaking his head in wonderment.

"Well done, little sister! I would not have thought you capable of such cunning."

The queen gave him a complacent look. "I have had an excellent teacher."

Montagor acknowledged her words with a slight bow. "Since you have all things well in hand, I will leave you."

"No, stay," the queen urged. "Zaor will not be back until tomorrow at the earliest. I would have your advice on how best to rid myself of that wretched Ilyrana. And while you're about it," she added in less pleasant tones, "you can explain to me why I never heard so much as a word of Amlaruil's latest two brats. And when you are through, then you can begin to think about how best to ensure that your future nephew will not be troubled by thrice a challenge to his rightful throne!"

* * * * *

As she fled from the palace, Amlaruil's first desire was to return at once to Craulnober Keep, and see once again with her own eyes that her sons were indeed safe from the Gold elf conspirators. She knew they awaited her there, hale and happy and dirty as a pair of piglets from their rowdy play, and that such a trip would avail nothing. It would be a personal indulgence, no more.

But she had a pledge to keep, whatever the keeping cost her. In a locked tower room, she consulted ancient books of folklore and herb craft, blending the old tales with the power of her own High Magic. She worked all through that night and well into the next morning. Finally she held in her hands two small vials which promised to be the fulfillment of Lydi'aleera's dreams—and the death of her own.

Amlaruil's heart was leaden as she called forth the magic that would once again bring her to the moonstone palace. This time, she found Lydi'aleera in the company of her brother, walking arm and arm with him in the wondrous gardens that surrounded the palace.

It struck Amlaruil that once Zaor was magically enthralled by the queen, Montagor Amarillis would have considerable power in the court. In all things, it was rumored, the queen deferred to her brother.

Well, it was not something that could be helped. Amlaruil gave the potions to the queen and left as quickly as she came. And when she left, she took Ilyrana with her—she did not trust Lydi'aleera with her daughter's safety. If the queen was willing to risk her own husband to bargain for an heir of her own begetting, what lengths might she take to remove any possible contenders for her child's throne?

With all possible haste, Amlaruil gathered her three children and entrusted them once again to her agent Rennyn. Before that day waned, she stood atop the walls of Craulnober Keep and watched as the ship bearing them to the safety of the Moonshae Islands disappeared from sight.

The mage's heart was heavy indeed as she returned to the Towers. Not only had she lost Zaor's love this day by magic she herself had fashioned, not only was she parted from her three children, but she felt estranged from Evermeet itself. The dire events in the forest glade had sundered her forever from the sense of security that she had always considered her birthright.

It seemed inconceivable that an elf would act the part of an assassin, or that her own children might have to take refuge elsewhere. It was a reversal of all that she held to be true—for was not Evermeet created by the gods as the ultimate refuge of all elves?

That night, as she sought rest in exhausted revery, Amlaruil had a terrible dream. In revery she stood once again upon the walls of Craulnober Keep, but the scene she gazed upon was not a white-winged elven vessel and a tranquil sea. The castle was scorched and blackened, utterly silent and eerily devoid of life, and the seas beyond were littered with the flotsam of a dozen shattered elven ships.

Amlaruil awoke from revery with a start, beset by the horrible conviction that there was more to her dream than her own troubled thoughts. Quickly she dressed herself and summoned the magic that would carry her to her kinsman's keep.

Dawn was breaking as she stepped out of the magic pathway and into the courtyard of the ancient Craulnober castle. Amlaruil had the oddest feeling that she was stepping into a waking dream.

All was exactly as she had pictured it. The ancient walls were blackened, crumbling. No sign of life greeted her. It was as if the entire thriving, vital community had been swept away by a burst of dragonfire.

A thin, piercing cry cut through the chill morning air. Amlaruil hurried toward the sound, which seemed to come from somewhere below the ground. She tugged at the heavy door that sealed the entrance to the castle's lowest level, then ran down a long, curving stairway. In a small room in the farthest reaches of the castle she found two living souls: an old elf, long past the age of warriors, and a small, squalling babe.

The elf looked up when Amlaruil entered the room, his eyes red in his soot-darkened face. A moment passed before she recognized him as Elanjar, the patriarch of the Craulnober clan and the swordmaster who had endeavored to teach the discipline to her own unruly sons.

"What happened here?" she asked, coming to kneel at the elf's side.

Elanjar's eyes hardened. "We were overrun by creatures from Below."

"No," Amlaruil said in disbelief. "How is that possible? Never have the people of the Underdark set foot on the island!"

"Nor have they—yet," the elf replied. "You know the island of Tilrith, do you not?"

The mage nodded. The tiny island, which lay just north of the Craulnober holdings, was much like northern Evermeet in terrain. It was a wild place, with rocky hills honeycombed with caves. The Craulnober and their retainers kept sheep on the island, and a few servants lived there year-round to tend the flocks. With a sudden jolt, Amlaruil realized that this was the season when spring lambs were born, and the sheep sheered of their winter coats. Most of the villagers and nobles would be on Tilrith for the work and the festivities that followed.

"They were attacked on the island," she murmured, aghast.

"Most were slaughtered along with the sheep," Elanjar said with deep bitterness. "A few escaped. The drow followed—not in ships, but with magic. They sent a firestorm upon the ships and upon this castle such as I had never imagined possible. Those few elves who remained behind were reduced to ash. I survived only through the magic of the sword I carry," he added, touching the glowing hilt of the Craulnober moonblade. "This babe, my grandson Elaith, was in my arms when the firestorm struck. He and I are all that remain of this clan." The elf's singed head sagged forward, as if this revelation had taken the last of his remaining strength.

Amlaruil lay a comforting hand on his shoulder, and then reached out to take the baby from his arms. She folded back the charred blanket to look at the infant. An involuntary smile curved her lips. Little Elaith was a beautiful boy, with large solemn eyes the color of amber and a cap of short, silvery curls.

"This child is kin to me," she said softly. "His parents sheltered my sons; I will do the same for theirs. Elaith will be my fosterling, and I swear before all the gods that I will hold him as dear as any child of my own body. He will be taught magic in the towers, and raised in the courts of Leuthilspar in a manner that befits a noble elf, and the heir to Craulnober."

She looked up at Elanjar. "Come. I must get the two

of you to the safety of the Towers. The drow will be back with the coming of night."

"Craulnober Keep is well-nigh impregnable," Elanjar said, a frown of worry deepening the furrows of his forehead. "If the drow gain control of this keep, they will have a stronghold from which to strike at the whole island!"

"They will not set foot on Evermeet," Amlaruil assured him as she helped him to his feet. "If it takes every warrior and every mage on Evermeet to complete the task, we will stop them on Tilrith and seal their tunnels forever!"

* * * * *

Alone and on foot, Zaor walked through the northern gates of Leuthilspar and set a brisk pace for the palace. He had not gone far before Myronthilar Silverspear appeared at his side like a small gray shadow.

"I told you to await me," the king grumbled.

"And so I have," his friend asserted. "This business that took you off alone, that which was so important that none could accompany you—it is completed?"

Zaor's face set into grim lines. "It seems it is just beginning. Is Amlaruil still at the palace?"

The warrior hesitated. "She has been and gone more than once since you left, and since she came bringing news that you were endangered, the queen's brother has been very much in attendance. He eyes the palace maids as if he were selecting his evening's entertainment, and he studies the chests as if contemplating which one would best hold his spare cloaks and boots. I tell you, my lord, I like it not."

"You were always cautious of Montagor Amarillis," Zaor said. "If he wished to lay claim to the throne, he would have done so twenty-five years before."

"Montagor is no king, and he knows it. But perhaps he desires a regency," Myron told him gravely. "His hope for an Amarillis heir is nearly gone, for the Princess Ilyrana nears the age of accountability. She will be crowned as your heir before the year is through."

Zaor stopped dead. "Do you think the princess is in danger?"

"The lady Amlaruil does," Myron said. "She took the princess and sent her and the twins away to safety. And she bid me meet you as soon as I could do so without breaking my word." His face turned grave. "Is it true? There was an attempt upon your life, here on Evermeet itself?"

"Do you doubt the lady mage?" Zaor said dryly.

As he expected, Myronthilar's face took on a look of near reverence. "Not in this or anything," he said quietly.

"Thank you for your faith, my friend," said a feminine voice behind them.

Both warriors jumped, and whirled to face the speaker. Their countenances wore identical expressions of chagrin that they could be taken unaware. Taking pity on the powerful blend of male and elven pride, Amlaruil reached out and touched the ring on Myronthilar's hand.

"The elfrune I gave you enables me to find you when needed," she explained. "Would that I had the sense to give one to Zaor, rather than worry about propriety and appearances! But there are other matters at hand that demand your attention, my lords." In a few terse words she told them about the invasion of Tilrith.

Zaor's face darkened. "All the forces of Evermeet will march north at once. Can you take us to the palace, my lady?"

Amlaruil called the magic that carried all three instantly to Zaor's council chambers. With the brisk efficiency of a seasoned war leader, the king sent forth messengers to all corners of Evermeet to gather the elves for battle.

At last he turned back to Amlaruil, who had stood silently by. "Can you bring a Circle to the northern shore? We will have need of powerful magic to close the tunnels.

If Tilrith must be dropped into the sea to ensure Evermeet's security, then so be it."

"It will be done," she assured him.

At that moment the doors to the chamber flew open, and Lydi'aleera swept into the room Montagor close on her heels. Her gaze kindled when it fell upon Amlaruil, and her smile turned feline. With deliberate motions, she took up a decanter of wine and poured two cups. She took the vials from her sash, holding them so that Amlaruil could see them and read her intent.

"Welcome back, my lord. Will you drink with me, to celebrate your return?" she purred.

Zaor shook his head. "I cannot stay. Have you not heard the news, or at least suspected that something might be amiss? The palace is in an uproar, and soldiers swarm the streets of the city. This is not a time for celebrations."

The smug expression on the queen's face faltered. "You are not leaving, surely!"

"At once. The northern shores are under threat of invasion—not from sahuagin this time, but from creatures from Below."

"No. It is impossible," Lydi'aleera said, her eyes huge with fear.

"I wish that were so," the king said in a grim tone. "But do not be concerned. You will be quite safe in the palace," he assured her, misunderstanding the true source of her concern. He bowed to the elf women and strode from the room.

Lydi'aleera whirled toward the mage. "This is your doing," she hissed. "You have always taken Zaor from me! And now you conspire against me, even if that means an alliance with the drow!" The queen drew back her arm as if to hurl the goblet at Amlaruil.

"Enough!" the mage said softly.

The chilling fury in that single word froze the queen in place. Amlaruil stepped forward, her eyes blazing in her pale face. "Do not dare to accuse me of crimes that you, and you alone in this room, have committed. Do you wish to speak treason? Then speak of a queen who would not lift her hand to save her husband, until she was assured of getting her will."

"I must give Zaor an heir," the elf woman repeated stubbornly.

"Perhaps you will, but not by my power, not now and never again," Amlaruil swore. "The magic of the fertility potion will not outlive this night; the magic of the love potion also diminishes with time. You might yet be able to lure Zaor to your bed, but you will not find your way into his heart! You have lost your chance, and I will not give you another." She turned away.

"I did not give you leave to go," the queen snapped.

The High Mage whirled back, her blue eyes dark with wrath. "I have more important concerns than your personal vanity and your need to resort to magic-aided seduction! Have you forgotten that the island over which you purport to reign is even now under threat of invasion? I am needed, even if you are not."

"You will fight at Zaor's side, I suppose?" scoffed Lydi'aleera.

Amlaruil's answering smile was cold. "Did you think the Tower magi spent all their time dancing beneath the stars? This will not be the first time I have used my magic in battle. And if the need arises, yes, I will take up a sword."

The High Mage disappeared in a sharp, angry crackle of magic.

After a moment's silence, Montagor came forward, shaking his head in bemused admiration. "Amlaruil in battle! Now that would be a sight worth seeing!"

Lydi'aleera's hand flashed out and cuffed her brother sharply on the side of the head. "Do your thinking with *this,* brother! You heard everything. Whatever am I to do now?"

Montagor considered her carefully. "You realize the importance of an Amarillis heir, do you not?"

"Yes, yes—of course! Would I go to such lengths to ensure one, otherwise?"

The elf nodded. "Then this is what you must do. You know Adamar Alenuath, of course. Have you ever noticed how closely he resembles Zaor?"

"No," she retorted. "He is nowhere near the king's stature, nor is anyone on this island."

"Perhaps 'closely' is overstating the case," he admitted. "But Adamar is a Moon elf warrior and strongly built, though not nearly of Zaor's height. He has the same odd coloring—the blue hair, the gold flecks in his blue eyes. If you were to seduce Adamar, the resulting offspring should be like enough to the Moonflowers to pass as the king's own."

Lydi'aleera gasped. "You cannot be serious!"

"Why not? Can you think of another way?"

"But even if I wished to do such a thing, Adamar would never agree to it!"

"Again, why not? You are very beautiful. He admires you—I know that to be so."

The elf woman shrugged impatiently. "And what of it? Adamar is loyal to the king. To lie with Zaor's wife would be an act of treason and personal betrayal. He would not do it, even if he desired me more than his next breath of air!"

A crafty smile twisted Montagor's lips. "Then it is time to test the potency of Amlaruil's spell. I will arrange for Adamar to come to the palace on some pretense. Give him the potion in a glass of wine, and he will not resist your offered charms."

Lydi'aleera wrung her hands. "But he will confess, after!"

"And besmirch his honor and that of his clan? To publicly dishonor his queen?" Montagor smirked. "I think not."

The elf's face grew deadly serious. "But do not concern yourself overmuch, my sister. Adamar thinks me his friend and consults me on all matters. Ofttimes I know his mind before he is entirely certain of it himself. If he is driven to confess, he will start by unburdening himself to me. If necessary, I will challenge him to battle over my sister's honor. And do not doubt that I will win."

She laughed without humor. "I have seen you fight, brother. You are not Adamar's equal."

"The duel will be a pretense," Montagor said softly, though his burning eyes acknowledged that her words had struck home. "Adamar is a noble fool—he will think he deserves to die. He will think his defeat the only rightful end, and will have more to do with bringing it about than I could think to accomplish. In fact, he may simply do the deed himself and save me the trouble of lifting a sword."

"But either way, Adamar will be dead."

"And Zaor will have an heir by his lawful queen."

Lydi'aleera was silent for a long moment, gazing out the open window over the city with eyes blinded to the turmoil of battle preparations below. "Very well. Send for Adamar, then," she said, the words coming out in a rush. She whirled to face her brother, hatred naked in her eyes. "But may Lloth claim you as her own," she said in a venomous whisper.

The curse, perhaps the most deadly and offensive words that could pass between two of the People, merely brought a smile to Montagor's lips.

"Be that as it may, dear sister. But bear in mind that the Abyss is a very large place. Be very careful whom you consign to damnation, lest you be judged by the same measure."

He turned and swaggered out of the chamber. At the door he paused, as if some new thought had come to him. Glancing over his shoulder, he said, "I have not seen Amlaruil for many years. She is wondrous fair, is she not? It is little wonder the king is so obsessed with her."

"Get out," Lydi'aleera gritted from between clenched teeth. She snatched up a gem-encrusted vase and brandished it.

But Montagor was not quite finished. "A word of advice, my sister. Save a few drops of that potion for Zaor's return. You'll need to bed him to complete this farce. And without Amlaruil's magic—even that which comes in a vial—you haven't a chance."

The queen hurled the vase at her brother. It missed him with room to spare and shattered against the wall. The tinkle of falling crystal mingled with the sound of Montagor's mocking, and triumphant laughter. He would have what he wanted at last, and why should he care that she had to pay the price for it?

Despite her anger, Lydi'aleera understood her brother's mind. He had worked long and hard for this, and would get what he desired: an Amarillis heir to the throne of Evermeet. Lydi'aleera would also have her due: a child of her own, the regard of her lawful husband, the esteem of Evermeet. What was a small, needed deception compared to such gain?.

* * * * *

Under the command of King Zaor, the drow were driven from the island of Tilrith and the tunnels sealed. The king also sent warriors and mages into the caves of Sumbrar and the Eagle Hills to explore and to seal off any possible openings to the world below. The only tunnels left undisturbed were those that led to the sleeping places of Evermeet's dragon guardians. If by chance the drow should ever find their way into those caverns, they would be well met indeed.

Within a year of the battle, a boychild was born to the royal family. If there were those who wondered at the begetting, they kept their suspicions to themselves. Zaor did not speak of the matter even to his closest friends, but he proclaimed Rhenalyrr his heir, and raised the young elf to be king after him.

Time passed, and Rhenalyrr reached the age of accountability. All the elves of Evermeet were to attend the ceremony that named him heir to the throne, and to stand witness as the young prince took an oath upon his father's sword, which he would one day wield as king.

As that day neared, not all of Evermeet's people rejoiced in the honor due to their prince. Lydi'aleera withdrew into silence whenever the ceremony was mentioned. And what the Grand Mage thought of Rhenalyrr, no one knew, for Amlaruil never spoke a word against Zaor's son or denied his claim to the throne.

Along with all of Evermeet, Amlaruil prepared to attend the high ceremony. She dismissed all the Towers' elves from their duties so that they might attend as well.

Shanyrria Alenuath, the bladesinger who taught this uniquely elven blend of swordcraft and magic at the Towers, was reluctant to go. She was a solitary elf by nature, and not at all fond of state gatherings or the gaiety of festivals. Indeed, she had not even stepped foot in her family mansion for many years. Yet her sense of clan was strong, and she stopped in Leuthilspar on her way southward so that she might attend the ceremony with the rest of her clan.

She walked into her childhood home to find it strangely silent. The mansion was deserted, but for one elf: her father Shanyrria could feel his presence. She had always been close to Adamar, and she loved her father with an intensity that bordered on rapport.

Thus it was that she felt the weight of his despair, and the sharp, bright pain that promised release. Her heart seemed to leap into her throat, fluttering like a caged lark as she ran up the curving stairway to her father's chamber.

Shanyrria found Adamar there, his hands clenched around the grip of the family's moonblade—which protruded from below his ribs. She stared in horror. This was beyond imagining! Never did an elf take his own life, and certainly not with the weapon that symbolized the family's honor!

"Why?" she asked simply.

In a few words, with the scant time remaining to him, Adamar told her.

The bladesinger listened in stunned, grieving disbelief as her father confessed his own dishonor, and told at last the terrible secret that he had never been able to bring himself to reveal: that he would be the cause of his own son's death. Prince Rhenalyrr was not of Zaor's blood. The king's moonblade, the sword of Zaor, was not his to claim, and soon all of Evermeet would bear witness to the disgrace of House Alenuath.

When Adamar fell into final silence, Shanyrria raced from the mansion and leaped upon her waiting moon-horse. Rhenalyrr might not be a true prince, but he *was* her own half-brother. She owed him the loyalty and protection due any member of the clan.

But when her lathered moon-horse pulled up in the valley of Drelagara, the bladesinger was greeted by a chorus of keening elven voices. She did not need to ask to know that Rhenalyrr had not survived the ritual.

Her face set with wrath, Shanyrria swung down from her mount and went off in search of vengeance.

She slipped into the pavilion where the queen sat alone, weeping silent, helpless tears. Quietly she walked up to the grieving elf woman. With a quick, smooth movement, she drew her sword and thrust the tip against Lydi'aleera's throat.

"I name you, Lydi'aleera Amarillis, false queen of Evermeet, to be a coward, a liar, a whore, and the murderer of my father Adamar Alenuath—and of my half-brother Rhenalyrr."

The queen stared up at the fierce bladesinger like a mouse awaiting the claws of a striking owl. "I did not know—"

"You *knew*," Shanyrria said vehemently. "You knew that Rhenalyrr was not of Zaor's blood, yet you remained silent while he took the trial of the moonblade! Surely you knew that he would not survive."

"He was a fine, noble young elf," she persisted. "There was

a chance that he might succeed. And if the moonblades are to be held as sole measure, Amarillis is as worthy of royalty as Moonflower!"

Shanyrria stared at the queen through narrowed eyes. "It is said that only those truly worthy of ruling can bear the sword of Zaor. Very well then. Come."

She put away her sword with a quick thrust and snatched a small knife from her belt. With one hand she grasped a handful of Lydi'aleera's hair and jerked her to her feet. She put one arm firmly around the queen's shoulder, and pressed the knife hard into the elf woman's ribs.

"I will support you in your grief, my queen," the bladesinger said with heavy irony, "and take you where you must go."

The elf woman struggled to pull away, but Shanyrria was strong and held her fast. "What are you going to do?" Lydi'aleera demanded.

"No more than what you did to my brother. You will draw the sword of Zaor and test your worthiness to rule Evermeet. You are Amarillis born, so your chances are as good as Rhenalyrr's!"

"I will not do it!" gasped Lydi'aleera.

"You will," Shanyrria asserted. "If you do not, I will proclaim before all of Evermeet what you have done. Zaor will put you away, and you and all your clan will be shamed. Or, if you prefer, I will kill you now, and then speak."

The queen stared at her, all hope draining from her eyes. "And if I draw, and succeed? Will you keep silent concerning all of this?"

"Whether you live or die is for the moonblade to decide. I will content myself with that. Either way, you will win: a kingdom or an honorable death. It is more than you deserve."

Since she had no recourse, the queen walked with Shanyrria toward the place where Zaor's sword lay, gleaming still with faint blue magic, upon the ceremonial pedestal. Before any could divine her intent, Lydi'aleera stepped forward and grasped the sword in her two hands and began to slide it from the scabbard.

433

A flash of terrible blue light lit the plain. When it faded, the elf woman was gone, but for a pile of pale, drifting ash.

Shanyrria nodded in grim agreement to the sentence that the moonblade had pronounced. The bladesinger felt no guilt over her part in the queen's death. She considered Lydi'aleera guilty, not only of her brother's death and her father's, but also of treason against the crown. It felt right to her that Lydi'aleera's fate was one that she had chosen, though her pride, ambition, and cowardly silence, for her own son.

Many were the witnesses to Lydi'aleera's death. In the stunned murmurs that swept the group, the elves surmised the queen had been maddened by grief, or determined to prove the worth of Amarillis after her son's failure. Shanyrria did not care what they thought, as long as they accepted one very important truth: Lydi'aleera Amarillis was not fit to rule. She was not and never had been Evermeet's queen.

The bladesinger turned to face the gathering crowd. Her eyes sought out Amlaruil, who stood pale and stunned among the Tower magi. Shanyrria bowed deeply, then pulled her blade and raised it to her forehead in a gesture of respect.

"The queen is dead," she said, and her words seemed to echo in the stunned silence. Then she strode forward and lay her blade in a gesture of fealty at Amlaruil's feet.

"The queen is dead," Shanyrria repeated. "Long live the queen."

Zaor understood at once the importance of this moment. He strode to the alter and drew the sword. Holding it high overhead with one hand, he held out the other to Amlaruil.

The mage hesitated only for a moment. She walked to Zaor's side and entwined her fingers in his. Then with her other hand, she reached up to grasp the hilt of the king sword.

Fey blue light poured through the moonblade and

enveloped them both. They stood together, in full sight of all of Evermeet, joined by the ancient magic.

One by one, the somber elves went down on their knees to acknowledge what no one could deny.

Evermeet had a true queen, at last.

To Lord Danilo Thann does Lamruil, Prince of Evermeet, send fond greetings.

Thank you for your latest letter, my friend, and for the lovely ballad that you sent for my Maura. Today is midsummer, and I have saved your song to sing for her as a midsummer gift. I have but little skill at the harp, but I have been practicing the simple accompaniment you fashioned for me and hope to do it credit. Maura is no critic where music is concerned. She is about as placid as a squirrel in autumn, and I have seldom seen her sit still the length of time needed to hear any piece of music from end to end. But few are the women who will not linger to hear their charm and beauty praised, and I feel confident that she will find enjoyment in this tribute.

It sounds as if you are progressing well in your endeavor. I can readily understand the frustrations you expressed, for the history of Evermeet's elves is so long and complex that no single work can do more than touch the corner of its shadow. But it is a worthy effort, for all that.

You asked me to speak of the queen. To do so is very much akin to the task you have undertaken: Anything and everything that can be said will fall far short of the possibilities. Amlaruil of Evermeet is revered and loved by the elves of the island and widely respected abroad. Even many of those who do not owe her political allegiance acknowledge that in a mystical sense she is indeed Queen of All Elves. The queen epitomizes all that the elven people value: beauty, grace, magic, wisdom, power. That is just the beginning. Just as your friend Laeral is Chosen of her goddess Mystra, Amlaruil is something more than mortal. She stands alone in a special place between elf woman and goddess. She is also my mother, and as such she often drives me to near madness in the time-honored manner of any mother and son. And in all candor, I must admit that I return the favor.

One of Queen Amlaruil's most remarkable accomplishments is that she has transcended many of the petty divisions between the elven races. Gold elves join with Moon elves to sing her praises. Green elves would set fire to their ancient forests if such could serve and protect her. The Sea elves adore her, and it is rumored that the Sea elven monarch of the Coral Kingdom has repeatedly asked for her hand in marriage. I can attest to this, as I was eavesdropping during one such appeal. Even some of the drow recognize Amlaruil as their rightful queen. Not many years ago, the queen secretly received a representative of the goddess Eilistraee. Though drow will never be permitted on Evermeet, the Moonflower family now has alliances with some of the goodly followers of the Dark Maiden.

Permit me to tell you a personal tale that I believe will illustrate the unique color-blind reverence that elves hold for Amlaruil.

Long before you were born, when I was a mere sapling and just beginning to feel my sap rising, I celebrated the summer solstice in the time-honored manner of my people—with feasting and song, revelry and dance. By custom, the royal Moonflower family attends revels in various parts of the island: that year, we celebrated amid the lush meadows of the Horse Fields that cover much of the northwestern part of Evermeet.

The morn of midsummer day was fine and bright, and I felt myself blessed by the bright attention of one of the spring maids who danced in the morning rituals. She was a Gold elf, a girl of good if not noble family. Before long it was clear to me that this year, I would join in the evening revels in a manner I had not before.

The girl and I, in our youthful exuberance, were ill content to wait for the coming of night—after all, midsummer is the longest day of the year! She was older than I, and wise in the ways of midsummer revels. Gifted with her soft smiles and sweet words of promise, I found myself in scant supply of that supposedly elven virtue: patience.

Before the dew was off the grass, we stole away and found a place for our private revels. I blush to admit that this place was her father's hay barns. At the time, however, we felt gloriously unburdened by this singular lack of originality and imagination.

Later, as we were picking bits of straw from each other's hair and laughing together at small things that would not, under any other circumstances, have seemed half as witty or clever, we were interrupted by her father. Yes. So far, this has all the makings of a second-rate minstrel's ballad, does it not?

The elf stood over us, grimly dignified and nearly shaking with controlled wrath. "By your leave, Prince Lamruil, I would like to have private speech with my daughter," he said in a tight, clipped manner.

I gathered up my clothes and fled from the barn. What else was I to do? Yet I did not go far, for though I respected the elf's right to rule his family as he wished, I would not allow the girl to come to any harm at his hands.

And so, as I hurriedly donned my festival garments just outside the barn door, I shamelessly eavesdropped upon the small drama played out within.

"You have shamed yourself and your family, Elora," the farmer told her in that same grimly controlled tone.

I could envision the pert, defiant toss of her golden head. "How so? It is midsummer. I am of age and promised to no male. I can do as I will—not even my respected father can gainsay me in such matters."

"That is not what I mean, and you know it well!" he thundered, his control suddenly spent. "How could you lie with a Gray elf? How could you?"

439

Elaine Cunningham

There was a moment of heavy silence—to which, I might add, I added the weight of my own surprise. Then my lass responded, "Lamruil is a prince of Evermeet. Who in your mind is an elf worthy for me to bed—the king himself?"

"Do not even speak of such treachery against the crown and the queen! With my own hands would I kill any elf woman who so betrayed Evermeet's Amlaruil, even my own daughter!"

"Then how can you object to Prince Lamruil?" she retorted, reasonably enough—or so it seemed to me. "He is his mother's son."

"What of it?"

Another puzzled silence, as the lass and I struggled to comprehend her father's logic.

"Well, Queen Amlaruil is a Gray elf too," she pointed out.

A ringing slap echoed through the morning air. "Have a care how you speak of Evermeet's Queen!" he snarled.

I was about to dash in to protect the girl from further mistreatment, but my intervention was not needed. The farmer stormed out of the barn, too consumed with wrath at his daughter's sacrilege to notice me standing there in my undergarments, wearing one unlaced boot and brandishing a ready and avenging sword. Admittedly, I doubt he would have been overly impressed by the spectacle.

And thus it is. Whatever enmities exist between Silver and Gold, Amlaruil the queen is truly Queen of All Elves. The efforts of a few stray zealots such as Kymil Nimesin have done great harm—to which my family can attest with sorrow—but I do not believe they will succeed in bringing down what Amlaruil has built.

But in all honesty, I must admit that I have been known to be wrong before.

By the sun and stars! What a dismal sentiment to add at letter's end! Let me then end by thanking you again for the gift of Maura's song, which I fondly trust will add sweetness and heat to my midsummer night. Give my regards to Arilyn and the little one. I look forward to seeing you all again soon.

Your uncle and friend,
Lamruil

Prelude: Nightfall

(1371 DR)

hanyrria Alenuath was among the first to see the approaching sky caravan. The bladesinger was drilling a new batch of potential students on a hillside not far from the Towers of the Sun and Moon. This was a particularly promising group, for perhaps half of them had the right combination of talent in music, magic, and swordcraft needed to become a true bladesinger. Of those, two or three might qualify for the specialized training offered by Sunrise Tower. There, skilled bladesingers honed their musical talents into a spellcasting art. The goal was nothing less than the revival of the ancient, nearly forgotten art of spell-song. This was but one of the efforts that sprang up in response to the challenge issued by Amlaruil, back when she was the Lady of the Towers. As queen she had continued to foster and support the elven arts, and Shanyrria was proud to have a part in this effort. She herself would never be a spell-singer, but she had made it her life's work to seek out promising students and direct them to Sunrise Tower.

But there was one loyalty even nearer to Shanyrria's heart. The sight of the pale blue rose emblazoned on the banner of the sky caravan was enough to make her drop her sword and forget her students. She stared in horror and consternation at the white-draped litter that was bourn southward by a team of four white pegasi. It looked like a funeral procession. The blue rose was the standard of the Moonflower family, and the pegasi were in the service of the Queen herself.

Shanyrria dismissed the students at once and sprinted down the hill toward the Tower of the Sun. Laeroth Runemaster, who had succeeded Amlaruil as Grand Mage of the Towers, would know if . . . Shanyrria's thoughts slammed to a stop, unwilling even to form the words. Yet she had to know the meaning of the white-draped litter. Laeroth would know what there was to be known.

She found all the High Magi gathered in the large spellcasting chamber awaiting the Grand Mage. Too impatient to wait, Shanyrria pushed through them and went in search of Laeroth. She found the aged elf in the upper tower, in the act of removing the Accumulator from its protective wrapping. Apprehension clutched at her throat with icy fingers as she contemplated a danger that would necessitate bringing out one of the greatest of Evermeet's defenses. An ancient artifact, it stored the power of the spells around it. Shanyrria's trained senses sang in harmony with the magic—the unique magic of Evermeet—which emanated from the artifact in silent song.

Laeroth turned to the bladesinger. "I am to take this to the palace," he said simply. "The queen is in need of all of Evermeet's defenders."

Relief flooded Shanyrria. "The queen lives! Praise the gods! But the royal litter?"

"The Princess Ilyrana," the runemaster said sadly. "She lives, but her spirit has flown—carried away to do battle in another place. They take her body to her mother the queen."

"How—"

"Ityak-Ortheel," Laeroth interrupted, his usually gentle voice dark with hatred. "The creature of Malar, unleashed upon Evermeet itself. Ilyrana carried it away—to Arvandor, I believe—but most of the elven clerics were slain during the battle I fear." He gazed down at the Accumulator. "There is much yet to come. Every child of Evermeet must rally to meet this threat, or we will all perish. We stand alone, for all the magical gates of

Evermeet have been blocked. The High Magi have gathered to see if this can be countered."

He looked up at her. "You are friends of the centaurs. Alert them, tell them to hurry to the river and hold back the sahuagin and scrags that have invaded the heartland. Then hasten to Sunrise Tower, prepare the spell-singers to defend the valley. A huge invading fleet approaches, and if any of the raiders manage to come ashore, you can imagine what prizes they might take."

Shanyrria nodded. Sunrise Tower stood in Drelagara, a Gold elf town in the midst of the lush measures that were home to the moon-horses. The wondrous beasts often played in the sea and the white-sand beaches east of the meadows; if raiders were to catch sight of such creatures, they would surely pursue them into the valley. A single moon-horse was worth more than a red dragon's hoard.

The bladesinger reached into the leather bag on her belt and took a small package of green powder from it. This she poured into her hand. She spat, then mixed it into a paste and streaked it across her cheeks with the fingers of her hands. It was not as elaborate a war paint as was her custom, but it was all that time permitted. Shanyrria was already a daunting sight. Her appearance was unusual for a Silver elf, for she was tall and broad of shoulder, with eyes the color of amber. Her reddish-brown hair had been plaited into dozens of braids and woven with feathers and painted stone beads. In her mildest mood, Shanyrria was fearsome to behold. Now, even the Runemaster, no coward or weakling, hung back from her.

"Send me to Sunrise Tower," she demanded. "I will rally the spell-singers, and then go to fight beside the centaurs."

Laeroth nodded and began to cast the spell that would carry the bladesinger to distant Drelagara.

Shanyrria accepted the whirl and rush of magical travel, and came out of the spell running at full speed. She dashed through the Tower courtyard, pushing past the

Gold elf guards who moved to block her way. They shouted that the Circle was casting and could not be interrupted.

She had barely cleared the door when an explosion of intense power slammed into her. Shanyrria staggered back, clutching at her bleeding ears. There had been no sound, no tremor, nothing that anyone other than an elf might hear or feel, but Shanyrria knew beyond doubt that every elf on Evermeet felt the impact of that terrible silent blast. She herself, so attuned to the silent music of magic, had been deafened by the force of it.

Horror gripped the bladesinger as she realized the implications for Sunrise Tower. In times past, entire Towers of High Magi had been shattered by a powerful backlash of magic. If this unknown spell could so effect her, what must it have done to a Circle of spell-singers?

Shanyrria slapped her face several times hoping to distract the terrible, ringing pain and focus her powers for the task ahead. She went with all the speed she could muster up the winding stair that led up to the spellcasting chamber at the top of the Tower, bracing herself for the sight of her friends' blasted bodies.

Astonishment froze her in the doorway. A group of Gold elves—each of them known to her, most of whom she had selected and trained—stood in a circle, their outstretched fingertips touching. The Circle was unharmed; even now the elves' lips moved in a spell-song that Shanyrria could no longer hear. In their midst stood a single female elf. Shanyrria recognized her as a Circle-Singer, a warrior-mage who could blend the magical song into a single spell, much as a Center focused a circle of High Magi.

Suddenly Shanyrria understood what had happened. These elves were traitors! Sunrise Tower had attacked. The destructive force she had felt was nothing less than the shattering of the Towers of the Sun and the Moon.

Grimly the bladesinger drew her sword and advanced into the room. Evermeet had developed no defense against such treachery from within, but neither did spell-song have a defense against the magic of a bladesinger. It seemed good and right to Shanyrria that many of them would die by her blade.

She seized the nearest elf by his golden hair and reached around to cut his throat. As she pulled the blade in a lethal slash, she spun so that the swing would take down the elf to his right. Shanyrria had no illusions about her fate. She would die in this tower room. But when she came to Arvandor, she would bring many traitors to present themselves before the Seldarine Council for judgment.

Her only regret was that she would die before the battle's end, not knowing what Evermeet's fate would be.

Book Five

Queen of Evermeet

"Amlaruil is not merely the Queen of Evermeet: Amlaruil *is* Evermeet."

—Elven Maxim

22

Amlaruil of Evermeet

fter an indecently short period of official
mourning for Lydi'aleera, Amlaruil and Zaor
were wed. She was crowned queen at once,
despite the outrage of House Amarillis and
the murmurs of a few of the other Gold elven
houses. But it was obvious to all that the moonblade had
chosen. That Amlaruil had borne children to Zaor was
counted in her favor.

Montagor Amarillis was furious at these events, yet
there was little he could do without bringing his actions—
and his sister's disgrace—to light. Besides, the formidable
bladesinger Shanyrria Alenuath sought him out and privately made it plain that she held Lydi'aleera responsible
for the death of her half-brother, the alleged heir of Zaor.
She vowed that she would keep an eye on him and his
house, and avenge any attempt on the royal family. The
bladesinger's fierce reputation was widely known, and Montagor had little desire to bring her wrath down on his head.
He suspected, even if he could not prove, that Shanyrria
had forced Lydi'aleera's hand. His sister would never have
taken such a bold and desperate step on her own.

Amlaruil left the Towers behind, leaving the rule of
them to the trusted war wizard Tanyl Evanara and to her
old friend Laeroth, now known as the Runemaster.
Although Tanyl was not among the High Magi, he was one
of the most powerful of solitary mages. Amlaruil was content that the Towers were in good hands, and dedicated
herself fully to Zaor and their joint rulership of Evermeet.

Though some of the elves worried that a warrior and a mage would make for a grim royal couple, the arts and music that had been the former queen's passion were nurtured as never before.

Elven minstrels began to travel abroad, bringing the lore and music of many lands back to Evermeet. In particular, the elves became intrigued with the many new instruments developed by ingenious human bards. The harp and the flute, the traditional instruments of elven music, were soon joined by a host of other instruments. Elven nobles and minstrels soon vied with each other in composing new verses to popular lute songs, and groups of elves began to delight in singing the exuberant, multi-voiced music enjoyed by humans.

As a gift to the new queen, the Tower magi cast magic that enlarged and transformed the Moonstone palace. A vast garden maze was added to the grounds and filled with magical displays, softly playing fountains, and wondrous flowers. It was Nakiasha, Amlaruil's mentor, who added to the palace the touch that showed a true understanding of the queen. In a feat of magic and forestry that consumed three years of diligent work, the forest elf had transported to the palace grounds the very forest glade in which Amlaruil and Zaor had first met. Set like a jewel in the midst of an ancient grove, this glade rapidly became the royal couple's favorite retreat, and the place most sought out by the children that filled the palace nearly to overflowing.

The union of Zaor and Amlaruil was unusually fruitful, and the coming of spring usually saw the house of Moonflower increased by yet another prince or princess. Ilyrana, who had no desire for court life, was content to remain upon the Moonshaes. There also the twins, Zhoron and Xharlion, grew to maturity learning the fighting arts of the elves of Sonoria. Although Amlaruil missed them sorely, she rejoiced in each new babe that filled her arms, and she devoted herself to their training.

The next-born son, Chozzaster, showed an early talent for magic and in time aspired to become a High Magi, like his mother. The following spring brought a daughter, a fierce, fire-haired lass that they named Shandalar in honor of the bladesinger Shanyrria Alenuath. Female twins followed, Tira'allara and Hhora, lovely, serious girls who devoted themselves at an early age to train as clerics of Hanali Celanil. Next came Lazziar and Gemstarzah, twin girls who seemed by nature and inclination destined to take the warrior's path.

Amlaruil's days were not all consumed with the raising of her brood, however. The chance to prove herself a worthy consort to a warrior king came all too soon.

Far to the west, off the coast of the fertile and troubled land known as Tethyr, a cluster of islands was drawing pirates as surely as bees to clover. The archipelago seemed designed for stealth, with its myriad small islands and hidden bays, and it lay between the ancient southern kingdoms and the thriving cities of the north. As the pirates grew wealthier and more daring, they turned their sights toward the sunset sky, and to the fabled riches of Evermeet.

From time to time, a pirate ship ventured westward, never to be heard from again. But there were successes, too, although the goods that pirates brought back to port were mostly wonders looted and exotic slaves taken from elven vessels on the open seas. When word came to the Nelanther that the elves of the mainland were secretly slipping away and sailing for their isle, the pirates began to patrol the seas in earnest.

One day in early spring, a young dragon sentinel brought news that an approaching elven ship was pursued by a small fleet of Nelanther pirates. Though the swanship was fleet and agile, the pirates were closing and would capture the ship before she could reach the shields of Evermeet.

Zaor called upon the trio of dragonriders to go out and meet the pirates. He wished to lead the eagle riders in attack himself, but the distance was too great for the giant eagles to fly.

Amlaruil, however, had an idea of her own. The High

Magi took to the sky in a chariot drawn by a team of six pegasi. With her she carried the ancient scepter known as the Accumulator, which held High Magic powerful enough to teleport the flagship away from the island. This she did, in a spectacular display of magical fireworks that lit up the sky and was seen from Evermeet to distant Waterdeep.

Exactly where the ship landed, the queen declined to say. That did not stop the minstrels from speculating, and their odes to the queen's bravery joined those that praised her beauty and grace.

But sorrow and tragedy soon befell the royal family. Malar the Beast Lord unleashed upon the elves of the Moonshae Isles his most fearsome creation. The monster known as the elf-eater attacked the once-secure valley of Synnoria. Many of the elves fled though the gate to Evermeet.

The princess Ilyrana was among them, but she brought with her terrible news. As she was pushed through the gate by the elven defenders, she caught a glimpse of a blue-haired lad gripped in one of the monster's many tentacles. She did not know which of her twin brothers was slain that day, nor did she ever learn the fate of the other. But Zhoron and Xharlion were lost to Evermeet.

Nor were they the only children of Amlaruil and Zaor whose fate was never determined. The ship carrying Lazziar and Gemstarzah was lost at sea while the twins sailed on a mission of diplomacy.

Even the simple passage of years took a toll. Chozzaster passed on to Arvandor at a young age, and Shandalar, Zaor's pet and favorite, was accidentally slain by a fellow student, a gifted spell-singer, during her training as a bladesinger.

Zaor, grieving and aging, privately began to feel the call of Arvandor. As the years passed, as security of Evermeet made the warrior king feel unneeded, and as his children slipped away from him, Zaor began to withdraw from the daily life of the palace.

More interested in gardening than in governance, he increasingly abandoned the rulership of Evermeet to his capable and apparently ageless queen.

23

Rapport

aor of Evermeet, now aged far beyond the years of most elves, busied himself in the palace gardens. He lowered the clippers and cocked his head to one side as he admired the effect. In the very center of the palace gardens, he had planted a hedge of pale blue roses and shaped it into a crescent moon. In the faint light of a summer twilight, the rare flowers seemed to glow with their own inner radiance.

"Very lovely," commented a voice behind him, a voice that still had the power to quicken Zaor's heart despite the passage of centuries.

He turned to face Amlaruil. A mixture of longing and pain smote him as he gazed upon her beautiful face. She looked exactly as she had when he'd met her more than four hundred years before. And he? He was an old elf, useless to Amlaruil and to Evermeet, homesick for Arvandor.

Amlaruil took a single step forward, her hands clenched at her sides and her face blazing with incompressible wrath. "I would never have thought I'd have occasion to call you a hypocrite!" she said in a cold voice. "Do you not remember the pledge you demanded of me, those many years past? You made me promise that I would remain on Evermeet for the good of the People, for howsoever long I was needed."

"I am old, Amlaruil," he said simply, "and I am very tired."

"Spare me your tales of creaking joints!" she raged at

him. "Do you think that it has been easy for me, or always pleasant, to do as you requested? If *I* could see my youth pass by, each year like a wasted spring day as I endured seeing you wed to another, can you not summon the courage to live your venerable years? You are needed!"

"You are Evermeet's queen, and all the ruler the elves truly need."

"What of my needs, my lord? And truly, what would befall Evermeet if I, like you, were to become so self-absorbed that I did not tend to the future? Which of our children could you truly envision on the throne? Tira'allara? Hhora?"

Zaor slowly shook his head. He loved his daughters, but neither would make a queen. Priestesses of Hanali Celanil, they were both completely caught up in the cult of love and beauty, so much so that at times he worried about them. Tira'allara was involved in a potentially disastrous liaison with a young Gold elf known as a rake and a wastrel. Zaor suspected that the youth's interest in the princess had more to do with her rank and wealth—for Tira'allara happily repaid his gambling debts with her jewels and dowry—than with the princess herself. Yet Tira'allara loved the elf with all her passionate, intense nature. Zaor wondered if she would survive the disillusionment that was sure to come. And Hhora was preparing to sail for distant Faerûn, for she was determined to wed a chance-met commoner with whom she'd shared a festival.

"Evermeet is without an heir," Amlaruil continued bluntly. "The sword of Zaor is a warrior's blade, and neither of our surviving children could draw it and live. We must give Evermeet an heir."

"I am old, Amlaruil," he repeated.

She came to him in a rush, framing his weathered face in hands as smooth and unlined as a maiden's. Tears filled her eyes and soul-deep grief softened her angry face. "Do not leave me, my love," she said with quiet intensity. "I could not bear it."

He stroked her bright hair. "You can handle anything. I have never known anyone as strong."

"Together we are strong!" she said urgently. "Do you not see it? What we have accomplished, we have done together. The bond between us is deep and unique, but it could be even more."

Zaor stared at her, stunned by what she was offering. The rare, deep bond of elven rapport would bind them together soul to soul. He would be sustained by the same divine fire that linked her to the Seldarine—at what cost to her, he could not begin to imagine. He could make, and make good, the pledge she demanded of him. He could vow to remain on Evermeet for as long as he was needed.

"It is midsummer," she whispered, clinging to him with an urgency that warmed his blood and sent it singing through his veins. "It is the time for making promises. Come with me to our glade, my love."

The king found that he could not deny the entreaty in his love's eyes. He swept her up in arms still strong despite his years, and carried her from the garden as if she were again a bride.

The palace guard parted to let them pass, the servants and gardeners melted away. Not a single elven face held anything but smiles of understanding and joy. None saw anything incongruent in the sight of beautiful springtime in the arms of late autumn. It was midsummer, and pledges made had a magic of their own.

Thus began Zaor and Amlaruil's new life together.

In the years that followed, four more children were born to them. First was Amnestria, who inherited her father's coloring and her mother's rare beauty—and something that came from neither. Alternately sunny and fierce, Amnestria possessed an intensity that seemed oddly out of place in the serene court of Leuthilspar.

Zandro and Finufaranell, the boys that followed, were cut more to the elven mold. They were diligent students both, and took to the Towers at a young age. And finally, there was Lamruil, the sunny, charming, spoiled baby of the family. By the time he was yet a lad, no more than thirty or forty, he had already taken up adventuring and wenching as avocations. Lamruil was much given to mischief; fortunately, his fierce love and admiration for his older sister Amnestria served to keep him somewhat in line. The year that he left the island in search of adventure and elven artifacts, many elves in the staid capital city—including Lamruil's tutors and swordmasters—breathed private sighs of relief.

The tenor of palace life changed yet again with the arrival of Thasitalia Moonflower. Near to the end of her mortal span, the adventurer had one task left to her before answering the call to Arvandor. As was the responsibility of every elf who wielded a moonblade, she needed to select a blade heir.

For weeks the sharp-eyed, sharp-tongued elf woman stayed in the palace, scandalizing the nobles and delighting the young with stories of her travels.

Amnestria, in particular, was enchanted by the tales of distant places and strange events. The king and queen watched their daughter as she listened to Thasitalia with shining eyes, and the fey Amlaruil felt a fear to which she could not give a name. She and Zaor were not pleased when Thasitalia proclaimed Amnestria to be the pick of Zaor's litter, and chose her as blade heir. Yet the honor of a moonblade was something that no one, especially a king and queen so chosen, could scorn. The choice was Amnestria's, and she embraced the sword with passion and joy: the sword of an adventurer, a solitary fighter. It was not an auspicious step for the daughter whom Amlaruil and Zaor fondly hoped to see upon the throne of Evermeet.

Even so, Amnestria seemed contented with life in Leuthilspar. The elf maid added a fierce regime of training for the moonblade's challenge to her studies of swordcraft and battle magic. But the girl's world shattered when her betrothed, Elaith Craulnober, left her and Evermeet without a breath of explanation.

For weeks after his departure, everyone in the palace tiptoed around the jilted princess, for Amnestria's fiery temper was legendary. Of all the royal elves, only Lamruil dared seek her out.

The prince found his sister in her chamber, her face set with determination as she flung clothes and valuables into a sea chest. When Lamruil entered the room, she looked up at him and grimaced.

"The door was locked and enspelled," she said pointedly. "I wouldn't have thought you knew magic enough to open it!"

Lamruil shrugged, and then nodded to the overflowing chest. "What's this about?"

The princess slammed the lid. "I'm going after him."

"Who? Elaith?"

She shot her brother a derisive look. "He sent me word from Waterdeep—wasn't that nice of him? He has taken up with a band of adventurers. Humans, mostly. He's off to see the world. Well, I'm going to become part of the scenery he sees!"

"Oh."

"Oh? That's it? You're not going to try to convince me of my folly?"

"Would it help?"

A reluctant smile softened Amnestria's face, and her shoulders rose and fell with a long sigh. "Well, it's comforting to know that at least one person in this palace understands me."

"I understand more than you think," Lamruil said, suddenly grave. He reached out and touched the weapons belt at his sister's waist. The clasp had been loosened a notch, displaying the well-worn notch to the right of it.

Amnestria's gazed followed his gesture. She frowned and shrugged. Though beautiful almost beyond measure, there was nothing of vanity in her.

"So? One notch is as good as another, as long as it keeps my sword on and my trousers up."

"Speaking of which, what was the manner of your leave-taking with Elaith?"

The princess's face darkened, and she turned away to snap shut the clasps on the trunk with more force than was needed. "That's none of your business."

Her brother saw that she truly did not understand. "Four moons have passed since Elaith left the island," he said gently. "Before too many more pass, you will have to set aside that belt altogether."

Amnestria spun back to him, her eyes wide with shock. She sank down on the bed and buried her face in her hands. "Oh, I feel such a fool! How could I not have known?"

The prince sat down beside her, hating what he must tell her next. "I know why Elaith left Evermeet. His grandfather passed to Arvandor, and the Craulnober blade passed to him. It went dormant in his hands, as there is no heir to Craulnober."

She sat up, abruptly. "There is now. Damnation! If only he had waited to draw the moonblade until after we—"

"If he had waited, he would be dead," Lamruil interrupted bluntly. "The sword did not accept him. If there had been an heir, it would have slain him and you would have kept the sword in trust for your babe."

They sat in silence for a moment as Amnestria tried to sort it through.

"There is more," Lamruil said reluctantly. He drew a letter from his tunic. "This came through the Relays, from a human ranger and a comrade of Elaith's. He says he feels he knows you a little, from Elaith's descriptions, and he urgently bids you not to come."

"I haven't told anyone I was coming," the princess muttered.

"Well, perhaps he does understand you. There is more. The adventuring group with whom Elaith has taken up has left the city. They seek to find the ancient burial grounds of Aryvandaar—and to despoil them."

Horror dulled Amnestria's eyes like mist, only to be rapidly burned off by the heat of her wrath. "And this human?"

"He does not approve. He will try to stop them, by whatever means needed."

The princess nodded, grimly approving. "And I will help."

"But what of the child?"

"I can still travel for a while, and I can still fight. When I cannot, I will find a place where I am not known, and bear the child in secrecy. For I swear to you before all the gods of the Seldarine, Elaith will never know of this child! I will give the babe up into the hands of another to raise, before I would link my house with a traitor and a rogue!"

She glared at Lamruil, daring him to gainsay her.

"That is your right," he said. "I will help you all I can, but you must promise me two things. First, you must tell me where the child is. Second, he must be raised in the skills and knowledge required of a potential king. Evermeet may have need of him."

Amnestria glared. "Damn it, Lamruil, that's the sort of thing our mother would think of! You're starting to talk like a king yourself."

A wide grin split Lamruil's face. "Not a chance," he said, genuinely amused by the idea. He rose and extended a hand to help her to her feet. "I'll help you slip away," he said softly. "Bran Skorlsun was not the only one to suspect that you would come storming after Elaith. There's a ship waiting for you off the shore of Ruith, and I've bribed enough of the palace servants that you can slip away in secrecy."

The princess thanked him with a brief, fierce hug, and then drew away. "Who is Bran Skorlsun?"

"The human ranger. I have sent word, and told him where to expect you. He seems a fine man, and I think you and he will do well together."

* * * * *

Lamruil was long to remember these words, and oft to rue them. Amnestria did indeed join with Bran Skorlsun, and they were successful in thwarting the efforts of Elaith and his comrades. The ancient burial grounds of Aryvandaar, the resting place of the mortal remains of those who died in defense of that wondrous land, remained sacred.

Elaith was never to learn of his son. The babe was born into the hands of a human, and hidden away to be raised in secret fosterage. Amnestria did all that she promised.

But she did not return to the island. The elven princess found a deeper love than that which she had lost, and she wed Bran Skorlsun. With him she established a rapport as deep as that shared by her royal parents. And in so doing, she inadvertently set in motion events that were to have grim consequences for her family, and for all of Evermeet.

24

The Elite
2nd day of Ches, 1321 DR

he elf emerged in a glade, a small verdant meadow ringed by a tight circle of vast, ancient oaks. His path had brought him to a spot of rare beauty that, to the untrained eye, appeared to be utterly untouched. Never had the elf seen a place more deeply green; a few determined shafts of early morning sunlight filtered through leaves and vines until even the air around him seemed dense and alive. At his feet, emerald droplets clung to the grass. The elf's seeking eyes narrowed in speculation. Dropping to his knees, he studied the grass until he found it—an almost imperceptible path where the dew had been shaken loose from the ankle-high grass. Yes, his prey had come this way.

Quickly he followed the dew trail to where it slipped between two of the giant oaks. He parted a curtain of vines and stepped out of the glade, blinking away the bright morning sun. Once his eyes adjusted to the light, he saw a narrow dirt path winding through the trees.

His quarry did not know that they were being followed, so why wouldn't they take the easiest way through the forest? The elf slipped through the underbrush and set off down the path. There was little to indicate that other footsteps had preceded him, but the elf was not concerned. The two he sought were, despite their deplorable origins, among the best rangers he had encountered. Very few could walk through the thick, deep grass of that sheltered glade and leave behind no more than a dew trail.

The elf glided silently along the path, his blood

quickening at the thought of the victory that lay ahead, so long awaited and now so close at hand. Elves, particularly Gold elves, were not hasty people, and behind this morning's mission lay years of planning, decades of discussion, and almost four centuries of waiting for the proper means and moment. The time to strike had come, and his would be the first blow.

The path ended at the stone wall, and again the elf paused, alert and observant. He crouched in the shadow of the wall and examined the scene spread out before him. Beyond the wall was a garden, as lovely as anything he had ever seen.

Peacocks strutted about an expanse of lawn, some with tail feathers spread to flaunt dozens of iridescent blue-green eyes. Brilliantly colored kotala birds chattered in the spring-flowering trees that ringed a reflecting pond. The elf's innate love of beauty welled up within him, pushing aside for a moment the urgency of his mission. It would be easy, he mused as he observed the garden scene, for elves to be seduced by such splendor.

As indeed they had been, he concluded as his gaze lifted above the garden to a distant castle, a marvel of enspelled moonstone and marble. His golden eyes glittered with hate and triumph as he realized that the trail had led him to the very center of Gray elf power. The ancient Gold elf race had succumbed to the rule of their inferiors for far too long. With renewed purpose the elf began to plan his attack.

His situation could hardly be better; no guards patrolled the outer palace gardens. If he could catch his prey before they got close to the palace, he would be able to strike and withdraw undetected, and return another day to strike again.

Between him and the palace was an enormous maze fashioned of boxwood hedges. Perfect! The elf flashed a private, evil smile. The Gray wench and her pet human had walked into their own tomb. Days could pass before the bodies would be discovered in that labyrinth.

The arrangement did have its disadvantages. The maze

itself did not worry him, but its entrance could be reached only through a garden of bellflowers. Cultivated for sound as well as scent, the flowers sent faint music drifting toward him in the still morning air. The elf listened for a moment, and his jaw tightened. He'd seen such gardens before. The flower beds and statuary were arranged to catch and channel the slightest breath of wind, so that the flowers constantly chimed one of several melodies. Any disruption of the air flow, however, faint, would change their song. In effect, the garden was a beautiful but effective alarm system.

Since his quarry was undoubtedly in the maze and heading for the palace, the elf knew he would have to take a chance. He vaulted easily over the low stone wall and raced past the inquisitive peacocks, then glided through the bellflower garden with an economy of motion only the best elven rangers could achieve. As he had feared, the tinkling song subtly altered with his passing. To his sensitive ear, the disruption was as glaring as a trumpet's blast, and he ducked behind a statue and steeled himself for the approach of the palace guard.

Several silent minutes passed, and eventually the elf relaxed. His lips twisted in derision as he pictured the palace guards—oafs too stupid and common to recognize their own musical alarm. Tone deaf, as were all Gray elves. The elf deliberately ignored the fact that few elves, be they Gold or Silver or Green by birth, had his keen ear for the subtle blend of music and magic. After all, he was a bladesinger, and one of the elite trained in the ancient art of spell song. With a silent chuckle, the elf slipped into the maze.

Garden mazes, he knew, tended to follow a common pattern. After a few confident turns, the elf began to suspect that this one was an exception. This maze was like nothing he had seen before. Vast and whimsical, its convoluted paths wandered from one small garden to another, each one more fantastic than the last. With a growing sense of dismay the elf passed exotic fruit trees, fountains, arbors, berry patches, tiny ponds filled with bright fish, and hummingbirds breakfasting amid vines of red trumpet flowers. Most striking were the magical displays depicting familiar episodes from elven folklore: the birth of the Sea elves, the flight of the dragons, the Starwing ship landfall.

He pressed on, running to the entrance of yet another garden clearing. One glance inside, and he skidded to a stop. Before him was a marble pedestal topped with a large, water-filled globe. Surely he couldn't have passed that globe before! He crept closer for a better look. A magical illusion raged within the sphere, a terrible sea storm that tossed tiny elven vessels about. Before his horrified eyes the sea goddess Umberlee rose from the waves, her white hair flying in the gale like flashes of lightning. By the gods, it was the birth of the Sea elves again!

There could be no doubt. Surely not even this ridiculous maze could have two such displays. The elf raked both hands through his golden hair, tugging at it in self-disgust. He, an elf as renown for his ranger's skills as his talents with sword and song-spell, had been running around in circles!

Before he could castigate himself further, the elf heard a faint clicking sound not far away. He trailed it to a large, circular garden ringed with flowers that attracted clouds of bright butterflies. Many paths led out of the garden, which was dominated by pale blue roses in a bed shaped like a crescent moon. At one tip of the blue-rose moon stood an elderly elven gardener, snipping away at the rosebushes with more vigor than expertise.

Again the elven intruder smiled. By all appearances, this was the maze's center and surely his quarry had passed through. The old gardener would tell him, at knife point if need be, which path the wench had taken.

The elf edged into the garden. As he entered a flock of the butterflies took flight, and the gardener looked up, his silver-blue eyes lit with gentle inquiry at the disruption.

His gaze fell upon the intruder, but he merely waved and cleared his throat as if to call out a greeting.

No, not that! thought the intruder in a moment of panic. He could not alert his quarry now!

A dagger flew, and a look of surprise crossed the gardener's face. The old elf's hand came up to fumble with the blade in his chest, and he fell heavily to the ground. His rough cap tumbled off. From it spilled an abundance of long, dark blue hair shot through with silver threads.

Blue hair!

Excitement gripped the assassin, and he sped across the distance between him and the fallen elf. As he crouched beside the corpse, a flash of gold caught his eye. He reached for it. From beneath the gardener's rough linen tunic he drew a medallion bearing the royal crest. The elf felt a clasp and flipped the medallion open. Within was a tiny painting. The exquisite, unmistakable face of Queen Amlaruil gazed up at him, a tender, very personal smile upon her lips.

It was true! The assassin dropped the medallion and sat back on his heels, dizzy with elation. Through the most fortunate of errors, he had killed King Zaor!

A keening scream, anguished and female, interrupted his private celebration. In one quick motion the elven assassin leaped to his feet and whirled, twin swords in his hands. He found himself facing his original quarry. So white and still was she, that for a moment she seemed carved from marble. No sculptor, however, could have captured the grief and guilt that twisted her pale face. The knuckles of one hand pressed against her mouth, and with her other hand she clung to the arm of the tall man at her side.

Ah, the fates were kind today, the elven assassin gloated. Swiftly and confidently he advanced on the pair, blades leading. To his surprise, the wench's oversized companion had the presence of mind to snatch a small hunting bow from his shoulder and let fly an arrow.

The elven assassin felt the stunning impact first, and

then a burning flash of pain as the arrow pierced his leather armor and buried itself in his side, just below the rib cage. He glanced down at the shaft and saw that the arrow was neither deeply imbedded nor in a vital spot. Summoning all his austere self discipline, he willed aside the pain and raised his swords. He could still kill the wench—kill them both—before making his escape. It would be a fine day's work, indeed.

"This way!"

A vibrant contralto voice rang out, very near. The female's scream had alerted the palace guard. The assassin could hear the rapidly approaching footsteps of at least a dozen guards. He must not be captured and questioned! He would die for the cause and do so gladly, but the Gray rulers would surely not grant him the dignity of death. With her foul magic, the Gray queen would surely pry from his mind the name of his master, and the names of the spell-singers lying in wait—here, in Evermeet itself— with Gold elven patience as they anticipated the signal to strike.

The elven assassin hesitated for only a moment, then turned and fled toward the glade and the magic portal that stood there.

Breathing hard and feeling lightheaded from pain and loss of blood, the elf plunged through the circle of blue smoke that marked the magical doorway. Strong, slender arms caught him and eased him to the ground.

"Fenian! Tell me what happened!"

"The portal leads to Evermeet," the wounded elf gasped. "King Zaor lies dead!"

A triumphant, ringing cry escaped the elf's companion, echoing over the mountains and startling a pair of songbirds into flight. "And the elf wench? The Harper?" he asked excitedly.

"They still live," the assassin admitted. The effort of speaking brought a fresh spasm of agony. He grimaced and grasped with both hands at the arrow shaft.

"Take ease," his friend consoled him. "Amnestria and her

human lover will soon follow Zaor into death." He gently moved the elf's hands aside and began to work the arrow out. "Were you seen?"

"Yes." The answer came from between gritted teeth.

The hands on the arrow stilled, then tensed. "Even so, you have done well." With a quick motion, he plunged the arrow up under the elf's rib cage and into his heart. When the flow of lifeblood stilled, he wrenched the arrow free and thrust it back into the elf's body at the original angle. He rose to his feet and gazed with a touch of regret at the dead elf. "But not well enough," he murmured.

The elf fled swiftly down the mountain, racing for the teeming anonymity of the human city beyond. It wouldn't take the elves long to trace Fenian back to the magic portal, but by then he would be long gone. He would lose himself in Waterdeep, and begin to fashion a way to exploit the discovery he had made this day. A gate to Evermeet was just the thing he needed to fulfill his life quest. And it was fitting that Amnestria, the former and disgraced heir to Evermeet's throne, would be instrumental in helping him reach that goal.

Kymil Nimesin smiled faintly as he ran, unaware of the two pairs of eyes that watched him go.

* * * * *

"He might be the one," Lloth mused, turning away from her scrying pool to eye her longtime comrade.

Malar the Great Hunter snorted in disgust. "He is an elf!"

"Who better?" she retorted. "The plans these Gold elves have put in place are quite ingenious, and they might be the added touch we need to accomplish what we have so long desired. Let us watch him, at any rate, and if he shows promise, we can bolster his efforts with our own."

25

Malar's Vengeance
(1371 DR)

he goddess Lloth was well content. In a tunnel far beneath the oceans surrounding Evermeet, she and Malar gazed with dark glee into a large scrying bowl, enjoying their long-awaited vengeance upon the children of Corellon Larethian.

Of course, it would be far more pleasant to observe in person, but this was as near to Evermeet as they could get. The weave Corellon had placed over the island barred all evil gods from entering. But it did not keep the drow from using the gate that Kymil Nimesin had so conveniently arranged, or prevent the passage of the deadly creature of Malar: the elf-eater.

The gate. Many elements had gone into this attack, but it was the gate that dealt the deadliest blow. A wonderful thing, this art of Circle-singing—using spell-song to combine many magical effects into one—especially when one considered the ingenious use Kymil had made of it. Under his direction, the circle-singers had gathered the power of all the gates to Evermeet, combining them into a single gate, effectively cutting the island off from outside magical interference.

It was a masterful plan, and Lloth was quite impressed with Kymil Nimesin. The Gold elf had nurtured his plans for years, gathering and training every talented elven spell-singer he could find. If only there were a way to imbue her drow followers with such patience! How quickly they would rule all of Aber-toril!

Well, they would soon overrun Evermeet, and for the time being she could content herself with that. No doubt Malar thought that his creature would destroy them, as well, thus giving him a victory over his dark-elven ally. Lloth, however, was ever alert to the possibility of treachery. To be on the safe side, she'd tried feeding a few of her faithful drow to the elf-eater, and found the monster had no appetite for them. Malar would disperse his creature soon enough, when there was no more sport to be had on Evermeet.

She glanced over at Malar. Although he kept an eye on the image in the scrying bowl, he paced in a short, restless path. That made Lloth nervous as well. Her drow had done well—they had lured many elven fighters into the tunnels with the coming of day, where they could slaughter them at their leisure—but she needed Malar's elf-eater to truly destroy Evermeet. The god was uncomfortable in these tunnels. If he left and took his fine toy with him, the game would be over before it was finished.

"There is fine hunting down here," she observed, her crimson eyes gleaming as she watched two drow slowly slice the flesh from the bones of an elven warrior. Wherever they looked, the tunnels were filled with battles.

Malar snorted, unimpressed by the spectacle. "I am no mole to tunnel through the soil in search of worms!"

Before Lloth could retort, the image in her scrying pool changed. A new fighter, an enormous elf maid thrumming with godly power, had entered the battle. Almost before Lloth could absorb this threat, the warrior maid neatly netted the elf-eater. Before her horrified eyes, elf maid and elf-eater disappeared.

Malar saw this, as well. The Beast Lord's fearsome roar reverberated through the tunnel, shaking rocks loose from the tunnel walls and causing a brief, startled pause in the drow's genocidal fun.

Lloth recovered quickly from the shock, her nimble mind seeing a possibility in even this. "A new avatar," she said excitedly. "But not an avatar of any of the gods I know. This is the spirit of a powerful mortal elf—therefore there is but one place it can go. Surely, the elf maid will bring the creature to Arvandor!"

"And where the elf-eater goes, so we might follow," Malar said, beginning to understand. "But we are two against the many of the Seldarine."

"It matters not," she said. "All we need do is watch and enjoy as the elf-eater rampages! I imagine that the spirits of the faithful departed will be as tasty morsels to your monster. If we are lucky, perhaps it will devour a god or two, as well!"

"We go," the god agreed. He snatched up Lloth's wrist in one enormous paw, dragging her with him as he followed his creature. The gods disappeared from the tunnel, taking the battle to yet another level.

* * * * *

In a chamber of the palace, Maura squirmed in the chair, restless even in her hard-won sleep. She had come to the palace along with the slumbering body of the princess Ilyrana, and she sat at the elf woman's bedside. But the terrible days of battle had taken a toll, and Maura had drifted into troubled slumber.

Even in sleep, the battle followed. In a strange dream, Maura watched as the warrior elf maid strove desperately to stop the monster that had attacked Corellon's Grove. The creature, bits of silvery web still clinging to it, thundered through a forest more beautiful than any Maura had seen and into a city of such wonder that even Leuthilspar paled. On and on the creature went, pausing only to snatch up the gallant elves who stayed behind to fight so that most of their people might flee. She watched as the creature advanced on a tall, blue-haired male elf. His resemblance to Lamruil struck her like an arrow to the heart.

The sleeping woman's palm itched for the feel of her own sword, though she knew there was little she could do against such a monster. Indeed, even the warrior maid did not fare well. She screamed a single word and threw herself between the blue-haired elf and the approaching monster. Maura flinched as the warrior maid went flying, struck aside with devastating force by one of the elf-eater's flailing tentacles. The elf maid got up, but blood dripped from her forehead where she had been cut in her fall.

A terrible, shrieking roar jolted Maura from her sleep. Instinctively she knew that this was not part of her dream, and she dashed to the window and looked out into the sky.

Hundreds, perhaps thousands of terrible creatures winged their way over the city, blocking out the sun with their loathsome bodies. She watched, near despair, as a swarm of them covered an airborne gold dragon. The battle was fierce and terrible, but in the end, the dragon was overcome. It plunged to the ground, its wings utterly gone, eaten away by the unnatural creatures that had attacked it. The dragon hit the island with a force that shook the palace—and no doubt leveled a good part of the city, Maura noted grimly.

She scanned the sky, trying to make some small sense of this strange attack. Here and there groups of the creatures, looking like dark, seething clouds against the sky, suggested that the rest of the dragonriders—even the aged Guardians released to combat the pirate fleet— might soon meet the same fate.

Maura drew a long, shuddering breath and turned away from the window. She fully expected to die this day, and she took comfort in two things: that Lamruil was safely away, and that the terrible slaughter of the elves she had just witnessed was only a dream.

She glanced down at the sleeping princess, and her heart thudded painfully. Ilyrana's white hair, in which usually glistened the pale colors of an opal, was dark and matted with blood, and on her forehead was a gash identical to the one dealt the warrior elf maid.

The single word that the elf maid warrior shouted now

made perfect sense, as did the blue-haired male's resemblance to Lamruil. Maura spun on her heel and ran from the chamber. If anyone could do anything about this new horror, it would be the queen.

And even if the queen could not act, she had a right to know.

* * * * *

All over Evermeet, the elves struggled to shake off the terrible lethargy that had fallen over them with the destruction of the Towers. Nearly all the High Magi of Evermeet had gathered in the Towers of the Sun and Moon, or in the Sumbrar Tower in the island east of Leuthilspar. These magi had woven a powerful web of magic that upheld the elven fighters and strengthened the island's legendary defenses. This web had not simply collapsed, though that alone would have been catastrophic. The Towers had been reduced to dust, the magi slain. The resulting blow to the Weave, and thus to all of them, was staggering.

Amlaruil stood in her council chamber, gazing out over the stunned and grieving elves who stood motionless in the city's streets, too stunned even to react to the appearance of the unnatural horrors that suddenly filled the skies.

"Darkenbeasts," she whispered, for her informants had been her well versed in such magics as the human mages fashioned. This was the work of the worst of them, the terrible Red Wizards who ruled distant Thay. Amlaruil did not need to ask what interest such humans might have in Evermeet. They had tried before to broach the island's defenses; of course they could join in such a devastating attack, hoping to take as their plunder some of the legendary magical wealth of the elven island. The thought of the elven treasures—the wands and swords, the magical art works, even the Tree of Souls—lent her new determination, and new strength.

475

Turning to Keryth Blackhelm, she asked that he give the report that had been interrupted by the silent magical explosion. The queen's calm demeanor seemed to hearten her advisors; even so, the news that the Silver elf gave was dire.

The northern shore had fallen to creatures from Below. The dragonriders of the Eagle Hills were making some headway against the sahuagin and scrags that swarmed up the Ardulith, but most of the centaurs and other forest creatures had fallen in battle. A mixed force of humans and elves had landed on Siiluth and were marching westward to Drelagara.

"Elves?" she asked sharply. "There were elves among the pirates? And they broke through our defenses?"

Keryth grimaced. "Yes, my lady, but not in any manner that we anticipated. The elven ships with elven crews, those that we thought were fleeing the invading force, were part of it. The holds of these boats were stacked with warriors and spellcasters, eager for battle. Even with the help of the lythari and the moon-horses, the people of Drelagara are having a hard time of it."

The queen took this in. "And the other ships? There were six, I believe."

"We do not know," he admitted. "Apparently the ships split up after what was left of our navy helped them through the magical defenses. Our ships are still offshore, fighting what remains of the pirate fleet. The decoy fleet," he added in deep self-disgust.

"You could not have known, my friend," Amlaruil said. "None of us expected such treachery from our own. We should have."

"There is more," the war leader said. "Three of these ships are approaching Leuthilspar. The leader is close enough to send messages through flag speech."

Amlaruil frowned. "The Starwing fleet could not stop them?"

"We did not send the Starwing ships against them," Keryth said softly. "I did not think you would wish it. The ship has sent word: Prince Lamruil himself is on board."

* * * * *

Kymil Nimesin turned an impatient stare upon the young human sailor. The youth was nearly dancing with ill-contained excitement. This annoyed Kymil. He had endured young Kaymid's enthusiasms for about as long he intended to. Once the battle for Evermeet was over, this wretched boy would be the first human to fall to Kymil's blade.

"You have something to say?" he asked coldly.

"The elf prince is asking to see you," Kaymid said importantly.

This interested Kymil. Young Lamruil had not spoken so much as two words to his former swordmaster since the day that he had stumbled into Kymil's trap. Glum and resentful, he had been the very picture of the spoiled, thwarted boy-prince.

The Gold elf followed Kaymid down to the hold, where Lamruil sat on the floor of his cell. For a moment Kymil gazed at the young elf, taking pleasure in Lamruil's wasted appearance. During the ocean voyage, they had given him just enough food and water to keep him alive. But even though the young elf was far thinner and less hale than he had been at the beginning of the voyage, he still outmassed most elves that Kymil could name.

"Well?" he inquired. "What do you want?"

Lamruil looked up, and the grim intensity in his blue eyes set Kymil back on his heels. "My life," the prince said coldly. "And I am willing to pay any price to have it."

Kymil was inclined to believe him. "What have you to offer? You are still a useful pawn to me—a pawn that if properly played, might be traded for a queen."

"You underestimate Amlaruil," the prince said flatly. "There is nothing she would not sacrifice for Evermeet's sake. Since she and I do not see eye to eye on many matters, I doubt she would shed many tears over me." He cast a derisive smile at Kymil. "Simple kidnapping, Lord Kymil? Expecting the queen to ransom me at the expense of her kingdom? I must say, that is by far the weakest part of your otherwise excellent plan."

There was some truth in that, and it galled Kymil. "And what would you have me do?"

"Free me," Lamruil said. "We will stage a mock battle on the deck of this ship, in full view of those who watch from Leuthilspar's docks. Then I, the victorious prince, will escape ashore, valiantly bringing with me the only other elf who survived the fight."

"Me, I suppose," Kymil said coldly, though in fact he rather approved of the prince's line of thought. "And then?"

"Then I will demand the queen's abdication. I have that right," he said calmly, holding up a hand to still Kymil's sarcastic laughter. "I am the heir, I am of age. All I need do is draw the sword of Zaor, and it is done."

"Oh, is that all?"

Lamruil smiled coldly. "You think I cannot draw the sword and live? Very well—say that I don't live. You have still accomplished what you set out to do. Every member of the royal family on Evermeet will be dead."

"But for Amlaruil herself."

"Ah. I forgot to tell you that part," the prince said. "I will kill her myself, before I draw the king sword."

"You would never get close enough," Kymil sneered.

"Who said I intended to use a weapon?" retorted the prince. "I know my mother, and I know her absolute devotion to Evermeet. If we present her with a task, a dangerous spell that only she could cast, she would do it. Even if it meant her death."

"Such as?"

"The other ships," Lamruil said bluntly. "We tell her where they are bound. Amlaruil has the power to cast a spell that can teleport a single ship away from Evermeet. She might be able to manage to send two away, and live. But more?" The prince shook his head. "She will try, all the same."

"And I lose my ships."

"And gain a kingdom," the prince said. "How many of the

elven survivors of Evermeet would follow you if your hand was raised against their beloved queen? Zaor might forgive you. But never Amlaruil. No, we go in playing the part of heroes. Amlaruil dies defending her people. I am no king," he said negligently, "nor do I wish to be. Nor, for that matter, will the people of Evermeet embrace me. I'll happily set aside the sword of Zaor—and take myself off to the mainland for a life filled with soft women and hard cider. It would suit me far better than a crown. Then you, in whatever guise you choose, will be free to restore the Council of Elders. We both get what we want."

Kymil stared at the prince, astonished by the grim tone, the venal light in his eyes. He had known Lamruil was a self-centered wastrel, but he hadn't thought him capable of such focused thought, even in the effort of self-preservation. He would test just how far the prince was willing to go.

"Convince me," Kymil suggested. "Tell me more."

"You have a spelljammer. I heard the others talking. Do not send it in until the island is subdued. Sumbrar has defenses that would bring it down with ease."

"The Guardians. The sleeping dragons have already been released, and most have exchanged their age-long slumber for a more permanent one. The same goes for the dragonriders. I am not troubled by the thought of a few pegasi."

"There is a Starwing fleet on Sumbrar," Lamruil said.

"Not so. The fleet was destroyed over five hundred years ago, during the flight of the dragons!"

"True, but it was rebuilt in secrecy. There are ten ships." Lamruil gave a short, concise description that left Kymil utterly convinced. He had spent enough time on just such a ship to know that only firsthand knowledge could prompt the prince's words.

The prince continued, describing the defenses of the island and the powers of its queen in such detail that Kymil was nearly convinced.

"Give me one thing more, and we will do as you suggest," the elf said.

A strange, almost mad light entered the prince's eyes. "It may be that for one reason or another you may wish to restore the throne of Evermeet. There is a lawful heir. The princess Amnestria had a child."

Kymil snorted. "Don't remind me! A half-breed bastard is no contender for the throne, by any elf's measure."

"Arilyn was my sister's second child. She had another— a son by a Moon elf of a noble family. No one on Evermeet knows this but me. The prince is not aware of his identity. I can tell you where he is. I can prove he is who I say he is. You can use him or slay him, as suits your needs."

The Gold elf nodded, convinced of the worth of what Lamruil offered. The truth of it, he already knew. After all, it was a small matter to cast a spell that weighed the truthfulness of what was said.

"We will do as you say," he said. "But be assured that a dagger will find your heart before one word of betrayal can escape your lips!"

The prince shrugged. "Just let me out of this hole, and I will be content."

* * * * *

The harbor guards brought Lamruil directly to the queen's council chamber, as she requested. A spasm of pain crossed her drawn face as her gaze fell upon her son's wasted form. Even thin as he was, clad in filthy garments and marked with several small wounds from the battle that freed him, he carried himself with an arrogance that brought frowns to the faces of all of Amlaruil's advisers.

Even so, he was her son, her last child. Amlaruil flew to him and enfolded him in her arms. He embraced her briefly, then took her shoulders and put her away from him.

"There is little time, mother," he said urgently. "I know where the other four ships are bound. One carries three score Red Wizards, determined to despoil Evermeet's magical treasures. With them are human ruffians who came for gold and elven wenches. There are more of their ilk on each of the four remaining ships. Human wizards, too, and as many fighters as they could pack into the hold like cordwood. I know what I am asking of you, but I know too that you would wish to know this."

Amlaruil's troubled eyes searched his face. "Ilyrana is gone," she said softly. "If I do this thing, will you take your father's sword?"

"Bring it to me," the prince said stoutly. "I will take it up if I must!"

The queen nodded to an adviser, who brought the sheathed weapon from its place of honor on the pedestal behind her throne. She laid it on a table nearby.

"All of you must bear witness to this. I name Prince Lamruil my successor. Now you must keep silent while I cast the needed spell."

Keryth leaped to his feet, shaking with rage. "You cannot, my queen! I know what you mean to do, and I know what the end will be. You are needed here! We will deal with these ships. Surely they are not such a threat as the prince tries to paint them!"

A hesitant expression crossed Amlaruil's face. "You have seen these ships, Lamruil. Must I cast this spell?"

Before he could answer, the sounds of a brief struggle and a woman's angry voice erupted from the hall. Maura burst into the chamber, her eyes wild. She gasped at the sight of Lamruil, but did not go to him. Rather, she ran to the queen and quickly told her all that she had seen.

"The warrior maid is Ilyrana," Maura concluded. "And she called for you! The elf-eater is in Arvandor itself! It attacks the spirits of the faithful. I saw Zaor among them."

Amlaruil's face firmed with resolve.

"We need you here," Keryth repeated.

"Not really," Lamruil said coldly. "Whether she casts the spell or not, I would demand her abdication. The sword is mine now, and the kingdom with it."

Maura rounded on him. "And what of your queen? What of me?"

A faintly puzzled expression crossed the prince's face. "What of you? I will chose an elf maiden of high family for my queen."

The woman's eyes flamed. "You are nothing but a . . . an albino drow!" she gritted out.

The prince shrugged again and turned to the queen. "Well, mother? What will it be? Duty as always?" He let out a brief, scornful laugh when Amlaruil nodded, and then turned to the cowled elf at his side. "Convinced, my lord? Will you tell her where these ships might be found?"

The elf slipped off his hood, to reveal a handsome but unfamiliar golden face. He spoke briefly and precisely. When he was done, Lamruil took up one of the queen's pale hands and pressed it to his lips.

"Farewell then, mother," he said lightly.

The queen stared at him a moment, and then turned and walked to her throne. She sat upon it, and closed her eyes. An aura of magic gathered around her as she began the casting that would send the dangerous ships from her shores—and that would send her to fight once again at Zaor's side.

The elves watched with tears in their eyes as their queen summoned her final spell in their defense. Silent power gathered, swirling through the room like a whirlwind and whipping the elves' hair and cloaks wildly about. Suddenly there was an explosion, a second terrible silent blast.

Amlaruil was gone.

In one quick movement, the prince lunged for the king sword and drew it from its ancient scabbard. The stunned and grieving elves were dealt a second shock to see the prince standing, alive and unharmed. The sword of Zaor gleamed in his hands, and the magical blue light seemed to hum with righteous wrath.

"I name you, Kymil Nimesin, traitor to Evermeet, and I call upon the magic of the sword to dispel the illusion you have cast. All of you, bear witness."

The features of the Gold elf's face shimmered and

blurred, quickly rearranged themselves into a familiar visage—that of the elf whose machinations had led to the deaths of King Zaor and Amnestria.

"He is revealed and accused. You, the advisors of Queen Amlaruil, say now what must be done. What judgment do you render?" Lamruil cried.

The traitor's sentence was passed in a single word, spoken as if from a single throat. The young king of Evermeet lifted the moonblade to pass sentence.

Kymil Nimesin saw death coming, and took the only escape he knew. He touched the gem Lloth had given him, releasing the powerful spell that contained the elfgates of Evermeet in a single entity. Some of this released power opened a gate he had prepared as a last eventuality.

The sword of Zaor swished harmlessly through the empty air. Once again, the Gold elf had escaped.

* * * * *

Amlaruil was thrust into Arvandor with a force that sent her reeling. Strong arms closed around her, familiar arms. She looked up into the face of her only love—Zaor, looking as vital and as young as he had when they first met in their glade. She touched his face, then reached out a hand to her daughter's powerful new form.

"Both of you, lend me your strength," she murmured.

The queen of Evermeet turned to face Malar's monster, not entirely certain what she would do to counter it. To her astonishment, two godly forms followed in the creature's shadow, their crimson eyes gleaming with malevolent delight.

A grim smile formed on the High Mage's lips, and she began to gather magic. No longer hampered by her mortal body, she drew lavishly from the power of the Seldarine, and from the strength of Ilyrana's faith and Zaor's love.

Magic flew at the evil gods in a streak of blue radiance. It enveloped them in a burst of bright light, and then just as quickly disappeared. In place of the huge, black-furred creature Malar once had been stood a tall being who, to any observer, might as well have been an elf. At his side was a dainty, white-skinned elven goddess.

Lloth, who had lifted her hands to hurl retaliatory magic at the hated elf queen, shrieked at the sight of her own hands.

The elf-eater whirled toward the sound, and then darted at this meal that had been presented so close at hand. The evil gods, sensing imminent destruction at the hands of their own creature, turned to flee. They disappeared with a burst of sulphur-scented smoke, and the creature of Malar followed in close pursuit.

Amlaruil smiled and turned to Zaor. "The spell will not hold in the Abyss—I have no power there. But oh, the look on her face!"

The united family burst into relieved laughter, holding each other close in the joy of an eternity begun.

After a few moments, Amlaruil pulled away. "There is something I must show you," she said softly. "A final message from our youngest son, the king. He pressed it into my hand during our final farewell."

She pulled a tiny note from her sleeve and showed it to him. On it was written a single phrase: "Once again, for the good of the People!"

Zaor looked into her eyes and smiled. "So you were right, after all. Lamruil will be a fine king."

The queen saw that her love did not yet fully understand their son's words. Lamruil knew of the sacrifices his mother had made. Once before she had renounced her love that Evermeet's needs might be met. Lamruil was urging her to once again set aside her deepest love; he himself would do so, if needed.

"Yes," she said softly, "He will be a fine king. But not of Evermeet."

Epilogue: Dawn

amruil and Maura stood alone together on the high cliffs where they had last taken leave of each other. Both knew that this farewell would be their last. The woman's eyes were sad, but set with determination.

"I am no queen, and you know it well," the girl said calmly. "Your destiny has been handed to you. You cannot turn away from Evermeet."

"You know I love you," he said. "What was said in the palace was a needed thing. I had to convince Kymil Nimesin of my perfidity."

"As well I knew," she retorted, "And I responded in kind."

"Yes. If I recall correctly, you called me an albino drow."

The woman colored and shrugged. "I wanted a really good, convincing insult."

"You did well," he said dryly.

They laughed briefly, then the sadness returned to Maura's eyes. "I must go now."

The young elf knew better than to try to dissuade her. Even so, he felt as if his heart had turned to ash and crumbled away. "Where will you go?"

Maura shrugged. "Somewhere new, someplace wild. That is all I know or care."

"Would that I could go with you!" Lamruil said with deep fervor.

"Perhaps, my son, you can," said a familiar voice, a voice like air and music.

Lamruil turned wondering eyes toward the sound. The familiar, much-loved form of his mother took shape in the air just beyond the cliff's edge. At first she was just a glimmering shadow, a transparent image. Motes of light like sparkling, multicolored gems—silver, gold, blue, green, and obsidian—winked into being and swirled through the glassy form.

Lamruil and Maura clung to each other, awestruck, as the apparition took on form. In moments, a ghostly Amlaruil stepped down from the air.

As her foot touched the soil of Evermeet, color swept through her, adding creamy tints to her white skin and setting the cloudlike hair aflame with red-gold fire. A tangible wave of power swept through her as the magical pulse that was Evermeet flowed through her and reclaimed her as queen.

Without a word, Lamruil took his father's pendant from around his neck and offered it to the queen.

Smiling, Amlaruil shook her head. "You have proved yourself Zaor's worthy successor, my son. The time has come for you to rule a kingdom of your own."

"But you *are* Evermeet," Lamruil said. "Why else would you return, but to rule where you are needed?"

A moment's sadness touched the queen's lovely face. "It was no easy thing to leave Arvandor, and Zaor. But you are right. I had to return, for the good of the People. Evermeet has need of me yet. The island's defenses are badly weakened, the confidence of the People shattered. Though perhaps the latter was a needed thing, we will have to rebuild. This undertaking must be mine. Yours, my son, is quite different."

Amlaruil lifted both hands and made a complex, fluid gesture. Suddenly she cupped a green bowl, in which was planted a tiny, exquisite tree with leaves of green and blue and gold. "Do you know what this is?"

The prince nodded, his eyes wide with wonder. He had long shared his mother's passion for the ancient treasures of elvenkind, and he knew the old legends as well as any seer or loremaster.

"That is the Tree of Souls, one of the greatest artifacts of Evermeet!" he exclaimed.

"Its time has come. The Tree of Souls will be planted on the mainland, creating a second stronghold for the elves," Amlaruil decreed. "Where would you place it, if the choice were entirely in your hands?"

Lamruil considered the matter. "My first thought is to restore Cormanthyr to its lost glory. But that time is past. No, the new kingdom must be more defensible. An island, like Evermeet, yet different in its strengths and defenses."

The prince fell silent. "I think," he said at length, "that I would set this kingdom in the midst of another vast sea, one even more forbidding than Umberlee's domain. There are vast, unexplored regions far north of the Spine of the World. A verdant island, surrounded by ice, would be a worthy haven."

"But unlike Evermeet, it would be a secret land, known only to the elves," Amlaruil added in an approving voice. "You have chosen well. Though this will be a hidden valley, strengthened by the presence of High Magic and protected by an ocean of ice, it will be a wild and dangerous land. This, perhaps, is the challenge that the People need."

The queen's gaze slid to Maura. "And for such a kingdom, there could be no better queen than she whom your heart has chosen."

Amlaruil extended one hand to Lamruil, and the other to the human girl. "I have no other daughter remaining to me," she said softly. "Thank you, my son, for this great gift."

The girl hesitated for a moment, then her small brown fingers curled around the queen's offered hand.

*　*　*　*　*

That night the streets of Leuthilspar were brilliant with festival lights, and a thousand forested hillsides flickered with bonfires and rang with the sound of music and celebration. The weary and battered elves found joy in the return of their beloved Amlaruil, and hope in the possibility that the elves of Evermeet would regain what they had lost.

And yet, there dawned in the heart of every elf the reluctant knowledge that Evermeet would never again be the same—that perhaps it had never been all that the elves had wished to make it.

The promise of a haven from change, the vision of a place where the passage of time and the sweep of distant events could be ignored, was ultimately an empty one.

Evermeet would endure. But as their ancestors had done so many times before, the elves would move on.

Most would remain and rally behind the queen, rebuilding Evermeet's strength and adding to it in new ways. Many of them would find a new homeland, as had the desperate Gold elves from another world whom Lamruil had surprised with a welcome and an offer of haven. Many of these newcomers would follow the restless Lamruil and wrest a new kingdom from a world of ice and solitude, as would some of Evermeet's natives. Still others would pass on to Arvandor, perhaps before their time, unable to adapt to their fuller understanding of the mortal world around them.

And perhaps still others would find ancient gates to other lands, and begin again as their ancestors had once forged a home in the new land of Faerûn. They would create still more legends, and do so knowing that they would never truly die as long as the old stories were told, and the ancient songs sung.

There is magic in such things, and where there is magic, there will always be elves.

30th day of Eleint, DR 1371

To Danilo Thann does Khelben Arunsun send greetings.

Thank you for sending me your manuscript of elven stories. Thank you, also, for your assurances that no one else would see it until I had the opportunity to read and approve the content. That you would think to take such steps shows a level of discretion and judgment that I had once despaired of you achieving.

I read your manuscript with great interest. As you surmised, there is much in it that is highly sensitive. To publish this work in its entirety would certainly arouse the ire—and endanger the security—of Evermeet's people.

You are quite right in saying that it might be wise to give one version to Arilyn, and submit another, truncated edition to Candlekeep as Athol's due for his part in this. I thought it best, however, that an elven scholar review the manuscript before it is reproduced in either format. Therefore I have sent the manuscript on to Evermeet for review by Elasha Evanara, a noted scribe and keeper of the Queen's Library.

This scribe is ancient even by elven standards, and is known to work slowly—again, even by elven standards. Although you've stated your eagerness to give this work to your lady as a midwinter gift, you should not count on its return in time for this year's festival. Or next year's, for that matter. You are familiar with the ways of elves, and I trust you will await the return of your manuscript with the necessary patience. Do not despair altogether of seeing it again. Members of the Thann and Arunsun families are known to be extremely long-lived.

I trust this letter finds you well. You picked an excellent year to remove to Silverymoon for a season of study. Winter has set in extremely early this year, and the roads and harbor have been closed by a barrage of early snow and ice this last ten-day. I assume that Arilyn is enjoying good hunting in the forests near Silverymoon. Give my fond regards to her.

I am enclosing with this letter several spell scrolls which I would have you learn. Yes, I do respect the bardic path you have chosen, but that does not preclude your need to attend to more important matters. (Laeral informs me that I am being pompous and insufferable—again. That may be true, but when one is right, one need not apologize or prevaricate. Magic is important, and you should not neglect your gifts.) You should know, Danilo, that I have not altogether given up my fond hope that you might return to a serious study of magic. Someone will need to hold Blackstaff Tower when the time comes for me to move on, and who better than my nephew and former apprentice? I know your mind on this matter, I urge you not to dismiss the possibility entirely.

Your news of recent events in Silverymoon was most entertaining. I nearly laughed aloud at your account of the student epics coming from your class entitled "The Satyr's School of Balladry." It is good to hear that the revival of the old bardic college at Silverymoon is progressing apace—and that not all the courses of study are as frivolous as those on which you lavished so much ink and parchment. In your next letter, perhaps a bit more information on the events surrounding the reorganization of Alustriel's palace, and the Queen's new political alliances? If that must be done at the expense of a bawdy tale or two, I believe I shall survive the disappointment.

Laeral sends her love, and asks for your condolences. I am not altogether certain what she means by that, but I will transcribe her words faithfully and leave you to divine their intent.

Yours in the service of Mystra,
Khelben Arunsun

R.A. Salvatore

The *New York Times* best-selling author of the Dark Elf saga returns to the FORGOTTEN REALMS® with a novel of high adventure and intrigue!

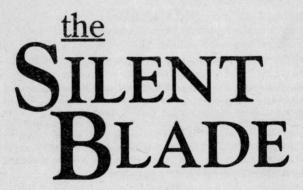

the
SILENT BLADE

Wulfgar's world is crumbling around him while the assassin Entreri and the drow mercenary Jarlaxle are gaining power in Calimport. But Entreri isn't interested in power—all he wants is a final showdown with the dark elf known as Drizzt. . . .

FORGOTTEN REALMS is a registered trademark of TSR, Inc.

FANTASY ADVENTURE

CRUCIBLE:
The Trial of Cyric the Mad
Troy Denning

The time has come for the gods of Toril to bring the mad god into line for the good of the world and all its people. But on this world, the gods are far from infallible. . . . The eagerly awaited sequel to *Prince of Lies*, by the *New York Times* best-selling author of *Waterdeep*. The legacy of the Avatar continues!

Edited by Philip Athans

An anthology of all new FORGOTTEN REALMS stories by **Ed Greenwood, Elaine Cunningham, Jeff Grubb, James Lowder, Mary H. Herbert, J. Robert King,** and a host of other talented authors that bring you tales of murder, intrigue, and suspense in the strange world of Faerûn. A world where detectives can Speak with Dead, and villains can animate a victim's corpse and have it cover the clues to its own murder. A world where the mystery story takes on a whole new dimension. . . .

the
Shadow
Stone
Richard Baker

A young apprentice wizard is confronted by the corrupting influence of power gone mad. Now, against all odds, he must stop his teachers from ripping the world apart with their unquenchable thirst for evil. The first in a new series of stand-alone novels: FORGOTTEN REALMS Adventures!

Available September 1998

FORGOTTEN REALMS is a registered trademark of TSR, Inc.